the Laguna Shores Research Club

a novel

LAURA KELLY ROBB

Relax. Read. Repeat.

THE LAGUNA SHORES RESEARCH CLUB
By Laura Kelly Robb
Published by TouchPoint Press
Brookland, AR 72417
www.touchpointpress.com

PAPERBACK ISBN: 978-1-956851-31-1

Editor: Kimberly Coghlan
Cover Design: ColbieMyles.com.
Cover Images exotic tropical palm tree landscape at sunset or moonlight by
dahabians (Adobe Stock)

First Edition

Printed in the United States of America.

To the Aero Caffe Writers Club: Erin, Glida, Judy and Kelly

CHAPTER ONE

Sunday, Day One – A Death at Laguna Shores

Laila spotted the HOA President, Bob Page, exiting the building. He paused under the portico to speak to a woman in trousers and an emblazoned shirt holding a clipboard. She jotted down whatever Bob was telling her and returned inside. Forrest held on to Alton, who had Laila's hand. The boys extended from her side, vibrating with curious energy, but curtailed by the gathering crowd. They made no move to break away to explore on their own. Laila waved to Bob, and he joined her on the sidewalk where knots of neighbors stood, murmuring.

"A bad day for the Research Club, I guess," he said.

Laila was dumbstruck. Only one member of her Research Club lived in this building, and Laila had seen her the day before. They spoke about the meeting to be held that Monday. Laila was scheduled to host, and they outlined the agenda together. She gaped at Bob.

"She was all alone," Bob said.

Laila squeezed her eyes shut, but the boys were tugging on her hand, and she couldn't keep her balance. She blinked open to find Bob with a knowing expression.

"Billie?" she whispered.

"Oh, you hadn't heard," he said.

"What hospital is this? Where are they taking her?"

An ambulance stood at the curb outside Billie's condo. The red lights rotated rhythmically. The siren had been turned off.

"It won't be right away," Bob said, watching her face.

"Was it a fall? They can't move her?" Laila asked.

"Laila," he said, "they're waiting for the coroner."

"No. No, it can't be."

Forrest and Alton moved in closer to her, each folding a hand around a fistful of the fabric of her slacks. Alton slipped a thumb into his mouth. Laila looked up to the curtained window of Billie's second floor bedroom. Her small condo was on the street side and was noisy, Billie complained, too noisy to sleep late so she ended up napping in the afternoon. Research Club meetings were bright and early Monday mornings mainly because it was Billie's prime time.

"Oh, no," Laila repeated. If the messenger were another neighbor, not Bob Page, they would have embraced, leaning on each other for a moment of oblivion, of erasure of all the considerations a sudden death forces upon the survivors. But in the recent past Bob had used his HOA position to ask Laila questions about David's travel schedule, which discomfited her.

"Quick," Bob said. "A heart attack, they think."

Laila looked up once more at Billie's window, taking in the whole building and its landscaped surroundings. So much of what Billie loved about Florida was right here at her doorstep. The tall palms that flanked the portico were mirrored in the graceful double row across the street. They curtained the Laguna Shores lane from the busy arterial and made her think of dancers.

Spidery ferns and birds of paradise flanked the building. Billie never felt the need to buy flowers, she told Laila, because they engulfed her whenever she stepped outside her home. Walkways threaded between the lush flowerbeds and led behind the building to a two-tiered deck that looked over the white beach and the endless blue ocean.

Billie wasn't one of the many older, retired beach walkers that logged thousands of miles each year, but she adored a late afternoon Scotch on the deck while dozens of skimming and diving sandpipers conducted their rituals. Laila understood completely. Never had she and David, in fifteen years of marriage, lived in a place so connected to natural beauty as Laguna Shores. The sun would rise the next morning, and the ocean would mirror the fresh light with blue diamond brilliance. How cruel that it could all go on without Billie!

"Who found. . . ." Laila began, but her voice caught, and she could only produce a sob. Her nose was beginning to run, and a tear streaked down her cheek.

"I saw she left her recycling container out after the pick up Saturday, which is not exactly unheard of, but then when it was still out this morning, I thought I'd better investigate," Bob said. "Her car was in its parking space, so I got to her door, and the newspaper was still on the mat at ten a.m. So, I went in."

"Oh, Lord," Laila said.

"I know," Bob began. "She was slumped half out of her lounge chair, her mouth hanging open, and the smell, I mean, bad." But Laila wouldn't focus on Bob's words. She was picturing the empty chair she and the rest of the Laguna Shores Research Club would face the next day.

"She's the foundation of the club," Laila murmured.

"What is it you guys do, anyway? You're all so closed-mouthed about your private little club," Bob wheedled.

Laila was fishing her phone out of the small cross-body bag she wore during all her vertical hours. She checked the time and grimaced, his needling left unanswered.

"I'm sorry. I need to go."

Laila took the hand of each twin and returned to the tennis courts the way she came. Regina would wait for Laila to return, and that was the problem. Sundays were long and closely scheduled days for Regina. She had back-to-back lessons at two other developments until eight that night. Laila picked up her pace, striding, if a woman barely five two and bountifully rounded (Regina's words) on top could be said to stride.

Jackson was pushing the ball collector around the court, and Eddie was loading Regina's collection of racquets into the back of her SUV. Laila and the twins got to Regina's side, Laila puffing and the boys laughing and twirling about, relieved that Laila's sudden upset had been quieted.

"You're fine," Regina said. "We just now finished up. I am merely lending you these future champions until next Wednesday afternoon at four o'clock." She pulled off her sun visor to smooth down her box braids and wedge them once more under the elastic band.

"Thank you, Reggie," Laila said. "I know you've got to run."

"Who was the ambulance for?" Regina asked.

"I don't know," Laila said, hoping her throat wouldn't constrict again from the shock.

A small lie and a justified lie. A merciful lie.

Regina knew Billie well through the Laguna Shores Research Club, and she wouldn't take the news of the death stoically. Laila would no more be able to tell Regina without both of them crying than she would be able to sing an aria. With the four boys in close proximity, each one likely to need a tailor-made explanation of what had happened to their grandmother stand-in, the moment would become complicated.

Besides, it was an honest answer since it was not clear if that particular ambulance would eventually remove Billie's body.

"It wasn't our building, and they hadn't come out yet," Laila managed to say.

"Stow the ball collector, will you Jackson?" Regina called toward the court. "God, I wish he weren't named for the most racist president ever," she said to Laila.

"He's not! I've told you! It's a wonderful name, and I won't cede it just because. . . ."

"I know, I know. The artist. I just like to see you get flustered," Regina said. "But if I could just call him "Poll" for short, I'd feel better."

"How about Jack?" Laila asked, hugging Forrest close while Eddie held Alton under his bony armpits and twirled him in a circle over the soft sand of the play area.

"It wouldn't bother you?" asked Regina.

"Not from you," Laila answered.

Regina gave her a quick hug.

"Can I call you tonight?" asked Laila.

"Of course," said Regina. "I'll be sitting with a glass of wine on my sofa by nine."

Laila sucked in a gulp of air involuntarily, like a sigh that had reversed course and made her gag. She thought she was in control, but her nerves were otherwise inclined.

Regina's brow darkened as she looked down at her. "Are you okay?"

Laila nearly relented. Their funny, unstylish, highly educated and generous friend was gone. The jagged news cut through Laila's calm, but the reality of Billie's death would dismantle Regina's day. Their grief had to wait until evening.

And I need time.

Billie's message, urgent and troublesome, clawing at her conscience, sat in her voicemail queue and made her phone seem now like a feverish thing she shouldn't touch. The little lie would buy her that time.

"I'm good," Laila said. "The sprint got me out of breath. What a wimp I am!"

Regina smiled at Laila, but Laila knew she wasn't entirely convinced.

"I'll pour one, too, right before I call," Laila continued quickly with what she hoped was a conspiratorial smile.

Regina nodded, took a quick swig from her water bottle and vaulted her muscular frame onto the driver's seat. Her Jamaican flavored goodbye had the lilt the boys loved, and they waved as she backed out of her parking slot.

"Aren't you hungry, Mom?" Eddie called to her.

"No, but I think I know someone who is," Laila answered.

Eddie shrugged.

"Let's take the beach path," Laila said. "Then I can test the temperature of the pool water for later."

"Great!" said Jackson.

They walked from the tennis courts past the handball courts towards the pool enclosure sitting prettily by the sand.

"I want to swim," called Forrest.

"Will Dad be home for a swim?" asked Alton.

Laila glanced sidelong at Eddie to see if the mention of David registered on his face. Yesterday afternoon, before David left for the trip to Vero Beach and then Miami, Eddie had been caught in an adult bookshop with the older brother of his best friend. The shop owner took their names and then shooed them out. He recognized Eddie's last name from newspaper reports about Harrow United's plans for new retail development, and he called David to report the incident.

David had a talk with Eddie, the two of them alone in David's office. Afterwards, when Laila asked David how it went, he said it was about as informative a session could be when one party wouldn't talk. David said the behavior was normal, but refusing to talk about it worried him.

Eddie caught Laila's glance and kept a straight face when she told Alton she expected their Dad at least by dinner.

"But, if traffic's good and he gets in early, we can swim together."

Delighted, the three younger boys sprinted around the community center, along the fencing for the pool, and on to the beach.

"I'm going," Eddie muttered, seeming relieved to leave her. He trotted after the younger ones in his often grumbled-about role of shepherd.

Laila slipped through the gate, dipped a toe in the pool, and found the water temperature reasonable. But checking the temperature was not the only reason she chose the back route into her building. It meant her family would enter the condo building from the beach and take the elevator to the top floor. The only room in their home that gave out to the front where the ambulance was parked was David's office and workout room, where the boys only entered if invited.

The news might reach them anyway. Friends would call, and neighbors might stop by. Plus, kids tended to gather on the building's outdoor patio Sunday afternoons in anticipation of the weekly family happy hour, and this pleasant, sunny day would be no exception. News of Billie's death would jump from person to person, a hot coal no one would hang on to for long. She would have only a short time to puzzle out the significance of Billie's last words to her and prepare her four sons for the loss.

The twins had not grasped the meaning of Bob Page's words, but the ambulance made them skittish. They had peppered her with questions, filling the air with noise to calm their nerves. Sudden events, like the arrival of an ambulance, made them twitch. She understood.

"Who drives? Does a doctor drive?"

"I could put lights all over the ambulance, like on a Christmas tree, couldn't I?"

"Do they come for pets? If we called for Ruffles, would they come?"

"Can you fall out the back? I saw it once in a movie."

"How many fit in there?"

"Are you allowed to cry in there? I bet a lot of people want to cry."

When she and David first got the twins, their dark, ropey bodies curled on opposite sides of the crib in the hospital, it was after their parents succumbed to dysentery during the raft journey from Haiti. David begged for them. Every leader in the Haitian community, every Human Watch manager, every refugee volunteer heard his impetuous, passionate plan to raise them as his own. Laila had loved them from the first time she saw them, but it was David and his determination to make something good come out of their nightmare that won over hearts.

The social worker suggested ongoing counseling to deal with the embedded traumas of hunger and loss. She was right, and counseling constituted a staple expense for the Harrow family. Still, Laila quaked at the job of telling them the woman they called Nona was gone.

Eddie and Jackson, her older sons, born in quick succession after David's completion of his MBA, were more solid emotionally, but the news would shake them, too. She would try to put it off until David got home—and until she dissected what had transpired during the previous twenty-four hours.

What had Billie meant when she called last night? The disjointed, rambling message, still on her phone, had bothered her, and she called back. Two tries, and Billie didn't pick up. Laila was worried enough to call Ken Lee. Since he lived in Laguna Shores and could easily walk to Billie's condo, she thought it the best option. She didn't think she should leave all four boys asleep and alone. Ken said it was no problem and that he would check on her.

What had Ken found? Why didn't he call after he checked on Billie? Was it too late in the evening? Ken had a streak of courtesy that Laila admired, but she admitted that sometimes he wore it like cardboard. And today he hadn't called either. Yes, it was Sunday, and he disappeared every Sunday, rain or shine, until late afternoon at best, when, occasionally, he'd drop by their building's happy hour. Such a devoted churchgoer, Laila fumed.

Immediately, she censored herself. It wasn't as if she and David had the most conventional religious practice, with David ricocheting between his ultraconservative Miami family members and their relaxed, almost casual, membership in the St. Augustine Unitarians. Harrow family unity depended on tolerance among conservative and liberal members of their clan. Ken's church life deserved the same respect.

Laila would call Ken again and leave a polite message. She was doubtful he would break with his routine and return a phone call on a Sunday, but she would try.

She hurried down the beach to her building, and found the boys waiting for her and the key to the elevator. They crowded in, all of them damp after more than an hour in the sun, the scent of sunblock mixed with sweat, Eddie's head now reaching above hers, his arm better able to extend to the third floor button, the twins scuttling their sandaled feet so that no one flattened their toes by mistake.

The thing to do, thought Laila, would be to listen once more to Billie's message. See if the words were so dire she should have gone over to Billie's immediately. She had no intention of sharing it with anyone, including David. She would hate to admit to him her failure to help a friend, and anyway, he had little part in the Research Club and the friendship that had sprung up among them, Laila, Regina, Billie, Ken, and Claire.

"Claire!" Laila exclaimed out loud.

She startled the boys with her cry. She startled herself, not realizing how much she had begun to care about the club's newest member.

"Mom, are you okay?" asked Jackson. He had David's curly hair and thick eyebrows as well as her olive skin, a complexion that would protect him in Florida's burnish or be-burned sunshine. She loved the way he made it his business to take the family's temperature when things seemed amiss.

"How many times have I told you, Mom, to keep a hat on when you're out in the sun," Eddie preempted. "It is sunstroke, boys. We're going to have to apply cold compresses to her forehead."

The twins giggled at Eddie's irreverence, and he folded his arms across his chest, imitating a doctor who has demanded that his remedy be followed. He gave a throaty "harrumph," and when the elevator opened on to the foyer of their apartment, he strode out first, snapping his fingers as if his minions would carry out his orders. Laila smiled, and the boys relaxed, even Jackson, each running off to his own corner and leaving Laila to the business of setting out their lunch.

CHAPTER TWO

Sunday, Day One – Regrets

For a few minutes after lunch, Laila listened to the phone message from the previous night. On the voicemail, Billie's voice vibrated with her peculiar nasal twang, the one heard from western Pennsylvania down through Maryland that stretched to a drawl in West Virginia. Accent or not, she used correct diction and grammar.

"Hello, Laila? Laila, dear? It's a bit late, but you said David was gone for the weekend, and you'll stay up, watching an old movie, something romantic, right? I admire you, softie that you are, good to your boys, your four handsome boys. And the internet, we have the best in St. Augustine Beach thanks to that husband of yours bringing it in and paying those set up fees then all of us getting a chance to, you know, what do we say, get a line in, it works for all of us. So nice. I mean, I don't want to upset you in any way. I've always been in favor of you living here. I'm a little tired, Laila, so I can't explain it tonight. I should call back. It could all be so complicated. She is our friend. And it's not good to get on the wrong side of anybody these days. What's her name now? All of a sudden I can't put my finger on it. Silly. I mean just this minute. Oh, dear. I'll call back tomorrow. I am tired."

The recorded message brought her calm but acute tones alive, only to dissolve into confusion. Laila backed up the audio to listen again to her friend's melancholy resignation.

"I'm a little tired, Laila," Billie said, and this time Laila heard the sigh.

Billie was not the kind of person who would run out of words. White-collar government work had made her learn to speak in a way that could be understood in any of the fifty states. She spent her career in Washington, D.C., in the heart of bureaucracy. She earned her retirement through forty years long of steadfast work within the system. The wording was awkward for anyone, let alone for someone as collected as Billie.

What did it mean to "get a line in"? Laila supposed she meant to go online, but it sounded more like a medical procedure. She must have been uneasy or distracted. What did she mean she was in favor of them living here? Because the twins are Black? She had never hinted at racism before, let alone exclusion.

Laila realized she had missed the signs. She had made a half-hearted attempt to respond by calling Ken. But he didn't know Billie as well, and perhaps after dark, Billie wouldn't open her door to a male caller, even Ken. Laila berated herself for not trusting Eddie just ten minutes while she could have run to the next building to check on Billie.

An imbecile could tell by that message that Billie was experiencing a health problem. What was wrong with me? What kind of friend does that? It was ludicrous. No one needs to know about this message. Well, Ken is aware, but not Claire or Regina, and I won't tell David. He would be surprised, disappointed. Telling people now would not change the outcome for Billie.

She couldn't be gone. But the ambulance was there. It doesn't compute.

Laila closed her voicemail queue and put the phone in its carrying pouch. She changed into her suit and gathered up a set of towels into her tote bag.

With the four boys slapping along in flip-flops and trunks, they went out to the pool. She hoped the temperature, barely creeping into the seventies, would keep most people away. Word of Billie's death would travel among the residents, and she wanted David at her side when she broke the news to the boys. They had two living grandmothers, but distance and personality kept them aloof. Billie was present and very interested.

"I'm their Florida Nona," Billie would joke.

Billie knew what school assignments bothered Eddie, and she kept track of his tennis team. She delighted Jackson with her range of scientific understanding, and she was one of the few people that Forrest would ask for a story, meaning he wanted to be cuddled. Alton called her Nona Next-door.

For over an hour, they had the pool to themselves. Alton and Forrest played tag with her. They showed off their new dog paddle skills and chased her from ladder to ladder in the shallow end. She let Forrest jump off the side into Eddie's arms, chug back to the side, climb out, and do it again. Jackson worked hard to perfect his cannonball off the diving board.

She took a breather, hanging on to the concrete edge, and Billie's words ran in a mournful loop.

"What's her name now? I can't put my finger on it."

What woman friend was she talking about? Had someone alarmed Billie? Her ability to convey a message was slipping, and she didn't deny it. She had given in to it. She wanted to consign the problem to another day, but there was no other day. This was Billie delivering a haunting goodbye.

She was living her last hours, and I didn't respond. I didn't help. What kind of friend does that?

"Mom, don't you want to play?" Forrest called. "Look at this, Mom. Look." He had figured out how to rest from swimming by flipping on to his back and using his hands to scull through the water. When Laila didn't respond, he turned back on his stomach and paddled over to her, hanging on her shoulders.

"Tired, Mom, are you tired? I'm not tired. I'm so strong," Forrest crowed.

Laila gave him a little splash. He yelped in response and pushed off. Alton called himself "it" again and started across the pool to tag Forrest. The older boys swam underwater to the shallow end, coming up under each of the boys to grab a leg or arm, whatever they could catch hold of, making the twins scream in pretend horror. They organized a chicken fight. Alton, who was the smaller twin, rode on Jackson's shoulders, and Forrest, huskier through his torso and shoulders, climbed up on Eddie's back. Lurching towards each other with their brothers wobbling above, Jackson and Eddie shouted comic threats. The tangle of sixteen limbs became an off-kilter dance.

She glanced up to her chair on the pool deck where her phone rested on her beach bag. The boys were enjoying their game. Perhaps she should take advantage of their activity to check to see if Ken had returned her call. The moment she got out there would be a hullabaloo, but with some luck, she'd have a few minutes to return his call, and if he hadn't called, to text him once more.

Nothing would change the awful finality of Billie's death, but she burned to know if Ken had gone to Billie's the night before, and if he had talked to her. It was possible, entirely possible, that Billie had answered Ken's knock, assured him she was fine, and gone back to reading in her easy chair. Whatever had killed her came as an unavoidable, unpreventable sudden and lethal event. Nothing Laila could have done would have changed the brutal end. It could have been Laila at Billie's door, and nothing would have changed. Laila would be off the hook for her unconscionable neglect. She could only hope.

Laila swung herself up the concrete ladder, grasping the metal railing, and stepped onto the deck. She skirted the shallow end of the pool and headed to her chair, when a woman and her daughter came through the fence gate in front of her.

The woman carried a plastic shark, blown up into a float for the little girl. They were the newest residents of her building, living on the third floor in a two bedroom with a balcony overlooking the pool. While some residents seemed to handle their children a little skittishly around Alton and Forrest, this child loved playing with the twins, and if her mother saw from the balcony they were out, she usually brought her daughter down to join the fun. It meant more work for Laila because the girl was allowed to paddle the shark float to water over her head, and with one or more twins on board, Laila needed to exercise special vigilance. It was a small price to pay for the girl's unbridled friendship. As much as Laila wanted to whisk by them to reach her phone, she stopped to greet them.

"Janet, how are you?" Laila asked.

"Good! How's the water?" the woman answered.

"I think Cara will like it," Laila said. "If you go in, I'll get the boys to choose a game that's not so rough."

"Let's give everybody shark rides, Cara. What do you think?" suggested Janet.

"I think so," said Cara.

A wave of relief came over Laila. Janet seemed not to have heard about Billie's death. She might hold off breaking the news to the kids until after David's arrival. She turned from her mission of communicating with Ken and hopped back in the water with Janet, Cara, and her sons.

A more confident swimmer than Laila, Janet towed the shark with the little ones on board. The older boys, warned to play gently with Cara and the twins, soon exited the pool and flopped on deck chairs, protesting their boredom.

"Call us when you want water monsters," Eddie teased.

"How about the monsters and me go for a swim in the ocean?" David's husky voice called from gate.

"You're back," yelled Jackson.

Eddie and Jackson catapulted off their chairs at the sound of David's invitation.

"How about it? First dip of the year in the Atlantic?" David said, directing the appeal to Laila. He knew that having her first and second born plunge into an unbounded sea would cause her dread.

"David," she called in welcome, but with a tinge of alarm.

"Daddy!" Alton clambered off the shark and paddled to the edge of the pool.

"Us too!" called Forrest.

"Not today, buddies. You're way too skinny. We have to get a few more dinners in you before I take you into the ocean in March."

Laila recognized David's masterful way of setting up a negotiation by presenting his offer as the safer and more conservative of two possible options. But neither choice was safe, she thought.

Maybe Eddie could weather the springtime ocean temperatures. He had developed wider shoulders and meatier thighs over the last few months; in fact, he sported a few chest hairs. But Jackson was only eleven, with a chest and back simultaneously concave. His legs had grown, but his hips were nonexistent. A good wave could flip him into the air. He shouldn't be in the ocean this early, and there was no way David could take Eddie and not him. She should hold them both back.

Too late. The boys grabbed their towels and sweatshirts, trotting happily through the gate and down the steps to the beach behind David. Forrest and Alton slapped the deck in frustration, but then turned back to their game with Cara in the pool.

"The sand is not even hot enough to require shoes," she said to Janet. "That should tell you something about the temperature of the water."

"They'll be fine," said Janet. "They'll body surf a few waves, feel the chill, and come back out. It's good for them."

"I suppose," said Laila. "I can't get used to the fact that my boys are braver than I am."

"You're not from Florida, are you?" asked Janet.

"Massachusetts," Laila answered.

"And him?"

"From Miami," Laila said.

"Southern boys have to have their adventures," Janet said.

"We're Southern, right Mom?" Alton asked. He had been lounging on the shark, but now sat up straight, watching Laila.

"You are Southern now, by way of Haiti. And that is a very good way to be."

"Haiti?" said Janet. "Haiti has more history in one square mile than almost any southern state. Not to mention a couple of extra languages that Southerners don't have."

Alton smiled shyly at Janet then lay down again on the shark.

"Mom, can you be from some place if you were there and then came home? Like, am I from Disneyworld?" Cara asked from her perch on the shark.

"Doesn't work like that," said Janet. "It means the place you were born. So you're from Savannah."

"So I am from Haiti but now Southern?" asked Alton.

"Yes," said Laila.

"And is Forrest?" Alton asked.

"I'm your twin, birdhead," called Forrest. "What do you think?" He was hanging on the side of the pool, kicking his legs to create the waves that would rock the shark and make Alton shout in fear.

"Stop! You're the birdhead," yelled Alton. He turned his back on Forrest and looked up at Laila again. "Are you sure we're Southern?"

"If we live some place long enough, we can become from that place. Daddy was born Southern, but I wasn't. I am becoming Southern here in Florida. You are becoming Southern, too."

"Like Regina? She's from Haiti, right? And now she's Southern?" Alton asked, and Forrest paddled to the shark, hanging on to the side, interested in the details of the conversation.

"Regina is from Jamaica. She's Jamaican, but really, she's from Florida because she lived here since she was very little," said Laila.

"How little?" asked Alton.

"Since kindergarten."

"So we're from Florida now. We're Southern," said Forrest. "We were here in kindergarten."

"But you're not from Disneyworld," said Cara. "We aren't, right Mom? None of us are, right?"

"Can we go with 'American'?" said Janet. "We're Americans, okay?"

"I might change to Disneyworld someday," said Cara. "When I'm big."

"I'm going to be whatever you are, Mom, okay?" asked Alton.

"The six of us together," said Laila. "A good plan."

Alton sighed and turned over onto his back again, at which point Forrest tugged just hard enough on the corner of the shark to make Alton slide off and into the water. He flailed and sputtered so that Laila had to grab him under his bottom and push him up, supporting him into a sitting position, until he caught his breath. Forrest was back at the edge of the pool, laughing at his misdeed.

"Shall we walk down to the beach and see how Dad is doing?" Laila asked once she got Alton to the pool's edge. "Happy hour later?" she called to Janet.

"I think so," Janet answered. "It'll be a good afternoon for it."

"Bye, Cara," the three called over their shoulders.

Janet had been right about short duration of the ocean adventure. By the time Laila got shirts on the boys, slipped on her sundress, and got out on the beach, Jackson was out of the surf watching Eddie and David ride a wave onto the sand by his feet. Eddie stood and turned, pulling up his Dad, the two of them shivering. The three got to their towels before they heard the shouts from Forrest and Alton, so it was too late to act as if the cold meant nothing and to get back in the water to show off their manly status.

Laila forgot her irritation with David's spontaneous plan when she saw the twins vault into David's arms, and he hugged them tightly, lifting one then the other above his head like envied trophies. They giggled and begged to be taken for a swim, but David held firm, insisting the cold would not be healthy for them.

"Let's have a game instead," he said.

They gathered up their belongings and moved toward the flat sand closer to the condo. Jackson volunteered to bring out his soccer ball, and he and Laila carried the beach towels home.

"I'll get the happy hour food ready," she called. Each Sunday the building residents organized an evening potluck on their common deck, and it was her turn to contribute.

"Tell your mother how beautiful she is," David told the boys.

"You're beautiful!" the four chirped at her. At least the twins sounded like they meant it, Laila decided.

But she knew she was spoiled. David worked hard and had learned the family retail business quickly. He had a long way to go to catch up with Sam, his older brother, but merely walking into their ocean-view condo proved to her that he could. A comfortable life was not the future she would have once predicted for herself, let alone for David.

In college, they played and dreamed more than they worked, and she loved him for it. The renegade and the poor girl – they were going to travel the world as art buyers and bring back only the wildest and most original works to upend complacent museum curators. The death of David's uncle changed everything. Called back urgently to Miami, David accepted that his father and brother needed him. Grad school followed, and Eddie and Jackson arrived, then the twins. Life was different, but life was good.

"Got it," Jackson said, the soccer ball tucked under his arm. "See you later."

When Laila told David she needed to get the food to the deck for happy hour, she only meant she would load up the cart and roll it into the elevator. Before she left on Saturday afternoon, Margaret, her housekeeper, stored the cold snacks and Sunday's meals in the fridge, with a detailed message on a clip on the door with heating times and other advice. Her efficiency meant Laila could handle four children and didn't need a nanny.

And she didn't want a nanny. She couldn't imagine inserting any distance between her and her sons. Too quickly they would be gone – she had seen it in her own family of origin. She, her sister, and her brother reached adulthood and flew off in three different directions, and except for one week a year with all their grandchildren, her parents spent most weekends alone in their Boston home. When the kids left her for their pursuits, Laila wanted a file in her brain for every single memory she had been lucky enough to live. She never envied anyone's live-in childcare.

Although it was still early, Laila loaded Margaret's trays of hors d'oeuvres on the rolling cart and added a few bags of chips and the veggies and dip from the fridge. After arriving at Laguna Shores three years before, Laila heard there used to be a Sunday get-together, and along with Bill and Barb from the first floor, she reinstituted the event. This week, she and David would provide the food – light fare that would tide over kids and adults until dinner.

With all in order, Laila had a few minutes to herself. From their balcony, through the wall of windows that shielded them from the ocean's winter breezes and summer's thick humidity, Laila saw her family playing soccer. David had a talent for parenting, and the boys paid him back with affection. Neighbors sometimes remarked to Laila that they wished they could get the response from their children that David got from his sons.

Today, that talent gave Laila time to try once more to contact Ken. He had not called or texted in reply, and she didn't want to be branded a nuisance, but this situation was extraordinary. She sat in her favorite living room chair, a floral wingback that had been chosen to hold her smaller frame. She liked that her feet did not dangle like those of a little girl. Dialing twice with no response, she sent another text. The silence was exasperating.

She had no choice. She dialed Claire. It was too strange to live out the whole day after Billie's death as if nothing unusual had happened. She didn't intend for Claire to be the first, after herself and the oily HOA President, to know, but so be it. Claire picked up on the second ring.

"Hi, is this a good time?" Laila asked.

"Yes. I just closed the door on an open house in Villano. What's up?"

"I have some bad news," Laila said.

"Tomorrow's meeting is off? Are you okay?"

"The meeting is on. I mean I think we should meet," Laila faltered. "It's not me."

"The kids?" asked Claire.

Laila thought Claire was the best salesperson she had ever met. She put herself in the other person's shoes, remembering their family situations, job titles, food preferences, city of origin, athletic interests, and just about anything that would constitute a fair subject for conversation. Laila figured there did not exist a Real Estate major in college because the skills needed were instinctual and could not be taught.

"No. Look, I hate to tell you over the phone, but waiting until tomorrow feels cold-hearted, too."

"What, Laila, what? Tell me," Claire urged.

Laila steeled herself. "It's Billie. She's gone. She passed away last night."

"Oh, God," exhaled Claire.

"It's awful," said Laila.

"No warning," Claire said mournfully. "No warning whatsoever. She looked fine last week."

"She looked fine yesterday," said Laila.

"She wasn't sick?"

"No, we planned out tomorrow's meeting. For about half an hour," said Laila.

"I didn't realize the meetings needed to be planned," Claire said.

That's Claire for you, thought Laila. She plans minute-to-minute, facial expression to facial expression, a practiced pitch and then spontaneous combustion. Flattery and psychology, creating a need and sensing vulnerability, knowing when to push and when to walk away: Claire had mastered it all.

Laila appreciated that Claire chose not to use her skills on her and the other club members, at least not in an obnoxiously obvious way. The Claire who showed up at meetings was a much less plastic version of the Claire who sold Laila and David their condo. Her comment about planning for meetings merely spoke to the habits of her personality, number one being "Just do it."

"No, just a brief discussion. It wasn't heavy duty. She showed me the Excel sheet she had put together for your searches."

"Why show you ahead of time?" Claire asked peevishly, and then she corrected herself. "Oh, it's not important. How stupid of me. It hardly matters now, does it?"

"I was probably the last person to see them. And I am pretty sure I wouldn't be able to tell you much about them."

"Damn, we are going to be rudderless without her," said Claire. "Ken knows a bunch, but Billie was the full meal deal. Programs, websites, archives, international organizations – you name it."

Until this conversation, Laila did not picture Claire as a full-throttled member of the Research Club. Claire's research interest, the one she brought to meetings in order to refine her search methodologies, wasn't complicated. She said she wanted to study building permits cross-referenced to road repair and construction plans. Couldn't anybody pick up the St. Augustine Register and figure out what was in the works?

Laila suspected the attraction of the club was to meet new clients. The demographic mix of an Asian in IT, a Generation X African-American, an older white woman, and an active mom were all people who could offer multiple paths into the St. Augustine community. But now her appreciative comments seemed sincere. Perhaps she had judged her too harshly.

"I haven't told Ken or Regina yet," said Laila.

"They'll miss her. God, Billie had just begun working on Regina's Bitcoin security program," said Claire.

Laila winced. Here they were calculating Billie's usefulness to the club members and the amount of work that would not get done because she was gone. What genie of callousness had taken them over?

"I'm going to miss her," said Laila. "My kids, too. On starry nights she'd bring her telescope out on her deck and teach them about the stars. Eddie and Jackson know more astronomy than David and I."

"How long has she been in Florida?" Claire asked.

"You didn't sell her the condo?" Laila answered.

"No. I've lived in Laguna Shores six years, and she was here when I got here. I thought you would know," Claire said, drily.

She has that way, Laila thought, of letting you know when you've gotten too big for your britches. Claire was the Laguna Shores real estate pro, the local guide and expert. Laila's implication that she and Billie were great buddies seemed to have rankled Claire and made her want to bring Laila down a notch or two.

Laila wondered why Claire got so defensive at times, but today she didn't have the energy to placate her.

"Perhaps you should look it up," Laila said with a tone drier than Claire's.

"She was president of the HOA when I first moved here, so I'd say she's had to be here at least eight years. Maybe more."

"I did not know that," Laila said, withdrawing from the conflict. Feeding Claire's ego wasn't that difficult after all.

"But you're right," said Claire, recovering her smooth style, " she was a great neighbor."

"Who will notify her sons?" asked Laila.

"The coroner does that," said Claire briskly. "Next of kin is listed on your HOA records. Our good friend Bob Page will have already given that info up."

Claire's gossipy turn in the conversation pleased Laila. Bob Page regularly violated boundaries between the various HOA members and himself, and Laila couldn't tolerate it. It was good fun to watch Claire box with Bob at HOA meetings.

Claire would rise to her feet, her long legs even longer in six inch heels, her pencil skirt and business blazer reminding Bob of her professional status, her librarian glasses poorly disguising her stunning face, and checkmate any move by Bob to enlarge his fiefdom as HOA president by quoting chapter and verse from appropriate legislation.

"Of course, that's only one woman's reading of the law," is how she would end her comments. Bob would table his suggestion for further study, and that would be the last it appeared on an HOA agenda.

"Bob said the ambulance people thought it was a heart attack," said Laila.

"Naturally, he was on the scene," said Claire.

"He found her," said Laila.

"What a feather in his cap," answered Claire. "We'll be hearing those gory details at the next HOA meeting."

The thought of Billie's sudden death, alone in her living room, no one to hold her hand or help her to her bed and make her comfortable, brought Laila to tears. She lowered the phone to her lap, but Claire had heard her sob. She lifted it back to her ear but couldn't talk.

"Oh, sweetie, you're crying," said Claire. "You're crying. Is anybody home with you? Is David back from his trip?"

"I'll be okay," whispered Laila. "He's on the beach with the boys."

"I can come over," said Claire.

If Claire came over, Laila might confess how she ignored Billie's Saturday evening phone call. As much as Laila would like an outlet for her grief, admitting her role in Billie's death would crush her. She wasn't ready to share her failure.

"No, I'm going to happy hour. I haven't told David or the boys yet. I have to get through the day until David and I can talk. But thanks. Thanks very much for the offer."

"And Ken and Regina?" asked Claire.

"I don't know. I've been calling him, but no answer. And Reggie doesn't stop to breathe on Sundays. They may not find out until we tell them tomorrow."

"Some meeting," said Claire.

"I'll see you," said Laila. She could feel the sobs welling up again. Claire signed off, and Laila sat with the phone in her lap until Eddie appeared in the living room, reminding her that the family was on the deck and eager for some food.

Chapter Three

Monday, Day Two – The Son

When she awoke that Monday morning, Laila calculated she had an hour to spend in private homage to Billie. She exited her building, trudged across the sand and up the outside stairs to a small balcony deck. This perch belonged to anyone in Billie's building, accessed through the second-floor hall door, but in reality, Billie had annexed it.

Laila placed a vase of flowers on the table between the two padded rocking chairs Billie had provided. The white lilies were stately, at the prime of their bloom, and Billie would have approved. She often held court on the balcony and decorated it for comfort and appreciation. Magazines and books were piled on the shelf under the tabletop, and she kept a notebook and pens in the drawer. If the weather were clear, she would set up the telescope at the corner railing.

Facing east, Laila rocked slowly next to Billie's empty chair, sipping her coffee and remembering their awe of a good sunrise, of the changing light and the illuminated clouds. Some days, heavy dew would chill the air and make the chairs drip as if with sweat. Other days, a smoky fog made by a night's long heat pushed the breeze offshore, leaving flat water and eerie quiet. The light, however, never disappointed them. Billie used to say it was like seeing a new production every day, run by a lighting technician who tweaked the colors for every show.

Conversation with Billie rarely flagged. They talked about marriage and kids, and compared their upbringings in different decades and different religions. They discussed Florida politics and environmental threats. Billie asked Laila about the art world, and Laila learned from Billie about economics and government policy. Later in the day, other residents rotated in and out of conversations, dragging out their own chairs for comfort.

Afternoons brought out iced tea, and later, towards dusk, wine glasses and often the famous bottle of Scotch. Laila had less availability afternoons and evenings, but occasionally, she would join in. There might be storytelling, or stargazing, or heated political discussion. With Billie, no two get-togethers were the same.

The night before, Laila confided to David how she dreaded telling the rest of the Research Club about Billie's death. Telling Claire had been hard enough, and she was a relatively new member, not like Billie, Ken, and Regina, who formed the original group when Laila and her family first moved to Laguna Shores three years earlier.

David had cradled Laila in their bed, and the two made love with a mixture of emotion and caring detail that took her back to the time after her grandmother died. David, like any other man, could be overly efficient in bed, especially when the demands of four children left them with the minimum of time and privacy. But he also knew well how to use sex like a balm. He colored his caresses with understanding and patience until it was Laila who urged him to capture her.

That kind of lovemaking left Laila with the feeling that David had traveled with her into her deepest desires because he wanted to be wherever she was. She hoped he felt as loved as he made her feel.

This morning, the sun dawdled behind the low clouds at the horizon, and Laila didn't want to leave Billie's deck. The wavering light created pastel tones. A lilac edge gilded one cloud, a smoky pink filtered through another. Over and under the clouds floated a creamy yellow, thickening here, diluting over there. Laila tried often in her painting to copy the swirls of colors, but she thought she only achieved some interesting puddles and nothing to equal a Florida sunrise.

"Today's sky looks like underwater fireworks," Billie had commented one morning.

Laila began to aim for that effect and had intended to give Billie her first successful sunrise painting. Now, when and if she achieved a decent painting, it wouldn't mean half as much.

She thought about Regina. She hadn't managed to talk to her the night before. Talking with the boys had been chaotic, and then, afterwards, David was by her side. She might catch Regina between workout and breakfast this morning, but Laila owed her a measured, unhurried call. Between getting the boys to school and coordinating the week's schedule with David, there would be no time. She resigned herself to a tough Research Club meeting – there was no other way around it.

The door opened behind Laila, and she turned, expecting one of Billie's neighbors. Instead, a tall, sandy-haired man stepped out, his mug of coffee steaming in the cool air.

"It's stunning this morning," he said.

"Hello," said Laila. She didn't recognize him as any of the residents, but it wasn't unusual to have visitors coming and going. Claire had told her that the condos at Laguna Shores were easy to rent to tourists, especially the ones directly on the beach.

"Do you ever get used to it?" he asked.

"I don't think that's possible," said Laila.

The man dressed more formally than a beach vacationer might. He wore beige trousers and a short-sleeve knit shirt. By his age, probably in his early thirties, she guessed he came on a business-golfing combination trip.

He stepped toward her and took a seat in Billie's chair. She flinched but tried to keep her smile steady. She wanted to speak sharply to him, but it wasn't this man's fault that she couldn't bear to have another person take Billie's seat.

"The flowers are beautiful," he said. "Are you a neighbor?"

"I love this spot and this view," she said. "But I live in the next building over. Are you visiting Florida for the first time?"

"I've visited before to see family," he said and patted the cushion on his chair. "Mom and I picked out these chairs. They were built to last."

Laila realized who had come out to sit next to her. She exhaled softly and put down her coffee. He rocked backwards, contemplating the slowly brightening blue of the sky above them.

"Benjamin?" she ventured.

His head jerked towards her. "Yes. You know my Mom? I mean, you knew my Mom?"

"I'm Laila Harrow. I'm sorry to meet you under these circumstances."

He looked at her somewhat stricken, as though it were Laila telling him for the first time about his mother's death. She wondered if she should try to soothe him, and she searched for words that might soften the encounter.

"I live next door, and your Mom and I had a lot of things in common. We talked often."

He stared at her, his face a portrait of alarm. "You're Laila. Wait a second." He rose, walked quickly to the door, and disappeared inside the building. She steadied her coffee cup with both hands.

When he returned, he had a small card in his hand, the kind sold at all the knickknack shops up and down the coast with a picture of a garish blue dolphin on the front caught in mid-leap against a harsh pink sunset. Cards like these made Laila want to pick up a pair of scissors and start cutting.

"It's written to you," said Benjamin.

The card flapped open, as if someone had pressed the fold flat, perhaps in an effort to write more easily. Laila took it from Benjamin and held it open in one hand. A single sentence started out in loopy letters that got sloppier with each word.

"Dear Laila, I think you would want to know about David," she read out in a soft voice.

It was as if Billie had wrapped her own cold hand around Laila's, causing her to drop the card. It fluttered into her lap. Laila stared at the card and then at Billie's son.

"What was she trying to tell you?" Benjamin asked.

"I don't know."

"I guess there was something."

"She was close to our boys, but David? It doesn't make sense," Laila said.

"Who is David?" Benjamin asked.

"My husband."

"Does he live here?"

"Yes, yes, but he's busy. I mean he and Billie didn't have that much time together," she said. "It doesn't make sense."

"Tell me about your children," he said.

"Yes, four boys. She liked telling them all about the stars, the moon, the tides. We liked your Mom a lot." Laila looked down at the message and back at Benjamin. "Where did you find this?" she asked.

"On a table, with a pen lying next to it," Benjamin said.

Laila hated to imagine what Benjamin had been through in the last twenty-four hours. She was sure he would rather think of his mother drifting off peacefully, not eking out mysterious last messages.

"I'm sorry you have this kind of disturbance to deal with," she said.

"Was there a problem?" he asked. "Anything I can help with?"

"No," said Laila. "Nothing like that."

Maybe Billie had been imagining things, reeling from whatever it was that killed her — her heart, an aneurism, a stroke. Yet she conjured up these words, fighting off death in order to warn Laila. Jolted, Laila smothered an instinct to run and hide. Billie had to have been mistaken, spying danger where there was none.

"I can't believe she was keeping any secrets. She was like a grandma to the kids. Like a mom to me," she said.

"I'm sorry. I should have thought before I showed it to you. It's all so strange. I should have thought it through," Benjamin said. "You're upset."

Laila stood and brushed off the seat of her jeans in what she thought was a business-like gesture but then began to feel like a fussy, nervous movement. She picked up her cup, but it slipped from her fingers and spilled on to the deck.

"I'm so sorry," she said. "I don't have a napkin or anything." She bent and picked up the cup.

"It's nothing," he said. "I'll get it. I've upset you, and I'm sorry." He pulled a handkerchief from his pocket and mopped up the brown splash.

"No, please don't worry. I have to go get the kids to school," she said. "I just came over to be closer to her." She tucked Billie's card under her arm.

"Can I talk to you again?" asked Benjamin.

His kindness, warm and unhurried under difficult circumstances, reminded Laila of Billie. She liked Benjamin for it.

"Of course. If there's anything I can do, please call," she said. "What will you do about a funeral? Here or maybe back in Maryland?"

"I'm waiting on my brother," Benjamin said. "He's out of the country."

"If you come next door and ring the Harrow bell, we'll buzz you up on the elevator," said Laila. "Any time."

"She talked about you," he said.

"Thank you," she answered. "She talked about you, too."

Laila turned and descended the stairs, feeling Benjamin's eyes on her back as she walked across the sand to her building.

CHAPTER FOUR

Monday, Day Two – The Club Grieves

Ken arrived first at Laila's home, a small blessing for which Laila thanked his work ethic. He came off the elevator in shorts, a T-shirt and running shoes, his leather computer bag hanging on one shoulder. Ken had a broad face and straight dark hair that disguised his forty-eight years. Under his shirt, there was a rumor of thickening at his waist, but his legs were muscular and his posture ramrod straight.

When he spoke, although he was polite and respectful, he used a lot of stock phrases and slang, staying away from artful or literary language. Billie loved him because he would share dirty jokes with her.

"Got any more?" she would ask him.

"Not that I can tell you," Ken would answer. "Not a lady like you."

Billie would laugh hard at that. "If Art were here, he'd crack a few," she would tease. "You'd blush."

Billie's husband, Art, died shortly after they retired to Florida, before Billie moved to Laguna Shores.

Laila searched Ken's face for a sign of shock or sadness, but he smiled and headed for the large, sunlit dining room. He knew the room well. She hosted the third Monday of each month. Billie, Ken, and Claire took the other Mondays. Since Regina didn't live at Laguna Shores, she didn't host. No one suggested that they venture out to her neighborhood west of St. Augustine's. In a month with five Mondays, they skipped a week.

Ken lifted the centerpiece from the table and set it on the credenza. He slipped the tabletop pad out of the closet and laid it out for protection from their computers. He brought his laptop out of his bag and fished around for his power cord. Laila should have been setting out the orange juice and bagels they all loved, but she stood staring at his back. He saw her when he bent to the wall outlet.

"What?" he asked.

"Did you go to Billie's Saturday after I called you?" Laila asked.

"Of course."

"What did she say?"

"She said she was tired. She was going to bed."

"That's all?" Laila asked.

"I kidded her. I told her she shouldn't stay out so late."

"Had she been out?" Laila continued.

"I have no idea. She made a joke, like saying I get around, too. Or you're not the only one."

"Was she sick?"

"Maybe. I mean I was standing in the hallway. She didn't invite me in." Ken looked up at Laila. "Why?"

"She passed away, Ken," Laila said.

Ken stood, the computer cord dropped to the floor, and he gaped at her as if she had insulted him. "When?"

"They found her Sunday morning. Bob Page found her."

Ken pulled out a dining room chair and sat heavily. Laila leaned back against the archway leading to the living room. She waited for Ken to catch his breath. His eyes wandered around the room as if it might hold some explanation.

"Ma'am?" Caya, the girl who filled in on Margaret's days off, stood at the door. She held a tray of juice and bagels.

Caya placed them on the table and straightened up, looking at them and assessing the moment. The boys had told her about Billie's death that morning. The ever-helpful Bob Page had crashed their happy hour and broke the news, amplifying it with an inappropriate account of how he found her. She kept her expression somber and padded out.

"What happened?" Ken asked.

"A heart attack, they think," she said.

"I'm so sorry," he said. "This is terrible." He rested his forehead on the heels of his hands, bowing his head in a moment of grief. "It's why you called, right? Why you called all Sunday?" he asked after a long moment.

Laila nodded again. "Also, I needed to know." She took a seat at the table.

"What do you mean?"

"I needed to know if she died because I didn't bother to go over," Laila said.

"A conversation is not going to stop death, Laila."

"I might have seen signs," said Laila.

"Maybe she would have invited you in," Ken responded. "Maybe."

"Was she eating? Or drinking?" asked Laila. They both knew that Billie was fond of good liquor.

"She seemed all right. Maybe she'd had one or two. Tired," Ken said. He looked past Laila, as if he were trying to picture something.

"What?" she asked.

"Well, she was leaning on the door. That's why I got the impression she was tired. But she also stood as if she were blocking something, as if she didn't want me to see inside. I've been in her place, I don't know, thirty or forty times. What didn't she want me to see?"

Was it the card she was hiding? What did she mean about David? What else did she want to say?

"She might have been working on something new," said Laila. "Something she wasn't ready to talk about."

More than once Billie had refused to discuss her research before she unveiled it. The group would be at a loss to predict her interests. She might produce a pictorial review of farmers' abuse of Florida waterways, or a comparison of cottons from around the world, or the discovery of diaries kept by technicians at Los Alamos. Laila never got used to her surprises.

"Well, the TV wasn't on," Ken said.

"She could have just been reading," Laila mused.

"I should have gone in," he said.

"And I should have walked over. After the call, I should have walked over there."

"How did she sound when she called?" he asked.

"A little confused. She sort of hinted at some problem with another person, a female friend. But she cut off the message, saying she felt tired."

"That's how she looked," said Ken. "Tired."

"That was all, right? Just Billie at the end of the day."

"It definitely wasn't Billie alone and staring into the jaws of death," he said. "But this friend? What exactly did Billie say?"

"She couldn't come up with a name. That's how confused she was." She shrugged. At least Ken had seen the same listlessness that she had heard.

"No name," Ken repeated, as if in a daze, staring at the unneeded computer cord in his hand.

The elevator bell sounded, and Laila drifted reluctantly to the foyer. Claire's voice came over the intercom, and Laila buzzed her in, but when the doors opened, Regina appeared with Claire behind her.

She didn't speak but only put her arms around Laila and hugged her close.

Regina was several inches taller than Laila, and from any angle her body was flatter. She had so much muscle control that her embrace pulled Laila up and held her as if she were about to float on air. Laila didn't want to be released. Regina's dreadlocks were tied on top of her head with a bright blue cotton band so that her soft cheek was bare against Laila's forehead.

"I told her," Claire murmured.

"I'm sorry. I wanted to call." Laila choked out the words. Regina held her tighter.

"It's terrible news," said Ken. He stood in the doorway to the foyer, his power cord still dangling from his hand. Regina loosened her hold on Laila and looked over at Ken.

"It makes no sense," said Regina. "She was not frail. She could drink any one of us under the table."

Laila remembered one late night drink with Billie. December lights had hung in double garlands along the deck rails. Billie recounted how Jackson had told her the tale of the Wise Men in Bethlehem.

"I'll have you know I did not prompt him," Billie said.

"Like any kid, he likes a good story," Laila answered. "But don't worry; he's a well-rounded Unitarian."

We could laugh at anything, ourselves included.

Led by Ken, now the group shuffled toward the dining room, and Caya brought in mugs and a carafe of coffee. They opened their bags half-heartedly and set out their laptops. Seated, they looked around the table at each other, no one opening to a screen.

"I guess there's nowhere to go but down," Regina said.

"It's like we're half a club now," said Ken.

"Oh, she'd have a laugh to see us," said Claire. "Lost sheep."

"She'd tell us to get our asses in gear," said Ken.

"Tell us about the agenda you and Billie planned," Claire said to Laila.

"What was on it?" asked Ken.

"She had an update of Regina's Bitcoin program, and then she wanted to show off the new stuff she was doing for you, Claire, on county construction."

"So, could we hear about that?" prompted Regina.

Claire sat unblinking, staring at Laila.

"I didn't understand half of what she explained." Laila lifted her shoulders in a gesture of helplessness. "She also agreed that if there were time, we could discuss my museum project."

"So you're done with your boys' history in Haiti?" Ken asked.

"Billie's already given me fifty ways to Sunday to get more information on Forrest and Alton. I feel like I know what I'm doing there," said Laila.

"What if we keep on with Claire's and Regina's?" asked Ken. "Can we wait a few weeks on your project?"

"Yes," said Laila. "Billie already gave me a skeleton program anyway."

"I can move ahead on Reggie's Bitcoin stuff," said Ken.

"You know how to program?" asked Claire.

"Not as much as Billie," said Ken. "If she were here, I wouldn't say a word."

"What about you, Claire?" asked Regina. "Ken could look at your project."

"She'd given me an Excel sheet, but not much more."

Claire often sounded unenthusiastic about her research projects. Her tamped down attitude contributed to the impression that the club was purely social networking for Claire.

"What she showed me was Excel," said Laila. "But she put in links to charts and budgets that could then go back and populate the Excel, and something about a projection model. It seemed to go on and on."

"It sounds like a Project Management program," said Ken. "Something she may have purchased and then tweaked just for you, Claire."

"Or something she created on her own," said Regina. "She didn't have much respect for the garden variety programs. She used to call them 'one size fits none'."

"So I'll try to finish up both Claire's and the Bitcoin." Ken looked at Regina. "Not with any fancy detail, but it might scratch your itch."

"If you put it that way." Regina smiled.

The moment between Ken and Regina lasted longer than expected, and Laila was pleased. She had often thought Ken and Regina would be a great couple, but with Ken's business demands and his intense interest in surfing, and Regina's very busy tennis life, they spent limited time in each other's orbits. Besides, Regina had a teenage daughter who occupied much of her time outside work.

"I can sit down with you, Claire," Ken continued. "You tell me what you are trying to accomplish, and I'll try to get you there."

"That's kind of you," Claire said. "But, I have another idea. It's just awkward to bring it up today."

"What?" asked Ken.

"It's about a new member," said Claire. "But today is not the day to discuss it, I think. I mean, it's cold-hearted to even suggest it."

Here we go, thought Laila. For Claire, the club only serves as a social group. She'll bring one friend and then another, and another. The Research Club will start meeting in the evenings, with wine served, and no one will bother to bring a laptop, let alone get into helping each other out of dead ends.

Billie would have discouraged diluting the club's purpose.

"The thing is, though," Claire continued, "he might help us cope with losing Billie. He's a retired cop. A retired detective," Claire said.

"And?" said Regina. "That's supposed to be a recommendation?"

"Because Billie had those skills. What would you call them? Sleuthing skills," said Claire.

"She was sharp." Regina sighed.

"I know. I couldn't begin to replace Billie in the research department," said Ken.

"Please let's not talk about replacing Billie," Laila said, her head folding down toward the table, her hands propping up her forehead.

"Of course," said Claire quickly. "Billie was unique."

The group went silent.

After a while, Ken spoke. "This sucks. We're acting like we don't all need time."

Laila rested her cheek in her hand, and Claire re-filled her coffee cup. The silence became heavier until Ken spoke again.

"Where in hell did Billie get her skills anyway?"

"I know, right?" Regina exclaimed. "She worked for Social Security for her whole career."

"She didn't tell me much," said Laila, "but she mentioned she was in the Forensic Division. It sounded like it was a fraud patrol."

"That explains the charts and spreadsheets," said Ken. "Fraud comes out when the details don't fit the patterns. The more neat categories you can establish, the more likely you'll find the sore thumb. What kind of detective was your friend, Claire?" Ken asked.

"Brick?" Claire said.

"His name is Brick? That's actually his name?" Regina said.

"He's a red-head."

"Cute," said Regina "Especially cute for a cop. Where from?"

"New York City."

"Did he want to join the club?" asked Regina. "Or did you recruit him because he was a detective?"

"So this was all before I knew anything about Billie," said Claire. "I met him at an open house because he's new to Florida and needs a place, and he asked about what people do around here, and the club came up. I suggested he come to a meeting to see if it suited him."

"Wow. New York boys work fast," said Regina.

"Or girls from Atlanta do." Claire smiled.

"It sounds like it wouldn't hurt any of us if he attended a meeting," said Regina.

"I agree," said Ken. "Because Claire knows him."

Caya entered the dining room and tapped Laila on the shoulder. "It's Billie's son," she said in a hushed tone.

"Here?" asked Laila.

"In the foyer," said Caya.

Laila jumped up, and Caya followed her across the living room to the elevator entrance. Benjamin stood on the marble tile, his sunglasses pushed up on his head, his trousers and knit top looking as pressed as in the early morning.

"Hello, Laila," he said. "Would you have some time?"

"Yes. In fact, would you want to meet some of your mother's friends? We're having a club meeting, and she is the focus."

Even if we are discussing how to replace her.

"Sure, if it's all right with them."

Laila didn't answer but led Benjamin into the dining room.

"This is Benjamin, Billie's younger son," Laila said to the group.

"Benjamin," said Ken. He rose, reached across the corner of the table and shook Benjamin's hand. "I'm very sorry."

"I'm sorry for your loss," Claire said. She was sitting next to Benjamin and offered her hand also.

"I'm so sorry to meet you like this," Regina said. "I'm Regina, and Billie was a good friend to me."

Laila explained the nature of the club and how, for the previous two years, Billie aided them in their search for information, while she, too, gathered facts about her wide range of interests.

"In college, I often asked her to review my papers," Benjamin said. "The first years, she commented on the writing, trying to straighten out my train of thought, but then, even through grad school, her help was with the bibliography. Any paper, any class, and she would add books, and sometimes journal articles that I had missed."

"What did you study?" asked Ken.

"At the time, it was archaeology, but I went on to law school. I have a family law practice now."

"So we weren't the first people she had to help out of a bind?" Claire smiled.

"Not by a long shot," he said.

Laila poured Benjamin a cup of coffee. "Has your brother arrived yet?" she asked.

"In a couple of days, I think. He works for Treasury, and he's on a project in Germany."

"Is there anything we can do?" asked Claire.

"Any way we can help?" added Ken.

"Actually, yes," he said. "We'll wait as long as necessary for the funeral. That depends on my brother. But he said to go ahead with a wake for her friends. She's at Berman's, here in St. Augustine."

"Do you need pictures or flowers?" asked Laila.

"Pictures would be wonderful," said Benjamin. "Any recent photos you have would be appreciated. But also, a list of people you think might want to attend, with contact information, if possible."

"You'll have it tonight," Laila said, looking around the table and getting nods from the other three club members.

"I was sure she had an address book or at least a contacts list on her phone. But, it's helter-skelter in her place," Benjamin said.

"What do you mean?" asked Regina.

Laila held her breath and begged the powers that be to keep Benjamin from mentioning Billie's card with the scrawled message.

"In the living room, things were spread around. Finding an address book would be like finding a needle in a haystack," Benjamin said.

Laila exhaled.

The rest of the group looked at Benjamin with surprise. When they met at Billie's place, her pristine sense of organization was on display. Her desk held two large file drawers, and she could put her hands on documents from projects, old and new. More than once, Laila and Regina admired her dedication to the orderly life.

"How peculiar," Claire said. "Your mom had a reputation for keeping it all together."

"Maybe I'm just not up to the task. I just need time," Benjamin said.

The four club members murmured their assent, and Benjamin stood to leave.

"Can we help with the announcement?" said Ken. "Do you have a time and date for the wake?"

"Berman's suggested two evenings, tomorrow and Thursday, starting at seven," said Benjamin.

"We'll let neighbors know," said Claire. The others nodded.

"Thanks for the help," Benjamin said. "I very much appreciate it."

Laila showed Benjamin to the elevator. She was grateful to him for not bringing up Billie's card to the group. In fact, she would have been happy to have him forget about it entirely, but she felt an obligation to apologize for her earlier behavior.

"I'm sorry I was upset this morning," Laila said.

"In my practice, I see many people dealing with stress, and, as in our case, with grief," Benjamin said.

"Grief," she nodded. "This won't be the same place."

"It's just hard," said Benjamin.

Laila reached up and gave him a hug. He stepped into the elevator and turned towards her.

"If you need anything," she said.

He started to speak, but he must have thought better of trying. The door closed on his saddened face.

When she returned to the dining room, the group had packed up. They agreed to each email Laila a list of contacts to convey to Benjamin. They would meet the next evening at seven at the funeral parlor.

CHAPTER FIVE

Tuesday, Day Three – Photo Memories

Tuesday, the day of Billie's wake, David set off early for a site inspection for the new retail complex Harrow United wanted to develop in St. Augustine. Laila got out of bed so they could share a cup of coffee before he left.

"Would you like dinner before we leave for the wake?" she asked.

"I'll text, okay?" he answered. "What I'd really like is about an hour to work out and then swim."

"Then I'll get the boys fed at six and leave here at six forty-five. And you don't have to be at Berman's right at seven. Later would be fine."

"Thanks," he said. "It'll be a long day for both of us."

He gathered his briefcase and camera bag, which were only some of the essentials for the day's task. He wore loose jeans, a plaid shirt with two large pockets in front, a ball cap, and his work boots. In the parking garage, he would load a pick and shovel into the back of his pickup.

Today's site inspection would be the third since David and his family announced their interest in building in St. Augustine. The project was costing Laila more of David's time than she liked, but in the overall scheme of things, the idea pleased her because it meant they would stay at Laguna Shores for years. David estimated another six months to finish laying out the site, then two years for construction, and five years to scale up full operations. That way, both Eddie and Jackson would finish high school, and the twins would be ready to start secondary. If they had to move again, those circumstances would help the family make an easier transition.

When David left, Laila set up her easel on the master bedroom balcony and threw a paint smock over her slacks and blouse. She had an hour to work on her latest effort, a mid-size canvas of birds in flight over the ocean waves. The swoop of the birds and the way they skimmed the water, expertly hunting a meal, beguiled her. She had been playing with the shadows created as they flew. Her goals were modest. Laila wanted to hang one of her paintings in the living room without anyone assuming that it was hers.

About a half hour after Laila began, Margaret arrived and put on oatmeal for the boys and coffee for Laila. Soon she heard Eddie in the kitchen, or more accurately, she heard Margaret and Eddie singing.

"Then I never will play the wild rover no more," they crooned.

Laila thought she would regret not recording the two during their morning duets, but it seemed too precious, too intrusive to take out her phone and catch them as they sang. Time was running out, she worried, because Eddie was beginning to sleep in more and was losing his taste for Margaret's baking.

"Puberty is robbing us," Margaret had mourned to Laila one Saturday morning when she stood alone rolling out pie dough without Eddie as her assistant.

Laila was capping her paint jars when Jackson slid the door open onto her balcony.

"Mom, I feel crummy," he said. "I didn't sleep."

"That's not good," she said. "What do you think is wrong?"

"Headache, and I feel like throwing up."

His forehead felt clammy, and his eyes were puffy.

"Back to bed with you," she said. "I'll look in when I come back from driving everybody to school."

"Tummy ache," said Margaret when Laila got home. "Had a nice upchuck, and he's sleeping."

Laila hoped it was nothing more than an upset stomach. She needed to pull up photos for the wake and had a bittersweet search through three years of memories ahead of her.

Her first week in Florida, Laila was bringing the sand-soaked twins in from the beach and Billie appeared on their deck by the door to the elevator. She held a half a dozen imaginative plastic molds.

"Hi, I live next door," she began. "Here's something for your boys."

She was sweet smelling, Laila remembered, and like wildflowers, unruly and unpolished. Her wiry gray curls framed an oval face and double chin, and her eyes were on the large side, deep blue with white lids that made them appear larger still. She kept her shoulders squared, but a shapeless blouse covered her middle and thighs. Her tennis shoes were orange; her cotton slacks were dark green. She bent down easily to talk to the boys.

"I saw how hard you were working on the beach," she said. "I hope these shapes can help you."

The boys took the molds, divided between two netted bags, and thanked her. They were smiling as if it were their birthday.

"Come in with us," Laila said. "I'm Laila, and this is Forrest and Alton."

"I'm Billie. Before we go up, I can show you a secret."

The twins kept their eyes peeled on her. She crooked her finger at them, and the three disappeared behind a non-descript rock wall at the far end of the deck. Laila waited, but when she heard running water, she peeked around the barrier. The three of them stood on a slatted floor near a low faucet, rinsing their feet in the handy flow. Billie helped Laila dry the boys' feet and legs, and followed the trio into the elevator.

Laila had a stream of questions about Laguna Shores and the wider St. Augustine community. Billie was glad to fill her in as she could.

"Can you see the beach from your condo?" Laila asked. That's how you noticed the boys playing in the sand?"

"From the deck," Billie said. "And the twins are hard to miss."

Laila appreciated Billie's company. Billie never joined them on the beach, but she welcomed Laila and the boys onto her deck and into her condo whenever she was home. Many evenings she played cards with David, Laila, and Ken, and it was Billie who conceived of the Research Club.

Today Laila made it her mission to find a photo from that first friendly card game. She was scrolling through her backups when Jackson joined her.

"How do you feel?" she asked. He looked more rested.

"Better," he said. He had gotten out of his pajamas and combed his hair. "What're you doing, Mom?"

"I'm picking photos of Billie. You know we are going to her wake this evening."

"I remember."

"I told her son that we would bring him pictures of her."

"Are you going to bring your computer to the wake?" Jackson asked.

"No, I'm going to print out the pictures I find and, I don't know, put them on a board, like a cork board or something."

"You should put them on the digital photo frame Grandma sent us. The one in the living room."

"What a good idea," said Laila. Jackson retrieved the gadget, and Laila started moving photos into a folder.

"It's faster if you take one photo, do a picture recognition of her face, and then use the search function to pull out the other pictures of her," said Jackson.

Laila stared at Jackson.

"What?" he said. "We do it all the time for reports."

"Next you'll tell me that Alton knows how to do this, too," she said.

"He is better than Forrest at doing stuff, but they're both still just playing games and watching YouTube. They like animal videos."

Laila reminded herself to spend more time overseeing the boys' computer activities. If Jackson's skills were outstripping hers, Eddie had surely surpassed her, too. She made a mental note to ask Ken what she and David should worry about when it came to their boys and computers.

Within an hour, they loaded twenty-five pictures of Billie on to the electronic device. Laila suggested they take the display to Benjamin for him to review, in case he wanted to add or subtract photos. When she called, Benjamin invited them over.

Jackson and Laila exited the front of their building on to the sidewalk. Benjamin could buzz them in if they approached Billie's from the street, and they would avoid dragging sand from the beach into Billie's apartment.

"Who will take her place? What will happen to your club?" asked Jackson as they walked between buildings.

"I don't know," said Laila. "It's hard to figure out things without her."

"So you'll stop looking for Alton and Forrest's parents?" he asked with a noticeable uplift in his voice. Laila stopped in her tracks and turned to him.

"How did you hear about that?" she asked Jackson.

"Billie."

"What did she tell you?"

"She just mentioned that Haiti was a hard subject to research and sometimes there aren't any answers."

"And that worried you?" Laila asked him gently.

"What if you did find their parents, and they wanted them back?" Jackson asked.

Laila put her arm around Jackson's shoulder and pulled him close to her. "We know their parents are dead. We knew that from the beginning," she said.

"It's for sure true?" Jackson asked.

"Daddy was at their funeral. It was in Miami," Laila said.

"Not in Haiti?" asked Jackson.

"No. They got sick during the trip to Florida. They were taken to the hospital, but they didn't make it."

"So you have pictures?"

"We have their passports, with pictures in them. But Jackson, we need to wait to tell the twins. They are still young, and they haven't asked."

"I know. I wouldn't tell them anything."

"It's not a secret," she said. "We just have to be sure they're ready."

"Okay, I don't talk about it anyway, even with Eddie. But what are you looking for when you research Haiti?" Jackson asked.

"Stuff about where the twins' parents lived, and who their grandparents were, and if they went to church. Things like that. Things they might care about later."

Jackson seemed satisfied, and they went on walking towards Billie's front door. Since he dropped the subject, she didn't need to disclose her larger reason for tracing the twins' lineage.

Yes, she was curious about their ancestry. But she also needed to know if they might have siblings, siblings who might need an adoptive home. She felt an urgent responsibility to discover if anyone had been left behind in Haiti. She dreaded a day when the twins might turn to her and ask, "Why did you let me abandon my brother? Why didn't you find out about my sister?"

Billie had understood her urgent interest. Laila hadn't shared her research goals with David, and not with the boys. Billie mapped out some steps to take, and Laila had kept her progress to herself.

Smiling tentatively, Benjamin opened the condo door to Jackson and Laila.

"Good morning, young man," Benjamin said in a kindly voice directed at her son.

"Hello, I'm Jackson Harrow." Laila smiled at her son's formality.

"Good to meet you. I'm Benjamin Farmer."

"I'm sorry about Billie," Jackson said. "I liked her."

"That's kind of you to say," Benjamin answered. "Come in. Please come in."

As they stepped into the living area of the small quarters, Benjamin's description of the disarray struck Laila as an understatement. Throw pillows from the sofa lay tossed in a corner. The contents of the bookshelves cascaded onto the carpet. Two drawers from the base of the coffee table sat upside down on a chair. The disk storage tower, knocked to its side, stretched across the shelf over Billie's desk.

Laila noted that signs of unsanitary neglect, such as dirty plates or abandoned take-out containers, were not visible. The place looked ransacked, but not abused.

"What do you think?" asked Benjamin, gesturing to the unkempt rooms.

"It's not like her," said Laila. Any explanation would involve some kind of mad behavior by Billie, or, at the very least, last moments of panic and loss of self-control. Her face darkened, and she shuddered. Benjamin shook his head dejectedly.

Jackson's eyes darted around the room, but he kept his thoughts to himself. He handed over the digital photo frame to Benjamin and fished the power cord out of his jeans pocket.

Benjamin set it on the small dining table outside the pass through to the kitchen and plugged it in. As he scrolled through the photos, Jackson named the people and locations he guessed Benjamin wouldn't recognize. When they finished, Benjamin placed the device in a large box that he was loading with other memorabilia to take to the wake.

"You've been very helpful," Benjamin said to them.

"Do you want a hand with the clean up?" Laila asked.

"No, but thanks. I changed the sheets and did some laundry. I'll get to the rest."

"How about her telescope?" asked Jackson. "Was it left outside?"

"No, that was stowed neatly in her closet," Benjamin said.

"Good." Jackson nodded with a smile.

"Will you be there tonight?" Benjamin asked Jackson. "If you could help with the pictures and answer questions people might have, that would be great."

"Yes," said Jackson with a gravity that both pleased and worried Laila. He was already a child unduly aware of melancholy in others. David once said that he feared Jackson would opt to become a social worker, just for the privilege of listening to sad stories.

"Look, I can help you decide what to keep and what to donate," Laila offered.

"I would be very grateful for that," said Benjamin. "My brother and I will want a few things, but that's all. We'll be selling the condo."

"Of course," said Laila. "I'll get started tomorrow. I'll bring boxes."

Returning home, Laila couldn't get the thought of Billie's last hours of confusion and mess out of her head. What had she lost that was so important she was tearing up her home to find it? Is that why she had barred the door to Ken? She didn't want him to see the kind of disruption to order that would have mortified her?

I was just next door. I could have helped her. I could have settled her down.

Jackson napped again after lunch, and later, when Laila was heading out to pick up the others at school, he was sitting up in bed, reading.

"I'm going to ask your teacher for tonight's homework," she chided him.

"Bring it!" he called, cheerily.

"Sounds like our boy is fully recovered," said Margaret from the kitchen as Laila waited for the elevator to take her to the parking garage.

"Thanks for adjusting the dinner schedule for tonight," Laila said. "I'll have everyone in bed by nine. I don't want the rest of the crew coming down with the twenty-four-hour flu or whatever that was."

"Because we all know what kind of nursemaid I make," said Margaret. "I'm closer to a serial killer than a nurse."

"I'm aware," said Laila as she hopped into the elevator.

CHAPTER SIX

Tuesday, Day Three- The first night of the wake

Laila and the four boys arrived at the funeral home at seven sharp. She had explained to the twins that at least two rooms would be open to friends of Billie. Alton and Forrest did not need to go into the second room with Billie's body. They could sit on the comfortable sofa in the outer room, they could serve themselves juice, and they could visit the plates of cookies two times, taking one cookie each time.

"It's nice not to take your whole share right away," Laila told them. "It's nice to say hello to people, and you can ask people how they know Billie. If someone asks you, you can say you are neighbors."

"Aren't you going to be there?" asked Alton.

"Yes, but I might be in the second room. I might be talking to other visitors," said Laila.

"And Daddy?" asked Forrest.

"He'll get there a little later," said Laila. "Maybe you could wait for your second visit to the cookie plate until he comes."

"Maybe," said Alton.

"But we don't have to," said Forrest.

"Correct," said Laila.

Eddie and Jackson were more difficult to counsel. Eddie had not been as close to Billie. He didn't have the same fascination with the night skies as Jackson. From what Laila could tell, Eddie liked Billie because of the off chance she might slip and use some colorful phrases that they had eradicated from their speech since becoming parents. Eddie would let out a belly laugh when he heard expressions like "ball-breaker" and "panty hound" that peppered Billie's stories.

Jackson could get the giggles, too, over her sailor talk, as David called it, but it was more the chance to use the telescope with Billie, who could explain what he was seeing, that made him eager to pay her a visit.

"What's out there, Billie?" he would call before his foot hit the top step to the deck.

"Come and see," she would answer.

Laila reiterated to Eddie and Jackson that they had no obligation to view Billie's body if they didn't want to, and she added that if the funeral home became too crowded, they could step outside. Berman's had a large front porch that often accommodated overflow crowds.

"I don't know about going in to see her," Eddie said to Laila as they were walking from the parking lot at Berman's. He lagged behind so the other boys could not hear him. She was relieved that he could confide his uncertainty to her.

"That's natural," she said. "Billie won't know the difference, and that's what counts. Just take turns keeping an eye on Alton and Forrest."

The funeral home was full, and as Laila expected, there was a healthy crowd from Laguna Shores. Friends on the St. Augustine Art Museum board told her they socialized little with neighbors, but Laila and David had a very different experience at their condos. .

Of course, they met people outside the development because David's business required familiarity with city and county officials as well as a multitude of business leaders. Laila met parents and teachers at the boys' schools, and she had become friends with a few local artists.

But for a relaxing social event, something as simple as a game night, she called friends at Laguna Shores. When she sent out the email announcements about Billie's wake, the great majority went to Laguna Shores. The remaining portion went to some of Billie's church friends whose emails Claire provided.

Billie's minister, a spindly woman with the leathered skin of a long-time Floridian, greeted Laila and her sons when they arrived at Berman's. She wore a navy shirtdress neatly belted and comfortable-looking canvas flats. She stood in front of a table with a plastic tablecloth depicting colorful fruits and vegetables. Plates of hummus with olives, chips, crackers and cheese, cookies, Bundt cakes sliced in generous portions, and pitchers of raspberry-colored punch filled out the buffet. She introduced herself as Reverend Krall.

"The refreshments look wonderful," Laila said.

"Claire's doing," the Reverend said with smile. "And Benjamin told me you provided the picture set-up." She glanced toward the other side of the room where the electronic picture frame rotated photos of Billie across its screen. Jackson took up a position nearby, faithful to Benjamin's request of him.

"Did you want to add some of your own?" Laila asked.

"How thoughtful," she answered. "I'll ask a few of her friends. But it's a wonderful tribute as it is."

An older couple appeared at the door, and the minister moved off. Laila caught Eddie's eye and tipped her head toward the twins to remind him of his responsibility as the eldest son, and she left the three of them eyeing the food. She turned into the inner room where Billie's body was laid out.

The first thing Laila noticed was how cramped Billie appeared in her casket. Her face was condensed, as if arranged to support her eyeglasses and maintain a closed mouth. Her arms, too, were fit tightly to her body, her hands crossed over her abdomen.

No one needs, when they are dead, much space around for airflow or for movement, thought Laila. Billie would need, if she were alive, space to make her signature gesture. She used to take off her glasses to extend them to her listener, as if to say, here, take these, so you can see things as I see them. The glasses might help you. Then she would put the glasses back on, as if to say, well, no, I need them more; I'm the one who needs to see more detail before I understand.

Billie had a wonderful conversational style. She depended on questions, each one drawing out an answer of more depth. Despite Laila's own belief that the here and now was all anyone got and that life was meant to be one's trial and reward, looking down at her pursed face, she hoped that Billie was an exception and that someplace, somewhere, she would continue thinking and asking.

"She never looked like this, did she?" Benjamin had walked to Laila's side and put his arm around her shoulders.

Laila sighed. "Her hair is nice, though. They did a good job with it. She always complained that the humidity ruined her bob. She called it a bob, as if hairstyles had not changed since the forties."

"Once, when I was a kid, I visited her at work," Benjamin said. "I walked by so many desks, and I thought the people were dressed like models. I'd never smelled so much perfume and aftershave. So, I thought Mom had been closed into the corner office because she was the odd bug, someone who was better off not out in the open."

"She was the boss?"

"The boss' boss," he answered. "Her door was closed because she handled the most confidential cases."

"When did you realize she was in charge?"

"In college, I think," Benjamin said. "When she retired, I was home helping Dad and her pack up the house to move here, and a guy from the Administration came to ask her, please, could she come back just for ten days to help unravel this one case."

"Did she relent?"

"Dad came down to Florida without her and went to work on their new house. The Administration kept her a month, not just ten days. Dad was digging in the garden when he had the heart attack. She didn't get there in time."

Laila put her hand over Benjamin's. She had never heard the story of Art's death. Billie only talked about the good times and about her sons' hard work. Laila missed the sound of Billie's voice, asking her to pass the Scotch.

"She always worked? Even when you and your brother were little?" Laila asked.

"Yes, but only at the office. She and Dad got a housekeeper, and we ate out a lot. She could have gone even farther in her career, but she wouldn't travel. When we were old enough, she paid us to learn new recipes and prepare dinner."

Laila felt a new version of Billie crowding out the old version of the kindly but outdated civil servant. The newer Billie had more experience. She had high-level responsibilities policing the seamier side of America's character.

A sudden chill passed through Laila.

The dolphin card.

"I think you would want to know about David. . . ."

What if the card Billie had been writing when she died wasn't a message from an over-imaginative mystery fan? Had she discovered something Laila needed to know? Something Laila wouldn't want to know? The garish card didn't make sense, but since when did ugly revelations make sense? Silently, she wished the card back to the stupid little tourist shop from whence it surely came. She didn't need to worry about David, did she? He was solid.

Laila felt a hand on her back and turned to see Claire. She wore a dark red blouse with a pocket and short sleeves over black cotton trousers, and black sandals revealing the red polish of her toes. She was what Laila referred to as 'Florida fancy.' Bright colors, Laila came to understand after three years in the state, did not mean a happy occasion. Bright colors, preferably solid bright colors, meant that the wearer wanted to look finished. Claire pulled it off with ease.

"Again, I am so sorry for your loss," Claire said.

"Thank you," said Benjamin. He let go of Laila and moved to his right to allow Claire space in front of the casket.

"This is hard," said Claire. "She was good."

"So, then you never played cards with her," said Benjamin.

Claire smiled. "This is true. I heard they liked her in the bridge group, but the poker players weren't so enthusiastic," said Claire. "I stayed out of that particular brouhaha."

"She didn't play that much," said Benjamin, "but she did cheat. She said it was the least of all evils, and God didn't mind. My Dad said she did it because games were too easy for her, but he didn't excuse it and said it was more than embarrassing."

"I don't know," said Claire. "I liked knowing she had her little vice. It made me trust her more."

Laila slipped her arm around Claire's waist and gave her a hug. She excused herself to let other mourners approach the casket. She walked into the outer room to check on the boys. Jackson stood answering questions about the photo display, but Eddie was not in sight. Regina had arrived and taken a seat on the sofa between Alton and Forrest. Laila sat in the remaining space, hoping that Regina hadn't felt obligated to sit there to separate two squabbling boys.

"Claire's inside," said Laila.

"I'll go in," answered Regina. "I just couldn't resist these handsome boys."

Alton leaned his head against Regina's arm, and Forrest blessed her with one of his megawatt smiles. "They each offered me a cookie. They are becoming real gentlemen," she said.

Laila had first met Regina at the Laguna Shores sports complex a few weeks after moving to Florida from New York. She introduced herself as the tennis pro but asked about the twins in a way Laila would forever remember. Regina referred to Alton and Forrest as "your boys," not "those boys" or "interesting twins," as so many had. Laila felt Regina's great generosity in the way she bestowed her approval, a Black woman's approval, of their multiracial family.

Her continued embrace of their family gave Laila a taste of legitimacy, a feeling that a white woman could be seen to create a family for boys of color. Between Regina and Billie, Laila had the two best confidantes a woman could want.

"I haven't seen Ken," said Regina.

"He has trouble with funerals," said Laila.

"Don't we all," answered Regina. She tipped her head toward Alton and lifted her eyebrows, as if in a question.

"I'm not sure about what's understood," Laila said. Alton avoided the topic of death, and Forrest's usual curiosity had also been replaced by a studious silence. David or she needed to probe the subject with them, she thought.

"I guess I'll go say goodbye," said Regina, smoothing the folds of her white linen dress.

"I'm going to step outside and look for Eddie," said Laila to the twins. "Come with me. Maybe we'll spot Dad's car when he comes."

"I'm sure they won't run out of cookies," Regina said when the boys hesitated, not moving from the sofa. "I saw women carrying plates into the kitchen. There's a lot more."

The boys smiled at Regina's understanding and went outside with Laila.

On the broad, painted planks of the covered porch, knots of visitors sipped punch and chatted. Curious, Laila took a few steps and spotted Eddie around the corner, leaned up against the railing, trading comments with friends she recognized from various school events. A blond girl, lithe in her form-fitting jeans, looked over Eddie's shoulder, and her eyebrows arched when she spotted Laila. Eddie followed her glance, letting his hand, which had been resting on the girl's hip, drop to his side.

Laila knew the girl, Bailey Hanlon, daughter of a county commissioner. She smiled indulgently at Laila, as if Laila had come across the finish line of the championship race in second place behind her own graceful youth. Eddie turned back at the girl and his friends, casually resuming the conversation. Laila stepped back around the corner onto the front porch, trying to wipe the shock of dismissal from her face.

The twins had taken over two rocking chairs, set back a few feet from a circle of residents from Billie's building. The group was talking amiably. Laila patted the boys on the head, grateful for their affectionate smiles, and joined the group of neighbors. Each one had a story ready about sharing an early morning coffee or an evening drink with Billie on the back deck.

"You never heard about her aches and pains," said one middle-aged man.

"She kept up on the news, even local stuff. She could give you a smart run-down," said another.

"Her son seems sharp," a woman said. "Definitely Billie's offspring."

The group knew Laila's close friendship with Billie and turned to her with questions about the sudden death. Laila was admitting ignorance about the exact cause, when Benjamin appeared at the French doors giving out to the porch. The interior of the funeral parlor had become warm and the air closer than is pleasant. Benjamin looked green around the gills. Laila walked over to him.

"Have you met your Mom's building mates?" she asked.

"Not many," he said. "Please, introduce me."

The circle of acquaintances expressed their regrets, and the conversation again turned to the cause of death.

"A sudden death is difficult, isn't it?" one woman commented.

"She had a grand total of one vial of thyroid pills in her medicine cabinet," Benjamin said. "I guess her doctor missed something."

"Doctor Lake?" said one of the men.

Benjamin nodded.

"Not likely," another neighbor said. "He's got a good reputation."

"I just didn't worry about her in that way," said Benjamin. "Other things, like if was she lonely, but not her health. Her own mother lived to ninety-six."

Everyone in the group began talking at once, assuring him that Billie displayed none of the characteristics of a lonely woman. She was a listener, they said, more interested in others' lives than going on about her own concerns.

"She must have put a lot of miles on her car," someone said. "Billie was always going somewhere, keys in hand."

"I don't know what the food bank will do without her. She spent a lot of hours there."

"Not lonely. Not by a long shot," said another.

Claire appeared at Laila's side, looking surprised at the gaiety of the group.

"Shhh, Laguna Shores, shhh," said Claire.

"It's all right. We're talking about Billie's energy," Laila said. "About how we'll miss her."

"Do you know she did not take the elevator?" said Claire. "I've been in her building many times to show units, and she'd come through the door from the back stairs. I mean, it was only the second floor, but still, she was seventy-two."

"Seventy-three," said Benjamin.

Claire looked at him with sympathy.

"I'd guess she had an apartment full of things, a lifetime's things."

"It's stuffed," he acknowledged. "Plus, the storage in the basement. Laila has offered to help me clean it out."

"Call me, if you want, Laila," said Claire. "I can help. I'm a flea market maven."

"I will," said Laila.

"Very kind," said Benjamin to Claire. "It's a small place, but she used every square inch."

"We'll get it in shape," said Claire. "Has Reverend Krall been available to work with you on Billie's service?" Claire asked, pivoting the conversation away from real estate. Laila admired Claire's good grace in not asking Benjamin if he were selling the condo.

"She and I haven't discussed it. It's more my brother's territory. He'll be here Friday," Benjamin answered.

From the corner of her eye, Laila saw the twins stop their rocking and scramble out of the chairs. She pulled away from the perimeter of the group to spy David moving toward the porch stairs. She felt her jaw unclench, and she realized how much the day had required of her reserves. She met him at the top of the steps, a few yards from their neighbors. Alton and Forrest had reached him first, and each had taken one of his hands.

"Things seem under control," he said, smiling down at the boys.

"They've been quite good," she answered. "I think it's fine for me to take them home now."

"No, you go," he said. "I'll stay with them. Take my car, and I'll bring everybody in the SUV."

"Are you sure?" she asked, grateful for the suggestion. "They're about to start the prayer service."

"We'll be fine."

Laila walked back to the group to arrange to meet Claire the next day and to say goodbye to Benjamin. Claire turned at Laila's touch, and for a moment, her eyes widened and shoulders tensed, as if Laila had said something harsh, when she hadn't opened her mouth. Her tight smile made Laila follow her glance. It was David she had seen first.

"We'll start tomorrow at Billie's?" Laila inquired softly. She could feel David walking up behind her, and she heard the twins' restless footsteps.

"Sounds good," Claire answered. She lifted her head solemnly and spoke slowly, as if she were only speaking because it was required by a formal protocol. "Hi, David."

"Claire, how are you?" he asked. He nodded to a few others in the group and stepped back to give Laila room to turn. "Go now, we're fine," he assured her. The boys were tugging him in the direction of the buffet table. He smiled stiffly, as if he were taking part in an unrehearsed skit. She patted his arm and thanked him before he went inside.

Reverend Krall had joined the group and was inviting everyone to return to the parlor for a prayer service. Laila made her exit, heading off the porch to the parking lot. She looked back once and spied Claire who looked quickly away at another neighbor, as if she had something pressing to say.

With her key fob, she lit up the brake lights of the Miata at the far corner of the parking lot and headed in its direction. She stopped about half way to the car and turned to stare back at the empty porch again. How had David angered Claire? Had there been an HOA meeting that Laila missed? Did they have a disagreement over some real estate issue? Laila could think of no way Claire's retail real estate life overlapped with David's commercial development. Or did Claire park in their guest spot again as she often did when she was showing a condo in their building? David could be touchy about his convenience, especially when stressed. His work might be impacting their social life, and she didn't like it.

Two cars away, a familiar figure stepped out between two vans.

"Jennifer Serrano!" Laila exclaimed.

"Am I too late?" the woman asked.

"I didn't realize we shared Billie as a friend," Laila said.

"I'm in her church," Jennifer answered. "And you?"

"Neighbors at Laguna Shores," Laila said.

"I guess it's no surprise. In her seventies, and all."

Laila's spirits sank in the face of this dismissal of Billie's death as an unremarkable turn of events, but she kept her smile in place.

"Her son Benjamin is still inside," she said. Jennifer nodded her understanding.

"We missed you at the board meeting this afternoon," Jennifer said.

Laila squirmed. She had completely forgotten her promise to attend. These past two days, her head was in a fog. But no one wanted to hear excuses, and Laila herself resented those who seemed to think excuses made up for poor performance. She noted Jennifer's irritation.

"I'm so sorry," was all Laila could manage. She was glad that she didn't have the boys with her, completing the image of the unprofessional stay-at-home Mom in the Board President's eyes.

"If you email me the report, I'll share it with the other members," Jennifer said.

"I'll do it tonight."

"You found something then?" said Jennifer.

"I found fifty or so leads," Laila said. "And I'm up to a dozen new Highwaymen paintings."

Laila enjoyed Jennifer's look of surprise. Billie had helped Laila uncover several sources of information on the Highwaymen, a loosely associated group of Florida painters who produced, by conservative estimation, one hundred thousand paintings during the second half of the twentieth century. Once discounted as rank amateurs, their works were increasing in value. It was an unexpected coup and could grow the prominence of the St. Augustine museum. Jennifer would want documentation on her desk as soon as possible.

"This is exciting news," Jennifer said.

"There is so much to explore," Laila said.

This wasn't the place, she thought, to go into the details of her work, and even if it were appropriate, she wasn't sure, now that Billie was gone, that she could backtrack and vouch for every thread.

What a gift Billie had been.

"So tonight?" Jennifer said eagerly.

"Yes, of course," Laila answered. "As soon as I get home."

Jennifer turned toward the funeral home, and Laila got into the car. She sat, her head resting on the steering wheel for a few moments, and gathered up her ragged emotions. Billie deserved credit for her selfless work on Laila's museum project, work that might lead to enriching the museum's collection of Highwaymen paintings. More than that, the Highwaymen's fantastic story of talent developing amid poverty and Jim Crow restrictions might come to the fore. Art critics and curators valued the originality of style and craft, and

Billie's research could add to the knowledge of the Highwaymen's evolution. So many might benefit – but not Billie.

It's the way of the world. This awfully sad world.

If there were any consolation to be had, maybe it would come from completing Billie's research, creating a small bit of legacy. In life, Billie would duck the spotlight, but if the Highwaymen catalogue ever happened, Laila would give Billie public credit.

She headed home to the common remedy for grief: sleep.

CHAPTER SEVEN

Wednesday, Day Four – Clean Out Begins

After delivering the kids to school, Laila let herself into Billie's to get started on the job of sorting through her friend's things. Claire had called to say she would be over as soon as she cleared up some paperwork at her office.

Benjamin had cleaned off a workspace on the dining room table and a small area in the bedroom closet. Otherwise, Billie's belongings remained as she had seen them the day before. Laila set to work on gathering up the scattered items, the things out of place in Billie's businesslike world so Claire could think clearly about what to take to dealers.

Pencils, notepads, files – everything had its nook or cranny. Laila recreated Billie's organization as she had known it and moved on to the coffee table. The drawers and the storage baskets underneath had been dumped out and the contents spread along the sofa and on to the carpet.

She combed through some of Billie's favorite items, like the deck of playing cards embossed with the various Washington D.C. monuments and a stargazer's guide. She found a compact world atlas, a U.S. atlas, a pad of bridge scorecards, and a tape measure. There were extra reading glasses in leather cases and a leather-handled nutcracker.

She dropped the odd pieces of mail into Billie's file drawer under "correspondence." Then she started to work on putting the bookcase back in order, wondering again what it had been that Billie was looking for that last evening of her life. Was it a pen to write those last words on the silly dolphin card?

Laila pictured her having a heart attack or stroke, searching in a panic for medication, even just aspirin, to stop the pain. She might have felt what was coming.

In contrast, Regina had confided doubts about that scenario the night before. She called as Laila was climbing into bed.

"Everything all right?" Regina had asked. "You left a little early."

"I know," Laila said, apologetic. "I'll go again Thursday night, maybe without the kids. Maybe spend some time with Benjamin and meet Billie's church friends. That was a side of her I didn't really know."

"Benjamin could use the support," Regina said. "He'll appreciate it."

"He's so much her son, right? Attentive, a listener," Laila added.

"Absolutely. But he's having a rough time."

"What do you mean?"

"After the wake, after most people had left, he was collecting some things. Those pictures, by the way, on that electronic thingy were wonderful. You really pulled together some great ones," Regina said.

"Thanks, but what did he say? I wish his brother would get here," she fumed.

"I don't know if his brother could help. It's the thing about Billie's health. No problems, no conditions, no surgeries. Not even a hint. And then a messed-up apartment, as if she'd been hosting a party, everything tossed around. He feels like something's not right."

Laila had no answer. Regina said goodnight, leaving Laila with the tumult of doubt and regrets she had been nursing for days. As she sorted through Billie's things, questions popped up from all sides.

Why, for what earthly reason, did the person who knew the most about Billie's last evening, about how she looked and what she said, not come to the wake? Laila tried to be forgiving about Ken's absence, but it was not working after her conversation with Regina. He said Billie looked tired. Maybe Benjamin and Ken should visit Billie's doctor together and sort out what might have been happening.

Laila could hardly make promises for Ken. He needed to show up. What was he thinking? Laila sat on her haunches, a book in her hand, a few more scattered at her knees, and her head dropped forward, her chin on her chest, her thick hair slipping in front of her eyes.

But now nothing could change that night. Nothing could bring her back.

She let her feet slip out from under her, and she slumped onto the carpet, propped up by a hand, weeping for the end of a friend who had been kind, intelligent, funny, and generous. If only she could have one more talk, one more cup of coffee, one more sunrise with her friend, one chance to say goodbye, one chance to say thank you.

The knock at the door did nothing to stop Laila's weeping. A deliveryman, a nosy neighbor, a kid selling cookies – Laila didn't care. They wouldn't change anything. The second knock irritated her more, and at the third, she called out, "Go away."

"It's me," came the voice. "Claire."

Laila pulled herself up and blotted the tears with the side of her hand. She opened the door to let Claire in and found her standing in the hall with a broad-shouldered, redheaded man beside her.

"Oh, my," said Claire. "You're having a rough time."

Laila opened wider so both could pass. She was wordless but tried to force her expression into a welcome of sorts. She tried again to fix what she knew were streaks across her face, and Claire produced tissues from her bag.

"Hey, hey," she said, handing them to Laila. "You're allowed. It's okay."

"I'm sorry," said Laila. "Just a moment." She walked through Billie's bedroom and into the bathroom. When she reappeared in the living room, Claire and the man stood gazing around the disheveled room.

"Laila, this is Brick. He's offered to help, and he has a truck."

Laila shook Brick's hand and offered both chairs at the dining room table. Brick seated his tall but slim frame carefully. Laila appreciated the tentativeness, as if he respected the apartment and the loss it represented.

"Laila lives in the next building over," said Claire to Brick. "She knew Billie better than the rest of us."

"I'm sorry for your friend," he said.

"I shouldn't have come over here by myself," Laila said. "I couldn't stop thinking about everything."

"We're here now," said Claire. "What's your plan? Just give us directions."

It was like Claire, Laila thought, to choose action over discussion. She was cool and direct like that. It's okay, Laila decided. Everybody has their own way of handling their feelings. Billie wouldn't have asked for a lot of wringing of hands. She'd be the first one to keep her tears to herself.

"I like your idea of a photo record," Laila said.

"I'll keep a running tally of furniture, decorations, and kitchen appliances," Claire said. "Brick can get good pictures, in case we want to post them rather than take them straight to the flea markets." She pulled out a thick pad of lined paper, a pen, and an iPad.

"Good," said Laila. "I'm about done straightening out this room; then

I'll move to the bath and closet to pull together Billie's clothing and personal items. Benjamin doesn't want to pack up her things. Too painful."

"You've got a job ahead of you," said Brick, gazing around at the apartment's scattered contents.

"It looks upended," said Claire. "Benjamin wasn't exaggerating."

"Who knows what was going through her head," said Laila.

She cringed at the thought of Billie's last call for help. Claire would be shocked to learn that at some point that evening Billie phoned Laila, and Laila didn't come running.

She smiled weakly at Claire and Brick and lowered her head back to her task, hoping to ward off any discussion of Billie's last hours. Brick and Claire cooperated, moving into the bedroom to start their inventory.

Within a few hours, clothes had been divided among a discard pile, a laundry pile, and several large boxes for donation. Laila chucked cosmetics and hygiene products into a plastic garbage bag but put aside the cleaning products for use by whomever Benjamin hired to come in before the sale of the condo.

Claire moved the radio from the kitchen to the dining area and tuned it to a local station. At first, Laila was irritated, thinking Claire, in her businesslike efficiency, would try to hurry the job along with an upbeat soundtrack. The station she chose, however, was classical music with few commercial breaks. An hour of Brahms was followed by an hour of Bach, and in Laila's mind, their work took on a feeling of ritual.

We're freeing her from these material weights, Laila thought. She'll coast away on waves of music, letting us take care of the minutiae. Believing that Billie approved of their efforts and was eager to take flight into the next realm was consoling. It was easier than believing that once they dismantled the apartment and sold it off, Billie would be nothing but ashes.

The peace washing over Laila as she worked at her tasks was not disturbed by Brick's presence. She noticed he paid careful attention to what Claire needed. He asked questions and made suggestions, but often, he worked without a word. She was sorting jewelry in Billie's walk-in closet when Claire and Brick started in on the bedroom. He dusted off the dresser and table, laying aside the odd knickknacks. She took a photo with her iPad, and they moved on to the bed frame, zeroing in for the carved details of the bedposts.

Laila was impressed with Brick's intention to be of service to Claire, but she wondered if that would be a good match for Claire. Independent, efficient, strong - the type to fight with David, Laila smiled to herself. Not the type to have a mutual partnership.

Mid-afternoon, Brick offered to get the three of them some lunch. Laila declined, but Claire agreed and stopped work to make coffee. Laila would have liked to stay, but she had to pick up the boys and take them to their regular tennis lesson with Regina.

"If you leave before I get back, I'll call you tonight, okay?" Laila said to Claire.

"What do you think of Brick?" Claire asked.

"He's pretty nice to put in all this time," said Laila.

"I've explained how much she meant," Claire said.

"It's quite a situation for a new guy to grapple with," Laila said. "The help is much appreciated."

"He really wants to join the club," said Claire.

"To spend time with you?" Laila smiled.

"I do get to running around. It's been so busy. I guess he sees it as establishing some common ground."

"Not a bad reason," Laila said. "Speaking of common ground, is there something up with David? Did you two have an argument of some kind?"

"No," she answered with a sharp shake of her head.

Laila stood looking at her, her head cocked to one side as if to say she didn't totally believe her.

"Well," Claire said, looking down sheepishly, "actually, he heard me telling a client that Laguna Shores has the very best residents. He said it sounded like code for rich and white. I see his point, but you know, a sales person's gotta sell."

"Well, you know, a Daddy's gotta protect."

"Of course, I understand. I'll do my best to change my sales pitch," Claire said.

"There are a lot of other things to point to. A beach, an ocean. No shortage there."

Claire smiled and nodded. "For sure." She paused and looked a moment at Laila. "Hey, please don't say anything to David about my comments, okay? He'll think I was trying to prolong the misunderstanding. I get it. Really I do."

"No problem," said Laila. "By the way, if Brick joins the club, what is he planning on researching?"

"What?" she said, caught short by the question. "Florida stuff, I think," she said after a moment. "Like places to go, parks, and stuff like that."

"Sounds good," said Laila. "Well, maybe I'll see you later."

Laila hurried into the parking garage, about ten minutes behind schedule.

Florida stuff? Oh, dear, Billie would have been appalled at the fluff of that topic. And when did David hear Claire giving a sales pitch?

CHAPTER EIGHT

Wednesday, Day Four – Hot Items

The boys retrieved and delivered, in Eddie and Jackson's case to the tennis courts, and in the twins' to the house for an afternoon snack, Laila stood considering Margaret's superb guacamole and chips. Spoiled, thought Laila. I am completely spoiled.

When her phone rang, Laila stepped out of the kitchen into the living room to take the call.

"Hi, it's Jennifer."

"Hello," Laila said.

"Thanks for the report," Jennifer said.

"It makes sense?" asked Laila.

"I'm flabbergasted. I'm not sure where to begin."

"If we want to proceed, we want to get as much photographic information as possible," Laila said. "Close-ups. Photos that show details."

"How much confidence do you have in these estimates?"

"Some of the Highwaymen are still alive. We could go to Fort Pierce and interview them," said Laila. "But, yes, I believe about thirty percent of their works are out of their control."

"But not all stolen," said Jennifer.

"Right," said Laila. "Approaching about fifteen percent of the thirty percent are stolen. The rest, who knows? In people's attics, or burned in house fires, or even painted over."

"We need another board meeting," said Jennifer. "Soon."

"I agree," said Laila. "Just set the date. I'll be there."

"You'll be available?" asked Jennifer, pointedly.

Jennifer's recruitment of volunteers left much to be desired, thought Laila. She could take it because the SAM had a decent reputation. When the boys were grown, she'd want to get back into the art world full time, and this project would provide a calling card.

Jennifer's ambition for the institution pushed projects further and faster than in most places, which was fine, except sometimes she scared off the more mild-mannered among the volunteers.

"You know you love it," said David, when she complained about Jennifer's drive. "You like tough standards."

"It's true," said Laila. "But I don't want to be the last volunteer standing when there's work to be done."

"You provide the charm," said David. "Let her be the taskmaster."

"Is that how you run Harrow United?" asked Laila.

"No, I'm the whole package." He laughed. "Charming and demanding. And it doesn't always work so well."

David might be right, thought Laila. Jennifer could pressure her even more and Laila would try harder. Let Jennifer do the hard work of running the institution.

"I'll be there," said Laila. "I missed last time because of Billie's passing. I don't expect to lose another friend soon."

A project as significant as locating, documenting, and cataloguing the entirety of works by the Florida Highwaymen made Laila shiver with anticipation. The energy with which they learned their craft, by-the-seat-of-their-pants marketing methods, and the joy of color that marked their canvasses turned the Highwaymen into a growing art phenomenon.

Growing? More like snowballing. Billie, who wasn't an art lover, immediately grasped the drama. A loose association of men straight out of the orange groves found in painting a catapult to economic freedom. Their story was hopeful and historic. Billie put the identification of hundreds of missing works within reach.

The catalogue, if St. Augustine's Art Museum ever publishes it, thought Laila, must be dedicated to Billie Farmer. Wilhelmina J. Farmer.

After their snack, Alton and Forrest found Laila in the living room, and the three decided to go back outside. The playground by the tennis courts attracted the twins, although Laila wished the climbing gym was not so high. Laila switched into hardy, rubber-soled shoes so that she could scramble up the ladders and slides, matching the boys' energy as much as she could.

"I see London, I see France, I see Forrest's underpants," called Eddie from underneath the climbing structure. He stood below, lesson finished, with Jackson and Regina.

Eddie was growing up, thought Laila, except when a chance to get his little brother's goat presented itself.

Laila and the twins reached the top of the gym and the mouth of its slide, a plastic-topped tube, twisting to the ground like a curled intestine. Forrest was first, but Alton and Laila were right behind, shooting down the slide with squeals and shouts.

"You can't catch us," Forrest yelled at Eddie. "Come on, Alton."

Eddie and Jackson comically counted to ten, as slowly as possible and then started climbing behind their brothers.

"What are you feeding them?" Regina called, and Laila walked to her side, keeping one eye on the climbers.

"You're the one that's building up their muscles," said Laila. "I saw how you run them around the court."

"I suppose," Regina answered. "Hey, it was nice to see David last night, even if it was Billie's wake."

"It's been a while since a game night," Laila said.

"Is it the travel?" asked Regina.

"He pretty much only goes to Miami now, to consult at family headquarters," said Laila. "But it still means he's out of the house. It's not great."

Plus, he's spending too much time under the tutelage of Sam.

The conservative religious haranguing by Sam Harrow was the obvious explanation for David's unusual comments the night before. For the first time in their married life, David expressed an interest in giving the kids a stricter religious grounding.

"That girl hanging on Eddie at the funeral parlor," David began, "looked a little too advanced."

"I thought you worked with her dad," she said. Laila pictured her unsettling face. *Cheeky, for sure.*

"What about a church with a youth group that's really organized," he said.

"Do you mean join Billie's church?" she asked.

"Not if Bailey Hanlon is a sample of their youth group," David said. "The Presbyterians have an enormous youth group that's always in the news. Can you look into that?"

She didn't like the girl's attitude either, but David's reaction seemed out of the blue. How long had he been thinking about this youth group thing?

Reggie was watching her intently, and Laila realized her wonderment and confusion with David's remarks had spread across her face. She shook off the worry and finished with a shrug.

"So older brother gets to stay at headquarters, but younger brother gets pushed out into the hinterlands of St. Augustine?" said Regina, only a half-joking probe.

"The company will build in St. Augustine. I mean build big. But you didn't hear that from me," said Laila, regaining her focus.

"The new Harrow United store isn't exactly a secret," said Regina.

"How about a Harrow mini-city?" said Laila. "He might be the younger brother, but he's got big plans."

Plans that will keep us far from Miami.

"Where do people get the energy? I can barely manage a slate of tennis students," said Regina. "And about that. I'm taking off next week for a vacay in New York."

"Just you? Or would someone named Ken be going along?" asked Laila.

Regina looked at Laila with astonishment. "Aren't you the detective!"

"The glances, the sighs – so cute," Laila said.

"Come on! We do not act like teenagers," protested Regina.

"You're my friends. I don't need cymbals to clang. Besides, you can't stop smiling."

"Amazing. You amaze me! But listen, it is new, and we want to keep it quiet until Mindy leaves for school. Five more months," Regina said.

"So, you're going to New York with Ken? That's keeping it under the radar?"

"I'm going with Mindy. It's her graduation present. We're going clothes shopping."

"Darn, I had you in a horse-drawn carriage in Central Park snuggled with Mr. Lee," said Laila.

"As if that's his style. Are you sure you're good friends with him?"

"Mom!"

Laila looked up to see Forrest hanging on one of the horizontal bars built over the open space between the ladders of the climbing structure. Between the two posts of the gym, Forrest hung down, his arms stretched to their limit but his feet yet dangling eight feet up over the ground. She took a step toward the playground, but Regina was quicker.

All Laila saw was the bottom of Regina's court shoes as she vaulted over the railing in front of the structure and positioned herself beneath Forrest. Eddie had crawled along the top of the horizontal bars, laid himself flat, reaching his arms to Forrest. He grasped at his brother's forearms. If Forrest let go, and Eddie yanked, he might dislocate a shoulder, or worse.

"The back of his pants," yelled Regina. "Grab the belt."

Eddie shoved one hand into the back of Forrest's pants at his right hip and took hold of his underwear. The other hand wrapped around his belt. When Forrest felt the support, he let his hands drop from the overhead bars and tumbled forward, his head lunging down towards Regina, his arms outstretched.

"Got him!" Regina yelled.

She gave Forrest as broad a target as possible, with her knees bent and her arms wide. Eddie let go, and Forrest tumbled on top of Regina, flailing towards her neck, the weight of his free torso and legs flopping towards the ground pulling them both down. Because of her strong frame, the only part of him that hit the ground directly was the toe of one shoe.

Laila got to Regina's side a moment after Forrest slipped from the bars. She got one arm under Regina's neck to break the fall that was coming, the fall that knocked her down as well. The three of them were splattered across the sand.

"Anything broken?" asked Laila, amid the grunts and moans of Forrest and Regina. On her back on the ground, Laila could see Alton backing down the ladder, rung by rung, until he gingerly placed one foot and then another on solid ground.

Eddie had swung down easily, and he and Jackson circled the three bodies. Eddie leaned over and lifted Forrest to his feet and brushed off his back. Forrest smiled up at his older brother.

"You couldn't tag me."

Eddie laughed at his brother.

"Tough guy, huh?" Eddie said, offering a hand to Regina and another to Laila.

"Incredible catch, Reggie," Laila said. "You saved him."

"I thought I saw a broken leg in his future," Regina said, taking the cap off her impressive braids and shaking the sand out of it.

Jackson put his arms around Regina and hugged her.

"Eddie, you're a fast thinker," she said. He laughed and elbowed Jackson as confirmation.

"Let's go take a break," said Laila. "Popsicles on the back deck, anyone?"

"I have to get going," said Regina. "Otherwise, I'd love to."

"We owe you," said Laila. "We all owe you." Regina accepted her hug.

The five of them accompanied Regina to her SUV. The sun waned behind them, warm light heating the early evening dew so that the grass was slick beneath their feet. Alton stayed close to Laila, but Forrest broke away from the group to try a running skid across the playground lawn. Laila's gaze followed his path towards the parking lot, and she spotted Claire and Brick climbing out of Claire's bright red car.

"Brick?" asked Regina.

Laila nodded. "We were working at Billie's together," she answered.

"And?" said Regina.

"They move fast." Laila smiled.

"Like Ken and me," she said with a straight face.

"You're deluded." Laila laughed.

Claire introduced Brick to Regina, and Laila introduced Brick to her sons. Eddie and Jackson started to squirm, as boys who fear an adult conversation may soon engulf them do.

"I've got some homework," said Jackson.

"Me, too," said Eddie, a little too slowly. But Laila understood and dismissed them to home.

"And, thanks, Eddie," she called after the two. Eddie raised two fingers to his brow in a salute, pleased, it seemed to Laila, for all the recognition.

"I'll be off, too," said Regina. "Nice to meet you, Brick."

"You'd better stay for this," said Claire. "I think you'll be interested."

Laila's attention snapped back from the departing boys to Claire's face. She noticed what she had first missed. Claire spoke in her real estate voice, and her face was taking orders from that voice. In this more formal stance, every glance and gesture felt planned to Laila. Telling Regina to stay was a reaction Claire had thought about before she exited her vehicle. Sometimes, Claire needed everyone to put attention wherever Claire directed it.

"What's up?" asked Laila. She inclined her head toward the twins as a warning to Claire to censor the conversation.

"Boys," said Regina. "While you're waiting, I'll give you ten cents for every tennis ball you can collect from around the courts. Look in the grass outside the fence. Lots that get lost there, too."

Alton and Forrest headed to the courts and out of earshot of the four adults.

"Have you checked your phone lately?" asked Claire. She tried to keep her tone light, but her arms were crossed tightly across her body.

Laila withdrew the phone from its pouch, lighting up the screen and pressing the touch recognition button. She brought up voicemail and saw a message from Benjamin. She hesitated to put it on speaker, afraid Benjamin might refer to the dolphin card mentioning David.

"I'm guessing he's telling you about the autopsy," Claire said. I wish we had gotten a heads up. Listen to it."

"Autopsy? He asked for an autopsy?" asked Regina.

At Claire's urging, Laila put the phone to her ear.

"Hello, Laila, it's Benjamin. Thank you so much for your help with the wake last night. I appreciate it. You can't imagine."

There was a pause, and Laila pulled the phone away, thinking the message was done. But Benjamin's words started again.

"Look, I visited Mom's doctor, and he said she didn't have a heart ailment. So, I asked for an autopsy. It's upsetting, and I'll be glad when my brother arrives. Call me if you'd like."

Another long pause. Laila kept the phone to her ear this time.

"Take care. Bye," came the voice finally.

"Poor Benjamin," said Laila. "An autopsy on his mother – it's got to be hard."

"I'm sure," said Claire. "But it would have been nice if Benjamin," and Claire pronounced his name as if he were a small rodent, "had given us, the day laborers, a heads up."

"What happened?" asked Regina.

"The police came to Billie's to take a look. When they found us there, they weren't cordial."

"Understandably," said Brick. "The three of us," he said, indicating Claire and Laila, "touched every item in the place."

"Benjamin asked us to!" exclaimed Claire.

Again, Laila had the feeling that Claire had purposely pushed her voice into a higher register. She was Claire imitating a Claire who felt outrage. Maybe she's trying to impress Brick with how strong she is, thought Laila.

"Still," said Brick, "it's a hassle for them. I've been there."

"If Brick hadn't identified himself as a retired policeman," Claire started.

"Retired detective," Brick corrected.

"Yes." She smiled at him, in a manner slightly less planned, Laila thought. "Identified himself as a retired detective. Without that, I had a feeling they would have put cuffs on us."

A tinkling tone, like a doorbell, sounded from Regina's pocket, and she took out her phone. A message lit up the screen.

"It's Ken," she said. "He says tomorrow's wake is cancelled and asks if I know why."

"Why is he texting you?" blurted Claire.

Laila, glancing at Regina, lifted her eyebrows.

"Oh," said Claire.

"We're all friends, right?" said Regina. "Friends call each other, right?" She shifted her weight from one foot to the other, trying to strike a nonchalant pose. It didn't fool Claire.

"Oh, right," said Claire.

"Well, so the wake is cancelled. Word travels fast, doesn't it?" said Laila.

She intended to cover over the awkwardness, but the sight of Brick, his eyes darting between Claire and Regina as if following a ping pong ball, his head cocked to one side, made her smile.

"I'll say," said Regina. She let out a defeated sigh.

"I like Ken. I'm happy for you!" Claire said. "Why wouldn't you want me to know?"

Now Claire sounds like the real Claire, thought Laila. Her reaction to the news of Ken and Regina as a couple was authentic. She appeared hurt that she might be excluded from the news.

"It's Mindy," said Regina. "It's better if we keep it casual until she's left for Chicago."

"Got it," said Claire. "My lips are sealed."

"I've really got to go," said Regina. She took two quarters out of her change purse and gave them to Laila. "For the twins," she said. "You keep the balls. And yes," Regina said, with a sidelong glance at Claire, "I'll phone Ken from the car and tell him about the autopsy."

Claire and Laila nodded sagely at each other.

Regina shook her head in pretended disgust, opened the SUV, and hopped up to the driver's seat. "Now stop standing around gossiping," she said.

The SUV headed for the main road outside Laguna Shores.

The twins ran toward the group, jumping and waving at her departing vehicle, their faces bereft, tennis balls bulging from their pockets and tumbling out of their arms so they looked like two jugglers for whom things were going very wrong.

"She left you the payment for your work," Laila said, trying to soothe their disappointment.

"I've got a bag in my car," Claire said, considering the small lake of yellow surrounding the boys. "Come on, Laila. I'll give it to you."

While Claire rooted around her trunk for a medium-sized shopping bag, Laila's head swam with questions. Benjamin's suspicions had to be acute for him to order an autopsy. Had he found something more in Billie's condo that suggested her death was not from natural causes? Had, God forbid, the dolphin card pushed him to seek police help? Could Ken shed any light on those last hours?

Laila wanted to ask Claire what to make of Ken's absence from the wake. Was there some reason beyond distaste for death that stopped so many people from doing the right thing by their departed friends and their families? But Claire had questions of her own.

"An autopsy, Laila?" she said sharply, pulling a bag from a tangle in the trunk. "Seventy-year-old women have been known to die. I don't get it."

"Billie wasn't elderly. See, even you couldn't pinpoint her age. Seventy-three."

"Of course, but come on. Age is age. Surely Benjamin wasn't shocked."

That was probably true, Laila thought. But she wasn't ready to discuss Benjamin's decision with Claire. She'd need to broach the subject of the dolphin card with David first before she discussed its possible meaning with others.

Nor could she trot out Billie's phone message. Besides the fact that the information would make her look like a cold-hearted friend, the identity of the woman Billie mentioned could be explosive. It had occurred to Laila that the woman in Billie's message could be Regina.

What if Billie had some information about Regina? If she didn't know about Regina and Ken, did she say something to Ken? Or if she already knew about Regina and Ken because she was more observant than most, could seeing Ken have surprised her that night? Maybe they even had harsh words? Laila had to get some things straight with Ken before she revealed that phone message to anyone.

"Laila, you look pale," Claire said. "Is David around? Is he helping you through this? Was he close to Billie, too?"

"You saw him at the wake last night. He cared a lot about Billie." Laila didn't like the bleat of defensiveness she heard in her own voice, but she liked Claire pulling David into any discussion of Billie's death even less.

"No, of course," Claire offered. "It's just I know he's busy. Always working. He even got in a work conference last night, talking to Jake Hanlon after the prayers and all."

Laila's brain felt like a beehive that had been poked by a broom, her thoughts flying half-cocked in circles above her head. Claire seemed to know a surprising amount about David's professional life, including who rubbed shoulders with him at any given event. And David! He acted as though she had let Eddie fall into the hands of a siren. Bailey Hanlon the girl-woman! All the while he was thick as thieves with Bailey Hanlon's Dad.

"Politics." Laila shrugged, as if the swirl of information that had been thrown at her that afternoon was simply business as usual.

Across the parking lot, she heard the boys giggling and turned to see Brick entertaining them by trying to build a pyramid from the uncooperative tennis balls.

"Benjamin will let us know what he's thinking when the time's right," she said. "If I hear anything, I'll call, okay? I have to run."

"Sure," said Claire. "Whenever you get a chance."

Laila thought she looked troubled again, in a way that was not planned.

CHAPTER NINE

Thursday, Day Five – Lost Art

Seven in the morning would be too early to intrude on Benjamin, Laila reminded herself, and she chose a walk on the beach instead. She could have occupied a rocking chair on the deck outside Billie's condo, waiting for him to appear, but that would be rude. She phoned him the afternoon before and left a message, and he hadn't returned the call. The cancelled wake and prospect of an autopsy for Billie worked on Laila's nerves, and her best recourse would be to move, not sit, for the hour before taking the boys to school.

David was gone, hoping to catch the road permit people in their lair, he said, before those officials set out to God knows what corner of the county for their day's work making honest businessmen sweat bullets to create jobs.

"Of course, the Harrows have no interest in profit. It's all about creating jobs," she had teased him. For as long as she knew him, he never wore pajamas, and he stood nude before the mirror as he shaved. "It will be the first non-profit retail center in the country," she joked.

He put down his razor and pulled her into the bedroom. "It's about jobs, and profit, and family, and me and you," he said. "Let me show you the me and you part."

"I can see the you part." She laughed.

David was quick, and slow, and then both of them were quick and quicker. Laila slid from him onto the bed, happily spent and with perspiration slick on her belly. She folded in on herself and caught her breath, reminding herself to try a smart remark on future mornings. Her time with her husband had been dwindling since this construction project had begun and work hours often took over the evening. Mornings had not been her favorite for lovemaking, but these circumstances might require changing her habits.

Now she walked on the beach, the endlessly peppy Ruffles running ahead to chase the gulls. Laila's taking Ruffles for a walk would disappoint Caya. She considered taking the dog for a long beach walk one of the most agreeable of her duties, and Laila didn't blame her. Laila also figured that more than one of the male residents of Laguna Beach timed their dog walking to Caya's, for a chance to see her trim body skipping through the waves and tossing Ruffles a tennis ball. Caya kept a bag full of cut-offs and bikini tops in the kitchen closet, which Margaret referred to as Caya's "bait bag." At twenty, Caya was too young to realize, complained Margaret, that the only thing she would catch on the Laguna beach were married men or Medicare recipients. Caya just laughed and continued buying adorable bikinis.

Laila reached the edge of the Laguna Shores section of the beach, deciding to walk another half mile, then double back along the street. The best neighborhood coffee came from a Vietnamese couple who cold brewed each cup and used sweet milk to cut their thick drink. There would be just enough time to grab a cup at their café on the main drag before driving the boys.

She bent to hook the leash on Ruffles when her phone rang. It might be too early for Benjamin, but Jennifer was awake and ready to do museum business.

"Jennifer, good morning," Laila said.

"Hi, Laila, can you make a ten o'clock meeting this morning?"

"That works for me."

"You'll bring your computer or whatever you have to store the additional photos you mentioned in your report?"

"I'll be glad to."

"And Laila, not everyone knows about this project. Not the receptionist at the office, or even my secretary. Not yet, anyway."

"Got it," said Laila. "See you then."

Laila couldn't see the harm in all of St. Augustine knowing that the museum wanted to catalogue the Florida Highwaymen paintings. A spotlight on the group of twenty-six Florida artists would delight collectors and everyday citizens. The passage of day laborers from subsistence to artistic success was a feel-good story at a time when Floridians endured the same fracture lines between the rich and poor as in the rest of the fifty states.

Laila was not looking forward to a fight about policy, but she wouldn't run from it either. She would get the boys to school and easily be there at ten sharp. A talk with Benjamin would have to wait until the afternoon.

The modest museum offices ran along a short corridor behind the ticket desk at the entrance. Inside the double glass office doors, a small conference room held a table accommodating up to twelve people. No objects except a pull-down screen decorated the walls. Laila was glad they didn't waste works of art on a space that the public would never see.

Around the table sat a group smaller than Laila had expected. Rather than the full Board of Directors, Jennifer introduced the members of a committee on collections: a board member, a staff member, and herself. Seeing her report summary already on the screen in front of the four of them, Laila realized that the meeting started earlier, and her ten o'clock arrival indicated they invited her as a guest, not a voting member. If there were to be a fight about the Highwaymen, she would occupy the low ground.

"I'll start by complimenting you on your speed," said board member Geoff Hardinger. Geoff had years of experience as a collector in Atlanta, and Laila had heard him talk about St. Augustine as a mere beach town. He showed little interest in connecting the museum to the community.

"Thank you," said Laila. "But I had help." The three committee members furrowed their brows.

"Who helped you?" asked Jennifer. All three board members turned their eyes on Laila.

"My neighbor – and your church member," she said to Jennifer. "I would have started with Florida municipalities, museum by museum, but Billie's aware of national and international data sources. Those resources that saved me from re-inventing the wheel."

"She *was* aware, you mean," said Jennifer gravely.

Laila nodded in agreement.

"Billie Farmer died last week," Jennifer explained to the others. They murmured their condolences, relief writ large across their faces. Laila understood why they wouldn't feel grief for Billie, a stranger to them, but she couldn't help being taken aback by their putting secrecy above decent human empathy.

They might have at least been less obvious.

"Billie helped without any thought of compensation. She just liked the idea of helping St. Augustine," Laila observed.

"She sounds like a fantastic contributor," said Grace Law.

Laila knew Grace from working with her on budget questions. She was surprised to see her on this committee because although Jennifer hired her, she kept her at arm's length from the museum's creative decisions. Grace would follow Jennifer's lead as long as the price tag was right.

"Without Ms. Farmer, will you be able to see this project through?" asked Geoff. His weak smile offered all the empathy Laila could expect from a man who insisted upon distance from the local nobodies.

"Progress will be slower, there's no doubt about that," said Laila. "Billie created a map of known locations of Highwaymen paintings and a map of the most likely locations. She used information on museum exhibitions, collectors, dealers, appearances on online markets, auction records, and even wills left by Highwaymen and their families. If she hadn't passed away, she would have helped me organize the leads into a strategic plan."

"What you're saying then is that this project involves some guesswork," said Geoff.

Laila flinched. She took a moment to assure herself that Geoff scoffed at most ideas that were not his but could be won over by reason and persistence.

"Billie used to say go with the best bets first."

Geoff lifted an eyebrow in interest.

"To help narrow down the search, she also came up with a style inventory for each of the Highwaymen," she said after a beat. "She identified how each artist evolved their techniques over time. Once we find a painting, the inventory allows us to make definitive statements about who produced it, and perhaps when it was produced."

"Fantastic," said Jennifer. "No such inventory exists now."

"Billie read at the speed of light. She read auction brochures from at least one hundred houses, not to mention international shipping documents and museum records," said Laila. "And blogs. She left me pages of links to blogs with at least one mention of Highwaymen artists."

"And?" asked Geoff. His collector's sense must have told him there were complications, Laila thought. And he was right. The treasures they were after appeared to be widely distributed.

"At least fifteen percent of the total known output of the Highwaymen is unaccounted for and presumed lost. Another fifteen percent is formally unaccounted for but probably available."

"Available?" said Grace. "Where?"

"The Highwaymen, before their art became sought after, gave away paintings in exchange for food and rent. Billie thought a search campaign centered on the Fort Pierce area would turn up a lot of paintings."

"A lot?" said Geoff, drily. "What constitutes 'a lot'?"

"Let's say only ten percent of the paintings are in the Fort Pierce area. That amounts to a thousand plus paintings. Finding only one hundred would be significant," Laila answered.

"Not something that would get done cheaply," said Grace.

"Billie and I volunteered," said Laila. "There might be others."

"But in Fort Pierce? Why would they want to help us?" asked Grace.

Laila expected the committee to hesitate before approaching the Fort Pierce community. The robust African-American population had once been marginalized, relegated to the other side of the tracks and subject to strict Jim Crow laws. Recent decades brought economic improvements, but the art community still looked segregated. Conducting a search for Highwaymen paintings would require cooperation and diplomacy, a coming together of the African-Americans whose lives had entwined with the artists, and the white community, who had the means to own the art but who had rejected the artists during much of their lives.

"It's a way to build their collection. We'd flush out paintings they might acquire for the museum."

"Of course, of course," said Grace and Geoff, studiously ignoring each other's glance.

"Our chief interest lies with the larger map you referenced," said Geoff.

Geoff was ducking contact with Fort Pierce. He started quizzing Jennifer about budget resources and the timeline of a catalogue. Laila's mind wandered. She pictured the excitement of working alongside the remaining Highwaymen and with family members of the artists who had already passed on. She knew that two of the Highwaymen had once established a small gallery in Fort Pierce to feature the paintings they owned in common. The son of one of the original Highwaymen had continued painting in the same landscape tradition.

A formally curated museum in Fort Pierce, the A.E. Backus, had hung a roomful of their works that Laila and David had taken the boys to see. The kids still talked about it, the twins especially dazzled by the portraits of the black artists who were honored in the exhibit. Now Alton called any pleasing landscape "as pretty as a Highwayman."

The men and women involved in the present-day collection efforts would add invaluable depth to the catalogue. Laila was making a note regarding a possible letter to the Fort Pierce families and art professionals when she realized Geoff was asking her a question.

"There's always a little bit of appropriation, right? An artist needs groceries and trades a painting for food. With time, the art acquires value and is best kept quietly, in the attic."

"I think the paintings in the attics of Fort Pierce are low hanging fruit," argued Laila. "Chances are their owners know details about their creation."

"Perhaps," said Jennifer. Laila was surprised Jennifer was reticent.

"St. Augustine working with Fort Pierce to create a Florida Highwaymen catalogue - that's a couple of news stories right there," Laila continued. "Free publicity."

"We'll get there," said Geoff. "All in due time."

Am I missing something? Did they have some reason to suspect theft or other deviousness in Fort Pierce?

"Wouldn't searching the auction and collector market online be easier than going door to door to Fort Pierce homes?" said Grace. "And more accurate?"

"And less expensive?" asked Laila. The sharpness of her answer was not lost on Grace.

"Yes, less expensive and more efficient," said Grace, continuing defensively. "That's the important part."

"Could you give it a try?" asked Jennifer. "Say you found one or two Highwaymen paintings online. Could you try applying the identification inventory to see if more popped up? We'd find out if it's efficient."

"Please keep track of your time," said Grace.

"I'd like the opportunity," said Laila. "But sooner or later, we need to reach out to Fort Pierce and start sharing information."

"If we blow our trumpet too early about this catalogue, a great many of these paintings may go underground," said Geoff. "They'll be lost to art lovers everywhere."

Somewhere, somehow, Laila thought, the committee members had acquired fears about what they might find in Fort Pierce. They were long time Floridians and might know more than Laila, a recent arrival. Maybe it was wiser not to press them to change their minds until more information was gathered.

Obviously, I have a little more research to do.

"A complete catalogue, an annotated complete catalogue, or complete as possible, would put the museum front and center in the Florida art world. It might extend to the national art world," said Jennifer. "You'd get a lot of credit."

"I hope the people in Fort Pierce will agree," said Laila, as neutrally as possible.

"Remember," said Jennifer, "we don't want to tip our hand to people likely to hide what they have. We'll proceed very quietly in the local market."

Laila could see she had argued as strongly as she could, given the little leverage she had. When she had more information and her research produced a considerable inventory, she would try again. She needed to hold more of the cards.

"I can spend about eight to ten hours a week on the search," said Laila. "I should have something to show you within two weeks."

"Fantastic!" exclaimed Geoff.

"Superb," said Jennifer. "Could you also, Laila, give us a copy of the inventory Billie created?"

"It's still a little unpolished," said Laila. "But sure, if you want it."

She brought out her computer and forwarded the document. Geoff beamed at her when she finished.

"You'll call when you're ready for the next meeting?" asked Jennifer.

Driving home, Laila's spirits soared. This catalogue would cut into her painting time but would re-acquaint her with the who's who of brokers and auction houses, and connect her with an exciting artistic group. The contact with Fort Pierce, which would surely come sooner or later, would bring her first-hand knowledge of the artists' creative process. Besides, volunteering with the museum would help fill the hole left by David's immersion in his work.

The whole enchilada! she thought, jauntily.

She studied painting at Bennington, a scholarship student whose portfolio brought a lot of faculty attention. When David abandoned his art career so he could finish his MBA, she worked for a gallery in New York.

The art community absorbed their leisure time. Her immersion in the world of famous art and artists intimidated Laila so that her painting didn't evolve as she had hoped. But they met collectors, attended openings, and Laila coordinated shows for the Harrow United gallery in their Manhattan store. She joked she was acing the art business but failing at art.

Still, walking away from the New York art world constituted an enormous sacrifice. The compensations, however, were major. She began to paint more, Florida's outdoor life pleased the kids, and David had the opportunity to slip out of his older brother's shadow.

For pure business acumen, no one shone like Sam Harrow. In an age when brick and mortar stores faced smaller and smaller margins, Harrow United prospered under Sam and their Dad. They anchored the stores in locations that had no downsides. They made sure access, demographics, retail neighbors, and store services fit their mission to sell products that rose above the rest.

David's contribution would have to be, if he were to make one, in building design and usage. So far, a Harrow store looked like any department store of the 1940s onward. David's ambition was to combine the appeal of a glittering bazaar with a blitz of individualized service. Where do you get your suit tailored? Harrow's. Where did you learn about hiking in Patagonia? Harrow's. How did your boy learn to skateboard? Harrow's.

David told Laila people are hungry for experience and fun. The St. Augustine store would become a city center, open twenty-four hours a day, and complement the enormous draw of the historic old town. Building it would make him Sam's peer.

When he wasn't out in St. Augustine negotiating construction subcontracts or wooing designers and other creative partners, he was in Miami talking finance and planning with Sam. Sam, his wife, Andrea, and David's parents, Edward and Sybil, made themselves available to David all day Saturday and Sunday afternoon. Their payoff? They were devout Presbyterians who got David to go to church with them Sunday morning

Two years, David said. In two years, the worst would be over. For two years, Laila could hang on. She would use the time without David to strengthen her connections in the art world.

Laila streamed over the causeway to St. Augustine Beach and Laguna Shores with a herd of other SUVs, the sun overhead and the liquid welcome mat of the Intracoastal Waterway sparkling below. The museum work made her feel as if she belonged in St. Augustine. Maybe Alton was right. They would become Southern. If not Southern, then at least Floridian.

CHAPTER TEN

Thursday, Day Five – The Dolphin Card

Laila set to work as soon as she got home. She spent two hours scrolling through the masterpiece of software that Billie had created. Tracking the immense output of the Highwaymen artists overwhelmed Laila, but not Billie.

Billie's orderly brain approached it as a geographical puzzle. Her goal was to create a map of known paintings, coded by artist and by owner. Billie and Laila had discussed how such a map could instruct them about the preferences of different galleries and collectors worldwide.

For instance, if she noted the year a painting was created and the year it was purchased, she might uncover when and to where an artist's work tended to sell. Patterns of known sales could be used, argued Billie, to predict the location of yet-to-be uncovered paintings.

Laila delighted in the search for the Highwaymen's works. A Highwayman offered untamed beauty and lots of history. Some of the artists had worked in close union, and others worked solo. Early on, several of the Highwaymen painted for speed, and they painted alike, copying one another, sometimes learning from one another and grinding out similar weekly paintings to sell along the Florida roadsides for a few dollars.

When they were most in a hurry, usually toward the end of the tourist season in May, they would paint assembly line style on each other's canvasses, one specializing in palm trees, another in beach grasses, another in clouds.

These rudimentary landscapes shared a distinctive quality. They used a palette knife, not a brush, to create a thicker, rougher texture that represented the uncultivated Florida savannah extremely well. Coupled with their attention to the slant and tone of the sunlight, their pictures tended to be wild and romantic. Framed or unframed, the pictures would be hustled out to the highway for quick sale at about twenty-five dollars apiece.

Some critics discounted the artists as rank beginners with little training or development. Laila admired their skill in creating a haunting mood, but she also realized the Highwaymen were pure Americana, a job creation project that had not needed government support. The production of one hundred thousand paintings constituted a phenomenon, no matter the varied effort and circumstances.

If Billie were alive, Laila would have rushed over to Billie's to give her a huge hug of thanks. Now it was not possible, and with a lump in her throat, she called Benjamin to tell him how wonderful his mother was. After two tries, he did not pick up, and Laila gave up. She had to get the boys. Combing her hair in her dresser mirror, she heard Caya's knock at the bedroom door.

"You'd better go down yourself," Caya said, her voice trembling. "It's the police."

Laila wondered for the hundredth time what experiences informed Caya's outlook. If there were a police car within three blocks, she walked with her eyes glued to the sidewalk, and in stores, she took such care to avoid the security guards that without fail followed her anyway. If Laila were driving and Caya spotted a police vehicle, she would grab the dash and not let go. If Black lives mattered, Caya hadn't heard about it.

Laila went down the elevator to the waiting callers, her purse under her arm, her keys in hand. In her experience, the St. Augustine Beach police excelled at beach patrol and tourist assistance. They enforced parking and beach cleanup, and they sponsored Jackson's Little League team. She assumed they were out for a donation drive, but the two gentlemen in suits and ties that greeted the open elevator had no ready envelopes or smart phones with credit card swipes. Each flashed a badge, not from the beach police, but from St. Augustine proper.

"Mrs. Harrow?" they asked, in unison. They tucked away the silver identification squares into inside coat pockets when she nodded.

They were both slender men, and neither was smoking. She would be unsurprised to see them lifting weights in the Laguna Shores workout room or biking along the shoulder of the coastal highway. More or less her age, they did not smile.

"Is there a place we can talk?" the white officer asked. "I'm Detective Borden."

"Were you going someplace?" asked the black officer. "I'm Detective Cranston, and we need to ask a few questions."

"To pick up the kids," said Laila. "What kind of questions?"

"We'd like to ask you some things about Wilhelmina Farmer," said Detective Cranston. "We need to set up a time to see you."

"No, this is fine," said Laila. "I'll ask someone else to get the boys."

She pushed her key into the elevator lock and pressed the call button. The detectives stood erect and alert, their heads turning casually to check out the darker corners of the elevator area. They didn't fidget, which made Laila fidgety.

Once in the elevator, she smiled and jingle-jangled her keys, but they remained serious and watchful. Billie would have gotten a laugh from the Dragnet vibe of the two policemen. When the door opened, she intended to hold it so they could enter her home, but they made it clear she should exit first.

In the condo, she had to search out Caya in the pantry where she sat, gazing at the view of the beach, as if contemplating escape. She asked her to run to the boys' schools.

"Glad to go," said Caya.

"It's fine. It's just about Billie," Laila assured her.

Margaret started a pot of coffee, and Laila returned to the foyer and led the men to the living room. They sat side by side on the sofa after she took up her easy chair. Again, they took in the surrounding room, each with a slow turn of the head and a steady gaze.

"How long had you known Billie?" Cranston asked.

"Almost three years," said Laila. "Since we moved here."

"She was quite a bit older than you," said Borden.

"Seventy-two?" asked Cranston, consulting a notebook he withdrew from his jacket pocket.

"Seventy-three," said Laila.

Cranston penciled a notation.

"Were you Church friends?" asked Borden.

"No, not church. We share the beach, and we're out on the decks a lot. Billie is very outgoing. It just seemed natural."

"Did everyone like her?" asked Borden.

"I think so. Except for her poker buddies," Laila said. She thought that at last the detectives would smile, but they didn't.

"Oh?" said Borden. He pulled out a notebook and a stubby pencil. "What happened there?"

"I'm sure Benjamin told you about it. It's nothing. She's so smart, she wins all the time," said Laila.

"Did you play poker with her?" asked Borden.

"No. I heard rumors, and Billie laughed about it. The others were mostly men, and she laughed about how her winning surprised them. She said she swindled them, and they never saw it coming."

"Swindled?" said Borden.

"She might have cheated, just to get their goat," Laila said. "But they played for small change. It was the bragging rights that got the others, not the money."

"Do you know any of the poker buddies we can talk to?" asked Cranston.

"Bob Page was one. He's the HOA President," said Laila. She took out her phone and read them Bob's number. "What prompted the autopsy?" Laila asked the officers. "Do you have a reason to think she didn't die of a heart attack?"

"Did you see her apartment after her death?" asked Cranston.

"Yes," said Laila. "It looked a mess."

Laila remembered Billie's last call and her disjointed message, the confusion and forgetfulness so unlike Billie.

"Did she have a temper? Would she throw things if she were angry or upset?" asked Borden.

"Not really," said Laila.

If she showed the detectives the message, she might help clarify the picture of Billie's last hours, but she pushed away the thought. How could she tell the police without also revealing Ken's check on Billie, making him the last person to have seen Billie alive? Then Regina, and of course, David would need to know. The echo of Billie's last appeal would come under scrutiny and be known by all, by David, by Benjamin, even by her boys. She needed time.

"But sometimes?" asked Borden.

"She wasn't terribly fond of animals. You got the sense that she didn't have a lot of that kind of patience. But never, I mean never, did I hear her raise her voice to anyone or even be irritated for that matter."

"Something seems to have irritated her that night," said Cranston. "Or someone."

"You mean someone was there?" said Laila.

Cranston gave a slight shrug and let his gaze rest on her for a few moments before he glanced back at his notes. "Books are heavy," he said, keeping his eyes down.

The amusement she first felt at their deadpan attitude had vanished.

"There were two things that we're wondering about," said Borden. "Her computer and phone are missing."

Perspiration gathered under her arms. If she didn't tell them about the phone call now, when they found out, she would look suspicious. Yet telling the detectives before she had a chance to talk to Ken was out of the question. She couldn't cast suspicion his way so thoughtlessly.

"That's odd," said Laila.

Both detectives looked up from their notes at her.

She tried to project a look of casual surprise. She would welcome a discussion of Billie's computer rather than her response to the phone call.

"She had everyone's research on her computer. Everyone in the Research Club, I mean," Laila said.

"What is the Research Club?" Borden asked.

"We meet and talk about our research interests," she said. "We all have projects we're working on in our spare time."

"Who's in the club?" asked Cranston, pencil at the ready, His pocket-sized memo pad covered with miniscule cursive.

"Five of us. Billie, Ken Lee, Regina Birch, Claire Benetton, and me."

"Don't the others have computers?" asked Borden.

"What? Yes, of course," answered Laila, perplexed.

"Then why did Ms. Farmer have everyone's research on her computer?" Cranston said.

"Oh," said Laila. "Because she helped each of us with our projects. Of all of us in the club, she had the best ideas."

"Did that seem to bother anyone?" asked Cranston.

"No," said Laila. "She was a very valuable resource."

"Did you help clean up the apartment Tuesday morning?" asked Cranston.

"Yes," said Laila. "No, I mean not Tuesday. It was Wednesday."

"So, you visited the apartment Tuesday to see Benjamin, and you returned on Wednesday to clean up," said Borden.

"Yes," said Laila.

When the detectives described her behavior, she sounded like a busybody. She began to understand Caya's fear of attention from the police.

"What was out of order?"

"Things were tossed around. I pictured her staggering around and knocking things down. I wondered how Bob found her in a chair and not stretched out on the floor if she had lost control like that."

"You were there twice and didn't notice her computer was missing?" asked Borden.

"I mainly concentrated on her clothes and her bathroom items," she said. "I was thinking about her suffering there by herself," she answered.

Both detectives looked up from their notebooks to Laila's face as she spoke. Her breath was coming out ragged, making her words catch in her throat and sound garbled. The men leaned forward in their chairs, as if to try to gauge her emotion. When Margaret came in with the coffee, she snagged a tissue from a nearby box and handed it to Laila. She had not registered the tears on her cheeks, and she dabbed them away quickly.

"Both power cords were plugged in, but the items in question were not there," Borden said, cocking his head as if he were stating something ridiculous. "And that wasn't strange?"

"No," said Laila. "I wasn't paying attention to those details."

"Did she often use her phone?" asked Borden.

"Yes. She brought it to meetings along with her laptop," said Laila.

"Tell us more about the meetings," said Cranston. He struck a note more soothing than Borden's, as if he were coaxing and not interrogating her.

"We met every Monday morning," said Laila. "We were everyday people, but we liked to discuss ideas that were bigger than us."

"Everyday people," muttered Borden with an obvious glance around the Harrow's well-furnished living room.

She looked out onto the balcony where the slanted spring light gave the clouds a grainy and distinct edge. Two large-winged seagulls perched on the railing outside the glass enclosure, happy for a resting place. Many times, Billie had envied the birds out loud for their ability to see into the distance and "get the whole picture." It was always Billie who helped the others get the whole picture.

"What did Ms. Farmer research?" Borden asked. "What were her subjects?"

The club members had agreed early on not to comment on each other's research interests outside the club. Billie wouldn't mind now if her topics were mentioned, but the others might. Laila hesitated a moment before answering, and she could feel her cheeks heating up.

"Does the club do secret research?" Borden asked when she paused.

"No, but it's like going to the library, you know, and expecting your borrowed books to be a private matter," she said.

To her relief, "Starlight," the ring she and David used for each other, harkening back to their time at Bennington, sounded on her phone. The call couldn't have come at a better time. If the detectives insisted, Laila didn't know how she would deflect them.

"Excuse me, I better take this," she said.

The men nodded their assent.

"How's my beautiful girl?" asked David. "How was the museum meeting?"

"That was great," said Laila. "Right now, I'm home and chatting with two detectives about Billie."

"Chatting," said David. "Sounds friendly."

"Well, they're wondering about Billie's missing things. Like her missing laptop," said Laila.

She noticed the sharp glance that passed between the two detectives.

"So, they are investigating it as a robbery?" asked David.

"I guess," said Laila, brightening at David's idea.

She had been focusing on Benjamin's call for an autopsy and her thoughts of possible foul play. Of course, the detectives settled on the more likely scenario of a robber breaking in to Billie's house! Perhaps that caused the heart attack. The death was tragic, but unintended. There might be a crime, but it wasn't murder. Laila was heartened. It seemed a less cruel end for Billie.

"Are they about finished?" asked David.

"I think so," she answered.

"Well, if I were you, I wouldn't draw it out. Answer questions, but don't go beyond that," David advised.

"Of course. Will you be home for dinner tonight?"

"About six, I figure," said David.

"Perfect," said Laila. "I'll see you soon."

Peculiar. He called to say he would be home at the same time he had already mentioned that morning. And he happened to have ready advice on how to handle the detectives.

But he was right. She would be glad to be done with this conversation with Cranston and Borden. She slipped the phone back into its bag and looked up at the detectives.

"I'd better get going on dinner," she said, as if she were going to do something beyond asking the boys to wash their hands before the meal.

"Right," said Cranston. "One other thing. Do you know what type of phone Billie used?"

"An iPhone," said Laila. "The latest one. She liked to have the best technology she could get her hands on."

"Thanks for your time, Mrs. Harrow," Borden said. "It's been helpful."

The three rose and walked toward the elevator. The movement caused the two gulls to drop off their perch, angling off toward the beach with an irritated screech. At the door to the hallway, Cranston stopped and looked back towards the large balcony.

"That reminds me," he said. "The card Billie was writing you, that dolphin card?"

"Yes," said Laila, fighting for a cool tone to her voice.

"Benjamin Farmer said he gave it to you. Could we have it?" he asked.

"Of course," Laila said. She crossed out into the hall, ducked into the master bedroom, and slipped it out of her lingerie drawer, from underneath the hosiery that was so seldom worn in Florida. She held it open with one hand and used her phone to snap a picture of the ominous message. She brought it to where they stood in the living room.

Gingerly, Cranston took it with two fingers, each on an outside corner of the opened card. Borden read the message out loud, as if it were mildly interesting. "Dear Laila, I think you would want to know about David. . . ."

"What did your husband say about the card?" asked Cranston.

"I haven't shown it to him yet," said Laila.

"And why is that?" Cranston asked. As he spoke, Borden placed the card in a bag, marked it, and slipped it into his inside jacket pocket. Cranston took out paper and pencil again.

"It doesn't make any sense to me," she said.

Cranston squiggled something in his notes, sharpening her impulse to end the interview sooner rather than later.

"I wonder why you haven't shown it to him yet," mused Borden.

"He's so busy," said Laila.

And Billie probably wasn't in her right mind. She babbled about some woman on the phone, then writes about David. I can't start down that path. The less said, the better.

She moved toward the hallway, hoping to lead the men out. Margaret came to the door of the kitchen and offered each man a bottle of cold water. They both turned her down and stepped onto the elevator. Borden held the door open for a moment.

"If you think of any reason Billie would have left that message, please give us a call." He extended a business card to Laila.

"Of course," she said.

"And we're asking people who've been in the apartment to please drop by the King Street station and get fingerprinted," Borden said. "Helps us narrow things down."

The door closed on the two men, and Laila turned toward Margaret. "Did you call David?" Laila asked.

Margaret didn't flinch. She stood about six inches taller than Laila and probably weighed seventy pounds more than her. Her hands hung at her sides, each grasping a water bottle. "Yes."

"And why?"

"You were crying. It didn't seem safe," Margaret said.

"Two policeman here, and you didn't feel safe?" Laila said, trying to keep recrimination out of her voice. "How was David going to help?"

"Not unsafe in that sense," said Margaret. "They were sounding very forceful."

She wasn't surprised that Margaret had been monitoring the conversation. Laila had long before learned that the price of household help included a loss of some privacy, but both Caya and Margaret had worked out so well in part because they displayed a minimum of interest in the Harrow's private activities.

"And again, how was David going to help?" asked Laila. She knew she sounded petulant, but she didn't like Margaret looking after her like one of the kids. Especially not if it left David as the only adult in the family.

"His call seemed to interrupt the flow, didn't it?" said Margaret. "They left."

Laila saw that, indeed, Margaret had assigned her junior partner status in the household. It came as a blunt force blow, and she struggled not to show she felt it.

"Well, at least we got some information from David. He'll be on time for dinner," Laila said as brightly as she could manage.

"Sounds good," said Margaret. "And that must be the boys."

The elevator cables hummed with movement. The door opened, and the boys tumbled out, followed by a more cautious Caya, her glance sliding towards the living room.

I'd tell her the coast is clear but I'm sure Margaret will fill her in on all the details, thought Laila, surprised by her own caustic reaction. She followed the boys down the hallway to their bedrooms to hear the news of their day.

CHAPTER ELEVEN

Friday, Day Six – Dinner with Friends

For dinner Friday, Laila had invited everyone for drinks at seven-thirty. Regina had lessons until seven, so they would hold the meal until she arrived. Margaret suggested serving bouillabaisse, Creole style, a dish Regina had taught her soon after meeting the twins.

"Are taste buds inherited?" asked Margaret, when she first saw the twins eat the dish as if ravenous.

"They are Haitian to the bone," said Regina. "I'm surprised they aren't answering you in Creole."

Margaret liked the seafood stew because she could prepare it midafternoon and let it bubble and simmer into the evening, long after she left for the day.

That Friday afternoon, she declared the bouillabaisse ready, stowed a dessert of chocolate éclairs in the fridge, and laid out the serving dishes and utensils. Laila looked forward to greeting her friends, her home fragrant with the mist of onions hovering over a mass of drunken shrimp. A good dinner in the company of Billie's friends might soften the pain, or at least, acknowledge the loss.

"What's the occasion?" asked Claire when Laila had phoned her.

"Missing Billie," said Laila. "I need my friends close."

"I'm honored," said Claire. "Look, I'll bring a candle to light, to put on the table."

"To keep her present," said Laila.

"Exactly," said Claire.

She fed the boys early in the kitchen, and they went to the den to wrangle over which movie to watch. The younger three would most likely bow to Eddie's choice, and as long as she held veto power, Laila let the dynamic work itself out.

Darkness edged along the waterline as the sun sank behind Laila's building. On the balcony, the long dinner table, covered with a cloth of purple and pink hibiscus that Billie had often complimented, held six settings. She pushed open the windows so the salt breeze freshened the room. The last joggers pounded the sand, making the birds skitter away in all directions.

One of them might be Ken; she'd recognize him if he passed by. When she first moved in, she would go the beach with the twins in the afternoon, which was Ken's exercise time. The third or fourth day they coincided, Ken stopped and complimented the boys on the mess of sand and shells they were calling a fort.

"Do you always run barefoot?" Laila had asked. David was an avid jogger, but he wore running shoes on the beach.

"Yeah, it strengthens my feet," Ken answered. "For surfing."

"Are you learning to surf?" she asked.

"No, I've been surfing a while. I grew up in Hawaii so I started young."

"But you need to get your feet stronger?" she wondered out loud.

"Well, I'm a little older now, and it doesn't take much to lose the touch," Ken said. "And it's habit. Shoes on sand don't feel right to me."

"I like walking my kids to the pier and watching the surfers," said Laila.

"A few more years and your little ones will be riding the waves," said Ken.

"Do you have kids?" asked Laila.

"I'm divorced," said Ken. He didn't offer details, and Laila didn't press.

They started talking about Laguna Shores, sports for her boys, attractions in St. Augustine, and how the Harrows had ended up in Florida after New York. She invited Ken to their Sunday happy hours. His condo was in a street-side building and lacked a deck or a view, so occasionally, Ken would sail in late on Sundays and bring a hefty platter of pulled pork he prepared Hawaiian style. The other building residents seemed fond of his company.

David's favorite sport was tennis, and Ken was a willing, if not fervent, partner. It was a good thing, David maintained, that Ken didn't play all out. With his medium height and stocky legs, David would be no match for Ken's quickness of step and long reach. It was Ken who introduced the couple to Regina as a potential tennis teacher for Eddie and Jackson. Lucky for their family, thought Laila, that Regina did play all out, in fact, did everything all out, including fall in love with Alton and Forrest.

Where Ken was reticent, Regina was full-throttled and confident. Her restless energy and easy manner got everyone talking. At their club meetings, she was curious, asking questions and trying out theories. Ken was inquiring, too, but he kept his feelings opaque and protected. The enigma that was Ken made it difficult to tell if he was hiding his feelings or camouflaging his impatience. It made her tread carefully around the subject of Billie's last night and his absence at her wake.

"Does dinner tomorrow night work for you?" Laila asked.

"Sounds good," said Ken. "What should I bring?"

"Yourself," said Laila. "Margaret's on a bouillabaisse tear."

"Wonderful," he said. "But I *will* bring wine."

"That's fine, but don't worry over it. You've been busy."

"I like busy. Anything new from Benjamin?"

"I haven't been able to get hold of him," she said. "Are you wondering about a second wake?"

"How long can her son stay away from his work? This autopsy is not anything he planned on, I'm sure."

Just like him. He answers a question with a question.

"Claire and I offered to help get the condo ready to sell," said Laila. "It's a small place, and she thinks it will go fast."

"Did I hear that another brother is on his way here?" Ken asked.

"Douglas arrives tomorrow evening. Benjamin described him as more formal, more church-going."

"If they need a hand with anything, I'm available," said Ken.

But not available enough to come to a wake, thought Laila. She knew it wasn't her business, and, at any rate, Douglas might not arrange another evening of wake after the autopsy. But the idea that there would be no more chances to say goodbye to Billie made her worry for Ken if, in fact, his absence at the wake had been unavoidable and not a deliberate choice.

One night, after an extra glass of wine at happy hour, Ken had told Laila that his father died young, of kidney disease, when Ken was still in kindergarten in Hawaii. His Dad was gone, his mother had told him. Ken thought he went to another island for work. He had not understood that it meant he was never coming back. For months, he expected his father's truck to show up in the driveway, until an older brother set him straight, incredulous he could be so thick. From that story, Laila suspected that working through grief was not anything he had learned.

"Reggie will be a little later, but I don't think she'll mind if we start with drinks, do you?" Laila had asked him.

"She told me she let the cat out of the bag," Ken said. Laila congratulated herself for getting a straight answer out of Ken.

"You don't know how happy this makes me," said Laila.

"She's pretty friggin' great, isn't she?"

"How did you figure it out?" she asked. "You're both busy all the time, you with work and church, her with tennis and Mindy. I had my hopes, but I thought you'd never get around to it, neither of you."

"Why did you think we'd be a good match?" he asked.

"Energy, I guess. You both have an aura of optimism."

"And?"

"You're fit. Anybody not fit would feel daunted by either of you."

"But she's also very smart," he said.

"That's the thing. You're athletic and bright. It's not so common to find both," she said. "It's wonderful."

"Thanks," he said. "But it's new, very new."

"Does Mindy have no idea?" she asked.

"It's a process," said Ken, his voice dropping, as if to close off the line of inquiry.

Friendship with Ken meant bumping into his protective perimeter and learning to back off without resentment. His relationship with Regina would make it that much more complicated, as the perimeter zigged and zagged around new territory. Laila knew something about blending family members together, but every family was different, and to be helpful, a friend must be invited into the circle. Because she had wanted Regina in her circle didn't necessarily mean Regina and Ken would welcome her into theirs.

"You'll do fine," she said.

"And no fuss about how I'm dressed up for dinner because of Reggie," he said.

"Of course not. I'll let Claire take care of that."

"Yeah, well, glass houses and all that," he said. "Brick is a surprise, right?"

"I think Claire only has to beckon and they come hither," she said.

"She's arm candy, all right. But a cop? She seems more, I don't know, worldly," he said.

"Sophisticated?"

"Cops tend to dominate, and Claire is kind of the bossy type."

"Ken! You, an anti-feminist! Wait until Reggie hears," she joked.

"It's not anti-feminism. It's physics. You can't have two dominators in one relationship. It causes fission."

"Claire's interesting that way," said Laila. "She shifts gears quickly."

"She's got a big playbook, you're saying."

"She's emotionally nuanced is a nicer way of saying it," said Laila.

"Dinner will be interesting," he said. "I look forward to meeting Brick."

Laila needed to talk to Ken in person. On the telephone, it seemed easier for him to deflect or change the subject.

"The police dropped by here. They were asking about Billie."

"Like an investigation?"

"Seemed like that," she said. "Asking about her activities. Asking about the Research Club."

"And?"

"I wonder if you and I could meet before dinner? Maybe we could talk a bit about what to say and what not to say," she answered.

"You think they'll be questioning me?" Ken sounded genuinely surprised.

"I think so. You're in the club," she said. "And," she added softly, "you were the last person to see her – that I knew about."

He must have been out on his patio because she heard a chair scrape along the floor and heard him open and close a door briskly.

"Sure, we can talk," he said after a pause. "But hell if I have anything of interest to tell them."

"I'm free now," she offered. There was silence for a moment.

"No," he said. "I've got meetings throughout the AM and PM."

She hesitated, not sure how to ask about her fear that Regina might be the woman referred to in Billie's phone message.

"Do you think they'll be back?" he added, when she didn't comment.

"I don't know. I haven't talked to Benjamin so I'm as surprised as you," she said.

Laila realized the irony of the fact her answers were as opaque as Ken's. If she were frank, she would tell Ken about the dolphin card and its implication that David was involved in Billie's death. The police questioning unnerved her, and she had no interest in sharing her fears. If Ken felt as strongly about Regina being a focus of concern as she felt about David's involvement, she had to be beyond careful.

"Well, I don't want to chat about this at dinner," said Ken.

"No," said Laila. "Not among six of us."

"Saturday, perhaps, then," said Ken. "We'll find some time. Not that I have much information to offer."

"Six-thirty for dinner then?" she asked, disappointed that her questions went unanswered, but relieved that she hadn't waded into the subject too far.

Another unpleasant conversation, Laila thought, as she hung up. Billie might be surprised if she knew the worry she had left in her wake. If things were uneasy with Ken, she and David weren't having an easy time of it either.

The previous night, after a quick dinner of pizza and salad, they had accompanied Alton and Forrest to a parent-teacher conference at the twins' school. Alton considered school a second home. Laila could tell by the way he arranged his desk, his favorite Disney figurine occupying the interior back corner where it was "less likely to be messed with" according to her son. The teacher mentioned a slight deficit in fine motor skills that he would grow out of, but otherwise, she had nothing but praise for his efforts.

Forrest, by contrast, already had a file on the teacher's desk, which she opened with a wince. He had a way, she said, of distracting and being distracted. He played fair and rarely intimidated others, she allowed, but he liked to talk much more than he liked to read and write. Although he only intended fun, Ms. Hennyson observed, he often disrupted the entire class.

David and Laila weren't surprised by the comments, but the conference stretched into an hour as the three adults discussed strategies to improve Forrest's academic life. By the time they got home and put the boys to bed, it was late, and they were past tired.

"The policeman that stopped by today were from Central Casting," Laila said as they rolled into bed, she without a pretense of skin care, he forgetting to brush his teeth.

"How so?" asked David.

"There was a rat-a-tat-tat rhythm to their questions. All business and no charm," she said.

"Were they aggressive?" he asked.

"Pushy? Not exactly," she said.

"Well, how exactly?"

"Abrupt. They would ask about one thing and then change to another," she said.

"Sounds like they were fishing for something," he said.

"Maybe."

David was under the covers, on to his side, his back to Laila. He seemed tired, and Laila knew he needed sleep. The detectives' visit had roiled her, however, and she gave in to her doubts.

"I know Margaret called you," she said.

He turned towards her. "She was worried about you," he said, his head still sunk deep in the pillow.

"About how I could cope."

"Yes," he said, his eyelids heavy. "With the autopsy, maybe her imagination ran away with the story. Anyway, sounds like the police suspect a robbery, not a homicide."

"Something minor I might be able to handle," she said.

David's eyes blinked open at the sound of her sarcasm. "You sound tired," he said. "You're tense."

"I didn't like being checked up on," she said.

"I knew you were upset, and I didn't want them to make you feel worse," he said.

"They did make me feel worse; you're right," she said.

"You're imagining someone robbing her and causing a heart attack. Of course, you feel worse."

"There was something else," she said.

Everything in Laila's experience told her there were about five hundred other, better ways to tell her husband about Billie's scrawled message, but she had let them slip by. It was late, he was tired, and she was irritated, but she had to get it out.

"Oh?" he said. "What?"

"They asked about you," Laila said.

"About Harrow United?" He rolled onto his back, his arms behind his head, listening.

"They didn't mention our last name," she said. "No, it was just about you."

"What about me?" he asked.

"About the dolphin card."

"Excuse me?" He propped up on his elbow now, wide awake.

Laila swallowed hard and swung her feet onto the floor by her side of the bed. "A card that Billie wrote to me before she died. They wondered what it was about," she said.

"They showed this card to you?" he asked, his eyes following her as she walked to her bureau. Her phone rested on top, plugged into its power cord.

"Benjamin had given it to me. I had to give it back to them."

"This makes no sense," David said. He fell back on his pillow, as if someone had pushed him down.

Laila brought the phone to his bedside, the photo of the scrawled message up on the screen. She held it as he read.

"I think you would want to know about David . . . ," he read in a monotone. "What?" he said, his face darkening. "Where's the rest of it?"

"That's it. The message stops there," she explained.

"What's that mean? What was she getting at?" David's tone was accusatory, and Laila didn't like it.

"I don't know what it means," she said. "She never said anything like that before."

"Where did this come from?" he asked.

"Benjamin," she reiterated. "He found it on her desk."

"Why didn't you show me it?" he said. "Why didn't you tell me?"

Laila knew David would ask that question, and she had hoped to have a good answer, but it still eluded her. "I got it Monday, when I first met Benjamin."

"And?" David was on his feet, standing by the side of his bed.

"Monday you worked late, Tuesday was the wake, and yesterday, the thing with Ken and Reggie getting together. There wasn't a moment," she said.

"But you told me about Ken and Reggie. And about Claire and whatever his name is. That you thought to tell me."

"It's not like I report in," she blurted. "I was thinking about it. Getting to it."

"Thinking about what?"

"What Billie meant." She was up on her knees on the bed, facing David as he began to pace.

"Do you have any ideas?" he asked.

"No," she said. "Do you? Do you have an idea about what it means?"

"Of course not," he said, more subdued and walking towards the bed, his phone in his hand. "Can I see it once more?"

David sent the photo to his phone and opened it up. He put on sweatpants and walked out to the balcony, standing and staring at the screen, his face impassive, but his breath rapid, his chest lifting and falling. Laila stayed on their bed, watching him through the parted curtains and wondering about his reaction, fear building in her about his fear. After a few minutes, he returned to the room. He had on his negotiator's expression, a smile with no warmth behind it.

"What kinds of things do you discuss at the Research Club meetings?" he asked.

"Our projects," said Laila.

"Why?" asked David.

"To get new ideas about how to approach our problems. Somebody might find only dead ends, so the rest of us try to figure out new directions to investigate."

"Investigate?" he said. "What are you investigating?"

"I've told you about this," Laila said. "I found Alton and Forrest's grandparents, and pictures of where they were born, and medical records on Isabelle, but nothing on Jean."

"And the others? Reggie? Ken? What do they investigate?" David asked.

Laila was relieved. She hadn't wanted to share with him her suspicion that Forrest and Alton had siblings or half-siblings still in Haiti. Now was not the moment for considered discussion. She was glad to talk about the others, as long as she could keep it to vague terms. Their promise to each other to keep their research confidential had extended to partners and other family members.

"Everybody has a project," she said.

"Billie, too?" he asked.

"She's been different," said Laila. "She picks exotic subjects, puts together information, but then moves on to a different subject. As if she's doing elaborate book reports on books nobody would read. Mostly, she helps the rest of us get a handle on our topics."

"And Claire?" he asked.

"Also different, come to think of it," she said. "She's new, and her interest was vague. From what I could tell, Billie was working one-on-one with her, to catch her up to the rest of the club."

"Didn't that make for dull meetings?" he asked.

"Claire offered great information on St. Augustine and the whole north coast of Florida. She knew the old families, the scandals, the hidden resorts and famous watering holes. The meetings are not dull; believe me."

"So, what did she need from Billie?" he asked.

"I'm not sure," said Laila. "But you can ask. The club is coming to dinner tomorrow night."

"It would be easier to hear it from you. I get the feeling the club doesn't like nosey people."

"With enough wine, we'll all spill our guts, as Ken would say," Laila joked.

"But not you to me," David said, no hint of a smile on his face. "You won't tell me."

"Billie's card has gotten you in a state," said Laila.

"Really?" David shot back. "I think I'm just fine. Time to go to bed."

Laila's mood had curdled at David's brusque responses. She knew she should soften the news of the dolphin card by sharing Billie's phone message and her mention of the unnamed woman. It showed how confused Billie had been and that her last words were likely not reliable. But she held off, not knowing if his response or her fractured patience would detonate more fireworks.

David got back under the covers and flicked off the bedside light in one movement. She did the same on her side, gazing at the thin light shining from the balcony through the slice of opening David had left in the curtains. The sharp conclusion to the argument played over and over in her head, until her dreams were suffused with angry colors and screeching gulls.

The next morning, David was gone before Laila awoke, but he had left a note on her bedside table.

"Dinner around seven, right? Don't mention Billie's card, okay?"

Of course, she wouldn't make Billie's message a topic of discussion at dinner. She didn't think she needed a reminder. She knew the dolphin card might give people the wrong impression - doubly so when they didn't know about the phone message. The phone message was the confirmation that Billie was muddled that night, to say the least. It would all become clear when David and she had a moment to calmly talk through all the information.

The uneasy night and unaccustomed harshness from David stained Laila's mood. She dressed and ran a comb through her hair without glancing in the mirror. Not bothering with breakfast, she drove the boys to school absentmindedly and needed to give them lunch money because she had left their bags of sandwiches and fruit on the kitchen counter. Arriving home, she consulted with Margaret about the bouillabaisse, took a yogurt out of the fridge, and retreated to her studio.

She made the call to Ken and hung up with his reminder to not discuss the police questioning at dinner ringing in her ears. Getting out her brushes and paints, she spent a few hours repairing the fissures in the foundations of her life, her marriage, and her friendships. Since she was a child, colors soaked up her emotions and smoothed all surfaces.

By the time she went back out to get the boys, she felt less vulnerable to her own recriminations. The fragrance of the bouillabaisse made her home welcoming and joyful. David would recover his sense of calm, she hoped. He was worried about a vague threat, and when he heard from the members themselves about their unconnected and harmless research interests, he would realize her discretion on the subject was not sinister. Her delay in showing him Billie's dolphin card was about grief and distraction, not about suspicion.

Billie's phone message means she was confused. He'll hear it and see that the dolphin card was more of Billie not thinking clearly. Last night was not the time, but I'll tell him soon about that message.

She finished preparing the balcony for her dinner guests and changed into black silk slacks with a gray top. Invisibility, she thought. Let the meal and the wine take center stage. David's natural friendliness would evaporate the previous night's tension, and all would be well.

CHAPTER TWELVE

Friday, Day Six – An Invitation to Surf

"Dad, you've got to!" Eddie stood at the wide doorway to the balcony, his eyes ablaze with excitement, his manners outdistanced by his enthusiasm, perhaps enjoying the attention of the adult guests.

He was in cutoff sweatpants, the waistband tie dangling below a faded yellow tee. Dark hair curled along his arms, held akimbo at his hips. The stance was all David, the words an echo of David's ebullient nature, Laila thought. When had Eddie gotten so cocky, she wondered.

The dinner guests tilted their faces to him. David raised his eyebrows, as if skeptical about his son's judgment, but Laila saw that at heart he was pleased with his enthusiasm.

"So, you think Ken's idea about surfing lessons is a good idea?" David asked him as he turned his attention back to the table. "I think everyone's met our oldest, Edward. Except for you, Brick," David said, as he rose from his chair. "Eddie, this is Brick Davison. Brick, our son, Edward Hopper Harrow."

"I did meet him yesterday," said Brick, "but I'm glad for the formality today. Edward Hopper Harrow? That's a mouthful."

"The artist and all that," said Eddie, dismissing any discussion of his name as a distraction from the more important topic at hand. "Dad, I think I'm the only guy in my class who doesn't surf," said Eddie.

"Sounds like your Dad might get some lessons," said Brick, gesturing towards Ken.

"And then me? Right, Dad?" said Eddie.

David smiled but looked straight into Eddie's face, giving him a silent nod.

"Enjoy your dinner, everyone," Eddie said, taking the cue. "It was nice to meet you, Mr. Davison. Again." He winked at Brick and turned back inside, but then faced the group once more. "Everybody's good, Mom. All asleep on the couch."

Eddie sent a quick smile Laila's way and glanced once more at David. As if she were observing someone else's child, Laila marveled at his equal measure of confidence in himself and dependence on David's masculine affirmation, and flashed on the idea that her role in raising the boys ended at puberty.

That's the wine talking. I'm exaggerating.

"Thanks, son. Good job," said David. Eddie headed to his siblings in the family room.

Any other night, if one of the kids appeared, he would look at her as if to say, "See what we're raising? He's a masterpiece." When he resumed the conversation without so much as a glance her way, Laila understood that last night's disagreement was still on his mind. The misunderstanding had festered.

Talk picked up more or less at the point when Ken had offered to teach David and Brick the rudiments of surfing.

"I'll bring the boards," said Ken. "No big investment needed."

"What about me?" asked Regina.

Ken's head swiveled towards her. "You'd do something besides tennis?" He laughed.

"I can't afford a broken arm, it's true," she said.

"I think you'd be great on the water. And we'll start small," he said.

"Could I bring Eddie?" asked David.

"No," said Ken, so abruptly that he immediately tried to soften the response. "Not until we have you up on a board and able to teach him. Kids can get overambitious."

Laila was relieved not to have to dissuade David on that point. She might try it herself, now that the kids' safety was not at risk, just to see what it was that captured Ken's imagination so thoroughly.

At Research Club, surfing was his only topic. He studied the supremacy of Hawaiian surfers and data about the contribution to the economy from surfing schools and the tendency towards monopoly in surfboard manufacturing.

"Can I get a lesson?" Laila said.

Definitely, the wine is talking now.

"Up on a board?" said David. He raised his napkin to wipe his lips, too late to hide the smirk.

"I didn't know you could swim," said Ken, heightening Laila's dismay.

"I swim. It's just usually in the pool," she declared.

"You and I will go body surfing," said Regina. But Laila didn't respond, recognizing that Regina was simply trying to avoid more taunting from the men. "That's the first step, right?" Regina asked Ken.

"The first step is getting into the ocean, isn't it?" said Brick. Claire laid her hand over Brick's arm, warning him away from a pile on, and further sparking Laila's pique.

"What's the big deal?" Laila shrugged. "I can lie on the board and ride a little wave. It takes more balance to ride the subway in New York."

"I neva tawt of it like dat," said Brick, tossing a half-baked Bronx accent into the conversation.

Laila threw him a dirty look. "Martha's Vineyard, plenty of times," she said to Brick.

"This is the first I've heard," muttered David, but Laila caught his comment.

"With my friends," Laila said, filling her glass. "We just didn't own boards. We body surfed all the time."

"I like your spirit," said Ken, still doubtful.

"It wasn't Miami, for heaven's sake," she said, rolling her eyes in David's direction. "But we had a little wave action."

"And if it's not a little wave?" asked David. "If it's a big wave, and it knocks you into the water?"

"Then you'll just have to trust me, won't you?" Laila said. "You'll just have to trust that I can swim to shore, won't you?"

Regina and Claire both took gulps of wine, while Brick looked sympathetically at David. Ken nodded in acknowledgment at Laila. David shrugged in Brick's direction, as if neither believed what amounted to a tall story. Laila felt unmoored.

"So, a lesson tomorrow? Would that work out?" David said placidly to Ken.

"Morning?" asked Ken.

"I believe we're free," David answered.

"I'll be there," Regina interjected, looking at Ken.

"It's supposed to be calm. Calm and flat," Ken said back to Regina.

Laila heard the comment as an assurance that things could be made safe even for an untalented beginner like Laila. She was furious at the whole exchange, the whole group acting as if they had to talk around her. What was she, twelve years old?

"Well, it won't matter to me," she said. "I'll be ready for it."

"I hate to miss it; I really do," said Brick. "I'm tied up."

He was suppressing a chuckle, and to Laila, it was the last straw. She stood quickly, a little too quickly, swaying slightly as she pushed away her chair. She steadied herself with one hand and started clearing the table by reaching defiantly toward Brick's plate.

Regina gathered her and Ken's plate, glancing meaningfully at Claire.

"Let's get the dessert," Claire said gaily.

"I'll clear everything to the sideboard," Regina chimed in.

Laila led with her chin, marching decidedly, if not steadily, toward the kitchen, grateful that Claire was leading the way.

In the kitchen, she ducked into the pantry, casting around for the dessert she thought Margaret mentioned. She opened cabinets and peered into the breadbox. She had the thought that if she couldn't find it, she could throw a few cookies on a plate and call it satisfactory. After rustling around, banging a couple drawers shut, and seething at Ken's condescension and David's smugness, she remembered everything was in the fridge. She walked back into the kitchen and faced Claire, who was leaning on the countertop by the coffee pot.

"Shall I make a pot?" Claire said.

Laila let out a sigh, deep and long. "I'd better make a cup over here," said Laila, indicating the Keurig.

"No, you take this," said Claire, filling a glass of water at the sink. "Down the hatch."

"Was I laughable?" asked Laila, gulping the lukewarm water, miserable now at ruining the party.

Claire busied herself with the coffee maker. "Oh, I'm sorry. I didn't realize you were the first person in Laguna Shores to drink an extra glass of wine," Claire answered.

Laila felt her shoulders relax. "You'll have to explain to Brick that I'm really a reasonable person," Laila said.

"Under no circumstances," said Claire. "He doesn't swim in the ocean at all. He had no business opening his mouth."

"You know this already?" asked Laila. The coffee pot began to hiss out its brew.

"It's Florida, baby. Either you're a beach person or you're not. And he's not."

"In that case, will you tell him I went to the surfing lesson and performed magnificently?" Laila said.

"Done," Claire said. She pulled cups out of the cabinet and turned toward Laila. "A tray maybe?"

Laila pulled one from a cabinet in the island, a cheery rectangle with laminated flowers.

"Kind of small," said Claire. She went rustling through the cabinets for something larger. Laila turned to the sliver of beach visible from the kitchen, imagining herself tossed from a surfboard into the pebbly bottom of the shore. She took another long drink of water and felt her equilibrium creep back as the alcohol diluted.

"Is everything else okay?" asked Claire.

"Who would want to hurt Billie?" asked Laila.

"The autopsy," said Claire. She stopped her search for a tray and turned to Laila. "It's upset you."

"And her computer and phone are gone," Laila said.

"I noticed the computer wasn't around," said Claire. "Actually, Brick noticed right away. I didn't think about the phone." She crouched to a lower cabinet and pulled out a large wood tray with painted birds.

Laila pulled the plate of éclairs out of the fridge. Claire smiled at the golden burnish of the pastry and the gleaming chocolate glaze.

"Do you have any mint?" asked Claire.

"Mint?" said Laila blankly.

"To garnish the plate," said Claire, opening the fridge to look for herself. "Never mind."

"Margaret thinks of everything," said Laila, as Claire pulled a baggie with sprigs of mint from the shelf in the fridge. "The police suspect a robbery in progress when she died," said Laila. "For a computer and a phone? It makes no sense."

"You know, her son is a prosperous, big-city lawyer. This might just be the police trying to put some doubts to rest," said Claire. "They want him to think they're thorough."

"They questioned you, too?" said Laila.

"And Brick. And Bob Page. I think it took approximately ten seconds for them to figure out that Bob Page was a sack of hot air." Claire patted the mint into place.

Laila tried to keep her face unreadable. She reached to refill the glass of water, feeling her throat tighten up. Claire might have been questioned about the dolphin card. Brick, too. Laila searched for a way to broach the subject without breaking the silence David had advised, no, ordered. Claire seemed oblivious, but Laila knew Claire could act almost any part.

"Could she have committed suicide?" Laila said. "Been angry, or desperate, and that accounts for the mess in her place?"

"Billie?" said Claire, brought up short by the question. "I doubt that, but anything's possible. Did the police hint at that?"

If Claire knew about the card, she would know suicide was unlikely. Was she truly surprised by the idea of suicide? Or was she faking it? Did she suspect a murder? Was that good or bad news? She would have to think about it when her head was clearer.

"No, nothing like that. No, you're right. She was anything but despondent," said Laila.

"Back to the table?" said Claire, holding the tray of cups and carafe of coffee.

"Sure," said Laila, feeling unsure of nearly everything this evening, including her own emotions. "Claire, do you miss her?"

Claire put the tray down on the island and looked at Laila evenly. She paused a moment before speaking. Laila was afraid she would dismiss the question with a light-hearted remark, or worse, with formulaic sympathy.

"She very generously spent hours with me to figure out what data I needed and how to organize it. She went above and beyond. But what you two had was more than the club. She seemed like a mother to you. You feel it more than the rest of us. It's just natural."

Laila leaned her elbows on the island counter and held her face in her hands. She could feel the burn on her cheeks. She wanted to remain the hostess, but her control was slipping away. Claire had given her permission to grieve, without pretending to mirror her feelings. She wanted to thank Claire, but she couldn't push the words through her tears.

"Hey," Laila heard Regina's voice and felt her arms encircle her shoulders.

"It's a tough loss," Claire said to Regina by way of explanation.

"I know," said Regina. "And there's no way to change it."

Laila heard herself sobbing.

Claire removed the cream pitcher from the tray and placed it on the island. "Reg, could you grab the éclairs and I'll take the coffee? We'll say Laila is looking for the cream."

"Sure," said Regina. She squeezed Laila's arm and picked up the pastries.

"You've got a couple of minutes, kid," said Claire. "Reggie'll come back for you and the dessert plates in a few."

Laila straightened and walked into the powder room on the other side of the pantry. She blotted off the smeared mascara and pushed a few damp hairs back from her face.

All right, my friends understand. So, I'm not crazy. David doesn't get it. Or he doesn't want to get it. He brushes off her death. I don't understand. And wine doesn't help.

Back in the kitchen, she collected six plates, six dessert forks, and the cream pitcher. She met Reggie half way back through the living room, and the two rejoined the guests on the balcony.

"Just in time," said Claire. "Ken is goading Brick into a bike trip."

"I'm fine on a bike," said Brick. "It's been a while is all."

David was circling the table with the carafe in hand, serving coffee. He leaned over Laila to fill her cup and took the cream pitcher, pouring her a dash of cream, just the way she liked it.

"Everything okay in the kitchen?" he said softly. She looked up into his face and nodded her assent. "Sorry about the teasing. I know you'll do great tomorrow," he added. He seemed sincere. She glanced at Brick next to her and willed herself to smile.

"What a fine dinner," Ken said. "Thank you both."

"Delicious" added Brick.

"Our pleasure," said David.

Laila gazed down the table at her guests and received Reggie's approving smile, then a barely discernible wink from Claire.

"Let's do it again soon," said Laila.

CHAPTER THIRTEEN

Saturday, Day Seven – Hang Ten

"And who is watching my precious boys?" called Regina. She stood close to the shore with her back to the water, her long, nut-brown legs planted in the sand, one of Ken's boards lying behind her.

"Too early for them," Laila said. She carried a bag and blanket, her small, bare feet leaving light impressions in sand that still wore a topcoat of dew. She was glad she threw a sweatshirt over her suit. "Anyway, they'd never sit quietly and watch, no matter what Ken asked," Laila added.

"Maybe Alton would," said Regina. "He's the observant one."

"Observant, but not abundantly calm," said Laila.

"I could take him swimming. Just Alton and me, every once in a while."

"I love that idea," Laila said.

"I'm head over heels for that boy. And for that guy, too," Regina said as she gestured down the beach.

David and Ken came trotting toward Regina's spot on the shore, each toting an additional board.

"Boards facing the water, and give yourselves a wingspan of separation," said Ken.

"Good morning to you, too," said Regina.

"Now don't pretend," David said, arranging the boards along the sand.

"You don't know." Regina laughed.

"I saw you two scamper out the door last night," David said.

"Fine. We had bagels and coffee together this morning, know-it-all," said Ken. He led Regina by the hand to the first board and indicated Laila should be on the middle board.

"Oh, David, when's the last time we had bagels and coffee together?" Laila cooed in a singsong voice. She and David bumped shoulders in triumph.

"Stop, or I'll send you both home without a lesson," said Ken.

"I'm leaving for New York with Mindy tonight," said Regina. "You won't have me to kick around for a while."

"Shoot, that's right," said Laila to Regina. "We are going to miss you so much. Alton will want to get you at the airport when you come home."

"That's my job now. Tell him sorry, dude," said Ken. "Eight days and counting."

"We'll be hanging ten by the time you get back," said David.

"Please don't use that phrase with anyone," Ken ordered. "The surfing crowd will make you a laughing stock if you do."

They got down to the business of beginner's surfing. Laila's expectations of success were slim, but it didn't matter. After the guests left the night before, David and she had regained their footing, and relief flooded in. He apologized for second-guessing her about Billie's card, and she admitted that she could have been quicker to show him the message.

"There's no point in creating a mystery where there isn't one," said

David. They had curled up together on their bed, their curtains and balcony doors wide open so that they could enjoy the salt-edged night as if they were sleeping under the stars.

David gave her plenty of encouragement about the surfing lesson, but in truth, she didn't feel the confidence she had boasted of during dinner the night before.

"Here's the thing," Ken began, "it's about balance. No surprise there. And what's balance? It's finding your center and holding it."

Ken had them sit cross-legged on the board and try to rock it in the sand. They switched to their stomachs, lying lengthwise and lined up with the center, again trying to rock the board.

"It's heavy," said Laila.

"You've got a lot of support underneath you," answered Ken. He had them practice the arm movements they would use to paddle the board. "Make sure your body is on the center line and your chest is lifted. Cup your hands, reach ahead as far as possible, and push your arm down into the water, to your elbow," Ken said. Walking from board to board, he adjusted each of them, urging them to keep a strong, arched back.

"It's not fair that Regina's arms are so much longer," said Laila.

"Height is not an advantage," said Ken. "Standing, her center of gravity will be higher off the wave and trickier to hold on to. I know."

"So, if we start losing our balance, we come back down to our stomachs?" asked David.

"That's jumping ahead a little," Ken said. "Let's take the boards in the shallows and paddle around. Paddle about ten strokes parallel to the beach, and then come back again."

Ken's three students did as directed and paddled on their bellies along the shore through the foam of broken waves. Ken stood among them in water to his knees, shouting encouragement and advice.

"Lift your chin, Reggie," he said. "You'll get more power."

"Keep your legs and feet together, David."

"Laila, get farther forward. The nose of the board is out of the water."

Several times waves that still carried some force brushed Laila toward the beach, and she would have to jump off the board and push it back out to the parallel course where David and Regina paddled.

"Man, I feel the paddling in my back," said David.

"Right," said Ken. "Laila, how's it going?"

"Is there such a thing as a lighter board?" asked Laila.

"Not so much lighter but shorter. Most boards are too long for an elf," he said.

She grinned back at him.

He watched them paddle a few more laps up and down the shoreline, then called them back to the beach, each with a board.

"Not much undertow on this beach, right?" David said.

"That's right," said Ken. "It's not a favorite surfing beach because the current pushes the bigger waves down shore towards Villanos."

"But for our purposes," said Regina with a smile.

"Exactly," said Ken. "For us, it's like a bunny hill for beginning skiers."

Each lay face down on a board in the sand. They practiced getting into a crouch; knees folded tight, feet flat but toes active and gripping the board. Ten times they repeated the movements until Ken said they looked halfway natural.

"Now, from stomach to crouch to standing," he said.

They all got upright, and Ken ordered them to rock the boards as best they could.

"Look at your feet," he said. "What do you notice?"

"One foot wants to go forward," said Regina.

"Yep, for balance," he said. "Your instinct is to spread out the weight. Watch how I go from belly to standing and keep my balance."

They watched Ken as he demonstrated how to establish a standing position.

"Right foot forward is the most common stance, and it's what I use. So, my arms support my torso, and my left leg moves first. The left foot crosses the centerline diagonally, and the leg pushes my body up. Then the right knee bends to the chest, and the foot shoots forward and grabs the board. Push up, and you're standing."

The three novices practiced the move a dozen times, as instructed. Regina and David both adopted the pull and hop movement that Ken had modeled. Laila followed suit, but she couldn't get the extension and balance she needed to stand up. Ken suggested that she try switching legs, keeping the right leg back and moving the left forward. On the third try, Laila surprised herself by reaching a standing position.

"It works!" Laila felt as though she had conquered Mount Everest. Her attempts at sports usually ran into the problems associated with short legs and a top-heavy figure. If it suits my body, surfing it is, she thought.

"Lean, Laila. Lean forward so the movement of the water doesn't knock you backwards," said Ken.

"You look adorable," said David.

"I don't think that's the goal," Laila answered.

"Works for me," he said. She turned to him and licked her lips, letting her tongue flick out at him, hoping she could make him lose his balance. He laughed, but he held his position.

"And if the wave rocks the board too much?" asked Regina.

"Crouch down or go to your stomach, whatever you have time for," said Ken. "Otherwise, fall off and start again. Your leg rope keeps the board attached to you."

"What if a wave just knocks us flying?" Laila asked.

"Go with it. Let the wave toss you. Its energy is coming towards shore, and you'll come with it. Panic is useless. Worse than useless. Hold your breath and try to get your feet underneath you as soon as the wave has passed."

Laila glanced at David. He was shorter than Ken, but molded, as if all of one piece. While Ken's limbs hinged at the joints, David's flowed without angles. His torso was broad but flat, and his arms muscled. She couldn't imagine him tumbled by a wave.

"All right, to the water," Ken said. "We'll use the broken waves first, where the foam is. We're going to catch rides in to shore, on our bellies first."

Ken walked with them as into water up to their waists. Light surf was breaking. The foamy water held the last parts of what had been mild but curling waves. They turned toward shore, pulled themselves on the boards, and started paddling with the push of the water. Ken watched, called encouragement, and motioned them back out to repeat the exercise a half dozen times.

"Looking more comfortable," he said. "How did that go?"

"Great," Regina said. "The board's heavy on the sand, but in the water, you feel like the wave and the board move together."

"That's the gist of it," said Ken. "The board wants to go with the wave, and you want to stay on the board."

Laila was exhilarated. She glided back to the beach on the light up and down roll of the modest waves. She was surprised by the grace of the movement; she had anticipated grabbing on with white knuckles while the board shoved about. Instead, she had hopped off easily when the wave was spent, and the board slowed.

"Okay," said Ken. "Back out to the beach."

They assembled once more on the sand. The tide was going out and left them plenty of space to line up beyond the water's edge.

"Now, we'll go out beyond the break and try to catch a wave, still on our stomachs, okay?" Ken said.

"With you?" Regina asked.

"Yeah, but I won't ride in with you. If you catch a wave, it'll be all yours. Regina first."

"Favorites. That's not fair," said Laila.

"Okay. You first," said Ken.

"Kidding! Just kidding," she answered.

Regina and Ken set off while David and Laila watched from the beach. Wave after wave crested, but Regina bobbed beyond the crests, with Ken on a board beside her. Sitting motionless, Laila began to feel a chill and slipped on her sweatshirt. They sat on the remaining board, watching their friends.

"The wind's picking up," Laila said. "Do the waves look higher?"

"You don't have to go out today. We've learned a lot already," David said.

"I know," she answered. "Let's see how Regina does. She looks like she's hesitating."

They stared as several more waves passed Regina by. Laila was counting as they rolled in, but David seemed distracted.

"What is it?" she asked.

"I'm going to have to go to Miami tonight," David said. "Dad texted this morning."

"But this was a weekend off." Her eyebrows knitted into a frown. Surely Sam Harrow was behind the request, not their father.

Sam and his wife, Andrea, were proud of being devout Christians. They served on several church committees, and their four children attended a Christian day school. Over each family meal, they prayed together. The eldest, Betsy, was nominated by her youth group to represent them at their national assembly this upcoming July.

Laila might have drawn closer to Sam and Andrea if they had accepted the twins. For her in-laws, Alton and Forrest were not true Harrows. They would inquire about Eddie and Jackson, but not the twins. Sam and Andrea talked as if they had only two nephews, and Laila was deeply offended.

She gritted her teeth and kept as much distance as possible from Miami. Regina led them to a small, progressive church in St. Augustine, a Unitarian community, in part because they had a youth program for all four boys, and because the members included plenty of kids the color of Forrest and Alton.

As payback, Sam delighted in breaking up their weekends.

"They're about to make big decisions on the retail areas, and I need to keep in the loop," David said.

"And Sam has nothing to do with it, right?" she said.

"Ah, well," he answered. "There's always that. Here she comes," shouted David.

Regina had caught one of the larger waves of the morning, still only about three feet, but for a newcomer, substantial. They watched the water surge under her board, capturing its full length, and tilting it skyward. Regina hopped to her feet, leaned forward, and rode down the brief chute the modest wave provided. She wavered at the end and folded into a low crouch, but she remained on aboard for the full ride.

"That show-off!" Laila was smiling at her friend. "She can do anything."

"Nice job!" Ken called from his water perch. "Let's go, David"

Laila hopped off the board, and David took it out toward Ken. Regina dragged her board from the water and sat next to Laila.

"That was a rush," Regina said.

"He's a good teacher," Laila answered. "You two are making me so happy."

"Thanks. I'm kind of regretting the timing of this trip to New York. We just got so fun so fast. I think I'm more surprised than anybody else."

"It's like you're leaving the nest, too," Laila said.

"Mindy seems to be resentful about Ken and me."

"You've been a Mom to Mindy with all your heart. She's solid. She's ready to spread her wings."

Regina gazed out at Ken. "I think I can walk and chew gum, you know what I mean?"

"Of course. You'll always be her Mom. It's just a big transition plus a new person in the mix," Laila said. "Hey, did everything resolve with the financial aid stuff?"

"For the first year. The scholarship people approve the next year after they've seen freshman grades. It's normal, I guess."

"The University of Chicago. You must be so proud. I'm proud, and I had nothing to do with it."

"Nothing else really matters now, does it? I mean I've done the hardest thing I'll ever do. And I hit a home run."

"If you do say so yourself," joked Laila.

"I have the most amazing child."

"Hey, now," said Laila.

"Four boys. Who has four boys and not one girl? That's just whacky," said Regina. She pointed at Laila in mock disbelief.

For a moment, Laila imagined that Regina knew about her search for siblings of Alton and Forrest. In her heart, Laila hoped there would be a sibling, a female sibling. Boys are fun, but having a daughter would be an extra pleasure, she thought. No, she's just joking. She's not thinking about more siblings.

Anyway, the idea of a sister for the boys is fantastical, as silly as the Spanish pirate show in old town St. Augustine.

"If I could have a daughter like Mindy, I'd have ten," said Laila.

"Oh, dear, watch out what you wish for. She wasn't that easy." Regina laughed.

"Here he comes," yelled Laila.

She was on her feet, cheering David as he positioned himself before a curling wave. He grasped the board by the rails and lifted his chest as Ken had coached them. He got his back leg in position, but the board rocked, and David remained crouched. It looked like he wouldn't stand in time, but before the last few seconds of wave, he hopped up and got his balance. He remained on his feet until the wave ran slack onto the shore.

It was Laila's turn. She felt a chill as she took off her sweatshirt. Regina helped her scoot the board into the water and affix the leg rope around her ankle. She pushed the board past the first line of foam until the water reached her knees. She climbed aboard and started to paddle towards Ken.

"Looking good," David called to her from the shore.

She would have been glad to hop off, turn the board around, and coast back to Regina and David on the beach. Yet Ken had put these hours at their disposal, and Laila wanted to hear him, hear them all applaud her success. She could justify Ken's investment by riding a good-sized wave on her belly, she thought. Just because David and Regina stood, she didn't have to get up. That accomplishment could come at later lessons.

Her arms ached, but she reached Ken. She saw him shiver and realized he probably hadn't counted on how long the three of them would take to choose a first wave. She'd grab anything that showed up.

Let's get this test over with.

Ken helped her turn her board to face the beach, and she positioned herself along the centerline as he had taught them. Her legs were too far apart, he said, and even though it gave her a greater sense of balance, it was a bad habit. She turned to look back at her legs, as if to order them to behave and pulled them in towards each other.

"You're too far forward," he said.

She grasped the rails and began to inch towards the back, concentrating on keeping her ankles touching as she moved. She felt awkward, as if this simple job required outsized effort on her part. Progress was slow, and she could tell she was still too far forward.

She felt a slight pull backwards, and she looked around to Ken, thinking he had grasped her board. Instead, she saw they were both in a trough, and a wave was looming above them, sucking them back. The pull shifted to a forward push.

"Go with it!" Ken shouted.

As if I have a choice, she thought.

Don't panic. Do not panic.

She flattened her belly to the board and held on, her arms wrapping underneath, her head resting nearer the peak of the board, far past any reasonable center of gravity. The power of the wave congregates at the crest, Ken had told them, and there was no fighting it. It pushed with total conviction, and for a lovely ten seconds, she and the board extended out into midair, forward and upward, flying wingless, propelled by a silent, spraying power.

The next fifteen seconds were humiliating. Her weight on the front of the board brought it straight down, at an angle steeper than the wave itself, so it hit the pebble floor while the wave still wielded its power. The board flipped forward, and she tumbled over on her back. The board and wave dragged her over the rough bottom. She flipped once more, let go of the board, and had her nose ground into the sandy gravel.

The spent surge deposited her in the shallows. She could feel the sand clumps inside the bra of her suit and wedged between her breasts. She pushed herself up to a sitting position. Still tethered to her leg, nearby the board swirled disingenuously in the eddies, as if it had delivered a ride exactly as ordered.

She sat by herself a moment, registering the pleasure of breathing in air instead of salt water. She uncoupled herself from the leg rope and pulled the board toward her, like she would a naughty child. Her elbow and nose stung from the salt on the scraped skin, but the rest of her was intact. Gathering herself up, she looked toward David and Regina, both on their feet, expressions of suspended alarm on their faces.

"I decided not to stand," she said. "I feel like belly boarding doesn't really get enough attention these days."

"Yeah, you could make a name for yourself belly boarding, all right," David said. She dug her feet into the sea floor and trudged towards the beach.

"Where are you going?" yelled Ken. He was paddling towards her, a smile broader than any she had seen on his face. "One more ride."

She scowled, but he didn't yield.

"I'm a mess," she said. "And you are turning blue."

"Get on," he ordered. "Another ride, or you might never go out again."

David gave the back of the board a shove, and she and Ken paddled out a few lengths beyond the first froth, turned the boards, and waited for a mild-mannered crest. They rode in towards shore, both on their bellies, grinning. Laila wondered if there was enough space in their basement storage locker for a board for her and another for David.

CHAPTER FOURTEEN

Saturday, Day Seven – Douglas Weighs In

Laila looked out from the living room balcony at the foamy shore and considered how Florida had shown her a new side that morning. The water held the power of daring and freedom. The surfing lesson gave back the old image of herself as an adventurer that her college dreams had stoked. She wondered if she would wake up tomorrow still enthused or shrink again from physical danger. So far, the brief victory gave her a feeling of strength.

She had been right, too, about how it affected her understanding of Ken. The surfing lesson opened her eyes to a part of him that had been nonsensical before. He pored over results of competitions, kept up on the newest hotshots, spent hours watching YouTube videos of Australian beaches. He rented a large storage locker for his collection of surfboards. Occasionally, when she was walking on the beach, she'd surprise him, standing on the shore, observing the waves as if he were powerless to move. If she could surf with the assurance he does, the ocean would mesmerize her, too.

The fact that Eddie was jealous also increased her interest. What an unexpected pleasure it was to see her son, her eldest who lately had less use for her than a dog has for a cat, turn and look at her with surprise envy!

"Where've you been, Mom?" Alton had asked when Laila and David came in from their lesson. The four were finishing up Margaret's stuffed French toast breakfast, lolling on their chairs with full bellies.

"Your Mom has been hanging ten with Ken," said David.

"What?" said Eddie. "I thought the lesson was for you, Dad."

"I gave it a try, but it was Mom who caught the big one."

"You mean it caught me," said Laila, but Eddie didn't hear the self-effacing joke.

"Mom, on a board?" Eddie was looking at David with disbelief.

"Oh, yes," said David. "And I wouldn't be surprised if she owns her own board by the end of the weekend."

"Mom!" said Eddie. 'I thought you were afraid of the ocean." He gave Laila an admiring glance and then had second thoughts. "Are you guys making a joke? Mom, did you go out by yourself? Did you actually surf or body surf?"

"I surfed enough to know a wave can toss you around," said Laila. "It's not so easy."

Eddie looked chagrined about getting sporting advice from his mother. "Please, Dad, please let me go with you next time," he said.

"We'll see," said David. "But it won't happen this weekend. I'm heading out to Miami after I get changed. Anybody got a hug that I can pass on to Grandma and Grandpa?"

Jackson and the twins circled David, taking turns wrapping their arms around him. Eddie waited until last and patted him on the back as David was releasing his hold on Forrest.

"Every weekend, Dad?" Eddie said.

"At least it's only down to Miami," David answered. "I'll be back here Sunday night for dinner." Eddie looked unconvinced.

His unscheduled departure left the weekend more or less unplanned. The twins would be easy to occupy as long as Laila took part. Eddie had a car wash for the tennis team, and Laila wondered if she wouldn't be wise to persuade Jackson to tag along with him. His quieter nature made him less compatible with Eddie's burly friends, and she wasn't sure that a forced fundraiser would benefit anyone. Still, she had nothing to offer but a dull afternoon playing Uno with his younger brothers. She was about to approach Jackson with her idea when Benjamin called.

"Hi, how is everything. Did your brother arrive safely?" she asked.

"Yes, last night. I picked him up in Jacksonville. That's what I'm calling about," he said. "I have a favor to ask."

"Of course."

"Douglas is the organized one, and this morning, he took a look around and said we need to sell the condo, plan a memorial for Mom, and say goodbye to St. Augustine."

"How do you feel about all that?" Laila asked.

"He said the autopsy will show a natural death, and we need to make peace with it. Sudden or not, we knew it would come one day."

"And you agree?" asked Laila.

"I tend to be an alarmist. He's the organizer; I'm the worrier."

Family dynamics, thought Laila. Who doesn't have to deal with them? Everyone clutching a role and marking territory. A crisis hardens the boundaries and fixes reactions to familiar patterns.

"Still, it's been a shock," she said. "I hope Douglas knows none of us expected this. We didn't see her faltering."

"I'm going to occupy myself with the condo and let the autopsy take care of itself. When the results come out, I might be closer to accepting everything."

"And Douglas?"

"He's more religious. For him, arranging the memorial will be the way he says goodbye."

"I'm glad he has that," said Laila. "And what favor can I do for you?"

"Claire mentioned the local flea markets. I wonder if you two would take charge of a couple of Mom's pieces to sell. You can't remove anything until the police finish their investigation, but maybe with photos, you can start the process."

"Yes, no problem. Claire knows her way around because of all the staging she's done. I'll call her and get back to you."

"So, there's a way I want to repay you," he said.

"Please, I'd do it in a second for Billie."

"You are so kind," he said. "The things she told me about you were all true."

"Okay, now you've signed me up for just about anything," Laila said, the edge of her melancholy softened by his comment.

"I know your boy, Jackson, enjoyed Mom's telescope. Would he accept it from us?"

"Oh, my goodness, yes," she said. "But you should tell him."

"Doug's over at the church, and I'm here at Mom's."

"I can come over to photograph the furniture, and I'll bring Jackson."

The twins were absorbed in a Lego project, and Eddie promised to keep an ear cocked for trouble. Jackson and she walked the short hop across the beach to Billie's. They climbed the stairs to the upper deck and entered the door leading to her condo.

"Why do you need me?" her son asked.

"There might be some things to carry," Laila said vaguely.

"Ah, the astronomer," said Benjamin when he opened the door.

Jackson blushed, and Laila put an encouraging hand on his shoulder.

"Hello," the boy said. "It's nice to see you again."

Inside the condo, Benjamin had pulled back the curtains and opened the blinds, letting in the morning light. Illuminated, the home seemed smaller. Benjamin had packed up Billie's books and photographs. Newspapers and magazines, the wide assortment that always impressed Laila, were bagged for recycling. The antiquated television, which had occupied a large chunk of the living room, had been removed, stand and all. Billie once told Laila that she kept it only to watch NASA space shots.

The telescope on its tripod stood by the wall in place of the television. Jackson took a few steps toward it as if drawn magnetically, and then he stopped, remembering his manners. He returned to Laila's side.

"Jackson," began Benjamin, "if you know anyone who may be able to take care of the telescope, we'd be grateful."

"Oh my gosh, you're kidding," he said to Benjamin. "You don't want it?"

"I think you should take it. I think it would make us happy," Benjamin answered.

Jackson stepped to the telescope. He tested the tripod for stability and examined the clasp holding the scope to the tripod. He rotated it on the tripod carefully, from one angle to another. He twisted the focus on the lens and fit the rubber lens guard on the end of the scope.

"She showed me Ursa one night," Jackson said.

"Major or minor?" asked Benjamin.

"Both," said Jackson, turning in surprise towards the informed question. "Are you sure you don't want it?"

"I have one," Benjamin answered. "I think it was the first piece of furniture I bought after I left home." His voice thickened on the last word, and Laila felt his sorrow.

Once when Laila asked Billie why she liked studying the night sky, she said that the stars teach us that anything is possible.

"Millions of years of light," she had said to Laila. "It makes you consider that there might not have been a beginning. At least, not the way we understand the word."

The comment had gone a long way to explaining her tilt of mind. And like her, Jackson liked whatever gave him the most room to exercise his imagination.

"It's a lovely present," said Laila.

"Thank you," said Jackson. "Thank you very, very much." Benjamin gave him a formal nod.

Benjamin pointed out the furniture he wanted to sell at the flea market. She took snapshots of each piece and made notes on her phone of his expectations on price. She told him Claire and Brick had more photos, so they could start the next day. Hopefully, she and Claire would have something to report by Monday.

"Claire knows how to bargain," she assured Benjamin.

While she worked, he helped Jackson fit the telescope into its carrier bag. They were ready to say goodbye when Douglas returned.

"My brother, Doug," Benjamin introduced him to Laila and Jackson.

Doug and Benjamin shared the same sandy hair, lanky frame, and erect posture. They were both trim, although Doug's shoulders and arms were more muscled, and his neck was thicker. He wore jeans and a shirt that remained untucked.

"The star-gazer," Douglas said after learning Jackson's name. "There's always one in the crowd."

If Jackson caught the deprecation in Douglas' comment, he didn't show it. She was proud of him. He wouldn't be undone by a bit of archness. If astronomy didn't impress Douglas, it didn't change Jackson's love of it. They shook hands, and Jackson thanked him for the gift. David, thought Laila, was teaching his sons well.

"You're helping us clean things out," said Douglas. Laila caught Benjamin's slight flinch.

Douglas conveyed a more hectic personality and left less personal space to those around him. He gestured often with his hands, and in the course of a few minutes, he clapped Benjamin on the back at least twice. But who's counting? Laila thought. Probably not Benjamin, after all these years.

"If you decide to sell other things, let me know. We'll be glad to help," Laila said.

"You can see the police have taken a lot already," Douglas said. "Notebooks, photocopies, random CDs. Mom had some really old stuff on floppy disks, and they took that, too. The police think they need my mother's records back to the invention of the file folder."

"I told them to take whatever." Benjamin frowned at Douglas. "What's the harm?"

"The question is what's the good?" Douglas said.

Benjamin answered him with a tight smile.

"What's done is done," said Douglas. He clapped Benjamin on the back once more. "I'm guessing they'll return it to us soon."

"I agree," said Laila. She supposed that was the answer Douglas most liked hearing.

Laila slid her phone into its bag, and Jackson shouldered the telescope carrier. He thanked the men once more, and the two of them left for home.

CHAPTER FIFTEEN

Saturday, Day Seven – A Day with her Boys

After lunch, Laila drove Eddie to the community center. She tried to ask detailed questions about the fundraiser, but Eddie gave brief answers with a minimum of information. Frustrated, she pressed harder, but Eddie continued to be tight-lipped.

"Maybe I'll discuss it with some of the parents," she said.

"For that, you'd have to actually meet them," he said.

He was right. Since David started traveling more, she participated far less in any of the kids' activities. The criticism stung, and she was sure her face showed her embarrassment. Eddie stared straight ahead, satisfaction settled on his face. She dropped him off and drove the three younger boys home.

Jackson set up his new telescope, and while he was protective of his new treasure, he was also a generous teacher.

She threw open the balcony windows, and he placed the tripod and telescope in the center, where he could swivel it from side to side for an unobstructed view. Laila got three stools from the kitchen for the young observers. On the large dining table, she laid out paints, paper, and books they could use for inspiration.

Jackson worked with Forrest first, showing him how to adjust the distance and focus and how to scan an area by gently turning the handle on the scope. The daylight discouraged any study of the sky, but the boys got busy searching out creatures along the shore.

"Look at this jellyfish," Jackson said, focusing on a spot by the water.

"Ugh, somebody stepped on it," Forrest answered.

"Can you see the kid making the sand castle?" Jackson asked. "He doesn't notice, but there's a crab on his turret."

"What?" Forrest yelped. "Let me see."

"Do you see it?" asked Jackson.

"Yeah, I see it now," the twin said, with a tone of dejection.

"What? Not big enough for you?" asked Jackson.

"I thought a turret was something else."

"What do you mean?" queried Jackson.

"He thought it was a piece of poop," said Alton.

"Did not," said Forrest.

"Yes, you did," said Jackson. They all laughed.

From time to time, the twins switched places. Alton took a turn at the telescope while Forrest sketched what he had seen. Often, one or the other would ask Laila to find a picture of the creature he wanted to draw, and with pencil, Laila would draw an outline, and a twin would complete it with brush and paints.

Jackson discovered that the telescope permitted him a view of the fishing pier a quarter of a mile south along the beach, beyond the Laguna Shores jutting breakwater. He went to his room and brought out a pictorial guide to Florida fish that David had gotten him for his birthday. He leafed through it trying to match the pictures to the fish being pulled out of the water at the pier.

"Grouper," said Forrest, peering through the lens all the way to the pier.

"Maybe," said Jackson, when Forrest pointed out the fish. "A pretty small grouper."

The boys' immersion in the details of the landscape amazed Laila. Margaret made sandwiches, and they took a break for lunch but quickly returned to the balcony and the telescope. They played a game of "What am I looking at?" where one had to identify what the other described from his perch at the telescope. They turned the game around by having one find a specimen in a book and the others trying to spot it through the telescope. It was three o'clock when they agreed to put everything away for the day.

While the boys got dressed to go out, she texted Claire about getting out to the flea markets to try to sell Billie's furniture. Although Claire had clients scheduled all day, she planned to come over that evening. Relieved, Laila tucked away the phone. She hadn't checked with Claire before assuring Benjamin and Douglas that Billie's furniture would quickly sell, and a disappointment on that account might aggravate the brothers' relationship further.

The boys came bounding into the hall, ready to go. Laila suggested a walk down the pier to ask the fisherman what they were catching, then a drive to the community center to get Eddie, and a dinner of pizza at their favorite nearby restaurant. They wished Margaret a happy weekend, hugged her goodbye, and loaded onto the elevator.

The pier was maintained by the Florida State Parks and attracted locals, but usually, a good crowd of tourists were eyeing the fish and irritating the fishermen with incessant questions. Laila didn't want the boys to be a nuisance, so she cautioned them first.

"People who like to fish like quiet, too. So, each of you can ask one question, and try not to ask the same person. Agree ahead of time what you're going to say, so you don't keep asking the same thing."

"What'll you do?" Alton asked.

"I'll stand here and watch you. You can ask on your own. Be polite, please," she said.

"Can I touch the fish?" asked Forrest.

"If you ask permission," said Laila.

"Does that count as one of my questions?" said Forrest.

"I suppose not," she said, "if you are very, very polite."

The pier was less than a quarter mile long, made of closely laid planks with a four-foot railing of wooden supports and a handrail. At the far end, a high, thatched roof set on poles created a shady utility area. Under the cover, there were sinks to clean fish and benches for onlookers to rest. Laila leaned against the railing as the boys consulted on which questions to ask.

They set off as she watched. She was pleased at the way they walked up and down the pier, each holding back on asking a question in order not to be the first one done. The sunshine was intermittent as afternoon clouds glided onshore, and Laila felt refreshed in the light breeze and mild temperatures.

She answered her phone when it vibrated. She didn't recognize the number, but it was local and could belong to someone in Eddie's crowd. He might have had a change in plans, or worse, some kind of trouble.

"Laila?" a male voice asked.

"Yes, that's me."

"It's Jake Hanlon."

Odd he would have my number, she thought.

"How can I help, Jake?" Laila answered. She moved away from the railing so that she could follow the boys' progress as they worked their way to the end of the pier.

"I can't get an answer from David. Is he around?"

"Has something happened with the kids? With Bailey or Eddie?"

"No, it's County Commission stuff. It's a 24/7 job, I'm afraid."

Relief flooded Laila. She didn't think she could handle a crisis about Eddie by herself, a thought she would certainly not share with Margaret.

"He's down in Miami until tomorrow," she answered.

"It's a pressing matter, Mrs. Harrow. Do you know where I can reach him?"

"I think you might have more luck after six," she said. "Saturday is a work day for David, too"

"Then wouldn't he pick up?" he said, an edge creeping into his voice.

"His meetings tend to go long," she said. "I could pass along a message."

Laila saw that all three boys had congregated around one fisherman, and she was anxious to check on the situation—and even more anxious to end the conversation with Jake, who happened to be a local bigwig, and who happened to be exasperated

"No," he said. "I'll text him again."

He made no apology for his abruptness so Laila couldn't resist an excessively cheery good-bye.

"Have a good day," she chirped.

She wondered if Bailey Hanlon got on her father's nerves as much as Eddie could get on hers, which might go half way to excusing him. The new territory of teen years looked rockier every day.

She reached the boys at the far end of the pier. They gathered at the base of a sink, crouched and staring at a hefty fish in one of the buckets. It had a mouthful of teeth, and its gills were still working, a sign that it had not yet given in to the inevitable end. The boys kept their hands to themselves but were close enough to earn an irritable look from the fisherman.

"Mom, look. It's got to be a shark," said Forrest.

"Do you think it's still alive?" asked Alton.

"It could bite your finger right off, right Mom?" said Jackson.

The fisherman, also on his haunches by the bucket, jerked his head up toward Laila. He did a double take when he saw her, not an unusual reaction. She gave a nod to the man, smiling and placing a protective hand on each twin's shoulder.

"Your boys?" questioned the man.

"Yes. This is Alton, Jackson, and Forrest," she said. "They are fascinated by fish," she added unnecessarily.

"I see," said the man.

His scowl disappeared as he adjusted to the situation. Physically, the dark-haired, heavy-browed, skinny-legged Jackson had little in common with the short and dimpled Laila. Add in the twins, with shiny, coal-colored faces, enormous black eyes, and high cheekbones, most people did not expect to be introduced to a family.

"Is it a shark?" Laila inquired.

"That's your one question, Mom," Forrest said, elbowing her. She laughed.

"It's just a sand shark," the man replied. "But I wouldn't put a finger in its mouth."

Laila got the hint and shepherded the boys off the pier and towards their vehicle. Each recounted his one question and its corresponding answer, and they mulled over additional questions they might ask if they had been permitted.

"When we get home, we'll find the answers online," she said.

They picked up Eddie and stopped for pizza. Back at home, after a few minutes of looking at fish pictures on the internet, then baths for the twins, and reading a couple of storybooks, Laila was free. The twins were tucked in, Jackson would read himself to sleep, and Eddie was allowed to watch television until ten.

Unfortunately, Claire called and begged off the evening visit. Brick had made it through a long bike ride with Ken, and she had the job of dispensing aspirin and massage.

"He's an aching, complaining mess." She laughed. "And I'm not much better. What a day!"

"Lots of showings?" Laila asked.

"Which is a good thing," Claire said. "But some people are so prickly. They act as though I purposely choose houses they don't like."

"So maybe tomorrow won't work out?" said Laila.

"Oh, no, no," she answered. "I'll be fine. I'm good from ten until one. Then I've got an open house."

"Are you sure you feel like it?"

"Mornings are best anyway," said Claire. "The markets get too busy in the afternoon."

They agreed to meet at ten at the largest flea market Claire knew. The place had at least a dozen reputable, long-time dealers, many of whom operated online antique and collectible sites and boasted considerable sales.

"With just a pinch of luck, we'll finish by twelve-thirty," Claire said.

Laila hung up and dialed Ken. She honestly had a tech question for him, but with any luck, the moment could be perfect for the other conversation they needed to have. She needed to lay out the line of inquiry the police would likely pursue about his last conversation with Billie. Yet how could she warn him without sounding like she was the one who wondered about a connection with Regina?

She'd simply plow into it, she thought. *We're friends, right?*

"What's up?" Ken asked, picking up on the first ring.

"Not much," she started. "I heard you had a good bike ride today with Brick."

"A lot to talk about, for sure, and I don't want to be rude, but Regina is leaving tomorrow for New York, and well, you know," his voice trailed off into the obvious.

"She's there?"

"Well, yes, matter of fact," he said.

"And tomorrow is your church day," she said.

"After the morning trip to the airport," he hinted.

"Now I know you're Presbyterian, she said. "They're the ones so large they have late services."

"Don't be jealous. You Unitarians have a cute little chapel." He laughed. "I'll catch up with you at our Monday meeting."

"Oh, I know you have to go, but one more quick question," she said.

"Okay," Ken said distractedly.

"Jackson was given Billie's telescope, and he is thrilled. He asked me for a cell phone to attach to it to take photos."

"I thought you didn't allow the boys cell phones?" Ken asked.

"Correct. David and I would only agree if it stayed on the telescope. No phone calls. No exceptions."

"So, the question?"

"Which phone has the best camera?"

"Most late model cell phones have great cameras. It's the synching between his Mac and the cloud you want, so an iPhone. No fuss. No muss."

"You are a jewel," she said.

Although she failed to work out the persistent knot in the story they shared of the night Billie died, she hadn't implied any accusations. Regina and he were drawing very close, very quickly. She needed an extremely deft approach, one she hadn't yet determined. She hadn't fumbled the ball.

"Thanks again," she finished.

She hung up and headed to the den to see Eddie. He interrupted the show he was watching, eyeing Laila self-consciously. The large screen held the suspended body of a surfer entering the curl of a towering wave. Young and muscular, the man was dwarfed by the wall of water. Laila sat next to Eddie, close enough to see dark hairs on his upper lip forming a phantom mustache.

"Go ahead," she said. "I want to see."

Eddie pushed start, and the man's thighs rippled as he steadied the board and entered the tunnel of water. For a moment he was curtained by the water, but he reappeared, still riding the skimming board, directing it up a crest and down a sheer face. His superb balance made him look as if his feet were attached to the board and unable to separate from it, no matter what loops and dives it executed. Laila couldn't imagine how one could acquire such confidence.

"Do you think Ken can do that?" she asked.

"Dad says he competed. And in Hawaii," Eddie answered.

"Is Florida as good as Hawaii?"

"I don't know about that. But there are schools here. And some champions."

"And you want to try?" she asked.

"Start, anyway. See if I can," Eddie said.

"Where are the schools?"

"So, I can?" Eddie said, a smile on his lips.

"I'm only asking," she said. "I'm just gathering data."

"Mom!" Eddie grunted. "Don't tease."

"And don't you pressure," she said.

"You don't even care," he said. He snapped off the television and got up from the sofa, heading off towards his room. "This stuff is important, and you don't care."

Laila stayed a moment, considering the dark screen and the empty room, the echo of her son's frustration bouncing from wall to wall. She had read books on child rearing and knew the arc of adolescent development included pushing away from parental authority. She remembered herself as a resistant teen, dismissive of her parents' attitudes and opinions. None of that helped her accept that her own boy, whom she had cradled and protected for thirteen years, would turn his back on her feelings.

I guess I have some toughening up to do.

She resisted the urge to follow Eddie to his room and try to remedy the tension. David would expect Eddie to build the bridge back into his parents' good graces, and not the other way around. She should divert her attention and occupy herself with something other than children.

She decided to work on the research report she promised Jennifer. It was a sad way to pass a Saturday evening, but it could work as an antidote to loneliness. Before her boys, before her marriage, she pursued art as a career and as a maker of meaning. If she could help the St. Augustine's Museum increase its standing in the community, she could claim some responsibility for bettering the world, or at least, her corner of the world.

She walked into her study and sat at her desk, shadowed by the feeling of being peripheral in her own home. She was alone because Claire was busy, and David was in Miami, and Billie was gone. Regina would most likely continue to spend Saturday nights with Ken, not the work widow, Laila. So be it. If one person deserved to ease up and enjoy her time outside work, it was Regina.

She owned what, probably five tennis skirts, two pair of court shoes, a windbreaker, and some hairbands? She had dark jeans and a white shirt for dress up. Regina didn't have cable and didn't go out to theaters, either. When her old television died, she chucked it and did not buy a replacement. In the annual run up to the Oscars, Regina and Mindy binge-watched the nominated films with Laila in her den.

Many times, Regina led her and Margaret down narrow roads to family farms where they bought oranges, peaches, corn, beans, eggs, and nuts for a fraction of city prices. She had friends on shrimp boats, and they filled up plastic bags for her at half price. She smoked tuna on her barbecue to use for sandwiches during the week.

Her car was solid, from the sub-SUV class, which she got after months of scrutiny of the used car magazines and online listings. She hoarded oil change coupons, and once a year, an old boyfriend, still apologetic for having cheated on her, checked the vehicle over, repairing leaks and worn brake linings when necessary.

Regina's parents retired from Miami to Jamaica, where Mindy spent many summer vacations and Regina didn't have to pay for daycare. Mindy spoke lovingly of these family times. According to her, the family loved music. Their playlist had Caribbean reggae, of course, and Cuban salsa, twangy rhythm and blues, and any pop hits that were danceable. Once middle school started for Eddie, Mindy took it upon herself to teach him some steps. As his reward for applying himself to the moves and music, she got him into one of her high school dances.

It was held outside on the football field one hot evening the previous September, and Eddie, pressed into the center of a cheerful group of Mindy's friends, slipped by security. Eddie did well, Mindy told Laila, and had little trouble finding dance partners. David and Laila weren't happy with the deception, but it was hard to punish Eddie for enjoying a simple pleasure of life. By that time, Mindy was a senior and had navigated high school without resorting to alcohol or drugs. They could think of worse ways their son might be introduced to the adolescent social scene.

Regina was about to embark on a new phase, spending time with Ken and learning to let go of Mindy. Laila would need to steel herself for the change. She told herself she would get used to the new normal and learn from the grace with which Regina relinquished her hold on Mindy.

Laila opened her computer screen and went to work. She added a dozen or more Highwayman paintings into the map data, paintings discovered as close as Jacksonville and as far away as Brisbane. As the map became more populated, she decided to find a photo of each painting. Billie's documentation showed her how to link each photo to a point on the map, which created an interactive program. She tried it with two test cases, and after minor adjustments, it worked.

The next step would be to find or create descriptors for each painting so that users could conduct searches by artist, year, or elements of the painting. Descriptions she found produced many possibilities. Some could be gushing, marveling at the effect of color and shading to create a melancholy mood. Some were unemotional, and the odd critic was dismissive, calling the settings stereotypical. Recorded sale prices added another level of categorization.

Laila cut and pasted into the Highwaymen data sheet. It was midnight when she glanced at the time on the top of her screen. She stretched, surprised at the length of her efforts.

The new normal. Maybe it's not so bad.

She checked once more on the boys. Eddie's room smelled like dirty socks, but he slept soundly, so she cracked open the window an inch and closed his door firmly. The twins were deep into slumber despite the nightlights plugged into all six of the room's sockets for Alton's benefit. Jackson, as usual, had fallen asleep reading and left his book splayed out on the blanket.

Laila went to bed grateful for the health and good fortune that had been granted her.

CHAPTER SIXTEEN

Sunday, Day Eight - The Flea Market

The parking lot outside the open-air flea market stretched across an unappealing field. Tired knots of grass poked out of a dusty earth. Laila wore sandals, and between her toes, rasping dirt accumulated. An occasional pebble lodged beneath her sole. Eddie's running shoes protected him well, and he strode toward the market entrance while she half-hopped, half limped behind him. Claire could have warned me, she thought churlishly.

The day had not begun well. She woke up late and rushed through breakfast with the boys. She had hoped to make church, but once again, Sunday would pass without their attendance.

The twins were clinging to her much more than usual, and Caya looked none too happy to have to supervise them. Jackson set up the telescope again, but it didn't exert the same magic over Forrest and Alton as the day before. The saving grace was Eddie's offer to accompany Laila to the market.

"You might sell the furniture and need someone to help you pick it up at Billie's," he said.

She doubted that a sale would materialize so quickly, but she didn't argue. She would have been happy with a few hours to wander the flea market with only adult company, but after some questioning, she accepted Eddie's offer of company, a rarity she needed to encourage.

"Don't you have homework?" she asked.

"I do, but I don't have plans for the afternoon. I'll get it done; I promise," he said.

"All right," she said. The twins let out a cheer, smiling for the first time that morning.

"We control the remote," they shouted. They slapped each other on the back, running from Laila's side toward the den. Caya brightened also.

Eddie knew the SUV's navigation system, and he talked Laila through the route without comment. When she asked him a few offhand questions about Bailey and a few other friends, he showed little interest in conversation. She felt his reason for accompanying her to the market had more to do with escaping his younger brothers than spending time with her.

They arrived without a hitch to acres of market stalls, introduced by an enormous billboard visible from the nearby interstate. The sign promised bargains on furniture, sports equipment, collectibles and art, along with a bouncy house for kids and "mouth-watering" food booths. Laila noticed that many of the cars in the parking lot had out of state license plates, giving her hope that sales were brisk.

They met Claire at the entrance as arranged. Brick accompanied her, a ball cap and white sun block shielding his fair skin. He shook Eddie's hand and kidded with him about guys being drafted for shopping expeditions.

"I don't mind looking around," Eddie said. "Mom, I'll meet you back here in an hour?"

"At twelve-thirty," she confirmed. "Sounds good."

Claire, Brick, and Laila consulted a map of the stalls posted by the front gate. Claire pointed out two of the furniture dealers she knew best and suggested they visit them first. The ground inside the market enclosure was better maintained than the parking lot, and walking in sandals was easier, but Laila noticed that Claire wore close-toed sports shoes. *Live and learn*, Laila thought.

"Which pieces should we start with?" Claire asked. Laila showed her and Brick the photos of a dresser and curio cabinet on her phone.

"Nice," said Brick. "That's the cherry and the oak."

"Good call," said Claire.

"I refinished a lot of furniture back in the day," he said. "Five kids and all that."

"I just noticed," Laila said to Brick. "You're not limping."

"Ken is a cruel and heartless man," Brick said with a grin. "But I bounce back quickly."

"How many miles?" Laila asked.

"Sixty," he answered.

"In one day?" Laila said.

"Why?" asked Claire. "Why do men do that?" She shook her head in sympathy for Brick.

"Ladies, have you met Ken? He follows surfing. There was a surfing competition at Flagler Beach. Hence, we had to cycle to Flagler Beach. End of discussion."

"Do you own a bike?" Laila asked.

"Ken has an extra. Ken has extra boards, extra free weights, extra scuba gear, extra water skis. . . ."

"Extra aspirin?" Laila broke in.

"No," said Brick. "Ken's answer to tired muscles is to ride ten miles farther. He says that muscles like to work."

"Poor Regina," said Laila.

"Poor Regina!" exclaimed Brick. "Have you seen Regina play Ken in tennis?"

"It's not pretty," added Claire.

"I'm not saying this will happen, but she might make him cry one day," said Brick with satisfaction. "My nightmare would be going with Ken *and* Regina on a bike ride."

"So, no more Ken outings for you?" Laila asked.

"I exaggerate," Brick said. "I came along today because I thought I might find a second-hand bike. I'll show that guy who's tough."

"And I wasted a Saturday night nursing your aches and pains?" Claire exclaimed.

"Now, sweetness, you know we had fun." Brick squeezed Claire's shoulders, and she rolled her eyes.

Laila laughed at the two of them. She found Brick to be heartier and more youthful than she thought, despite the self-deprecating complaints. He might be a decade older than Claire, but he talked and walked like a man in his forties. She chalked up her negative reaction towards him at dinner on Friday to the wine.

The first of the dealers Claire knew had a double booth, enclosed on three sides by long tables holding small lamps, decorative bowls, and porcelain figurines. Within the border made of tables, smaller pieces such as vanities, desks, benches, and rocking chairs crowded together like a reunion of friends, each marked by a long life. Laila's impression was that Billie's furniture would be out of this vendor's price range, and he confirmed her conclusion.

"No," he said after glancing at the pictures on her phone. "I handle what will turn over in a week or less. High-priced pieces take too long, sorry."

They skipped over two rows to find the next dealer, and the response matched the first. The thin margin of profit for second-hand goods caused dealers to put a premium on quick sales. The second dealer suggested they try an antiques specialist new to the flea market who might have more room and more tolerance for slow-moving, high-end items.

"She's over at the far corner, across from the west entrance. It's where they stick the newbies," he said. "But nice things, and very nice art."

"Thanks," said Claire. "All right, group, you heard the man. To the west!"

Scuttling along the warren of booths, the three moved at different speeds. Claire showed little attraction to any of the displays and would get ahead of Brick and Laila. She stopped every few booths to wait for the two to catch up. Brick craned his neck left and right at every intersection of rows, looking up at the signs announcing the type of vendors.

"I don't see any sporting goods," he complained to Laila.

Laila counted on Claire to draw them along in the right direction. She kept one eye on Claire and let the other take in the individual style and contents of booth after booth. She surveyed stacks of Persian rugs. Another vendor had mirrors in a variety of frames made of wood, iron, ceramic tile, and in one case, feathers. They came upon three booths in a row full of clocks that made her want to toss out the digital alarm on her bedside table.

"We'd better pick up our pace," said Brick.

She had stopped to view a table of ceramic ballerinas, and he spoke over her shoulder into her ear. Laila caught sight of a slight expression of irritation on Claire's face, and she reminded herself that Claire had limited time.

"I'm sorry," said Laila when she caught up with Claire. "This is like the best candy shop ever."

"I know," said Claire. "Let's take care of business, and you can spend the rest of the day here."

When they found the recommended antiques booth, Brick peeled off.

He had spotted a sporting goods sign, and said he would be back in ten minutes. Claire seemed close to exasperation with her helter-skelter companions, but she agreed to stay put for the ten minutes.

They inserted themselves into the long and narrow booth. Several tallboy dressers and a few dark cherry desks created an aisle to the back where the vendor had set up a makeshift counter for transactions. A laptop was open at one end with an iPad and card swipe by its side. Three or four cartons full of dusty-looking leather bound books were on the floor behind the counter, and they could see the back of a woman stooped over them. She stood and turned at the sound of their footsteps.

Laila and Claire both stopped short and stared. To an uncommon degree, the woman resembled Regina. Her light brown hair wrapped around her head in plaits and was held up in a joyful bunch with a bright scarf tied tight at the base.

Her eyes had a generous almond shape that called attention to their misty shade of green. Her skin was cocoa-colored, and sprinkles of freckles crossed from one cheek over to the other. The feature that distinguished her from Regina was her youthful complexion. She was ten, maybe fifteen, years younger than Regina.

"Can I help you?" she asked.

The sound of her voice made Laila and Claire turn to each other in surprise. Her tone was the same gravelly alto as Regina, but with a stronger Jamaican lilt.

"You look like a friend of ours," said Claire.

"Let me guess; she's Jamaican," the woman answered.

"Yes," they admitted. "She's been in Florida a long time, though," added Laila.

"Well, I'm bound to run into her," she replied. "Meanwhile, my name is Elizabeth Powell. And I haven't been here long."

"Nice to meet you, Ms. Powell," said Claire. Both friends extended a hand, shook, and offered their names in introduction.

They showed her the photos of Billie's furniture, and she agreed to accept them on consignment. Her booth, although small, was not overloaded, and Laila thought they would display well given the available space. Ms. Powell took Laila's phone number and promised to call her with a suggested price range.

"It's an estate sale?" Ms. Powell asked.

"Yes," said Laila. "A neighbor's."

"Are there more items?" the vendor asked.

"There's a lovely queen bed frame and six upholstered Queen Anne dining room chairs," Laila answered.

Ms. Powell cocked an eyebrow and twitched her mouth to one side. "I might have room for those."

"Thanks," said Laila.

"We'll keep that in mind," said Claire.

Leading the way out of the booth, Claire covered her mouth and whispered back at Laila, "Maybe you can use those additional items to sweeten the deal."

"What do you mean?" asked Laila.

She trailed behind Claire, anxious to catch her advice on price negotiations. Laila leaned forward, and her legs barely kept up. She almost missed it.

The painting was leaning against the curtained wall of the booth, resting behind a desk. If it hadn't been for the illuminated sky of gilt clouds, their warm, diffuse colors peeking above the table, she would not have noticed it. The picture had the trademark tones of a Highwayman.

Laila stopped cold. She looked back at Ms. Powell whose interest was masked by a polite smile, and she stepped toward the painting. She leaned over the table and saw the signature and date. A smile broke over her face, and she turned back to the vendor.

"You like the Highwaymen?" she called.

Ms. Powell stepped from behind the counter and headed toward Laila. "I'm sorry? What did you say?"

"This painting you have. It appears to be an original Highwayman. By Alfred Hair."

"Is that a good thing?" she answered. Her smile looked fixed to her face.

"Laila?" Claire called from the open row outside the booth. Brick was standing by her side. "Coming?"

"Excuse me," Laila said to the vendor. "I should talk to my friends."

Laila stepped out of the booth towards Claire.

"She has a valuable painting in there," said Laila. "And I'm not sure she knows it."

"Are you looking for art for your house?" asked Claire.

"Not exactly, although I'd definitely consider that one. It's a Highwayman painting, and a rare one."

"I'd stay and help you bargain, but I have to go," said Claire. "And what or who is a Highwayman?"

Laila glanced at Elizabeth Powell, who was pulling the painting from behind the desk. She hoped she hadn't tipped her hand to the vendor. Alfred Hair was one of the very first Highwaymen, an innovator with a flair for color. He was a popular man in his community, but when he died in a bar fight at twenty-nine, his works acquired more value.

"It's the project I've been working on at Research Club," said Laila. "You know, the Florida artists."

"And you found one at a flea market?" said Claire.

"They find Rembrandts in people's attics, so I guess anything is possible," Laila said.

"I hate to be talking out of school," Brick broke in, "but I ran into your son in the sporting goods aisle negotiating his own deal."

"Eddie? He's buying a bike?" asked Laila.

"A surfboard," said Brick. "Comes with its own wax kit."

"Did you drive here in the SUV?" Claire laughed. "You'll need the space to get it home."

"Does he have his own money, may I ask?" Brick said.

"Could be," said Laila. "He's good at saving his birthday money. And thirteen was a big birthday."

Laila hated to admit that she didn't know her own son's financial details. The boy who had been an open book, who had held her as a confidante and secret sharer, turned opaque the moment he had been inducted into the teen world.

Laila glanced back into the booth. Carrying the painting, the vendor was slipping through the curtains behind the counter. Laila wanted to run to her and call out. Was the painting sold? Not for sale at all? Were there others? How did she obtain it? This Ms. Elizabeth Powell might tell her more than all her research so far.

Brick patted Laila on the back and smiled consolingly. "Whatever happens, he seems to have a good head on his shoulders. Don't worry."

"Oh, dear." Claire sighed. "You might as well tell a hound not to hunt as tell a mother not to worry."

"You've always got Ken to guide him," Brick said.

Brick's comments conjured up an unsettling image of Eddie crashing through the surf on a rocky beach somewhere in Hawaii. Laila wondered if she could persuade Eddie to put off any purchases until David got home.

"The flea market is open weekdays, too, right?" Laila asked Claire.

"Yeah," she answered. "There's more booths open on the weekends, but the market itself is here seven days a week."

"Point me to the sporting goods, please," said Laila.

Reluctantly, she turned away from her discovery of the Alfred Hair. Brick and Claire walked her towards the correct aisle, and the two of them took off at a trot towards the exit.

"Thank you!" Laila called to their backs. "See you at tomorrow's meeting!"

Claire lifted her hand in a wave without turning back.

CHAPTER SEVENTEEN

Monday, Day Nine – Research Meeting #2 (Cancelled)

The late morning storm was not unexpected but impressive all the same. Laila watched from her favorite chair while the purple clouds bulged along the horizon. The sky went to a midnight dark. Lightening flashed, first to the north, then the south, electricity descending from above, unbidden and uncontrolled.

"Unplug everything," Caya told her.

She left by the back stairs, going home to the apartment she shared with her mother and grandmother, just a few blocks away.

"My Grandma's alone," she said. "Just stay far from the windows, and I'll check in later."

When Caya left, the thunder was still a distant drum roll, and Laila calculated that Caya had gotten home before the brunt of the storm struck. Now it exploded overhead. The bolts crackled, spearing into the ocean along the Laguna Shores beach. Ruffles had retreated into his kennel, which Laila had carried into the boys' bathroom where she lulled him to sleep under a substantial blanket.

Laila found the darkened room calming. Alone, she didn't have to fear for loved ones. The boys were safe in school, miles inland. David had gone to Jacksonville for the day where he caught only the benign edge of today's storm. The rain, he texted, came down like a "gully washer." The thunderheads, however, had snagged on the coast, rumbling and heaving above St. Augustine's Beach and more precisely, over Laguna Shores.

"No one likes a show off," Laila whispered to the sky after a bright flash coincided with the deep-throated roar of thunder.

Jackson might sit with her and explain the physics of an electric storm, but the twins, and, if the truth were known, Eddie, would be keeping Ruffles company inside the interior bathroom. It was good timing, she decided, that she was on her own. Hunkered down, she had time to think about her conversation that morning with Ken.

He had come by for the regular Research Club meeting, unaware that Claire had cancelled, which of course meant Brick would not attend either. Regina had sent word that she and Mindy arrived safely in New York.

"Mindy's not sure there are enough stores here," she joked in her text.

"There's five Mondays in this month anyway," said Ken when they decided to cancel. "We'll meet on that last Monday to make up for this."

Laila agreed, and texted Regina back about the new date.

"I heard you gave Brick a run for his money on your bike trip Saturday," she said. "If he expires because you run him into the ground, Claire might drop out of the club, too," she teased.

"Did he say that?" he asked. "Did he call you?"

"He and Claire and I took photos of Billie's furniture to the flea market."

"Nice of him to help."

"He said he was looking for a second-hand bike, but I think he is just attached at the hip to Claire," Laila said.

"I guess." He nodded.

"What?" she asked.

"What nothing," he said, hunching his shoulders. "I guess romance is good."

"You don't like him?" she said.

"I like him fine. We spent the day at Flagler, and he was fine."

"But?"

"Okay, so maybe this is nothing. But we went into a bar after the competition, and he knew a couple guys," Ken said.

"A couple of surfers?" she asked.

"A couple of gamblers."

"People bet on surfing?" she asked, incredulous.

"Oh, yeah," said Ken. "Not as common as horses, but people will bet on just about anything."

"So why wouldn't Brick know some gamblers?" she asked.

"Okay, well, they weren't just gamblers."

"Bookies?" she asked.

"Well, if you put it that way, yes. Bookies. From Miami."

"How did you know them?" she asked.

"I've been up and down the Florida coast for years watching surfers. I've seen these guys at every big event. You get to know things," he said.

"So why does a man who just retired from New York know them?"

"Exactly," he said. "It's odd."

"But he's a cop. It's possible he knew them from some investigation or something, right?"

"I guess," said Ken. "But they are in a kind of Florida niche, very specific to this area. It's just odd."

"Should we ask him?" said Laila.

Ken heaved a deep sigh. "I went looking," he said.

"You checked on Brick?" she said.

"Just a couple things—things Billie taught me how to do."

"For instance?"

"He was a cop. That's for real. Thirty plus years in Brooklyn."

"Like on a beat?"

"At first, then promoted to detective. A few years on narcotics and then ten or more on white collar crime—bank fraud and scams, that kind of thing."

"He'll come in handy for our research," Laila said.

Ken's look was not heartening.

"What?" Laila asked.

"So, I don't think he worked on vice cases. He didn't investigate gamblers out of Miami."

"So, you think he's a gambler himself," she said.

"Yeah, which is not a crime, but it's not a character reference either."

"True. Should we talk to Claire, then?"

"One more thing," he said. "There's no obituary or death notice for Mrs. Brick Davison."

"Oh, dear." Laila stood up and started to pace the length of the living room. "Wait," Laila stood with her hands on her hips, addressing Ken. "Brick's wife could have another last name. And Brick is certainly not his given name."

"Right," he said. "I could have missed it."

Laila continued to pace.

"All this, it's nothing you can hang your hat on," he said. "But neither piece of news is good for Claire."

"Billie's gotten us into a fine mess, hasn't she?" said Laila. "Taught us how to go poking around in people's lives, and she's not here to tell us what to do next."

"So, we don't share, right?" said Ken.

"No."

"Not with David?" he asked.

"And not with Regina," she countered.

"No, let's not poison the well. If something else weird turns up, we'll reassess."

Laila told Ken about her discovery of a Highwayman painting at the flea market and about Eddie's bid to buy a surfboard.

"He's pretty mad at me," she said. "He had one picked out, but I wouldn't let him buy it without consulting David."

"And what did David say?"

"We're talking about it tonight. We promised Eddie after dinner we'd sit down and consider the options."

"This isn't the best section of the coast for surf," he said. "Cocoa Beach and south are much more popular."

"Why did you choose St. Augustine?" she asked.

"Business reasons," Ken said, briskly.

As far as she knew, Ken ran his business online, remote from customers and suppliers. Why not choose Cocoa Beach over St. Augustine Beach, if surfing is your passion?

"It's not easy to find an instructor," she said. "Would you be willing to teach him?"

"I don't know," he said, turning away from Laila to gather up his things. "It's not the best place to learn. A school down towards Melbourne, maybe in the summer. That would be better."

Laila hadn't expected a refusal from Ken. But he seemed uncomfortable with the request, and she didn't insist. He changed the subject.

"Are you going to buy the painting you found?" he asked.

"I don't know if it's for sale," she answered. "Once I pried Eddie away from the surfboards, I didn't think I should stick around the market."

"But I bet you'll go back."

Laila thought better of telling Ken about the likeness of the vendor, Elizabeth Powell, to Regina.

What if Claire and I are two white girls who think all blacks look alike? What if Ken sees Ms. Powell, and to him, she doesn't bear any resemblance at all to Regina? What if I'm more stuck in my white bubble than I think?

"Definitely," she said. "She is supposed to call with a price for Billie's furniture."

"Nice work," he had said, getting up to leave. "Your art stuff is on the agenda for the next meeting. You'll have an interesting story to tell."

"Have the police come round to see you?" Laila asked, a bit too anxious to escape Ken's notice.

"Not that I know of," he said. "Have they been here again?"

"No. Maybe they're too busy running down her dangerous poker buddies," she joked, but Ken didn't laugh. "Ken," she continued, "at some point I'll have to give them the voice mail the night she died."

"Okay." Ken looked perplexed. "Why tell me?" He sat back down on the sofa.

Because it points the police away from David.

The bleak thought shocked her. It was unsayable.

"Well, she mentions someone who seemed to have been giving her trouble. Some woman, but of course we don't know who that was," Laila said.

"Or, *if* she existed," he said. "She sounded completely confused, right?"

"What if she was warning us? What if it's someone we know?"

"That's crazy," Ken said, getting up. "You're overthinking those last hours because you feel guilty. I'm telling you; Billie wasn't Billie that night. She was ill, and you couldn't have done anything."

Maybe he was right. And Regina would be the last person anyone would fear. She didn't have a mean bone in her body, and Billie would know that. Wading into some discussion of Regina with Ken would be a ridiculous foray. She pulled back from the precipice.

"Everything will be all right," he said. "You'll see."

"And if it wasn't a heart attack?" she asked.

"It was," he said.

In three strides he was at the elevator, and she waved goodbye.

The storm moved south, and a light shower followed behind it, freshening the air and dousing the sparks of electricity. Light seeped into the living room from behind the shifting clouds. Laila walked through the condo plugging in lamps and electronics, kitchen appliances and workout machines. Caya would be back soon. Laila would pick up the boys and bring them home for a snack and homework time. David would roll in around six, and they could have a cocktail before dinner. There was so much to talk about.

CHAPTER EIGHTEEN

Monday, Day Nine – Autopsy Results

Dinner went well Monday evening. Jackson described his science teacher who had been a marine researcher for the Navy and was signing up kids for a field trip to his old lab. Alton had a new friend that Forrest and Eddie teased him about because she was a girl. David told them about the mini-amusement park he was planning for the new retail area, and he asked which rides they would recommend. A robust discussion of roller coasters versus log flumes ensued. They concluded four votes versus two in favor of a roller coaster.

The older boys went off to do homework while David volunteered to read to the twins. Laila stayed on the balcony, content to consider the cloud formations and how one might render them on a canvas. David's obvious enjoyment of the family time calmed Laila's worries. Maybe things at work were improving. Maybe whatever it was had blown over.

Glancing down at the beach, she saw Benjamin walking with Doug, the two brothers enjoying a slice of Florida as best they could.

Laila hesitated about disturbing their conversation but then dialed Benjamin. She thought she should explain the delay in selling Billie's furniture. She watched as he pulled his phone from his pocket and read the screen. Casually, he put the phone away. Laila was stung. She quickly ended the call.

Of course, it's only furniture. It hardly matters next to the other tasks they're facing.

She tucked her phone in its pouch, thinking herself rude for attempting to intrude on the grieving brothers, but it hurt just the same. She decided to use this pocket of free time to work on her laptop, and she headed to her studio. She got halfway across the living room when the elevator bell rang, and she answered.

The resonant voice of Detective Cranston came over the intercom. She buzzed him into the elevator below and waited impatiently for the ding as the doors opened into her home. If there were something they needed, something that would help Benjamin and his brother settle their mother's death, she would be happy to hear about it.

Cranston was with his partner, Borden. Borden's pale face showed fatigue more blatantly than Cranston's. The skin pillowed up under his eyes in reddish ridges. The coarser hairs in his eyebrows grew wildly askew. On the other hand, Cranston's dark skin stretched over prominent cheekbones, and the whites of his eyes gave him a more vigilant appearance. Still, Laila noticed his step was slower than the first time she met them. The end of a long day for both of them, she guessed.

"Can we talk with you and Mr. Harrow?" Cranston asked. Borden was already peering into the living room.

"He's with the boys right now," Laila said. The detectives' stiff formality provoked a sudden defensiveness.

"Could you ask him to come out just for a few minutes?" Cranston answered. The idea she would collaborate with the police was withering under Borden's steely gaze.

"Of course," she said.

Laila extricated David from the twins' bedroom by promising the boys there would be more reading in a few minutes. She pulled pajamas out of a chest of drawers and instructed them to change and brush their teeth.

"What do they want?" David whispered as she led him down the hall toward the living room.

"They haven't said," Laila answered.

Looking back at him, she expected to see exasperation with yet another interruption caused by an old lady's passing. Instead, she read a look of dread. He pressed his lips inward, as if readying his game face. She felt her throat constricting.

Breathe, breathe. This is nothing. We're a normal family.

After the introductions were made, David sat in his favorite armchair across from the detectives, and Laila sat in her smaller chair, placed at an angle to David's.

"We have some difficult news," Cranston said. He looked from David to Laila, and back again.

"Yes?" said Laila.

"The autopsy on Wilhelmina Farmer indicated her death was caused by cardiac arrest provoked by a lethal dose of fentanyl," Borden said.

Laila recoiled. The words nauseated her, and the officers became an unwelcome presence. It was an offensive movie script written for the wrong cast. She doubted the officers' knowledge.

"That is unpleasant," David said.

Laila felt the dry comment prickle her skin. He was taking this information on face value. Certainly, he didn't believe someone had hurt Billie on purpose?

Not here. Not in Laguna Shores. Not our friend.

"Do you know who would want to hurt Mrs. Farmer?" Borden asked. "Did she have any enemies?"

Laila leaned forward. They meant it. They believed Billie was murdered. *Someone watched her die.*

"No one. No one at all," Laila said. "She had friends. Piles of friends."

"Mr. Harrow?" Cranston asked. Both detectives were looking at David.

"I barely knew her," David said. "She was a neighbor who liked to drink Scotch; that's all."

His comment felt like a blow to Laila. She could feel the color rising in her face. His cold-blooded tone sounded as though it came from another man, a stranger, not her husband. She turned and stared at David.

Somehow the news isn't sinking in. David's not processing this news.

Cranston surveyed the two of them back and forth. Borden sat back on the sofa, his legs crossed, mirroring David. Their scrutiny alarmed Laila, and she turned her full attention back toward the detectives. Any reaction to David, she realized, needed to be muted. His comment must have been a lapse, a small mistake from an otherwise superb man—a man whose strength and warmth radiated through their home and was personified in their children.

"So, you wouldn't be aware of any information she might have that would anger someone? We ask because both her computer and her phone are gone," commented Borden.

"She was pretty old, right?" David said. "I mean, what could she be involved in?"

Borden was watching her carefully as David spoke. She tried to keep calm and hold an undisturbed expression on her face, but her breathing came in sharp, shallow intakes. She fought against the trembling she was feeling through her torso and down her arms. She was glad that she hadn't served any coffee because her hand wouldn't hold a cup without shaking.

"That is our question," said Cranston. "That card she left made us think she was looking into something that Mrs. Harrow, and possibly you, Mr. Harrow, might be concerned about."

Before David could reply, Borden leaned forward toward Laila. "Did you mention the card to Mr. Harrow?" Borden asked.

"Yes, she did," said David, reaching a hand to pat Laila's shoulder, as if thanking her for her help. "It didn't make sense, though."

David's touch communicated anything but gratitude to Laila. He never patted her in that condescending way, as if she were a hapless partner to his firm leadership. He was asking her to follow his lead, to say as little as possible, and to end this interview.

"What do you mean?" asked Cranston.

"We know the worst about what?" said David, his voice even. "What was she talking about?"

"You remember the card clearly," said Cranston. "Where were you the night Mrs. Farmer was poisoned?"

"In Miami," said David. "With my brother and his family."

David sensed it first. This is an interrogation, not an interview.

"Without Mrs. Harrow?" Borden asked.

"On business. I go most weekends," said David.

"And you, Mrs. Harrow?"

"I was here, with the kids," she said.

"Any visitors?" asked Borden.

"No." Laila wanted to say more, but David's approving smile told her that less was better.

She thought about Billie's phone message. If the police heard the message, they might understand more about Billie's thoughts that night. She was thinking about someone, some woman, but not David—and not Laila.

Why didn't I let David hear the message? Stupid pride, that's all.

"There's something about the card that's strange," said Laila. She could see David turning sharply toward her, as if to warn her into silence, but she kept her eyes on Cranston.

Talk about the card and forget the phone message.

"What do you mean?" asked Cranston.

"It's silly, but I've been thinking about it," she said.

"We'd be interested," Borden said.

David shifted in his chair, uncrossing his legs and fixing his eyes on her.

"Billie didn't like animals. Not pets, not wild animals."

Borden and Cranston looked at her stone-faced, but she continued.

"She would not use a card with a dolphin on it. She would never have purchased a card like that," Laila continued.

Borden and Cranston exchanged a cautious look, as if one was waiting for the other. Finally, Cranston spoke. "That brings up a point," he said. "The card had only your fingerprints and Benjamin Farmer's prints."

"Well, Benjamin handed me the card," Laila said.

"So, Billie didn't write the card," said David in a brisk tone.

"Correct," said Borden.

"But who would have written it? And to me?" Laila cried.

"We think whoever poisoned her wrote it. The card was meant to confuse us," Borden said.

"Whoever wrote the card knew you and Mr. Harrow," Cranston said.

"Yes," said Borden. "Any thoughts about who, in your acquaintance, might need Mrs. Farmer's computer and phone? Someone who would like to do you harm?"

"But she had backups of everything!" Laila blurted.

"Everything?" echoed Cranston. "What do you mean by everything?"

David's mouth tightened, but Laila saw she had to answer Cranston's question. As far as Laila knew, Ken was the last person to see Billie. Most likely, Billie had Ken's surfing research on her computer, but so what? Ken had that research also. Unless Billie had some research about Regina – something Ken would want or need. It was late, and Billie was tired, Ken had told her, but if the woman Billie was warning about was Regina, Ken might not have been willing to go away.

That's insane. What kind of scandal would involve Regina? But Ken's story was murky, claiming Billie was secretive. He let Saturday night and all of Sunday go by without contacting me, as if he knew the worst had happened.

"Mrs. Harrow, do you have an idea of who would want to hurt Mrs. Farmer?" Borden pressed her. "We've searched her apartment, and there are no backup drives. What research would be on her computer and phone?"

"Well," said Laila, fumbling for something bland to say. "She liked to research different topics, but they were things like astronomy or local history. Things you could read about at the library if you were interested."

David patted her hand, and she tried to keep her head up and her smile fixed. She held her shoulders back, keeping her throat open, calming her breathing and slowing her heart.

Borden wrote a few words in his notebook and closed it with a sigh. "If anything else occurs to you, either of you, we'd like to hear about it," Cranston said. "Anything you think might help Wilhelmina's family."

"Of course," David said. Laila nodded in agreement.

When the elevator doors closed behind the detectives, David turned to Laila.

"The boys," he said.

The two of them found the twins wrestling in their bedroom, as far from exhaustion as David and Laila were close to it. They settled each down with a book. David read to Alton a story about a fox, while Laila and Forrest paged through a picture book on fire engines. After reading, they completed a search for a favorite stuffed animal, served up a drink of water, and gave numerous hugs and a last kiss. They turned off the light and closed the twins' bedroom door. Checks on Jackson and Eddie produced promises that both were headed to bed as soon as they finished their homework.

Laila and David retreated to the master bedroom and closed the door. He sat in an armchair facing the bed.

"My God, she was killed," Laila said. She sat on the bed, her legs curled under her, her head in her hands. "No, no, no. It's not possible."

"Who wrote that card, Laila? Who wrote it to you?" David asked.

"We know a ton of people at Laguna Shores. Who would do that?"

"Did you know about the autopsy results?" he asked.

"No, of course not!" she answered.

"I thought Benjamin might have told you," he said.

"No, I called him this evening, and he didn't pick up. I guess this explains why. Suddenly, the neighbors are suspects," she said.

"I wish you weren't in that Research Club. I wish I'd never heard of the Laguna Shores Research Club," he said.

"That's crazy. I've been in the club for three years. No one in that club suddenly decided to murder Billie. That's impossible."

"Everyone's been in the club for three years? All of you?" he asked.

"Except Claire," she said.

"How long has Claire been involved?" he said.

"Months. Several months."

"Not that long, right?" he asked. "And what does she research?"

"Nothing she ever wants to talk much about. Something about building permits and new housing. Real estate related, of course."

"Permits?" David echoed. He rested his chin on his hand and studied the floor.

"I think I told you about it before," she said.

"I guess I wasn't clear," he said.

That's an understatement. I told you how smart Billie was, and you made her sound like a decrepit alcoholic to the police.

"I need to show you something," Laila said. She stretched across the bed to disconnect her phone from its power cord. She queued up Billie's voice mail and handed it to David. She could hear a faint version of Billie's voice— Billie's confused voice warning her about some unnamed woman.

He listened twice and handed the phone back to Laila.

"When did she leave this message?" His tone was level, but his eyes were focused unblinking on her face.

"The night she died."

"But you didn't tell me," he said.

"I called her, and she didn't answer. I didn't go over to see how she was. I didn't want to leave the boys."

"But why not tell me? Why not tell the police?" David asked.

"I left her alone. I left her alone, and she died." Laila buried her face in the comforter on the bed. "Now we know she was murdered," she murmured into the fabric.

"No, Laila, it's not your fault. You're a neighbor not a daughter," he said.

"That's not how I feel." She lifted her head up and sat upright.

"We need to get this to the police. It's about some woman, someone else. Not about us," he said.

"That night, I called Ken. He said he would go and check."

"Ah, Ken," David said. "Your good friend, Ken. Ken who won't bother to help us with Eddie. Good old Ken."

She sat back down on the bed, her feet on the floor, watching David.

"And did Ken check on Billie?" David asked.

"He did. But he didn't call me back that night—or the next day. Later, after we heard the news, he gave me the details."

"So, you have this that shows I'm not involved, or at least, I'm not on Billie's mind, and you don't show it to the police because you're protecting Ken?"

David got up from his chair abruptly and walked toward the balcony windows. The evening light was fading, and the sky showed a delicate pink reflection of the setting sun.

"So is the friend Billie mentions Regina? Are Ken and Regina up to something? What did Billie have on Regina?" David asked. He kept his back to Laila.

"What?" she asked, her voice rising. "No, that's not possible."

"Did Ken go into Billie's place? Was he there when she died?" David asked.

"David, stop," Laila said, getting up from the bed and taking a step toward the balcony. "Ken said he didn't go in. Billie was tired, and she didn't invite him in."

"That's what he said. But you aren't sure," David answered. He kept his back to her.

"I know Ken, and he liked Billie. Ken researches surfing. You don't kill somebody over surfing," she said.

"You think you know Ken, but you didn't know about Ken and Regina. That surprised you. You told me that yourself."

"David, you're making trouble where there is none," she said. "Stop!"

"What was Regina working on in your club? In the *great* research club."

"Bitcoin."

"What?" said David, turning his face to her. He looked astonished.

"She only just started that project," she said, taking a step back.

"What's a tennis pro need with Bitcoin?" he asked. "And for that matter, what's she doing on a week-long trip to New York?"

Laila retreated to their bed and sat down heavily. David's angry volley of words accusing her friends felt like an assault in a war he had declared without warning.

"We don't know these people," he continued. "We don't know what they're up to."

"We've known them for years," she said.

"*You've* known them. Or you *think* you've known them," he said.

She sat staring at him. He stood straight but moved stiffly, as if some other force controlled his responses.

That's what's been going on these last few months. You've stepped away from me, from our life. You've had less time for these friendships, and now they seem like a threat. Why?

"So, congratulations. Your great friends have gotten me a place on the list of suspects," he said, staring back.

"No, David!" she cried. "The police are making routine inquiries. You were in Miami. There isn't anything else you have to worry about."

Brusquely, as if he had made a decision, his head cocked to one side, he spoke with cool calculation. "Tomorrow, you're going to give the police that message, right?" he said.

"Yes." She paused. "Are you thinking of hiring a lawyer?" she asked, her voice trembling.

"For me or for your Research Club?" he growled. "No, what I'm going to do is stay as far away from those people as possible, and you should, too."

He walked past her towards the bathroom, staunchly ignoring her tearfulness.

Misery hung over Laila. She couldn't bear to watch David shut her out.

"I'm going to paint for a while," she said.

"I've got a report to write," he said, calling back over his shoulder.

"For Sam?" she asked.

"Yes," he said. "He wanted it yesterday."

"Right," she said. "How unusual."

He shut the bathroom door without answering. She left the bedroom for her studio, walking as fast as she could away from David's anger and unreasonableness. The night's turmoil seemed to wash around her, along the hallway, and it surged with her into the living room and across to her studio.

Murder, police, strange half-messages, tragedy. Billie's dead, and it's the shock and surprise. But it can't be our fault! No one I know could have hurt Billie.

The light was gone from the sky, but she picked up a brush and tried to work on finishing some clouds. Shadows were always tricky to bring off, and she was less successful than ever before.

Her hands grappled with the paints, while her mind darted from Billie's last moments, to Ken's silence the night of the murder, to Regina's reticence in telling her about her romance with Ken, to Claire's on-again, off-again attitude towards the research club. She found herself staring at the canvas, her brush tossed aside. Concentration was impossible.

Billie had never spoken ill of any of the club members. Her message had to be referring to someone else, some other Laguna Shores resident. Had she had a run-in with someone in her building? Laila tried to remember their last conversations. Billie would laugh sometimes about some members of her church, including the minister, Reverend Krall. She was irreverent about everything, but kind to everyone.

But David's right about one thing. We don't know everything about our own friends. I don't know everything about my own husband.

After Laila gave up and put away her paints, she found David in bed, his lamp turned off. His breathing was shallow, and she thought he was still awake, but she didn't want any more argument. She climbed under the covers and concentrated on thoughts of clouds and shadow, drifting into sleep.

When she woke, the room was pitch black and silent. She knew without moving that David was gone. She turned her lamp on and rose from the bed. Walking in the low light offered by the security system panel, she found her way to the living room. David was lying on the couch but sat up at her approach.

"Can't sleep?" he said. He checked his phone. "It's a little after three."

"Bad time," she said. "The dead of night." She joined him on the couch.

"I haven't slept yet," he said.

"Did you finish the report?"

"Sent it off," he answered.

"Is there a problem?" she asked.

"There's always a problem," he said. "I wish there were only one problem."

"Money?" she asked.

"Time," he said. "And I guess that means money, eventually."

"Are we in trouble?" she asked.

"No, nothing like that," he answered. "It's nothing we can't handle."

"We?" she asked.

"Sam and me," he said. "But I hate asking for his help."

"Ah, pride," she said. "I understand that."

"I think you are one of the least proud people I know," he said. "You have beauty and talent, and you seem unaware of both."

"You believe that?" she asked.

"Yep," he said. He put an arm around her shoulder and pulled her to him. "Pride and you? It doesn't compute."

"I hid the message from Billie because I didn't want you to find out. She called for help, and I didn't go."

"That again," David said. He dropped his arms and stood up.

"It was pride about having to be the best friend all the time," she continued.

"Look, you weren't involved with that whole mess. Go to the wake, sell the furniture, and Claire can list the condo, whatever. That chapter is over. Billie is gone. I'm sorry, but you need to stay away from that mess."

Claire is listing the condo? I hadn't heard that from anyone. Wouldn't I know, too?

He stood looking at her with his arms folded tightly across his chest. Laila was tired, and confusion had taken hold. David seemed to know more than she did about Laguna Shores, but he acted as if Billie were trouble, something he wanted no part of. She wanted to calm David but help Billie. Billie and Benjamin deserved the truth.

"Billie is dead. Nothing can change that. I understand; believe me," she said in a whisper.

"Yes," he said. "You'll explain about the message, and we'll both be out of the story. That'll be good." David walked back to her on the couch and pulled her up into his arms. "Let's sleep. We've got work tomorrow," he said.

"Yes," she said. "Work tomorrow." She put her arms around his neck and laid her head on his chest. His heartbeat seemed to slow the longer she embraced him. They were good together, and they were good for each other. Secrets were not healthy.

"We've got a family to take care of," he said.

"Yes," she answered.

And I have questions to ask.

Chapter Nineteen

Tuesday, Day Ten – Back to the Flea Market

The next morning Laila brewed a pot of coffee and brought two cups out to their bedroom balcony where David sat looking down at his bare feet. Weariness pulled his eyelids down.

"County Commission meeting tonight," he reminded her. "I'll grab a burger out."

"Okay. I'm going over to get fingerprinted later," she said. The station just happens to be in the direction of the flea market, she thought.

"You'll tell the detectives about the phone message, right?"

"Them and Ken. I've got to give him a heads up."

"Oh, naturally," he said, shaking his head in disapproval. "So, you'll find surfing instruction for Eddie this week?" David continued. The early gray light outlined a jogger on the beach, but David had yet to look up or out.

"I suppose," she answered.

"He'll go out on his own if we don't. His friends have boards."

"Probably right," she said. "Brick said there are worse pastimes."

"What would he know about the subject?" David frowned.

Laila had promised not to tell David of Ken's juicy suspicions about Brick, and as long as he was in this state of mind, it was easy to keep the secret.

At least David's work life seemed to be stable. He had arrived back from Miami late on Sunday saying the project was going well. His brother secured financing for the first phase of the St. Augustine retail center. Both his brother and his father approved of the site selections. They all agreed on which other retailers they would approach with lease agreements.

But when she remembered the rude call from Jake Hanlon and asked if Hanlon had managed to reach David, he nearly bit her head off.

David had been bent over his desk, reading the mail from Friday and Saturday, and his head swiveled abruptly toward Laila.

"How did he have your number?" The question came out like a bark.

"I assumed that his daughter got it from Eddie. He didn't call me back, so I guess he got through to you," Laila had said, wanting to make him understand she paid careful attention to his business concerns.

"For Christ's sake," David said. He massaged his forehead. "What did he say?"

"Apparently, he's not aware that some people work weekends." She tried to keep her tone light.

"He's a county official, not a career counselor," David said.

"Sorry, but he was more curt than necessary," she said.

"Maybe he had his reasons," he answered.

David stuffed the mail in a desk drawer and stalked off to the bathroom to brush his teeth before bed. Subject closed.

Sipping her coffee on the balcony, with the memory of the unnerving questions from Borden and Cranston the night before adding to their dark atmosphere, Laila made one last attempt to distract them from the tensions of the past few days.

"I'm going back to the flea market this morning. I'm intrigued by that vendor with the Highwayman painting. Besides, she didn't call me back with a price range for Billie's furniture."

"Please don't pay an ungodly amount for this Alfred Hair thing," he said. "I don't see where we would have room for it anyway."

David had once pored over Monroe's book *The Highwaymen* with her, pointing out the reproductions he liked. Now he discounted them, and by extension, her work for the art museum. She stood, unable to disguise her hurt feelings, and walked back inside. She dropped her coffee cup off in the kitchen and busied herself in her studio until he left for work. He pecked her on the cheek and walked out the door with a one-word goodbye. She didn't crack a smile.

You're not the only one who has a brain. We'll see what I can do on my own.

Laila took the boys to their schools and approached the flea market from the interstate, driving up the service road to the rear entrance. She passed up the vendor parking lot, planning to park in front as she had on her first visit, but on second thought, she made a U turn. She was curious to see if the vendors had any storage facilities. It was ten in the morning, and all of two cars were in the vendor lot.

Laila got out of the car. She walked toward the chain-link fence that enclosed the flea market without seeing a storage warehouse or individual sheds. Two feet of razor wire trimmed the top of the fence.

A gate, mounted with a digital lock, built wide enough to let a vehicle enter the grounds, blocked her entry. A narrow, paved access path ran a quarter of a mile along the back of the stalls, enabling pickup and delivery of merchandise by and for the hundreds of vendors.

The back end of the market had a white canvas roof pulled taut and jutting out from the canvas walls, like one long circus tent. Poles held up the extended roof over the access path and created a covered space protected from sun and rain. Lines driven into the ground secured the poles. They built the structure to stay put in any weather less than a hurricane.

Laila could see that numbers posted over each stall identified the individual vendors. She hadn't noticed an identifying number when she first visited Elizabeth Powell's stall, but she could remedy that problem by revisiting her stall. She headed out of the lot on foot, following the sidewalk that skirted the market and led to the front entrance.

The morning was warming up, and the cement stretched ahead unmercifully. Laila wore running shoes, having learned her lesson on Sunday, but the shoes didn't ameliorate the heat. She could have driven to the front and the customer parking lot, but she had plenty of time this morning. Besides, the idea of an Alfred Hair within her grasp gave her nervous energy that needed an outlet.

At the flea market entrance, she passed a sleepy security guard who rifled through her purse disinterestedly. The aisles were quiet. Nine out of ten booths were shut. Most of the vendors at the open booths engaged in tasks other than serving customers. She slipped across the rows until she reached Ms. Powell's booth. The canvas door was drawn tightly closed and secured with a lock and chain. Tacked to a post, the stall number read two sixty-five.

She retraced her steps, reading the section signs as she walked. The designations were more specific than at most markets, and she approved. "Fine furniture," "floor coverings," "window finishing," "porcelain and ceramics," "antique appliances." No doubt a little of everything was mixed in, from people selling cheap costume jewelry to traders of rare coins. People who shopped flea markets expected to have to sort through many items before finding what they wanted. This market, however, had a professional, organized caste to it.

Back at the entrance, Laila noticed the "Manager" sign. She peeked her head into the larger-than-average booth and was greeted by a friendly gentleman, a white man, slender, goateed, about sixty years old.

"Yes, ma'am?" He embraced the old Florida, redolent with Southern charm. "May I be of service?"

"Good morning," she said. "I wondered if vendors generally post their business hours."

"Yes, of course," he answered, approaching her from his workstation. "It's part of their contract with the market."

"Could you tell me what hours booth number two sixty-five has?"

"I believe so." He gestured for her to follow him, and he returned to his desk and computer. "I'm sorry, the number again?"

Laila repeated it, and he consulted his screen.

"This is a new lease. That's good for you," he said.

"Why?" Laila asked.

"New vendors are more likely to keep their hours as promised. Sometimes the old timers get a bit lax."

"That makes sense," Laila said. "But I'd guess everybody wants to be here Saturdays and Sundays."

"Now that is the truth," he said. "We're building something of a reputation. We're getting folks coming from Georgia, Alabama, and up from Miami, of course." He looked back at his screen. "That lease has the vendor committed to Thursday through Sunday, from ten to six. On Saturday, you can add an extra hour. Open until seven."

"Thank you," she said. "You were very helpful."

"You're welcome," he said. He walked with her out of the booth, as if he thought there would be no more questions.

Well, maybe I do have others.

"Are vendors supplied with storage space as part of the lease?" she asked.

The gentleman's brow darkened for a moment. "Why would you need to know something like that?" he asked.

"I have several large pieces Ms. Powell indicated she could handle, but I don't see how she could display them all," Laila fibbed.

"Ah," he said. "I see." He looked at her doubtfully.

"It doesn't matter." Laila shrugged. "I guess I don't have to do business with just one vendor. Just wondering."

"From what I can tell, two sixty-five has a load of paintings and not much else. If there's one thing she has, it's room."

"Paintings?" she asked, as if the word were foreign to her. "I don't understand." Her heart was pounding like the thunder of yesterday's storm.

"Ms. Powell leased a booth in the furniture aisle, and she calls it an antiques booth, but as far as anybody around here can see, she's an art dealer. It's somewhat confusing."

"Should I find another vendor?" Laila asked in her most innocent tone. She desperately wanted the manager to tell her more about Elizabeth Powell and her dealings.

"Don't let me dissuade you. The last thing I want to do is get between a vendor and a customer. She does have a few pieces of furniture."

"But the art?" Laila asked, raising an eyebrow.

"Yes, what about the art?" he said, his tone growing impatient.

"Don't people like to keep more or less to one category? Art, or furniture, or jewelry?" she asked.

"Roughly, yes, but there's overlap. And dealers help dealers. I think she's placed a few paintings already with other dealers. Maybe she's making room for furniture like yours."

She had a dozen more questions, but the manager seemed to have marked her in his mind's eye as someone to handle carefully. She'd rather not stand out as a troublemaker.

"Thank you again for your time. I'll be back on Thursday," Laila said.

"I'll tell her that a furniture customer stopped by. She might like that," he said.

Laila followed the sidewalk to the vendor parking lot. Before she got in her car, she peered through the fence at the access road along back of the stalls. Across the narrow road, more like a wide path, stall two forty-one was the first number by the gate, and the booths proceeded by odd numbers. Elizabeth Powell's booth would be the twelfth one along the row. It would be roughly a block and a half from the gate.

How many Highwaymen paintings were in the back of that booth? To whom did they belong? Were they authentic? If so, were they some of the many assumed to be stolen? If Ms. Powell had the authority to sell the paintings, why wasn't there a sign as big as a house on her booth? Was she aware of the value and provenance of the paintings, or was she an inexperienced salesperson?

Laila had legwork to do. The sooner she could get to her laptop, the better.

CHAPTER TWENTY

Tuesday, Day Ten – The missing pieces of the catalogue

Back home, urgency pressed in on Laila from all sides. Ken had to get a
heads up that the police were on the track of a murderer. The poison
found in Billie's system required a frank discussion with him about what the
police would say when they heard Billie's voicemail.

Yet the surprising news that Elizabeth Powell was selling paintings to
other dealers meant the Alfred Hair could be soon gone. With some timely
research, Laila might uncover the existence of a trove of Highwaymen.

One hour online, she told herself, *and then I'll call Ken.*

On Laila's laptop screen, red plumes of light blossomed across the map
of North America. Billie had loved the pictorial, and the Highwaymen map
showed it. A white pinprick showed the presence of one painting, and a
yellow meant two. For three presumed paintings, the pinprick got larger and
turned orange. Above three, a red spot bloomed, which could represent a
gallery, a museum, or a private collector.

Laila zoomed in on the Florida portion of the map, but on second thought, she widened her focus to include Georgia. Money talked, and if the market manager were correct, the St. Augustine Flea Market was on the radar of collectors all the way from Miami to Atlanta. Atlanta's throbbing growth and large African-American professional class provided a likely pool of admirers for the Highwaymen.

Twenty red locations came into focus, twenty dealers or buyers who did enough volume or dollar value in regional art to make them targets. Any one of these red dots might either have supplied Ms. Powell with the Alfred Hair painting, or, on the other side of the ledger, be an interested customer. She executed the report command and sent the list to the printer. By phoning these contacts, she hoped to create an investigatory guide for Jennifer and the museum acquisitions committee.

Before launching any phone blitz, tracking down Elizabeth Powell seemed a logical step. If she mentioned only one gallery or collector, Laila would head the right direction.

She worked, it turned out, at Flagler College in St. Augustine, in the Fine Arts Department. Laila portrayed herself to the receptionist as a potential student whose friend recommended Professor Powell. She was put through immediately.

"May I help you?" The pretty Jamaican lilt confirmed her identity.

"Hello, I am Laila Harrow, and I met you the other day."

"Hello, Ms. Harrow. What can I do for you?"

Laila knew she should mention her volunteer position with the St. Augustine Art Museum, but her memory of the scene at the market, the haste with which Ms. Powell retired the Alfred Hair from view, stowing it somewhere behind the back curtains of her booth, made her wary. If Ms. Powell were involved in art theft, the last thing Laila wanted was for her to think an official investigation was in the works.

"I caught sight of the lovely landscape painting you have at your booth, and I wondered if it was for sale?" Laila asked.

"My booth? I'm sorry, I thought you were interested in registering at Flagler College."

"I've heard your program is quite good," Laila said, trying for a disinterested tone. "I just love Florida art."

"We try to keep our studies at Flagler as broad as possible." Ms. Powell's words took on a singsong quality. "We take a classical approach in our Art History and Fine Arts programs."

"But that Florida sunrise, it's just what I would like for my lanai." Laila aimed for a tone that was respectful but also relatively clueless.

"I'm not sure what you're talking about," Ms. Powell said.

"I met you at the flea market, and you seemed so helpful," Laila said.

"I see," Ms. Powell said. The warmth disappeared from her tone when she continued. "I'm helping out a friend at the flea market, and I would like to keep it separate from my work here at the college. I'm sure you understand."

"Is that painting for sale? Or maybe there are some others like it?" Laila said. She feared the woman would hang up on her at any moment.

"I'm not sure what painting you mean. My friend deals in antiques and furniture. From what I can tell, she's not much interested in art."

Laila had a sense that she had overreached. The intensity she felt at coming close to pinning down a rare Alfred Hair must have translated to her voice. Ms. Powell, or Professor Powell, might truly resent Laila's intrusion into her Flagler College office. On the other hand, she may have other reasons for not informing Laila about that valuable painting.

"But I have furniture I want to sell, too," Laila added. She was doing a poor job of keeping her own desperate tone under control.

"Oh, you're the one with the curio cabinet and the dresser," Ms. Powell said coolly. "My friend is not interested. I'm so sorry." She bid Laila goodbye and hung up.

I'm too clever by half, Laila thought. *What am I doing using subterfuge? All it did was cost me a good look at an early Alfred Hair. Even if it weren't for sale, it would have been a great addition to the catalogue.*

Billie would have had a trick or two up her sleeve. She'd somehow track down a bill of sale or a shipping receipt that could refute Elizabeth Powell's protestations of innocence. She would discover where she worked before coming to St. Augustine and come up with contacts to call. Billie knew so much about so much.

Is that what got her killed?

The thought sent chills up Laila's spine. Or did someone simply carry a grudge too shockingly far? She knew a lot of people, and she was pointing at someone in her phone message. Was it Claire? She wouldn't forget Claire's name, would she? Or a person they knew from the HOA? Or someone Claire and she knew at church, and Billie was confused, thinking Laila went to her church.

She was sidetracked, off on a bunny trail, but Laila didn't care. The questions were too compelling.

Laila pulled up the home page for Billie's church. Several times, Billie's face appeared on the membership pages, passing out bulletins before service or stocking shelves in the food pantry. Claire appeared in one, too, sitting in a lecture by a visiting missionary, but no one else sparked Laila's interest.

Would the police extend an investigation to Billie's church? Could a church member have been the woman troubling Billie's last hours? It made as much sense as thinking Claire, barely in the Research Club long enough to get any research done, had something to do with it all—or Regina.

It had never occurred to Laila that Regina might belong to a church, but there were great swaths of her life she didn't discuss. Maybe she joined Ken's church since they became a couple. That would be fun to kid them about!

The website for St. Paul's Presbyterian was more polished than Billie's smaller Methodist church. The menu included a page dedicated to youth group activities, which detailed a dozen events all scheduled for that month. David's idea to change churches for the boys' sake might make sense, she thought ruefully.

She clicked to the schedules page and was brought up short. The hours of service on Sundays had begun to follow a summer schedule, pared down considerably from the year-round version. The late service Ken had said he attended after taking Regina to the airport had not been offered last Sunday.

She scrolled through the remaining pages of clubs and activities, as well as events and retreats. Of course, with a large membership, not everyone would appear, but given the time Ken devoted to that church, she expected to see him in at least one photo. But there was nothing. He wasn't named on their list of financial supporters either. No trace of Ken in any facet of the life of the church.

Peculiar, she thought. What does he do on Sundays? A sect? A cult to which he's sworn secrecy?

We're adults. I get it, and we all have baggage, secrets, unknown facets of our lives, whatever you chose to call it. But I'm not fond of a hollow shell of a friendship, either. When was I downgraded from friend to acquaintance?

It was as though she couldn't quite see the boundaries any more.

Time to make a phone call, I guess.

"How ya doin', surfer girl?" Ken picked up on the first ring.

"Very funny," she answered. "I'm more likely to become a surfer Mom."

"Eddie?"

"Yes. He's very interested. David wants me to find an instructor."

"For the three of you?" Ken asked.

"For Eddie, and maybe me. David is neck high in Harrow United right now."

"I'll ask around, but this really isn't the best town."

"You could do it. Eddie would be so grateful," Laila said.

"No, really, I can't commit. I'm not a teaching pro, and I'm often tied up with the business. I'd let him down. It wouldn't work out."

Laila wished she hadn't begun the conversation with a request she knew Ken would turn down. Now breaking the news of the autopsy results would seem heartless, as though her kids came before the murder of their friend.

If you want to be a trusted friend, maybe try not botching the conversation.

"I do have some good news," Ken continued.

She gathered her resolve. "No, Ken, I have to tell you something first."

"Okay."

"Ken." She paused because the words were heinous. "Billie was poisoned. She died from fentanyl poisoning, not a heart attack."

The long silence made Laila think Ken had walked away from the phone. She called his name twice before he answered.

"What the hell," he said finally.

"Hard to hear," she said. She was tearing up, and her throat burned.

"She didn't deserve that," he said.

"Who, Ken? Who would have done that?"

"Did Benjamin tell you?"

"No, the police."

"Crap," he said. "Damn, this is ugly."

What did he mean, she wondered. Ugly for whom? Is he thinking of Billie or of people he knows who may be involved? Does he know something? How can I possibly ask?

Ken led the way while Laila tried to steady her breathing. "Why are the police talking so much to you?" he asked.

Here goes, thought Laila.

"Maybe because I haven't shared the fact that she telephoned me the night she died, and I asked you to check on her. They don't know you were the last person to talk to her."

"That you know of," he retorted quickly.

"Well, right. Nobody knows what really happened."

"I told you my part, how she seemed, that she was tired. Why haven't you told them?"

It was Laila's turn to answer a question with a question. "Why didn't you get back to me Saturday or Sunday? You dodged me."

"You know Sundays are very busy for me," he said.

"At church. At that Presbyterian church?"

"It's a very big, busy place," he said.

Laila's heart sank. If he was lying now, it was highly probable he was lying about the night of Billie's death. If his lies had anything to do with Billie's death, Laila would be terrified. If his lies had anything to do with Regina and Billie, Laila would be crushed.

"Of course," she said. "Actually David's been talking about visiting the church. What kinds of things does that huge youth group do?"

"Tons of trips and sports things," Ken said, without much conviction.

"Bible study?"

"Well, sure, I think so, sometimes. But you really want to talk about this now?"

Ask him, she could hear Billie prompting her. *Ask him the name of the youth minister. Make him falter. Make him know you know. You'll get to the bottom of where he is on Sundays.* But Laila couldn't summon Billie's self-assured voice. She was more full of caution than Billie and needed to figure out what to do next. She changed the subject.

"What was that good news you had for me?" She tried not to sound as listless as she felt.

"Brick is okay, I think. I talked to Claire."

"You just called her up and started asking questions?"

"Would Billie have ever done that?" he said. "No, I called her to talk about the next Research Club meeting, and other things came up."

"Very smart."

"I don't know about that. I was far off track about him."

"What did she say?"

"She brought it up. She said Brick wants to go biking more. He liked it even though he was a little sore. His wife's death came after a prolonged illness. For a year, he didn't get out of the house."

"But still, no obituary?" she asked.

"She had Alzheimer's. Not many friends left, so no wake. He and the kids don't belong to a church, so no funeral. Apparently, they took the ashes to her hometown in Rhode Island. They scattered them at a beach she played on as a kid."

"So, he still owns their house in New York?" she asked, her skepticism not completely dissipated.

"You can bet that Claire the real estate agent told me about that, too," he said, laughing.

"What's so funny?"

"I'm just laughing at us, well, at me, at us, thinking we're Sherlock Holmes."

"We're protecting Claire," she said. "We weren't wrong to investigate."

If he thinks I'll stop asking questions about Billie, he's mistaken.

"Anyway, one of the kids is renting Brick's New York house and hoping to buy it, so no transfer of title. Claire said that's why he's not ready to purchase in St. Augustine."

"At the risk of sounding ridiculous, what about those bookies?"

"I didn't ask. I couldn't quite figure out how to bring it up. So, it's just his thing. Some people like to bet, and he might be one of them," Ken said.

"I guess so. The widower part was the most important. The betting, well, everybody has some vice, right?" she said.

Ask him if he gambles, whispered Billie's guiding voice. *He might be part of that world. It might be what he really does on Sundays.*

But Laila couldn't. She didn't know the first thing about gambling. She wouldn't know truth from fabrication.

"Exactly," said Ken. "It's best not to turn over every rock. But there's a piece of bad news, too."

"And this was going so well," Laila said.

"Lighten up on the sarcasm, there, Inspector," Ken said.

Laila didn't say anything.

"Not huge," Ken continued. "But Claire said she is done with her research project. Billie's software wasn't close to being completed, and she doesn't have the patience to piece something together. And she doesn't have any other ideas, at least not now."

Laila had thought that Billie's program for Claire, as hard as it was for Laila to understand, had substance. The last time they met, the day before Billie died, she talked about a decision matrix within the city and county government. One could use it to determine who was proceeding on which funding and permit questions. Claire was throwing it out, like yesterday's news.

Well, that's not so out of character for Claire. Her interests in men and computer programs changed without much notice.

"You, Regina, and me," said Laila. "Brick wouldn't stay in without Claire."

"Nope."

"I don't like the thought of recruiting new members, but it might be necessary," Laila suggested.

"How about Bob Page?"

"You're a million laughs today," Laila said. "A million and a half."

Let it come out as sarcasm, thought Laila. Better sarcasm than accusations.

"Look, I know the autopsy news is disturbing. But the police will get to the bottom of this. Fentanyl is a street drug and a medication. If the cops are calling this a poisoning, maybe they know something. But I can think of many ways she could have overdosed on Fentanyl accidentally, without anyone trying to do her harm."

"I can't stand to think of her murdered," Laila said, and once again, her voice caught, snagged on her emotions.

"Hold on," said Ken. "Don't cry. Hold on until the police do their job. They might uncover a reasonable explanation for everything. Tragic, but reasonable."

She felt that finally her long-time friend was talking, the Ken who thoughtfully responded to her ideas, the Ken who worked hard but put friendship ahead of business, the steady-as-you-go Ken. She knew he had been lying, but she also knew he spoke sincerely about Billie and that he cared about his friends.

"I hope you're right," she said.

Lying doesn't make him a suspect. Everybody keeps secrets about something.

They said good-bye, and she returned to her work on the museum report until it was time to pick up the boys at school.

CHAPTER TWENTY-ONE

Tuesday, Day Ten – Claire and Brick shed some light

Laila grabbed her keys and purse to pick up the boys. She got the twins and Jackson first and continued to Eddie's school. His school delayed dismissal because of a late-afternoon assembly, and the kids became disgruntled by the long wait and lack of a snack. She promised them pool time that afternoon, which helped keep them calm until Eddie climbed in to the SUV.

On the ride home, the twins sang "The Wheels on the Bus" enough times to get everyone riled, which was the point. Eddie growled at them until they stopped, and he would only answer Laila's friendly inquiries with monosyllables.

No one talked in the elevator up to the eighth floor. The boys descended on the kitchen for Margaret's mid-afternoon sandwiches and homemade chips. Laila got changed into a swimsuit and sundress. She alerted Margaret that she'd be at the sports center pool, and with beach bag in hand and the twins at her side, she waited for the elevator. She would have gotten on if hadn't been for Eddie's darting eyes.

Jackson and Eddie were on the living room balcony where Jackson had set up the telescope. Jackson was refining the focus, and Eddie was standing at his side. When the elevator bell rang, Eddie's eyes veered toward Laila. There must be a reason he needed to check she was getting on the elevator. She pulled the twins back from the door and told them to stay put.

Out on the balcony, she bent to the telescope without a word, before either boy could change its angle. It was trained on the breakwater, on the end of the rocky outcropping, where two young ladies had spread towels on the flattest rocks, lay down in the shadow of the boulders, and removed their bikini tops.

"So, planets are not the subject this afternoon," Laila said. Jackson stuffed his hands in his pockets and studied his shoes.

"You can go to the boardwalk and rent one," Eddie said. "It's not like it's illegal."

"Are you saying this was your idea?" Laila said to Eddie.

"No," said Jackson. "I told him about the girls. They're always there."

"They intended to find privacy," she said sharply. "Take this down and put it away. I don't want to hear about it. And please don't talk to me about a phone for at least a week."

"A phone?" Eddie said.

"You can put a phone in the holder there and attach it, and then you get digital pictures of the moon and stars," said Jackson.

"You would get him a phone?" Eddie said. "I'm older, but he would get a phone first?"

"He'd be getting a digital camera that happens to look like a phone," Laila said.

"Oh, man, that's not fair. He would use it to call people, or his friends would call him. That is so not fair!"

Laila's temperature rose.

Why am I justifying myself to these adolescents? Would the boys be acting like this if David were around more? Is this what life is going to be like for the next ten years? Fifteen years?

"Go to your rooms," she said. "Stay there until I get back, and expect a conversation with both your parents tonight."

She circled back to the kitchen, told Margaret the situation, and got Forrest and Alton, who knew enough to maintain silence, on to the elevator. At the poolside, the boys slipped into the shallow end, and Laila sat with her phone on her lap.

She hated to text David for help when he had been making it clear lately that she was not totally capable as a family manager. But Eddie and Jackson had used Billie's telescope to be peeping Toms, and not for the scientific work Billie would have admired. She missed Billie's support and guidance. She felt disappointed in her lack of self-reliance, but the boys needed to see a united front.

She texted David that she would like him home as early as possible.

"What's up?" he texted back.

"Your sons need male authority!" she answered.

"Late meeting, remember? Bring out the brass knuckles," came the reply.

"And then some," she wrote and hit send.

Laila tucked the phone away in her bag and got in the pool with the twins for an energetic game of Marco Polo. The heated pool kept the game comfortable despite the cooler air temperature. When two boys the twins' age joined the game, their mother in tow, Laila took a break, wrapping herself in a beach towel for warmth. Behind her, she could hear the gate creak open and close.

"Hi," Brick said.

Laila looked around for Claire, but Brick was on his own. He tossed his lanyard with a Laguna Shores keycard on a side table.

"How's the water today?" he asked, sitting on the end of a lounge chair.

He lives here now. He must have moved in with Claire. Wow, that was fast.

"Hey, Brick," Laila said. "Are you a swimmer?"

If Claire's happy, I'm fine with it. It's not my business. Wait until Ken hears!

"The most boring kind," he answered. "Laps in a pool. No ocean, no beach, just contained, safe pools."

"I get it," she said. "Believe me; I get it."

"That reminds me. What happened Sunday? Did you talk Eddie out of a surfboard?" he asked.

"Hardly," she said. "I don't think I could talk him out of anything now."

"How old is he? Fourteen? Fifteen? Physical activity is good."

"Only thirteen. And headstrong," Laila answered.

"Yep, developing as expected," he answered. "You've got a run ahead of you." He gestured towards the twins in the pool, splashing frenetically with the other boys.

"Oh, please, not today," she said. "Too much good news for one day."

"Well, did the other thing pan out? Did you sell Billie's furniture? Claire didn't hear back."

"No. The vendor told me this morning she couldn't handle those pieces. It's back to the drawing board for us. I mean, if Claire has more time to help."

"She's busy, but she likes markets and antiquing and all that," he said.

"Great because I'm going to need her. Benjamin is counting on us," she said.

"I thought you hit it off with that vendor. Wasn't there a painting or something?"

I could sure use a detective.

"It appeared to be an original. Exactly what I've been researching." He looked at her blankly. "You know, my club research," she added.

"I don't know, but it sounds good."

"These artists I'm searching for, they're Florida natives. There are thousands of their paintings but they've been circulating under the radar."

"Whose radar?" he asked.

"They're not Picassos or Warhols. You can't look them up and find out where they are, who owns them, what they're worth. Nothing like that exists for these artists."

"And you want to track them down?" he asked. "Thousands of them?"

"As a gift to the art world. The museum wants to create a catalogue and, by the way, give the artists more attention and more standing."

"So, you should put out a call to the art world types and ask who's got one," Brick suggested. "Or maybe a few hundred."

Laila smiled at Brick's attitude. He didn't seem to take much seriously, and that was fine. There was too much seriousness in her life lately.

"That's sort of what Billie did, before she died. She gathered likely locations for these paintings, and I need to reach out and see what's there," she said.

"Problem solved," he said. "Kudos to Billie. I wish she were here so I could meet her."

Laila watched the boys playing, channeling some kind of metabolic process into kinetic energy and joyous movement. She wondered how it worked, how we could exist on the same plane, all feeding on the same oxygen, and then, without warning, a person can disappear. The twins used to romp around Billie's chair, and she would reach out to tickle them. Laila and Billie would sit on her deck watching the birds, each holding a twin, feeding them cookies, telling them stories.

"She would have picked your brain," Laila said. "Asked you what to do next."

"Next?" Brick said.

"People won't report stolen paintings. We think about fifteen percent of the Highwaymen's output was stolen."

"Is that normal? It seems high," he said.

"It riles you," she said. "In the beginning, the artists were vulnerable. They had no security, I'm sure, just living hand to mouth."

"And you think you saw one at the market?" he asked.

"It looked like an Alfred Hair, and he was an early Highwayman with a distinctive style and a tragic story. His work goes for more."

"Let me get this straight. You use Billie's program to guess where these stolen pieces might be. But you see one for real, and you don't know what to do?"

"That's about it. I'd be happy with just taking a picture and adding it to the catalogue. I don't have to ask embarrassing questions."

"No 'under the radar' art dealer would believe that," he said. "But I do."

"So go back and ask to photograph it?"

"Photograph it," he nodded. "But after hours. Don't ask."

Alton was walking towards her, dripping, his arms wrapped around his bony chest, his lips a shade closer to blue than Laila liked. She stood and took a dry towel out of her bag.

Is he making fun of me? Is the detective laughing at the amateur sleuth?

"It's chilly," she said to Alton. She wrapped him up and sat him next to her on the chair.

"Forrest! Forrest, come out and get warm," Alton called to his brother. He huddled into Laila's arms.

"I'm okay," Forrest called. "Come back in!"

"I'd better do my laps before these athletes use up all the water," Brick said, giving Alton's close-cropped, brushy hair a pat.

"Don't drink it," Alton said. "My brother peed in it. He told me."

"That's what chlorine is for, young man. I'll be all right."

Laila shook her head in disbelief at Alton. "I'm so sorry," she said to Brick. "Are you sure you don't want to reconsider the ocean?"

"As if there aren't fish out there doing who knows what." He laughed.

"Think about my idea," he added. "It might help."

Brick got in the water and began his laps, swimming in the deep end, away from the splashing boys, doing widths instead of lengths, with a smooth freestyle stroke. His cropped red hair and muscular shoulders made it look as if a teenager were getting his workout.

I've got to get Claire to stay in the Research Club. Brick could be so much help.

Forrest finally climbed out of the pool and let her wrap him tightly in a towel. He lay on a lounge chair, smiling. "I feel great," he said. "What's for dinner?"

At home, Laila meted out the punishment to Eddie and Jackson, a week without the telescope for Jackson and a week without television for Eddie. Eddie's sullen air and Jackson's grief at losing the telescope made their meal seem endless. Laila climbed into bed soon after the boys said good night.

She heard David come in around eleven and not trying to be quiet about it. He would want her to wake up, she knew, and he would ask her if she turned over the audio of the voicemail to the police. He wouldn't care, she was fairly certain, about how she had lost her nerve because Ken seemed protective of some unnamed thing, and she had lost sight of the parameters of their friendship. She pulled the covers over her chin, sunk into the mattress, and faked the snore David occasionally ridiculed.

CHAPTER TWENTY-TWO

Wednesday, Day Eleven – Brick and Laila's Plan

The next morning, David backed her up about the boys' misuse of Billie's telescope and was happy to have it stowed away as punishment. He would reinforce the decision, he said as they dressed, with a firm rebuke of his own.

"Thanks," said Laila. "The 'Respect for Women 101' class, I hope."

"Oh, we're on 102," he said. "Not until tonight, but yes, definitely."

She was buoyed, and she smiled.

"Did you turn over the audio to the cops?" he asked briskly.

"The voicemail? Yes, I emailed the audio to Borden, no Cranston. I forget which."

Lying, she thought, was best done vaguely, so that no one could remember what exactly had been said. Miscommunication could be blamed for so much.

"What did he or they say?" David asked. He was slipping his keys and wallet into his pocket watching her all the while.

"No response yet," she said.

"And Ken?" he asked.

"I'll get to Ken. He's been busy, I guess."

David jetted off to work and another round of meetings with only an energy bar for breakfast. Laila got back from dropping off the boys and retreated to her studio.

She had no choice but to send the audio to the police now that she had told David it was done. She had her hand on the phone to make one last try at telling Ken what consequences her action might bring, when Jennifer called.

"Laila, I've been thinking about you," she greeted her.

"Good things?" Laila said.

"Naturally," Jennifer answered. "The development committee met to discuss fund raising for our new wing, and I sat there pondering how the Highwaymen catalogue could help the museum. It gives us one more reason for being."

"I agree. Not to mention benefitting the artists. Imagine a debut party for the catalogue, with two or three of the surviving Highwaymen there to discuss their work," Laila said.

"Right," said Jennifer. "It might be hard to pull off, but sure. Good idea."

The Highwaymen artists were aging, and from the small bit of coverage Laila read in the Fort Pierce press, she guessed they didn't travel much anymore. Still, their participation in promoting the catalogue would be worth pursuing. Jennifer should surely see the merit in including them.

"I came upon something that might interest you," Laila said. "Here in St. Augustine."

"A collector?" said Jennifer. "A collector with deep pockets?"

"Not exactly," Laila answered. "I found a flea market dealer who owns an Alfred Hair. She might have other Highwaymen works."

"On display at the St. Augustine's flea market?" Jennifer asked, her voice rising in disbelief.

"Stored at the flea market. When I saw it and commented, the dealer squirreled it away behind a curtain."

"It's a fake," Jennifer said.

"What?" asked Laila.

"It must be. There's nothing but junk at that market. I've been there a dozen times hoping against hope that somebody has something decent, even some local artist just starting. It's all worthless."

"Well, this was an Alfred Hair. I'd swear it."

"Who was the dealer?" Jennifer asked.

"Elizabeth Powell. New to the market, according to the manager."

"New to St. Augustine's, I think. I've never heard of her," Jennifer said.

"She may have some connections. She's an Adjunct Art Professor at Flagler College."

"My, you have done your homework," Jennifer said. "Where is she from?"

"I think Jamaica. I mean she has a Jamaican accent."

"Oh," said Jennifer, pausing a long moment. "Is she Black?"

"Yes, she's Jamaican," Laila answered. "Why?"

"You saw just one painting, or a group?" Jennifer continued, ignoring Laila's question.

"One. A great sunrise scene, signed by Hair."

"How do you know there are more?"

"The manager mentioned that she is selling them through other vendors. For a commission, I suppose, but he didn't offer details."

"If they *are* real, they're stolen. I'd bet the house on that," said Jennifer.

"Or Ms. Powell doesn't know what they are or what they're worth," suggested Laila.

"Oh, come on," said Jennifer. "She thinks she's distributing worthless paintings to eager dealers? Unlikely."

"She's respectable. She teaches at Flagler," Laila argued.

"So, she knows what she's doing," said Jennifer.

"I suppose that's true. She's only an adjunct, however," said Laila.

"That's a great cover," said Jennifer. "It's probably her first semester there. In and out of town in a wink of an eye."

"It is somewhat suspicious," Laila conceded.

"Look, we didn't share this before, but Geoff and I got the idea for the catalogue precisely because of these suspicions. We've known someone's been leaking Highwaymen into this area. Collectors are quiet about it, but you hear rumors, and Geoff, he goes to a lot of parties and sees a lot of private art."

"Would it help if we identified her inventory?" Laila asked.

"And how would you do that?" Jennifer asked with a quick intake of breath.

"With a camera," Laila answered.

"Excuse me?"

"So, the booth is not open every day, but the flea market is," said Laila.

"The booths are locked. Chained and locked," Jennifer said. "I've been there on the off days."

"I know, but. . . ."

"I can't consider this idea. It would be completely wrong. I'll talk to the others on the committee, and we'll see if we can follow up some other way," said Jennifer. "I'll call you. Are you home?"

"Yes," said Laila.

Jennifer's sudden rejection of the idea stunned her. She felt like a naughty child, soon to be led into the time out room. Perhaps Jennifer was doing her a favor, saving her from her worst instincts. Laila had railed at Jackson and

Eddie for ogling girls, and here she was proposing breaking and entering. It was the kind of thing for which she and David would ground the boys indefinitely.

But Jennifer insisted Elizabeth Powell was doing something wrong. Don't we have the right to investigate?

Fine, we'll do it the electronic way, she fumed. She opened the Highwaymen program and went to work populating the red-highlighted centers with the names and descriptions of paintings unmistakably identified as Highwaymen. For each painting she entered, she added a link to the photograph provided by the museum or dealer. For paintings confirmed as part of a private collection, a photo was not always available.

She hoped the more people learned about this art, the greater the fascination with the movement, and the greater the value that would accrue to each artist. If nothing else, the painstaking work gave her a deeper knowledge of each piece and a feeling that the art deserved its day in the sun.

Margaret stood at the door, watching her intently.

"What's up?" Laila asked.

"I've been standing here watching you," she said. "You're always cheery, but when you're at that computer, you look downright happy."

"Really?" Laila said. "I'm smiling?"

"With your eyes," said Margaret. "The kind of smiling that counts."

"Thank you for noticing," Laila said. "That's sweet."

"There's a woman calling from downstairs. A Jennifer."

Startled, Laila saved her work and headed toward the elevator with Margaret.

"So, you know her?" Margaret said, trotting to keep up with Laila.

"From the museum," Laila said.

"I should have guessed," she said and disappeared into the kitchen.

Laila buzzed Jennifer up, and she stepped into the foyer with a bag over her shoulder and her phone in her hand. Her head turned to the view of the sparkling ocean, and she raised her eyebrows at Laila. "Oh," she said. "Unbelievable. Your place is fantastic."

Laila ushered Jennifer into the living room and went to the kitchen to ask Margaret for coffee. Returning to the living room, she saw Jennifer had left her things on the sofa and was walking along the far wall, admiring the paintings.

David and Laila agreed that owning art of great value did not make sense. It belonged in museums for all to see. Instead, they hung work by local artists, usually men and women getting a start in their careers. The exception was a work by Paul Klee, a small oil painting. When Jennifer got to the Klee, she turned to Laila with admiration.

"My God," Jennifer said. "That's an original."

"A great aunt passed it down to us," Laila said.

"It's lucky such beauty could escape the Nazis."

"The owner traded it for passage out of Germany. It turned up after the war in a looted collection, but its owner didn't have the same luck."

"I'm sorry to hear about that kind of background," Jennifer said. "I'm not sure if that makes the art more valuable or history more pointless."

"Both," Laila said.

Jennifer nodded and walked to the sofa, settling in next to her bag. "So, tell me about your idea," Jennifer said. "And let me warn you; you had me at photographs."

By the time the two had finished coffee and several of Margaret's orange rolls, Laila had laid out her suspicions about the Highwaymen paintings that might be under Elizabeth Powell's management.

"If you find out it is stolen merchandise, we can go to the authorities," Jennifer said. "The Board would be grateful, but we'd remain anonymous. The credit for the discovery would go to you. But you should move quickly. Stolen property has a way of disappearing."

Energized and laser-focused, Laila called Brick as soon as Jennifer left. He agreed to meet for a walk on the beach. She had over an hour before she had to leave to pick up the boys. The day was sunny, so she padded along the edge of the water barefoot, carrying her sandals. She saw Brick approaching, his nose coated in white sunscreen, his khaki shorts revealing his knobby knees and the fine coat of red hair up and down his legs.

"You left your ball cap at home," Laila said.

"People don't like the Mets around here," he said. "It's shocking."

They walked beyond the Laguna Shores breakwater, south towards the St. Augustine pier. Laila described the flea market security gate and the access road. She told Brick that the booth with the Alfred Hair appeared to be a short distance from the gate, perhaps two- or three-minutes' worth of steps. Its canvas flaps were secured with chains and a padlock.

"Daylight would be best," he said.

"You're kidding! Why?"

"You wear navy blue slacks and a white, square cut shirt. You're a delivery person from the local florist. Carry a tin vase with a bunch of lilies. You have been given the gate code by one of the flea market vendors."

"How do I get the gate code?" she asked.

"I can get it. One of my poker buddies drives UPS," he answered. "Carry a pair of sharp garden snips, and your phone camera, of course."

"They wouldn't have guard dogs roaming the market, would they?" she asked.

"Can you imagine the lawsuits? Market management would rather have you empty out a whole booth into a van and drive away."

"Alarms?" she asked.

"I can check, but it's hard to install a security system when there aren't walls to hold the wires. And I didn't notice any surveillance cameras when I was there, but then again, I wasn't looking."

"Does Claire know you're helping me?" Laila asked.

"Who's helping you?" Brick said. "We never had this conversation."

The thought of Brick denying their plan gave Laila pause. She looked down at her feet being tickled by the timid surges of foam and walked wordlessly for a few steps.

"Cold feet?" Brick joked.

"What's the worst that could happen?" she asked.

"Somebody stops you. You give them your florist's card. They take out a phone to call the number on the card. You put down the flowers, smile, and walk quickly to your car."

"Then they have my license plate number," she said.

"There are sheaths that fit over plates. Buy two. When you park, cover the plates. As soon as you leave, pull over and uncover them."

"The sheaths?"

"An auto parts store," he answered.

"Where do I get a florist's card?" she asked.

"Oh, for God's sake. I'm going to let you answer that one yourself." He laughed.

They were getting closer to the pier where umbrella huts and candy stores popped up along the beachfront. From the several bars, pop music floated out toward the water, and customers began to fill the thatched roof locales.

"If I get photos of even a few paintings, it'll be worth it," Laila said.

"If she's stealing, you've got to do what you've got to do," Brick said. "Be quick, and it'll be okay."

In front of Laguna Shores once more, the two friends separated. Brick headed north along the beach to Claire's building. Laila went up the elevator, grabbed her keys, and drove to the boys' schools.

Calling Ken to discuss Billie's phone message once again got pushed to the back burner. Laila suspected her subconscious had other ideas on how to proceed. Talking to Regina directly might be easier, but her trip to New York complicated things. She had to turn over the phone message to the police before David exploded. *Tomorrow*, Laila thought. *Tomorrow will be the day, like it or not.*

When she got home and took all four down to the pool for an afternoon swim, Claire and Brick sat reading in two lounge chairs. Brick nodded, looking absorbed in his book.

Laila had an odd feeling, as if a cold wind that only she could feel were sweeping over them. A dull wash reduced the bright colors of her children and friends to pale gray. Something was setting her apart from herself and from her normal life.

Maybe this is how actors feel. You walk on the set and become someone else. Like cell division, another persona appears.

"So, Brick said we're back at square one with Billie's furniture?" Claire asked. She glanced at Brick, but he remained immersed in the novel.

"Do you have another place in mind?" Laila asked.

"In the strip mall behind the railroad station, there's a guy with a fairly large shop. I'll call."

"That'll be great. Thanks," Laila said.

"Come on, Mom," Forrest called. "Watch me touch the bottom."

"I thought you had a ton of open houses this week," Laila said. She slipped off her beach cover and shucked her sandals.

"A big one got an offer." Claire smiled. "I'm rewarding myself."

"Congratulations," Laila said. She had the feeling that Claire could use a couple of big sales. She seemed nervous lately, pressed for time and rushing through the day, as she did at the flea market. Backing out of commitments like the Research Club meeting could be another symptom of financial pressure.

Brick tore himself away from the book long enough to pat Claire's thigh. "That's my girl," he said.

"Back to the salt mines tomorrow," Claire said. "But I'll call that furniture shop."

Laila gave Claire a thumbs-up and joined the boys in the pool. By the time the five of them pulled themselves out of the water, Claire and Brick were gone.

That night, when the house had quieted down, Laila vibrated with the thought of the risk she would take by breaking into Elizabeth Powell's store of paintings. She sat on the couch turning over the possibilities for an embarrassing misidentification of her stock, or worse, someone stopping her at the gate before she even got close to a painting. On the other hand, scenes of celebration as she coolly presented the catalogue to the public also played in her imagination.

"You're quiet tonight," David said. She looked up startled, caught in mid-fantasy.

"Picturing my next art endeavor," she said. It wasn't a lie.

"Good," he said, sitting in the chair across from her. "I'm glad for you to be painting."

"Why?"

"It's something you care about. Something beautiful."

"I appreciate that," she said. It was true that David's pleasure in her painting was important, but she could tell he wasn't relaxing into the conversation.

He leaned toward her, his arms on his thighs, his eyes on her but his knee bouncing to an insistent beat. Something else was coming. "Did you happen to hear back from the detectives?" he asked.

"Not so far," she said.

"Did you point out to them that on the voicemail Billie talks about a woman she's worried about, not a man?" he asked.

"Don't you think it's obvious?"

"I say leave nothing to chance," he answered. "Maybe you should call tomorrow."

"I can do that," she agreed. "For all I know, the audio quality wasn't any good. So I'll check."

"Well, it's just something Sam suggested," he said. "If you have time."

"Sam?" Laila wasn't sure she heard correctly. She didn't expect to have Sam weigh in on a Laguna Shores situation.

"You know how he likes to give advice," David added. "Asked or not."

Laila nodded, alive now to the depth of worry David had to feel to share news of this aspect of the investigation with his high-flying and thoroughly judgmental brother. If David thought he was safely beyond the reach of the investigation, he would have called the detectives himself.

"It's no biggie," he said, reacting to Laila's watchful look.

"Does your Dad know, too?" she asked.

David stood and casually brushed off his slacks, as if suddenly bored with the conversation. "It was nothing. A casual conversation. I wasn't going to mention it. Really, it's nothing."

He left her, saying he hadn't yet done his treadmill for the night and then he would have to clean up a few email odds and ends. Laila sat pondering David's evident wish to put as much distance as possible between him and the investigation of Billie's death. It would be a nasty piece of irony, she concluded, if after losing Billie's openhearted guidance she had to follow the narrow-gauge tracks of her in-laws.

CHAPTER TWENTY-THREE

Thursday, Day Twelve – Confronting Ken

Margaret squeezed the last dab of icing on the thirtieth cupcake and dropped it in the plastic carrier as Laila watched. Jackson and Eddie had already gone down to the basement garage while Forrest and Alton remained in the kitchen.

"You're packing them all?" Forrest asked, his voice trembling with tragedy.

"Hush," said Margaret. "There's a dozen in the oven, which I'll decorate once you two scavengers leave." They squealed when she squirted a blob of icing on each boy's nose.

Caya picked up two containers, and Laila held the third in one hand while she called the elevator with the other. In the garage, they loaded the car, and Laila wished the four boys a good day.

"Jackson, who will help you with the cupcakes?" Laila asked as an afterthought.

"I will," said Caya. "I'll drop him off last and go in with him."

"Thank you," said Laila. "And I'll see everybody this afternoon. Remember, we're going to Jackson's science fair right after school."

"Are the cupcakes going to get you a medal, Jacks?" asked Eddie.

"Won't hurt. Not like this will," he said, pinching Eddie's arm.

"Like I can even feel it," Eddie said, curling his lip at Jackson.

As Laila closed the door, she heard the twins asking Jackson to pinch them to see if it hurt. She was grateful that Brick had called her just in the nick of time that morning and gave her a reason to foist today's chauffeuring on Caya.

"Do you have time for a coffee?" Brick had asked. "I think I can help you with your art investigation."

Laila had quickly assented. Good news would be more than welcome that morning.

They met at the small patio outside the Vietnamese coffee stand on Beach Boulevard, a place where Laila filled up a frequent flyer card every few months. She held the small cup in both hands, warming herself in the morning breeze. Brick did the same.

"My friend came through," Brick said.

"A code?" she asked.

"One time only. They change daily."

"It's good today only then," she said.

"Tomorrow only. I figured there'll be more shoppers on Fridays, so slipping by the gate will be easier."

"But more people mean more questions, right?" she asked.

"You don't want anyone to see you slice open the canvas. The rest of the time, though, you are just one more person getting ready for a busy weekend. A florist, a friend, whatever."

"Was your friend curious why you need the code?" she asked.

"He thinks I'm playing a practical joke on someone."

"This may turn out to be a joke on me."

"I don't think I can ask again," Brick said. "If you can't use it, tell me now. I'll tell him something came up, and I'll need it another day."

"Tomorrow is all right. David will head down to Miami, and I've got nothing planned. It'll work," she said. "Thanks."

"Have your phone juiced up. In and out, okay?"

"Maybe this is silly," she said. "There might not be any paintings stored there."

"You're just checking it out and getting a quick look."

"Two or three photos, and I'll be happy," she said.

"I believe in serendipity," Brick said. "And you seem lucky." He gave her a slip of paper with the five-digit code. She was about to put it in her wallet but he put his hand on her arm to stop her. "Memorize it now, and give it back," he said.

"But, why?"

"If you have to stop at the gate to look at the numbers, you increase your risk," he said. "Someone might notice."

"All right," she said.

When they got up to leave, he quizzed her, and she repeated the code without hesitation.

"You are a godsend," she said. "I think I can get you two year-long passes to the art museum."

He smiled at the compliment.

"Don't mention it," he said. "I'm doing it in Billie's memory. Claire had a high opinion of her."

The sentiment was unexpected. Claire had liked Billie more than Laila realized.

"I guess that's what's motivating me, too. Billie wanted to get the facts right," Laila said.

Laila and Brick bussed their coffee cups, and he headed off in his vehicle to chase down a lead on a used bicycle. She walked back to Laguna Shores, thinking over her plans. Considering how new Brick was to the Research Club, his help was impressive—and timely.

Brick put the lie to David's paranoia about trusting the Research Club. The job of calling Ken looked easier. The explanation for his absence the Sunday after Billie's death would most likely lay her fears to rest. After that, with the clear conscience of a good friend, she could do what she already promised she had done and relay Billie's phone message to the police.

In her studio, with the door closed, she called him.

"Hello, how are you?" His voice rang out with optimism and energy, qualities she felt lacking that day.

"I'm glad to hear your cheery tone," she said.

"It's been a long week, but Regina's coming home tonight."

"That *is* good news. I'll be happy to see her," she said.

"I feel like celebrating, " he burbled. She steeled herself for a change in attitude.

"I wonder if I could talk to you. Today, I mean," she said.

"I'm home all day," he said, surprising her. "Come on over."

Ken's condo mimicked the floor plan of Billie's. An L-shaped living room led off to two bedrooms, and a third door led to the bath. Ken's second bedroom served as an office, and much like Billie's, all the rooms had at least one floor to ceiling bookshelf. He opened the door as soon as Laila rang the bell.

Inside his front door, Laila had a view into the dining area and the sliding doors beyond to a stand of palm trees. The trees added a degree of beauty to the otherwise bare bones interior of Ken's sparse condo.

They sat at the hardwood dining table, the place where he hosted club meetings. On the wall hung a framed picture of twenty-year-old Ken riding the face of a daunting wave. It was the only art he had hung on his walls.

"What's up?" Ken asked. "I'm thinking you didn't come over for coffee."

"That night," she said. "I'm stuck thinking about that night."

"She was more than a friend to you," he said.

"They say fentanyl is fast," she said. "A shot, or a pill, and it works right away."

"So, she was just tired when I saw her. Or worried," he said.

"You mean she sensed she was in danger?' asked Laila.

"She might have already known there was a threat. But if she was afraid, why wouldn't she tell me? She couldn't have feared me."

"What if she had been drinking?" Laila said. "What if she were confused or panicked about something?"

"Something *was* wrong. She called you, right?" he said.

"That's right." Laila handed him her phone queued to Billie's last phone message.

Motionless, he listened to Billie's words. He lifted his eyes to Laila and started the message again. His face was the picture of concentration. He handed the phone back to Laila and sat with his head resting on his folded arms.

"Yeah, this is more or less what you told me," he said finally. "Who is she talking about? What woman does she mean?"

"It might be twenty different people. Or nobody, if she wasn't thinking clearly."

"She was definitely on the tired side when I saw her," Ken said.

"This confusion, that's why David wants the police to see this message and hear about your going over to Billie's afterwards. He wants to clear up any suspicions about him."

"David? How is he under suspicion? What are you talking about?" Ken lifted his head and looked at Laila with alarm.

"There's something I didn't tell you before," Laila said. She reached out and touched his arm. "I'm sorry. But I was afraid."

"What?" he asked. "What happened?"

"When I first saw Benjamin, he gave me a card that he found on Billie's desk. A message was scrawled inside. It was a message addressed to me."

"You never said anything," Ken said.

"It felt as though Billie were reaching out to me, asking for help. The phone message, the card, and I didn't go to her. I was, I mean I still am, embarrassed. Mortified."

"You think she wanted to tell us she was in trouble?" Ken asked.

"You say she seemed secretive, like she was hiding something from you," Laila recalled.

"There was that leaning on the door. Was she tired? Was she confused? Was she actually trying to block my vision?" he asked, exhaling in frustration. "Can I see the card?"

Laila brought out her phone again and showed him the photo.

"Where's the actual card?" Ken asked.

"The police took it."

"'I think you would want to know about David,'" Ken read on the phone screen. "What's that mean?"

"When Benjamin gave it to me, I was angry with Billie for writing something so horrible. At that time, I thought she had died of a heart attack, and the message came from some crazy last thoughts, some kind of confusion," she said.

"So, the police are pointing a finger at David," he said.

"But when Cranston and Borden hear the phone message, they'll be sure Billie was not pointing a finger at David."

"Well, at who?" he asked, his face skeptical.

"Someone else. Someone in our circle," she said. She looked down at her lap at her tightly clasped hands.

He sat, his chin supported, looking at her. Suddenly, he jumped up from the table and started pacing back and forth. He ran his hands through his hair nervously, as though searching his brain for ideas. After a few minutes, he turned towards her.

"Me?" he said, his steps lengthening and his glare unwavering.

Laila kept her eyes averted. Ken stopped in front of her, his face as flushed as if he'd been running.

"So," he said, "you got a message, you sent me to check on Billie, and no one saw her alive again. And now we find out she is poisoned."

"Yes," said Laila. "And the police think it was someone who wanted what was on Billie's computer. Someone who took her phone and computer."

"She writes a warning about David, but I'm a prime suspect?" he said through gritted teeth. "I'm sorry. I don't get it."

"Here's the thing," she said. "The only fingerprints on the card were Benjamin's and mine. None of Billie's. It doesn't seem that Billie wrote the card."

"So, *you* could have written the card. *You* could have been the last person to see Billie," Ken said.

"What? That makes no sense, Ken!" Laila said. "I wouldn't write a card to myself that makes me or David look suspicious!" She glared at him, as though he had lost his mind.

"But someone did! The card has your fingerprints on it!" he retorted.

"I wouldn't have killed Billie," she shouted.

"But I would?" he shouted back.

He slammed his hand on the table, and she jumped in fear. She pushed her chair back as he strode into the living room and threw himself into his armchair. Laila searched for a way to unwind the situation and calm it down, but she felt helpless.

"Wait, wait, wait," he said, getting up and heading towards her. "The card is false, and the phone message mentions a woman. How am I possibly implicated?"

"If Billie was talking about Regina, she might have said that to you. You might have gotten angry. You were the last person to see her."

"This is insane," he said. "*Regina*? Are you crazy?"

"If Billie found out something that wasn't good and she told you, maybe you got mad."

"Regina works. I work. We do not do this kind of thing. Are you nuts?"

"It's not me," said Laila. "It's what someone else could think. I'm just trying to warn you. In the eyes of the police, we could be connected to the poisoning. Any of us could be connected."

"Sunday morning you discover Billie's dead, and you don't tell Regina. You don't call David, and you don't tell your boys. Isn't that suspicious? Regina was hurt. She was standing right there in front of you, and you let her go on her merry way without a word." Ken flopped again into his easy chair.

"Not in front of the boys, and not in the middle of the street. And Regina was leaving for more classes. It wasn't the right time," she said.

"The boys, the boys," Ken fumed from his chair. "Your only job is those four boys, and that's it. And you have hired help. What do you do all day?"

Laila's head burned. Pain shot across her brow and roiled under her scalp. Ken was being hateful, and she didn't deserve it. The fury was boiling behind her eyes.

"You were certainly no help," she raised her voice. "I called and called. Oh, but excuse me. It was Sunday. Supposedly, you go to church on Sunday."

"I have commitments," he said coldly.

"You were absolutely no help at all," she yelled in frustration.

"And guess what? No servants. Nope, not a one," he sneered at her.

"That's some beautiful church you go to," she said. "It doesn't exist. You aren't a member of the Presbyterian Church. Or the Methodist. Or the Unitarian. Should I check the Lutherans?"

Ken came out of his chair like a shot. He hurtled toward her chair but stopped, snared by an unseen power. His arms dangled down, and one hand clenched the fabric of his slacks, as if he were barely able to keep from swinging at her.

He looked long and hard at her. Laila wanted to say more, but they had reached a point of no return. Whatever more she would say might provoke the worst in him.

Without a word, he turned and walked to his office. She heard him rustling around, opening drawers. He might be looking for a weapon, and their deteriorating standoff could become much worse. The sliding glass doors were the nearest opportunity for escape, and they were unlatched. The sound of his footsteps got her up on her feet. She sidestepped toward the doors, putting the table between her and Ken's path. She waited, with her fingers grasping the door handle.

He came into view, around the corner of the living room, carrying a white photo album, the kind with a window on the cover. He no longer seemed to be in the grasp of angry passion. He placed the album on the table in front of her.

Laila saw a color photo of a young girl, shiny dark hair, an angular and exotic face, a female version of Ken. She wore a wet suit, almost as black as her hair, and she supported a surfboard with one arm. She hugged it like a best friend and smiled at the camera. Ken ran a finger over the picture and then pushed the album closer to Laila.

"That's my daughter," he said.

"Ken," Laila said. "A daughter. You have a beautiful daughter." She looked up at him and gingerly opened to the first page. "Oh, Ken."

Several photos showed an infant on a blanket, a baby having her first soft food, a baby crawling behind a comical stuffed duck. On the next pages, the girl toddled behind a dog and built a tower with blocks. On a sunny day, she squinted at the camera from her beach blanket. From then on, pictures contained water, sand, surfboards, or all of the above.

She rode on her pudgy baby belly, then her legs lengthened, and she stood on the board. Barefoot in a graduation robe on white sand, the teenager was submerged by dozens of leis. In the last photo, taking up a full page, she appeared at the edge of the water with medals around her neck.

"What's her name?" she asked.

"Lindsay."

Laila was afraid to ask, and her voice cracked with the next question. "Where is she now?"

"She had an accident," he said. "She lives in Jacksonville."

"She's what you do on Sundays," Laila said.

"Yeah, I go to Jacksonville," he said.

"How old is she?"

"Twenty-seven," he said.

"Ken, I apologize," Laila said. "I made an assumption."

"What are you doing this morning? For the next three hours?" he asked.

"Going with you?" she asked. "To Jacksonville?"

CHAPTER TWENTY-FOUR

Thursday, Day Twelve - Jacksonville

The care facility in Jacksonville was unmistakably Floridian. Built low and long, the smooth masonry veneer drew a clean line below the Spanish tile roof. A circular drive to the entry passed under a breezeway of plaster columns faintly reminiscent of the Old South. A wide ribbon of robust plantings, lilacs, hydrangeas, hostas, iris, and honeysuckle surrounded the building and softened the lengths of walkways and ramps.

Laila got out of the car, and they walked toward the building. Large windows decorated with ironwork panes gave the center a stylish finish. As she got closer, Laila saw a long, sunny hallway that appeared to lead to a solarium adorned with hanging baskets of flowers and ferns.

"I'll make up an excuse for why I'm here to see her on an unscheduled day," Ken said. "You won't pass for family, so I'll say you're my accountant and only free today. Something like that."

Inside the facility, they greeted the receptionist and signed the visitors' book. According to her individualized calendar, Lindsay was participating in a physical therapy class, so the receptionist asked them to wait for an escort.

"We won't speak with her," Ken said.

"But you came all this way," said Laila.

"I would introduce you today, if there were an urgent need, but generally, changes in the schedule disturb her. She gets anxious, and it takes days to get back into a routine. I've got to respect that."

"But I won't meet her?" she said.

"I want you to see her. Because you're my friend, I want you to see how lovely she is. But I want you to see the situation, too. I want you to get it."

In the car on the way to Jacksonville, Ken had talked about his daughter's condition. Lindsay had finished high school nine years before and began to surf competitively. She had a backer, a surfboard manufacturer who underwrote the cost of her travel. Eight to ten months of the year, she did the circuit of the big championships. Ken's business kept him tied to his Hawaiian clients, and he missed many of her star moments. The surfing magazines could be counted on for feature stories, however, and twice a year, he made it a point to be at whatever big event she had.

The accident happened in Hawaii on the Big Island, a short plane trip from their home on Oahu, about six years after her graduation. At the time, Ken was married to Brett, Lindsay's mother, and she had flown from Oahu for the first day of the qualifying heats. Ken intended to join them on the weekend. He got the phone call Thursday night.

Lindsay had been knocked off her board by the curl of an overhead wave in relatively shallow water, and she must have been pounded into the ocean floor. She surfaced briefly but wasn't able to swim and went under once more. Onlookers dove in after her and brought her out, but she was still unconscious when the ambulance arrived. At the hospital, they determined her injuries required surgery, and Brett consented. When Lindsay had a stroke on the operating table from a broken rib puncturing a lung and throwing off a clot, the orthopedic surgeon and anesthesiologist upped the blood thinners drastically, but ten minutes passed before she had relief. The damage was severe.

"I taught her to surf. I got her excited about it. Then I stood by her bed in the hospital unable to help," Ken told Laila. "I don't want you to feel sorry for us," Ken continued. "I've done plenty of that. I just want you to know something more about my life. So, you'll understand how ridiculous it is to think I am a killer."

"I didn't think you were a killer," Laila said.

"Then stick up for me when the cops come calling," he said. "And they will."

Before Laila had left with Ken for Jacksonville, she had called Detective Cranston and told him about the phone message from Billie and her call to Ken. At his request, she emailed the audio of the message and the time it was received. Ken said he understood why she needed to do it.

"It's ridiculous to think because of Regina I would attack Billie," Ken said as they drove the interstate into Jacksonville. "But I get that the police look first at the closest friends."

"Poison," Laila said. "Who could be so cruel and cold to inject an old woman?"

"Not me—and not Regina; that's for sure," he said. "If for no other reason than we have plenty to worry about. We're both tied up supporting our kids. The last thing we need is more trouble."

"So, Regina knows about Lindsay?" she asked.

"Yeah, she actually guessed it on her own. When I met Mindy, I started talking to her about her life and school and friends, and Regina figured I must have had experience with teenagers."

"Has she met Lindsay?" she asked.

"Sundays are terrible for Regina, and Sunday visits are all the staff want Lindsay to have, for now," he answered. "Regina's seen all my pictures and newspaper clippings, and she's been able to have a short observation like what you'll have today."

Laila's observation of Lindsay was indeed brief. The social worker, Penny, let them into a room behind the physical therapy studio. Through a one-way mirror, they watched Lindsay working with heavy plastic stretch bands. She worked on a floor mat and then from a wheelchair as the therapist ran her through a series of muscle strengthening exercises.

"She hardly has any speech," said Ken, "and for years, I accepted the diagnosis that she had low cognitive function. But then this therapist got hired by the center, and things have changed radically."

Ken leaned forward in the metal folding chair, unconsciously flexing his arms and legs as Lindsay worked her limbs. He gritted his teeth and held his breath when she stopped. When she started up again, goaded by the therapist into more reps or heavier weights, he moved his limbs along with her.

Laila saw Lindsay's muscles quivering with the strain, but her face was turned either toward the therapist or toward the wall holding the exercise bands. She saw her straight black hair, shiny and thick, and her long, slender torso. In her cotton shorts and t-shirt, she looked like any young athlete or gym rat. At one point, she slammed her hand against the mat and let her leg drop limp, but the therapist squatted and spoke to her, and Lindsay started again, pulling her leg against the constraint of the band.

"Most of the damage was to speech and to her right side," said Ken. "She didn't walk, and no one tried to teach her how to use a motorized wheel chair. She had to be pushed everywhere she wanted to go."

"And now?" Laila asked.

"This therapist recommends braces that allow someone young and light

like Lindsay to walk. But her left side, the good side, has to
Lindsay has to want to learn how to operate the mechanical

"But if she couldn't operate a wheelchair, how will
asked.

"No one explained the chair to her, and without speech
a clue," he said. "And maybe she was confused. This therap
medications changed."

Casually, because Ken was watching, the therapist turned Lin
the one-way mirror. Laila immediately saw the toll the accident h

Lindsay had a delicate face with dramatic, deep brown eyes
lashes. The straight bridge of her nose and a dimpled chin were des
frame sweet, symmetrical contours. The stroke had distorte
construction by slackening her cheek and mouth, so they collapsed
downward towards her neck, pulling on the surrounding flesh. Her head
canted slightly to the right also, adding to the appearance of imbalance.

Despite knowing about the probable effects of a stroke, Laila had not
prepared herself for the sight of Lindsay's face, and she wasn't fast enough to
control her reaction.

"It's okay," said Ken. "But you don't know what she looked like this time
last year. That was bad."

"She's changing then?" said Laila.

"Last year, Penny took Lindsay to the ocean with a girl who learned how
to use the new braces. The girl put on a wet suit and swam. Lindsay erupted.
She used to wear a whistle around her neck that she was supposed to blow
when she needed something in a hurry. She blew the whistle all the way back
to the center and into the night. They had to call me to come and calm her."

"When do you think she'll get the braces?" Laila asked.

"If it were just about muscle tone, she'd have them already," he said.
"She's lost twenty pounds or more since last year and grown stronger. But

manipulation of the brace. You won't see it today, but they

hat teaches her how to handle steps and things like getting

d."

o hug her for trying so hard," Laila said.

roadly at Laila. "She's got some spirit, doesn't she?" he said.

see it."

oes her Mom say? She must be bursting, waiting for these

a said.

s not here anymore," Ken said, his smile erased. "She passed on

r years ago."

u always say you're divorced," said Laila.

was suicide."

"I'm so sorry," Laila said. "I am so very sorry."

"I thought I was a tough guy. I competed around the world in my day, like Lindsay. The crowd I ran with played hard. You learned how to make trouble afraid, not the other way around. Then Lindsay. Then Brett. The life you used to have comes back and laughs at you. Just busts a gut laughing at you."

"I don't know how I would survive it."

"Brett did what she could, and then she couldn't any more. She went under, but she went with a fight." Ken took a last look through the window at Lindsay. "We better get you back to your kids. Your plate is full, too."

Laila took one last look also through the one-way glass and turned to go, but Ken caught her arm and pulled her back towards him.

"Look, I'm sorry I made that comment about your work raising the boys."

"Apology accepted," she said.

Before they left, Ken showed Laila the pool and dining room and an art room where residents were working with clay and paints. In a small meeting hall, a woman played the piano while a group of residents, sitting in a circle, sang together.

On the way home, Laila told Ken how impressed she was with the apparent quality of Lindsay's care.

"I brought her to Jacksonville after Brett died, mostly because of the hospital. It's lucky that the facility had room and even luckier that they have this new therapist."

"You must have great insurance," she said.

"Some," he shrugged. "The rehab is more or less on my dime. My business is good, but I can't let it lag. The bills must be paid."

"You're right. Between you two, Regina and you have a load to shoulder," she said.

"We haven't talked money yet. We're not that far along," he said. "I'm putting it off as long as possible."

"Regina's a hard worker. I don't think she's looking for a man to support her."

"Hah!" Ken said, with a bitter chuckle that startled Laila. "What I'm worried about is she might do better *without* me."

"She's used to a budget," she said. "Look at her with Mindy. She's saved so hard for so long."

"I get the feeling she has help from Mindy's father," he said.

"Really?" said Laila.

"I'm guessing. I mean this trip to New York. It seems bigger than Regina can afford with tuition bills coming up in September."

"She's never mentioned child support, but she doesn't mention money, period," she said.

"Support might drop away now that Mindy won't be living at home," Ken said.

"I thought it was too early for you to have this conversation?" Laila chided.

"I think about this stuff. Maybe too much."

"But you wonder," said Laila. "It's natural."

The idea of Mindy's father having a role was new information to Laila. In the past, Laila had offered Regina support for Mindy's studies. Regina consistently demurred and said that Mindy had access to enough scholarships and grants. As long as she had known her, Regina was close-mouthed about finances, so Laila didn't push the issue. Money from Mindy's father would answer a lot of unasked questions.

Was Mindy's father Regina's true love? Does she still see him? Love him? Is Mindy aware? Will this go badly for Ken?

They were about to exit the interstate when Ken's phone rang. He answered on the car's Bluetooth. Detective Borden asked to interview him later in the afternoon. They agreed on a four o'clock appointment at Ken's home.

"That was fast," said Laila.

"Have you talked to this guy? Borden, is it?" he asked.

"He has a partner, Detective Cranston," she said. "I've met them twice."

"So, what are they looking for? What will they ask about?"

"They're going to start with the night she died. Where were you? What time did you see her? How long did you stay? Why didn't you check back in with me?" she suggested.

"Wait, now, that last one is your question. No one else would expect me to call after eleven at night," he said. "I figured that if I didn't call back, you'd realize Billie was fine."

"Okay, if they ask, tell them that," she said. "They'll probably ask anyway about the rest of us in the club. How do we act? Did someone have a problem with Billie?"

"The million-dollar question seems to be what did Billie have that someone killed to get," he said. "If she was trying to keep me out of her apartment, what was she working on? What was she hiding?"

Laila tried to picture Ken's last encounter with Billie. Why would she feel defensive with Ken? What would have been on the other side of that door?

"Was someone in there with her?" she asked, struck by the sudden thought.

"The female friend she was talking about in the phone message?" he said.

"Or a male friend of the female in the phone message—a male friend who knew Billie had something of value, something of importance," she said.

"You're making me nervous. They can't be thinking that," he answered.

"But they are," said Laila. "They're coming to talk to you because they're considering every possibility."

"Then it could be David, too," he said. "Why couldn't Billie have found out something awful about David? He's not off the hook."

"He was in Miami," Laila said. "He was three hundred miles down the interstate."

"Was he?" he asked. "Who vouches for him? You?"

"They checked his SunPass. He was on ninety-five until Miami. Cranston told me when I called about the phone message."

"Nice of him to put you at your ease," said Ken.

"Don't do this," Laila said, her hand on the dash as she turned to Ken. "Don't let this happen."

He pulled the car into an empty parking lot and killed the motor. "You're off the hook," he said. "It's easy for you to say."

"You didn't do it, and David and I didn't do it. The police might not have cleared you yet, but they will," she said.

"Are you sure?" he asked.

"Yes, I am absolutely, positively sure. The only reason I came over this morning is because I am absolutely sure."

"So, who did it? Was it someone from Laguna Shores?" Ken asked.

"The killer had to have gotten into her home at some point in the night. She might have let him into the apartment willingly," she said.

"Or after a struggle. The mess left behind could have been from a struggle, or from the killer looking for something," he said.

"How will anyone know until they find her computer?" she asked. "Obviously, the police are as hard up for suspects as we are."

"We haven't talked about Claire. She could be the female friend," he said.

"And what? Brick, a man she's known for a New York minute, went in and killed Billie for her?" she said.

"Claire couldn't administer a poison? She's perfectly capable."

"You won't say that to the police, will you?" Laila gasped.

"No!" he barked. "What do you take me for? An idiot?"

Laila sat back into the bucket seat. The car felt like an oven, the temperature dangerously high, close to boiling.

"God, Claire? Claire barely knows Billie," she said. "We're all friends. Just friends." She looked over at Ken, who was leaning his head against his window, his eyes closed against the bright sun. "We're asphyxiating ourselves," she said.

He started the car, and the air conditioning powered on. He pulled back out into traffic. Two traffic lights later, they pulled into Laguna Shores, and he parked in front of his condo.

"Are you okay for time?" he asked. "Do you want to come in for a sandwich? I forgot about lunch."

"Thanks," she said. "But there's a school event this afternoon."

"I'll call you after I talk to this Borden guy," he said. "Maybe tomorrow. Regina will be back tonight."

Laila smiled when Ken blushed over his own comment.

"Call whenever," she answered. "And thank you for Jacksonville. For letting me see Lindsay. I appreciate it."

"We'll go again," he said. "One day we'll go and watch her swim."

Laila got out of the car and walked the two blocks back to her building. She was glad she had held back her tears until Ken could no longer see her.

CHAPTER TWENTY-FIVE

Friday, Day Thirteen – Flea Market Snafu

Laila pulled her SUV over to the curb two blocks from the St. Augustine Flea Market. In the early morning quiet, she turned off the engine and tried using the deep breathing exercises from yoga classes to calm down. The street ahead led to the entrance to the vendor parking lot and the secure entrance at the rear of the market. With each breath, she recited the five-digit code and pictured her index finger darting from key to key.

When she talked to Jennifer and consulted with Brick, the idea of cutting her way into Elizabeth Powell's back storage area to take a few pictures had seemed like a minor breach of etiquette. Daring, to a degree, but you could make a case for it being what any diligent researcher of lost and stolen paintings would do. Jennifer endorsed the plan, and Brick had made it sound like the logical thing to do.

Her investigation could produce a groundbreaking report on the whereabouts of missing Highwaymen paintings. Finding Highwaymen landscapes would not be equivalent to finding a Goya or Picasso, yet museums throughout the state and region would be grateful. They might name her to the museum board, a remarkable feather in her cap since people in her world gained seats on museum boards due to large donations, not for their research.

David would not be the only person in the family with a laudable public profile. He worked hard, Laila knew, and deserved the respect of the community for developing the commercial core responsibly. Laila hoped for a taste of that purpose and accomplishment, too. Not to show him up, but to stand by his side while standing up for herself. David had contacts throughout St. Augustine and into the upper echelons of government. How pleasant for her to introduce him to the local stars, and not the other way around!

Now, only a few blocks away from her target, doubts about the plan gripped Laila. Technically, well, no, more than technically, she'd be breaking the law. Her intent was one hundred percent honest, but her methods were not exactly kosher. Wouldn't it be better to wait and ask more questions? Perhaps visit these vendors to whom Elizabeth Powell supposedly sold paintings? Or would that alert the whole flea market to an investigation that was supposed to be under the radar?

She hadn't asked David's advice, in part because he had been absorbed in his own work and worry. Also, and perhaps more compelling, was her tendency to compare herself to David. If it were his plan, he would know a raft of people to consult, she thought with some bitterness. With his charm, he might elicit all the information he needed without anyone being the wiser.

She sat at the wheel of the SUV, her fingers trembling in anticipation of this unlikely infiltration of Elizabeth Powell's world. To be perfectly honest, David would not approve it. In fact, the night before, he urged her once again to distance herself from not only the Research Club, but also from her own research.

She had told him about Ken's daughter and their trip to Jacksonville, and David's response was to zero in on the dangers surrounding the investigation into Billie's death.

"You need to disband the research club," David said.

She was in their bedroom watching the late news. He had just begun his nightly half-hour run on the treadmill, but appeared in the bedroom after less than five minutes of exercise. She muted the big screen when he joined her on the bed.

"Why? What do you mean?" she said.

"Or at least suspend the meetings," he said.

"What are you talking about? That's the last thing Billie'd want," she said.

"Of course not," he said. "But now you don't know where it could lead."

"Probably nowhere without her," she lamented. "She had a hand in each project."

"There's the rub," he said. "You know what she was doing for you, but not for the others. You don't know what she was delving into for people."

"Like surfing stats for Ken?" she said with a grin. "So dangerous!"

"The police aren't buzzing around because of the surfing report. You're right," he said.

"Then what? We were the most unexciting researchers on the face of the planet. How about Regina's thrilling look at Bitcoin? The Highwaymen research would beat out the others hands down, and that's not saying much."

"Maybe she had a project you don't know about. Could be anything under the sun," he said.

"What's worrying you? I told the police about Billie's phone message. They're questioning Ken. You are not their focus."

Instead of the expression of relief she expected, David's response sounded like another round of accusations. "You don't know that. You have no idea of what direction the police will take this. Belonging to this stupid research club is like walking around with a target on your back." He shook his head as if she were a hopeless fool.

Laila searched for some reasonable explanation of his unreasonable attitude. "Is this about the dolphin card? Is there something weird about you she could have known? Something someone else suspects?"

Laila didn't intend to say something that sounded as if she were answering accusations with accusations, but David's objections baffled her.

"Billie? Not at all," he assured her, as if the thought had never occurred to him. He smiled, as if his mood had changed.

She was encouraged but still doubtful.

"Unless she was secretly taping my tennis game. That could be a disaster for me." He laughed.

She smiled at his charm. They could, she thought with relief, discuss this situation sanely, as they always had discussed problems before.

"You haven't mentioned Claire," Laila said.

"Yeah, Claire," David said. "What was she researching?"

"Remember, new housing developments and such," she said. "She's dropping it, though."

"And you believe her?" he asked. "You don't know her." The edge was back in his voice.

"What's to believe?" she asked. "She just fiddles around a bit. She's never given a serious report to the club."

"But Billie was helping her, right?" he said. "She developed a permit tracking program for her?"

Laila was confused. David had vague ideas about the Research Club, and he told the police Billie was less than an acquaintance. Details about Claire were another story. He pretended he didn't know, and then recalled specifics.

Well, I can play cat and mouse, too.

She stretched out on the bed, propping up her head and directing her gaze out the window. After a few moments, she looked back at him. "That Claire is a bit of a fake, if you ask me," she said. "I like her and all, but have you seen her even once at a meeting?"

"Yeah, I've seen her. Usually, I'm leaving by the time she's arriving. She's not exactly religious in her attendance."

Laila was glad to hear David offhandedly dismiss Claire as a serious participant in his world. But at the same time, his report on her didn't jive with Claire's drive and persistence in all matters concerning real estate. She generally kept her eye on the ball.

"I got the idea that research is not her thing, but if she's going to zoning meetings and all that, maybe I'm wrong," she said.

"Don't obsess over it. Let the club slide for a while, and maybe later, it'll start again. If people are interested, you could start up in the fall."

Silently, Laila dismissed the idea of disbanding the club. The meetings comforted her. She was doing something Billie liked. Besides, with Ken and Regina forming a couple, the meetings might be one of her few contacts with them, at least as long as they were in a courting phase. She could only take so much loss at once.

"I'd probably lose my initiative on the Highwaymen project if I did that," she said.

"So, spend more time on your own painting. The Highwaymen will always be there," he answered.

So that was that. My museum project – take it or leave it.

Laila tried not to let any rancor creep into her thoughts. Communication would collapse completely if she couldn't keep a steady attitude. She had nodded as though she were considering David's suggestions. He returned to his exercise routine, and she climbed into bed with a book.

Now at the wheel of car, she sat at and considered her alternatives.

Maybe David was tired. Construction on the retail center had picked up. The rainy season would begin in a matter of weeks, and they had to hurry. He had little energy for this intrigue about Billie's death, let alone any interest in the Highwaymen. He needed her undivided support.

"Cut the man some slack," Laila said out loud. She put her hands on the wheel. She'd make a U turn and go home. She would return to where she belonged. She should think about what her family needed.

But is this art research solely for my benefit?

The Highwaymen deserved a champion, a protector of their rights. If there were a culprit, it was whoever hid the whereabouts of those paintings. Billie would have wanted her to get to the bottom of these suspicious sales, wouldn't she have? The museum report, no matter what it turned up, could only bolster their profile.

David will be proud. He doesn't see it, but my success will do the family good.

She started up the engine. She could get this little job done, find out what Elizabeth Powell was or wasn't hiding, and get back home before anyone had missed her. It was simple, and she could do it.

She was so early the vendor parking lot was completely empty. She went up the driveway entrance and into a parking slot without seeing anyone at all. She left the car unlocked so that her departure could be that much quicker.

The keypad was affixed to the gate above her line of vision. She punched in the numbers while balancing on her toes. Each press of a button elicited a high-pitched note, and the buzz of the gate opening was also louder than she expected. She noticed a current of vibration in her legs as she walked into the market and headed down the alleyway to number two sixty-five. It was difficult to walk a normal pace, as if her body wanted to jump ahead of itself.

Breathe in, hold it, and breathe out. No one is here.

The canvas flaps on the back of Elizabeth Powell's booth overlapped snugly. Laila could shove her hand behind the outer flap but couldn't reach beyond the inner one. Along the ground, the chains securing the flaps were taut and fastened with a padlock. She saw she could use the tautness to slice a hole in the canvas in a lower corner. She would have to crawl in and out, but her size presented an advantage. The L-shaped slash she needed to slip inside might not be discovered for hours, even days.

She took a box cutter out of her purse, applied pressure to a spot in the canvas about two feet from the ground, and pulled, ripping material as she went. Laila had cut plenty of canvas, albeit much lighter grade, during her employment in New York galleries. Canvas, they used to say, wants to comply.

The box cutter went back in her purse, and the heavy-duty garden shears came out. Crouching to find the most effective position for her cutting arm, and a few inches before the scissors would have cut dirt, she angled left and sliced another two feet. She had created a small door into the booth.

She dropped the shears in her purse and shoved it through the opening. She took off her shoes and pushed them through next. With one leg through the hole, she pushed off with her hands and propelled herself into the darkness on the other side. The scratchy plastic of a tarp lay under her hands and knees. Her flashlight beam lit up an orderly collection of framed works, stacked in rows of four or five, each leaning on the one before, like windows for sale in a big box hardware store.

The frames had cardboard guards stapled together around the outside and plastic sheathed the paintings. The beam couldn't penetrate the plastic, and Laila had to hold the light in her mouth to use both hands to shimmy off the covering so she could see the landscape beneath. Golds, yellows, browns, and blues of a Highwayman sunrise shined back at her. She pushed her fingers behind the cardboard on the lower right and pulled it out far enough to see the iconic signature of Harold Newton. Harold Newton was central to the entire Highwaymen school.

Elizabeth Powell, who are you?

Using the phone she always carried slung over her body, she snapped a photo. The result was poor, so she fumbled to put on the flash. She took another shot, and while it would win no prizes, it identified the piece. She let the plastic drop and set the painting to one side as best she could.

The next three paintings, once uncovered, produced the same joy for Laila. Another work by Harold Newton, one by Roy McClendon, and a third by Willie Daniels used the characteristic low clouds and unruly vegetation to convey wildness and melancholy, hallmarks of these artists. She photographed each one and restacked them, one supporting the other along the wooden posts that held up the canvas walls.

She flashed the beam greedily around the storage space, calculating the number of paintings stashed there and the time it would take her to photograph the whole lot. At three or four minutes a painting, the fifteen remaining Highwaymen would take her an hour. She hesitated. Getting all the photos would mean getting back after the boys needed to leave for school. Better to work diligently for thirty minutes and leave unobtrusively, happy to have gotten ten paintings documented.

Who knows? I might be come back another day.

The next stack held at least five frames, and Laila duck-walked towards them, her phone camera at the ready. Laila could smell the warm grass underneath the tarp, and she sensed the moisture in the air. The warm and clammy feeling made her wonder about the protection from humidity these paintings would need. She hoped this storage was a temporary resting place while they were awaiting sale.

"Who is over there?" a woman's voice called.

Laila turned off the beam and remained crouched on the tarp. If she budged an inch, the tarp would rustle under her feet. Looking up, she noticed for the first time the gap between the canvas wall and the ceiling, where light from the neighboring booth spilled in to the storage space. Sound, like light, would also float from one booth into another.

"Is that you, Elizabeth?" the neighbor called again.

Laila could hear the person moving to the rear of her booth, putting down whatever bags or packages she was carrying and opening the canvas to the outside, which, by all indications, involved a zipper and some ties. Laila held her breath.

"Oh, Lord!" The woman's voice came through the back of the booth, precisely it seemed, where Laila had cut her small door.

"Who's in there? You better scat! I'm calling the manager!" The woman returned to her booth, on a search for her phone no doubt, swearing as she barged around the small space. Laila turned on the beam, found her purse, stowed her phone, grabbed her shoes, and crawled out the canvas hole.

Maybe she's large. Large and slow.

Laila scooted down the pathway toward the rear gate. Passing three booths, she turned to look back and saw the woman who likely discovered her, standing with her phone to her ear, one hand on her hip, and gesturing at Laila. She was an older woman, but slim not heavy-set, and not at all slow to report an intruder. Laila began to run.

She reached the gate and could see her car in the lot, still one of very few parked there. She punched in the numbers and pulled the gate toward her. No buzzer sounded, and when she tugged it toward her, it stayed firmly closed. Repeating the code like a litany in her head, her hand reaching above her head, she tried the combination once more, to no avail. A third time she pushed the gate with all her weight, managing to rattle the posts that held the rest of the fence, but the gate did not yield.

Directly behind her, a walkway led into the flea market. If she could wend her way to the front entrance, there might be someone, a vendor or an early customer who would let her out as they came in. To reach the entrance from this far corner of the market, she knew she had to jog from one narrow row to another until she found the main arterial. As she backed away from the gate and turned into the market, out of the corner of her eye, she could see the woman in the alleyway pointing at her, and this time, there was a uniformed man by her side, following her accusatory finger.

Laila changed her plan and ran, not toward the main entrance, but parallel to it, until the row ended in a T. She scooted to the next parallel row, doubled back toward the rear gate, passed it, and ran toward the opposite corner of the market. The security guard wouldn't expect her to take a zigzag path. She might dodge out the front while he was still chasing along her helter-skelter route.

At the last turn, she found herself only two rows from the entrance. She ran up this long row. At the end, with one turn and one sprint, she might get through the front entrance. She tried to increase her speed and get her short legs to stretch forward farther and faster. Her purse was knocking awkwardly against her ribs, and she looked down a split second to move it toward her back. When she looked up, an alarming scene made her pull up and stand stock-still.

The older gentleman she had talked to earlier in the week, the market manager, stood conferring with the woman who had just chased her out of Elizabeth Powell's booth. Laila was mere yards away from the entrance and escape, if only she could get by them. They hadn't seen her.

To her right, between closed flaps, a light peeked through the gaps in the canvas covering. She pushed aside the flaps and stepped inside.

Three rows of long tables extended deep into the booth. On display, kitchen items from past decades jumbled together in no particular order. Tin sieves, wooden mallets, rolling pins, coffee grinders, and hand-held juicers filled in the spaces among incomplete sets of dessert plates and teacups. Laila ducked down and fit herself beneath a table, hoping she could rest there until the guard got tired of searching.

She heard the dog growl before she saw it.

"Molly, what's bothering you?" a man's voice reproved the dog.

Undeterred, the dog's growl grew deeper as it approached the corner table where Laila hunched low. When its snout passed the first leg of Laila's table, she gasped at the powerful jaw of a German Shepherd.

Its growl became a high-pitched bark, one of panic and anger mixed. It lunged toward her, disregarding the table legs and cross bars. The dog jerked up its head when a paw knocked a bar, and it struck the lip of the table, giving out a cry of pain.

Laila bolted onto the top of the table, shoving aside the kitchen utensils and trying to get her ankles tucked under her and away from the dog's teeth. It lunged and retreated, then lunged again, jostling the table and rattling the messy collection of ancient appliances.

"Look here, young woman," the man began.

On hearing his master's angry tone, the dog barred its teeth and pawed the top of the table where Laila huddled, her purse in front of her for whatever protection it might provide.

"I won't hurt you," she cried.

"Molly, Molly, come here," the man ordered, less emphatically than Laila wished.

"Please call it off," Laila begged.

"Who are you?" the man shouted.

"I'm sorry. I thought someone was chasing me," Laila said.

The dog continued pawing and snapping.

"Come here," the man said again. "Right now." He grabbed the dog by the collar and herded her toward the back of the booth. "And why would someone in here be chasing you?" the man cried. "And please get down from my table, if you don't mind."

"Is the dog going to back off?" she asked.

"She's better behaved than you," he said.

Laila jostled the piles of merchandise as she attempted to rearrange her body to a less awkward position. The table swayed when she shifted her weight.

"Could you walk me to the exit?" she asked. "I am really scared."

"Look, I don't know where you think you are, but any monster you imagined will surely let you exit in peace. Go already! My dog is upset."

She pulled her legs out from under her and sat on the edge of the table. Her feet dangled, not quite finding a landing. She pushed off, hopping to the ground and creating a landslide of kitchen paraphernalia in the process. The clatter and crack of tin and ceramics started the dog growling once more.

"Can I replace any of the items?" Laila asked, opening her purse to pull out a wallet.

"Just get out," he said.

She took a step to the canvas curtain leading out to the aisle. She turned back to the aggrieved vendor. "So sorry, really," she said, backing up towards the opening. She felt the heavy canvas flaps on her back and leaned too hard into them. Losing her balance, her weight shifted to her heels and her purse, heavy with the flashlight, cutter and scissors, swung behind her through the flaps. It landed squarely on the thigh of the security guard, who was striding back to his post at the entrance.

"For Christ's sake!" he shouted at her as she stumbled backwards through the flaps.

"You! What do you think you're doing?" shouted the manager down the aisle when he spotted her.

The guard grabbed her by the arm, hiked her up to the balls of her feet, and hustled her to the manager's office inside the front gate at a double time pace.

"I thought you were suspicious the last time you were here," the manager said after the guard deposited her in front of his desk. "I should have gone out and gotten your license plate then."

"I think I can explain," Laila said. She wasn't sure, but she thought she might look as though she just stepped out of the tumble cycle of a dryer.

"Let's see in that purse," the manager said.

He pulled out the cutter, the scissors and flashlight, turning the last item towards her and flicking on the beam so that it hit her eyes directly. He scoured around in her purse, pulled out her wallet, and read her name to her from her driver's license. She tried to smile, but it felt like a grimace. Yellow circles, caused by the glare of the beam flashing on her retinas, dodged back and forth across his face.

"Harrow is a familiar name," he said. "Should I know it?"

"I don't think so," she answered. "I'm new in the area." For the first time, it occurred to Laila that this escapade was more likely to get David's name in the newspaper than hers.

"What did you want in that antique booth?" he asked.

"I collect Highwaymen paintings, and I got carried away. It's not every day when you see an original Alfred Hair."

"So, to do it justice, you thought you'd cut it out of its frame and take it home. How devoted to art you are!"

"I would never do that," she said. "I would never deface a piece of art."

"God, it takes all kinds," he said, rolling his eyes. "I'm supposed to believe you?"

He picked up the walkie-talkie from the corner of his desk and asked the person on the other end to take a photograph of the hole cut in the back of the booth. He also requested that the person enter the booth, photograph the scene, and count the number of framed paintings. As he spoke, he opened a desk drawer and pulled out a form.

"Fill in all the blanks," he hissed at her.

The form header read "Incident Report." As Laila wrote, he took out his cell phone and moved away from her and out of earshot. When she finished, he returned to his chair and faced her across the desk.

"The owner is coming in. She'll examine the paintings. When she's done, the police will take you away."

"I've got to call home," she said. "I've got kids."

"Won't they be proud of mama," he snapped. "Go ahead."

She pulled her phone out of her carrying bag and got Margaret on the first ring. She said she would take the boys to school.

"Are you having car trouble?" Margaret asked.

"Nothing like that," she said. "It's fine. I'll be home soon."

She hung up and faced the manager again. He shook his head at her as if after so many happy moments together, she had disappointed him with this malevolent turn.

"How did you get in?" he asked.

"Through the rear gate. It was open, and I guess it hadn't clicked shut," she lied. "I couldn't resist."

"You just happened to try the gate at around, I don't know, say seven in the morning?"

"Gosh, was it that early?" Laila said. "I was going for a cup of coffee, but I didn't realize it was that early."

"So, someone gave you the key code to get in," he said. "Who would do such a thing? Give you the key code to get in, but not the code to get out?"

"Pardon," she said. "There is a key code?"

"No," he said. "In the plural. *Codes.*"

The information felt like a slap. Laila tried not to betray her surprise. Why would Brick omit the code for her escape?

A cop doesn't make that kind of mistake.

"I'm sure I wouldn't have come in if I had known I was breaching security," she said in a meek tone.

"Who the hell are you?" he asked.

"I just wanted to see the painting," she repeated.

"Let's look," he said, opening up his laptop, "at how much an Alfred Hair is worth."

After a few clicks, he leaned in toward the screen to read. He scrolled down pages on one site and double-clicked into several other sites. He took a couple of notes and went back to scrolling.

"What sites do you use to search for an artist's work?" she asked.

"Finish writing," he said, ignoring her inquiry.

"Done," she said after a few minutes. She handed him the pen and completed form.

He scanned it with irritation.

"How much do they say an Alfred Hair is worth?" she asked.

"A lot," he said. "You say here you broke into the booth because you are an art researcher."

"Yes, and I'm working exclusively on the Highwaymen."

"For whom? Who is paying you?"

The idea that Brick may have been setting her up, coupled with Jennifer's unexpected secretiveness, shook her awake to the danger of what she was doing. Laila had assumed that her attempt to track down the Alfred Hair had a socially redeeming purpose, even if she strayed into sketchy territory. But now she realized Jennifer and the other committee members might or might not testify to her intentions.

Naïve. I've been totally naïve.

Not having the Acquisitions Committee's support could be discouraging, but the museum making their disapproval public would be a disaster. She couldn't risk using Jennifer's name.

"I work for myself. I try to sell the research once I'm done."

"That's a first," the manager said. "A rogue art researcher comes to my little market."

"I'm not rogue. I'm independent."

"Yes, and I do this job for free because I love antiques. Please don't insult my intelligence."

Laila's face burned under the glare of the manager's anger. She sat unmoving, staring down at her shoes. She had no idea how she would explain an arrest to David's parents. Their name would be dragged into the report of wrongdoing. David's position in the company would suffer.

They might know a lawyer who specializes in keeping things quiet.

"May I make another phone call?" she asked.

"I'll let the police decide that," he said.

"May I go to the restroom?" she asked.

"No," he snapped. "Just sit tight."

Vendors began trickling in to the market, waving to the manager as they passed by his open office. A few looked curiously at Laila. She was dusty, parched, uncombed, and sweaty, but most of the vendors gave her a friendly smile.

Sales people make sales, not judgments.

The manager's cell phone pinged, and he answered. "Hello. In my office. Let me see." He picked up the form Laila had completed. "Laila Harrow," he said. He furrowed his brow and read once more from the sheet. "Yes," he continued. "Five-foot one inch."

He listened a moment and puckered his mouth in disapproval.

"I don't recommend it. Not by yourself. The security people are going to be hopping mad."

He listened a few moments longer, sitting forward in his chair, like a man receiving unpleasant news.

"Fine. Suit yourself." He put on his jacket and slipped the phone in his pocket. "Let's go," he said to Laila. "And take this purse with you."

"Where?"

"The owner's here. She wants to talk to you."

He led her through the market, put in the exit code at the rear gate, and directed her toward a small SUV in the corner of the vendor parking lot. The driver's door opened, and Regina stepped out.

"Thanks, Mac," she said. "I'll get to the bottom of this and call you shortly."

Laila, wordless, gaped at Regina, and the two of them watched as the flea market manager took his leave and walked stiffly across the lot to the gate.

"Please get in, Ms. Harrow," Regina said stoically.

CHAPTER TWENTY-SIX

Friday, Day Thirteen – Regina Has Her Say

Laila climbed into the passenger seat of Regina's SUV and saw Ken in the back seat. Relieved, she smiled at them both.

"You two! How did you know where I was? I'm so glad to see you," she said.

Regina shook her head and returned the smile with an expression of frustration. "I don't know where to begin with you," Regina said.

She was sitting sideways in the driver's seat, resting her head on the neck support and looking at Laila as if she deserved both pity and a smack on the face.

Regina looked at Ken pleadingly. "Help me out here," she said.

"Laila, what possessed you to break in to the booth?" Ken asked.

"Do you guys know Elizabeth Powell?" Laila asked. "Is she your friend, Regina?"

"She's my cousin," Regina said.

"And her *employee*," Ken added.

"You own the booth?" Laila asked, drawing back from Regina. "*You* are selling Highwaymen paintings?"

"I own thirty-six Highwaymen. I used to own fifty. I sell them to augment my salary. I'll be selling quite a few to pay for the next four years for Mindy," Regina said.

"But that's not really your business," said Ken brusquely.

"They are beautiful," said Laila. "Why are you hiding them?"

"It's not your business," Regina said, less gently than Ken had.

"It's for my research project," Laila said. "For the museum."

"For the museum?" Regina laughed bleakly. "Tell me about that."

"We'd like to do a catalogue of all the Highwaymen paintings. It's a huge project, I know, but it will bring attention to them, and maybe more value," Laila explained.

"We?" asked Regina. "Who is 'we'?"

Laila looked questioningly at her, then at Ken. "The St. Augustine Museum board," she said. "I'm volunteering to help the Acquisitions Committee."

"Laila, you're working for Geoff Hardinger, plain and simple," Regina said. "There's not ever going to be a catalogue."

"Yes, there is!" Laila reiterated. "I've located dozens of the Highwaymen paintings. Billie helped me create a location map, and some of them could be stolen." Laila stopped short and looked at Regina with dismay. "You know Geoff?" Laila asked.

"Quite well. I've seen him in action."

Laila ignored Regina's flare of anger and continued her search for an answer. "Regina, do you know where those Highwaymen came from?"

Regina turned away, shaking her head angrily. She opened the driver's door, got out, and closed the door behind her. Laila turned and looked at Ken.

"You'd better give her a moment," he said. "She's pissed."

"At me?" Laila said. "Why?"

"You and your friends at the museum. She explained it to me on the way over, but it's better coming from her," he said.

They sat in silence for the next few minutes. Laila checked her phone again. It was only nine-thirty, and she felt as if she had lived a week in the past few hours. The morning was warming up, and she opened her door to get the air circulating. She looked back at Ken, but he was sitting back, his eyes closed, his face showing the strain of the conversation. In Regina's side mirror, Laila could see her friend resting against the SUV, her arms folded, her head bowed in meditation. Finally, she rejoined them in the car.

"Look, Laila, you've got serious trouble coming up, and I don't want to make it more complicated," Regina said. "So, I'll be brief."

"What trouble?" Laila asked.

"I'm going to get to that," Ken said from the back seat.

"I own each and every painting that I sell. That you had to ask me is very difficult," she said.

"Insulting," said Ken. He was leaning into the gap between the front seats, his hand on Regina's arm as if comforting her.

"It's not uncommon," Laila began.

"How would you know about the Highwaymen? How would you know anything but what you read in a book?" Regina asked. "Please don't tell me about my paintings."

"The museum could help preserve them and increase their value," Laila protested.

"Laila, the museum is using you. Geoff Hardinger is a broker, and he's in the business of making money from art. Everything you tell him is for the purpose of him collecting art at the best prices he can," she said. "Ask any vendor in the market."

"A catalogue is for everyone, for members of the public," Laila said.

"Laila, listen. There's not going to be a catalogue. There was *never* going to be a catalogue," Regina said. "Let me take a wild stab at it. They told you to keep the research confidential because thieves might get wind of it and hide paintings."

"Something like that," Laila admitted.

"Well, here's something confidential," Regina said. "Mindy's father was one of the Highwaymen. He was married when we were together, but the paintings were his way of taking care of her. *Confidentially.*"

"Does Mindy know?" Laila asked.

Regina grabbed the steering wheel and shook it. She stopped and rested her forehead on the wheel and took some deep breaths. Ken reached over and placed a hand on her back in sympathy.

"Laila, I'm going to drive home with you now," said Ken. "Regina has a full day of work."

Ken said goodbye to Regina and hopped out of the car. He opened Laila's door and offered her a hand down. They walked to Laila's car, and as she rooted in her purse for her keys, Regina pulled out of the parking lot without waving goodbye.

"Let's go to my place," Ken said. "I have something you must see. I'll drive." Laila tossed him the keys, and they climbed in her car.

"I'm making a mess of everything," Laila said, looking to Ken, hoping for forgiveness.

"Pretty much," Ken said.

The whirl in Laila's mind roiled her stomach, and it lurched sickeningly at every turn and sudden stop. Her face burned with guilt. They rode in silence while worry and shame convinced her that Regina would no longer be a friend. When the causeway arched over the Inland Waterway, she looked down mournfully at the flat blue water. A malign component hid among the sandbars and palm trees. "The enemy of my friend is my enemy."

What if I can't tell the difference: friend or enemy?

Ken and Regina, deeply disappointed with Laila, had still plucked her from the threat of prosecution at the flea market. Ken was upset, but in the worst of circumstances, he showed a core of control and consideration. Regina was also hurt, but not in a blind fury.

They are friends. They've got to stay my friends.

If anyone was furious, it was Laila. Furious at herself. That realization calmed her enough to form some questions.

"Why was she upset with me?" Laila said.

"Why didn't you ask *her* that question?" Ken replied. "You asked her things that weren't your business instead of asking what was very much your business."

"What can I do?" Laila asked.

"Do you love your boys?" Ken asked.

"As if they are the limbs of my body. Four boys, four limbs," she answered.

"So, you know how Regina feels about Mindy," he said.

Laila's chin dropped to her chest, and tears burned at the corners of her eyes.

I was asking her to explain, when I was the one barging in.

"I didn't know Regina was involved. If I had known she was the owner of the booth, I never would have done this."

"She knows that," said Ken. "She'll calm down about that. It's the museum she's mad at."

"And me?" asked Laila.

"To the extent you act like them, sure," he said. "Just the idea that you and the committee could undertake research about these artists and not consult the painters themselves, many of them still living nearby, I mean, it boggles the imagination."

"The committee members thought that should wait until we knew more locations of the paintings," Laila said.

"Laila! You of all people! That's so white! It's so rude," Ken exclaimed.

"The paintings are beautiful. I just wanted to save them," Laila murmured.

"Save them from whom? From their black owners? For whom? For white collectors who have recently discovered there's money to be made?"

"That wasn't my plan," Laila said. "What should I do?"

"I don't know the answer. But I suggest you leave Mindy out of it," he said.

"I know. I know," Laila cried. "That was so stupid. God, so stupid."

"You'll have a chance to tell her that. I promise," Ken said.

"So, Regina called off the police? The flea market manager isn't reporting me?" she asked.

"Yeah, you might begin there the next time you talk to Regina."

"I expect so," Laila answered.

They turned off the main boulevard of St. Augustine's Beach into Laguna Shores. Ken's building faced the sports center, close to the main entrance, but across the road from the beach. Less costly and relatively plain, the condos there tended to be inhabited by financially modest residents, most of them working full-time jobs, leaving the building abandoned most of the day. The sight of Bob Page, propped up against his car as though waiting for their arrival, surprised them both.

"The Research Club is still meeting?" Bob called as they got out of Laila's car.

"What's up, Bob?" Ken answered, his keys in hand, intent on bypassing Bob to get to the building entrance.

Bob cut across the parking lot to the sidewalk leading to the main door. He stood to the side as Ken and Laila walked straight ahead.

"I was just out for a walk, but I'm sorry. I have to ask." Bob smiled knowingly. "So, it's officially a murder investigation?" As he got closer, Bob registered Laila's appearance. "Did you two go hiking or something?"

"Did the police pay you a visit?" Ken asked, disregarding the question. He rattled his keys as though they had no time to dawdle.

"Maybe," Bob answered cagily, a smile playing on his lips. "Seems Billie was deep into research, huh? Laila, what's this about Billie leaving you a note right before she died?" he continued. "Crazy, huh?"

Laila froze in her footsteps. The idea of the dolphin card and David's name bandied about in every conversation around the pool or on the tennis courts loomed before her, and she felt unsteady on her feet.

Ken laughed loudly. "Bob, they're going to deputize you, I'm sure," he said. "By the way, is Billie's son planning another night at Berman's?"

"I have no idea," Bob said.

"I think people would want to know. Can't you find out?" Ken asked with an air of incredulity.

"I can check," Bob allowed.

"Call me, will you, when you find out?" Ken took Laila's arm and ushered her past Bob and inside the building entrance.

Inside Ken's condo, Laila flopped down on the sofa, grateful to be safe and sound—and wondering if she could regroup in time to pick up her boys.

"Don't get too comfortable," Ken warned. He brought his laptop out of his office and sat it on the coffee table in front of the sofa. Laila sat up and leaned forward as he clicked to a grainy photograph.

An image of David and Claire in a watery moonlight, face-to-face and deep in conversation spread across the screen.

"What is this?" she asked. "Where is this?"

"David would have to tell you that. I don't know."

Laila sat staring at Ken, misery in her eyes and anger in her clenched fists. "How'd you find it?"

"This," Ken began, "is from the cloud. I accessed Billie's cloud storage."

"Her cloud storage? Why? When?" Laila asked.

"After the police asked me to take a polygraph test," he said. "I'm not cool with being a suspect."

"It doesn't even look real," Laila said. "It could be doctored. Anybody could have made it." She touched the screen and traced David's head as though measuring it. She stared a long moment at Claire's face.

"You know how Jackson asked you for a phone to attach to the telescope? It made me think about Billie's phone and why someone would want it. I realized she might have been taking pictures without people knowing—or at least without their permission."

"This was taken through Billie's telescope?"

"From the graininess, I'd say yes. Taken at night," Ken said.

"On the beach then," said Laila.

"Or the fishing pier," Ken said.

He paused, and she sat quietly with shallow intakes of air, feeling as if the business of living had become other people's concern, not hers. She needn't bother breathing. It brought no pleasure.

"I have to give it to the police," Ken said.

His words hit her heart like a shot of adrenalin.

"What? Why?"

"Billie wasn't interested in idle gossip. If she kept this picture, it's because she suspected something serious."

Laila felt the day was spiraling out of control. A turning, spilling feeling grabbed her, and an impulse to smash the computer was at war with an equally strong need to scream and cry.

"Why you? Why do *you* have it?"

"The police asked how the club shared information, and I said we delivered oral reports at each meeting. I said that sometimes Billie engineered a program for another club member, but each member kept their own files," Ken explained.

"Well, of course," Laila said. "But, how did you get this?"

"Last month, Billie found a photograph of a surfing championship that I had been looking for. She put it in her Google docs drive and sent me the link and password."

"She shared this photo with you, too?" Laila asked, horrified.

"No, but I kept the password. It worked on her cloud storage. It was as if she wanted it to be found."

"That's your assumption," Laila said angrily. "You didn't have a right to go into her personal files. You have no right to this photo. The police don't. No one does!"

"Benjamin does," Ken said quietly. "He deserves to know what's going on."

Stay alert. Don't panic. You are needed now.

"Was there a date associated with the photo?" Laila asked.

"It's the last photo in her cloud storage, taken Thursday night."

"What else? Was there anything else in there? Something someone would want to kill for?" Laila asked. She knew she raised her voice, and by the look on Ken's face, he wasn't sympathetic.

"Documents," he said tersely. "They looked like things she had gone looking for to help us with our projects. Surfing championships, an explanation of Bitcoin transactions, County Commission budgets, your Haitian genealogy stuff – all that was saved and labeled."

"My art project?" she asked.

"Nothing I saw. But she did have links to Haitian birth records from way back before the twins were born. Were you looking for a sibling of the twins?"

"What? Why were you looking at that?"

Ken didn't respond. He picked up the laptop and walked back to his office. When he returned, he sat on the edge of the chair opposite the sofa, keeping his distance.

"You can cut your way into Regina's antiques booth, but I can't look at research into the boys' background? Do you get how unbelievably obnoxious that is?"

"I'm sorry. I'm sorry," she said. She searched through her bag for a tissue. Ken retrieved one from the bathroom for her.

"You're saying that a lot today," he said.

"Nothing is making sense," she said. "All of a sudden, nothing in my life is making sense."

"David and Claire?" he asked.

"How could that be a thing? How could that be possible?" she cried. "Then who is Brick? What is she doing with Brick?"

"Brick is married," Ken said.

"Was that in Billie's Google drive too?" she asked.

"No. I did more research," he said.

"I hope I never hear that word again," she groaned. "I never want to hear about research again."

"Sometimes, it's better to know. Anyway, it wasn't all that difficult to find out. Those guys in Melbourne who recognized Brick told me he's got a wife so far gone into dementia she doesn't recognize anybody."

"How would they know that?" she asked.

"Because they know he's in debt, and they make it their business to know why and how much in debt their customers are."

"So, Brick is desperate for money, and Brick and David are fighting over Claire, and two strangers in Melbourne can tell you about it? " she cried. She stalked to the window, and then whirled on Ken. "Am I the only person who walks around not knowing what the fuck is happening?" she asked.

"Laila! Language!" Ken said. For the first time that day, Laila saw him smile.

CHAPTER TWENTY-SEVEN

Friday, Day Thirteen – David Reveals His Problem

Laila left Ken's to drive the short distance home, tears misting her vision. She grazed Bob Page's heels as he crossed the road to the community sports center, giving her the fright of her life, and by the way he jumped, giving him a scare, too. She hit the brakes hard and pulled over to the curb.

Why doesn't that man stay home? He's everywhere.

"Bob!" she said, stepping over to the sidewalk. "I'm so sorry! I was distracted. Where are you headed?"

"The office. Bills to pay. Insurance to arrange. Speed limits to enforce." He slid his sunglasses down his nose and looked sternly over them at her.

Wait. He might be useful.

"You're the best, Bob. You're like the backbone of Laguna Shores."

"You pay on time," he said. "Not like some knuckleheads around here."

"I admire your patience, and I'm so sorry if I scared you." She walked to the driver's side of the car while Bob watched, basking in her attention.

Reaching for the door handle, she gave him one of her gentle smiles. "Bob, I have a little favor to ask. It's kind of a secret."

"I'm great with secrets," he assured her.

"It's about Claire Benetton. Do you know Claire?"

"Of course. She's sold condos here. Really, Laila, what a question!"

"So, she's being very mysterious about her birthday. We wanted to make a fuss because she always does for everybody else, but she won't divulge the date. She's so stubborn!" Laila managed a giggle.

"Sounds like Claire. She's all business, no charm," he said.

"Can you peek in some file someplace and find out the right day for me?"

"You're inviting me to the party?" he asked.

"I thought maybe a surprise at the community meeting room? She'll be shocked."

"I'll call you later," he smiled conspiratorially.

She had scarcely reached the building elevator when he called. He gave her the date, birth year included.

"So, she's no spring chicken, huh?" he said.

Laila clicked off with a shiver of disgust as much toward herself as toward Bob Page. But when the doors opened, she stepped out with her game face on.

"Finally!" Margaret greeted her.

She could manage last minute guests, failed soufflés, spilled trays of hors d'ouevres, hungry boys underfoot, and Laila's intermittent dieting, but Margaret couldn't handle a household without a schedule.

"Life is unpredictable," she would say, "so meals need to be on time."

Laila's surprise foray that morning must have knocked Margaret back on her heels. Laila needed to smother her concerns and burrow away for a moment to think uninterrupted.

"Did you miss me?" Laila asked.

"Did you get a job delivering the morning paper?" Margaret retorted.

"I've started running," Laila said. "I'm going to lose ten pounds."

"Is this about the surfing nonsense?" she said. "You do *not* need to lose any weight."

"That's kind," Laila said. "But I do need to shower and rest."

"No argument there," Margaret said. "We'll talk weekend food later."

Laila closed the door to her bedroom and dropped into a chair. In this room, the previous night, she and David made love. They had taken turns making the other moan, laughing about muffling each other's pleasure, proud of how late it was when they rolled away to separate sides of the bed. What did that mean to him?

Was their sex something he did so he could compare her with Claire?

Her fear was real, but the thought of David as Claire's lover created no image in Laila's mind. No picture formed of David in bed with another. It was inconceivable. But, still, there it was—a meeting in the dark on the beach—late nights that David worked, and extra days in Miami that appeared excessive—irritability that cropped up lately for no good reason. And his slip ups! He knew details about the program Billie created for Claire. He found out Claire was listing Billie's condo.

That information didn't come from me. That's something he discussed with Claire. Behind my back.

Laila showered, dowsing from her curly hair to her heels, scrubbing hard and rinsing as though she had been exposed to radioactive dust. She felt dirty and betrayed, a pathetic victim. At the same time, she felt conniving and manipulative. If she was vulnerable and exploited, she had also been greedy for success and willing to lie to get it. If she had been cheated on, she also violated the privacy of others. She had been brave but was terrified of what she now knew.

She toweled off, combed through the unruly mop of hair, and sat at her office computer. Billie had taught her some things about checking a person's background. Armed with Claire's birthdate, and after a small charge to her credit card, thirty minutes later, she had a few notes.

Ten years before, a woman named Claire Bennetton Franklin began serving two years in the Georgia state prison system for reckless endangerment. Newspaper accounts told the story of wrong-way driving under the influence. While no one was injured, police had rescued two young boys from her vehicle. It was her third DUI, and the judge imposed a heavier sentence than expected.

Her divorce from Patrick Franklin became final while she was in prison. Two years after Claire Franklin's parole was lifted, approximately six years ago, a woman named Claire Bennetton received a real estate license in the state of Florida. Laila found no record of property ownership for Claire Franklin or Claire Bennetton in Georgia or Florida.

Laila thought about the possibilities. The two boys in the car would be teenagers now. Claire might owe support payments or may have committed to providing college tuition. She may have racked up credit card debt while she reestablished herself after prison. The story about meeting Brick at an open house could be nonsense. What if she met him at a casino because she also has a gambling problem?

David has no idea who he's dealing with. She must be desperate for money. She'll take him for everything she can.

Laila's hair had dried wild, and hasty efforts to tame it were not successful. It didn't matter. David had returned her text and could meet her for lunch. He had an hour before he needed to leave for Miami.

Or wherever he really goes.

She hurried past a surprised Margaret and down to the parking lot. The place he named was near his office, a dockside café they liked for its shrimp cocktail. She arrived before him and chose a table inside since most of the restaurant's customers crowded onto the outside deck.

"Hey, babe," he greeted her. He was clean-shaven and sturdy, his sleeves rolled up as if he had been outside, inspecting a site. Most of his day was still ahead of him, while she felt battered, as if she had already lived through a year of days since that morning.

She stood to kiss him and rested her hand on his arm to keep her balance. The muscle of his biceps reminded her how hard he worked for what was supposed to be their shared future. Could he have thrown it all away for Claire?

It doesn't matter what he could do. I won't let him ruin us.

"What's up? Did I forget an anniversary?"

A waiter came by, and they both ordered the shrimp cocktail and sweet tea. The man brought crackers and bread sticks and withdrew.

She couldn't bear to look at him. She leaned forward, her arms folded on the table and her eyes on two comical daisies stuck in a vase between the place settings.

"Before I say anything, you have to promise me to be one hundred percent honest, no matter what."

"Of course," he answered. "Is this about my family?"

"*Our* family," she said.

"Has Eddie done something?" He sighed.

Laila had practiced a half-dozen ways to arrive at the core of the issue and without giving in to anger or jealousy. They escaped her now, and she charged down the most direct path.

"How did you know Claire had gotten a program from Billie? Do you see her?"

"Claire?" he asked, his tone betraying no emotion. He lifted a breadstick to his mouth and thought better of it, letting it drop and bounce off the corner of his plate. "Why?"

"Just tell me," she demanded.

"I see her when she comes over—and at happy hour."

"I saw a picture of you with her at night." Laila tried to control them, but the tears welled up, and she couldn't talk without sobbing first. She angled her face toward him.

His smile vanished. He pulled out his wallet, signaled the waiter with urgency, and gave him a credit card.

"We need to talk," he said. "Privately."

He signed the receipt at the hostess' station and walked her to the door, with no expression but a brief nod to the wait staff.

"I've got to re-park the car. I saw your car, and I'll meet you there."

Laila got in her car and let a flood of tears soak her cheeks. She gave up trying to control her desperation, and her shoulders shook as she buried her face in her hands and sobbed. By the time David opened the passenger door and got in, the temperature in the car had reached sauna territory.

"Can you drive?" he asked.

She nodded and pulled away from the curb.

"Bell Beach would be best. It's lonely in the early afternoons."

She looked at him wide-eyed, horrified by why he might know such a detail.

"No, Laila, it's not like that. I run there some days, instead of eating lunch."

They drove the few blocks in silence. Laila didn't want to talk without being able to look David in the eyes to judge his reactions. David looked straight ahead, as though he were driving, not Laila.

No one was in the beach parking lot. Nevertheless, she chose a far corner, put down the windows, and let a cool breeze cross through the car. She turned toward him.

"Claire is complicated," he said. He gazed towards the sand and the ocean.

"Yes?" she said. The words she was thinking were larger, faster, and uglier, but she was helpless to get anything past the sobs in her throat.

"We're involved in a transaction," he said. "And sex is the last thing on our minds."

"That doesn't mean you don't do it, and what kind of 'transaction' are you talking about?"

"God, Laila, how could I cheat on you? How could I do that to you? Risk losing you? I'd be crazy."

He leaned his arm on the open window and propped up his chin with his hand. Laila almost smiled at the mournfulness of his expression. There was a picture with Claire, however, whether he regretted it or not.

"Is this about gambling?" she asked.

"No!" David looked at her, unbelieving. "Why would you say that? When have I ever gambled?"

"Brick gambles," Laila managed.

"Brick! Who is he? A cop? A gambler? Who is he?"

"He's married," she said.

"How did you find that out?" he asked.

"Ken."

"He knows about Claire?"

"He showed me the picture of you and Claire on the beach at night."

David cradled his head in his hands and groaned. "Did Ken tell you Claire and I are having an affair?" he asked.

"What else would he think?" she cried.

"It's totally not true. If I thought she could ever tell the truth, just once in her life, I'd tell you to ask her."

"What were you doing with her then? You're nose to nose in the picture," she said.

"Claire and me in bed? Even if I were slightly interested, which I'm not, why would she bother? I don't have what she wants."

Laila was getting her breathing under control, and her tears were slowing.

David was stressed and mixed up with Claire, but not, she decided, in a way that indicated betrayal. He wasn't apologetic enough for that.

He lifted his head and loosened his tie. He turned toward her. "Why has Ken gotten involved?"

"The police asked him a lot of questions, so in self-defense, he broke into Billie's cloud storage, and that photo turned up," she said. "We came to the same conclusion."

"It's not a bad conclusion," he said. "It's better than the truth."

"Then, what's the truth? It can't be worse than you having an affair with one of my friends," she sputtered.

He reached out and took her hand. "I'm sorry. I'm so sorry. But listen; erase any idea of me in bed with anybody else. It didn't happen with Claire. It's never going to happen. *You* are the one person I love."

She wanted to believe him. She squeezed his hand back, but he hadn't explained the photo, and he was dodging her questions about the 'transaction' he mentioned. What were he and Claire doing out at night together?

"I have to go to Miami today. I mean it's key. I have to see Sam and Dad—and figure this out."

"Figure what out?" she asked. "Tell me what's going on."

"Look, please, don't go near any of these club members. I don't care if you and the boys have to hide at home all weekend. Don't exchange even one text with anyone. Please."

"David, please. What's going on?" she asked.

"It's bad, but it's not terrible."

"Then, tell me what's going on, so we can get through it together," she yelped.

"No. With help, I can handle this, and then, I'll explain everything. But, I swear, I have nothing to do with Claire romantically or sexually or anything.

Nothing like that. It's a money thing, and it has to do with the business, and it's complicated."

"Did she ask you for money?" Laila guessed.

He sighed. "It has to do with greasing people's palms, and it wasn't much money, but it got out of control," he said. "It's not anything any contractor doesn't do, but it's still trouble, and I'm going to take care of it."

"Bribes? You're talking about bribing someone?" she asked. "What would Sam say? You're crazy!"

"It was just to get a left turn lane into the mall. It's something the county would do eventually; I'm just hurrying up the process a little bit. Sam and Dad aren't thrilled, but they know how things work. It'll keep us on schedule, and that's important."

"And Claire knows?" she asked.

"Claire is about Claire. She thinks because I get things done, I can help her get her hands on real estate to sell. Apparently, she wants to move into commercial properties. I'm not interested, but she's pushy."

Bribery, combined with a sales pitch? Laila had never sold real estate, but she found David's explanation unworkable. Fishy, actually, if she was being honest.

"She needs money. I think she might be really desperate for money," said Laila.

"Aren't we all?" He smiled. "And the question is—'Is she desperate, or just greedy?'"

"I don't believe you and Claire were talking about a possible career move," she said.

David shook his head, waving a hand as if he could dispel the trouble with a wand. "Of course not, " he said. "But nothing with Claire is what she says it is. She's trouble."

"And Sam can help you? Sam and your Dad can help?"

"Consider it taken care of," he said. "But just to be clear, did Ken know how Billie got the photo?"

"She attached her phone to her telescope. Like Jackson wants to do to get pictures of the moon."

"Were there more photos? Photos of me?" he asked.

"Ken didn't show me more than that one," she said. "Would there *be* more?"

Laila could tell that David didn't like the question and that he tried to disguise his reaction with another wave. "Whatever," he said, which was a phrase he did not permit the boys to use. He scratched his head and gave Laila a weak smile. "It's not important."

"You're not telling me everything. Who else is involved?" she asked.

"No one!" he said quickly. "Harrow United, but no one else." He gave her another faux smile. The relief she had felt at his denial of an affair began to fade with his forced confidence.

She wanted to tell him what they discovered about Brick and how she suspected that Brick tried to sabotage her foray into the flea market. She would have to admit how stupidly she risked the family name by playing detective and breaking into the booth. But she had gotten out of the mess, thanks to Regina and Ken, and if David had financial trouble involving Claire and whoever else, she didn't need to sidetrack him. Later, she could think through what would become of her friendships.

"I was so afraid. You with Claire – it would have broken me," she said.

He turned toward her and put his hands together as in prayer. "Please, trust me. We'll put this right, and things will calm down. I know it's been hectic. I've been preoccupied. It's going to get better. Success is just around the corner."

Laila wiped away a tear and nodded. With all her heart, she wanted to trust him.

"When I get back to the car," he said, " I'm going straight to Miami. I need Sam's help to work out this tangle. But really," he continued, his tone low and serious. "Keep your distance from Laguna Shores friends. Not Ken, not Claire, no one! Promise me."

"Of course," she said. *Why is he so threatened by them?*

He put his hands on her face and pulled her to him, his kiss as sweet as any they'd ever had. What she couldn't do was let him slip into the arms of another woman. If he had a problem, she could help.

Problems come into everyone's life, and they could solve them together. Harrow United – the exact name for what they were.

CHAPTER TWENTY-EIGHT

Friday, Day Thirteen – Claire and Brick Have a Plan

Afeter leaving David at his car, Laila went home to regain her routine as best she could. Friday afternoons with the kids usually went well. This Friday, Eddie brought a friend home from school, and with five boys, she trooped down to the pool for a swim. She imagined that anyone passing by would be discouraged from taking a dip by the gaggle of shouting and splashing kids.

She took a break from a water fight to check her phone. David had not called, and she ignored the call from Ken. He might have information on the direction the detectives were taking Billie's murder investigation, but that discussion had to wait. David asked for a promise of silence, and though she wasn't sure why, she intended to comply.

She cannonballed back into the pool and upheld her end of another ferocious water battle with Alton and Eddie on her side, and the rest lined up against them. Eddie's pal had a wicked aim, and at one point, her eyes stung with chlorine so badly she pulled herself up on the edge for some relief. Through her blurred vision, Laila thought she saw the familiar red of Brick's haircut slipping out the side door of the sports center and around the corner toward the parking lot.

I'll catch up with him eventually. We will definitely have a talk!

Refraining from calling Brick and Claire would be the hardest part of her bargain with David. She'd like to have a few moments with Claire to discuss keeping secrets from friends and the danger her shenanigans posed to David. And that Brick! Why would he want his plan with the key code to backfire? She seethed thinking about how close she had come to arrest that morning because of his idiotic idea.

At least the flea market fiasco was behind her. Regina had convinced her to stop sleuthing against owners of Highwaymen paintings. Jennifer and Geoff would be called to account for their intentions and secrecy. When she had time, she'd visit Fort Pierce and view whatever collection was on display at the city museum. She'd act like a proper patron of the Highwaymen, not a spy.

The boys complained of hunger, so they returned home to a barbecue on the balcony. Margaret knew they ached when David was away weekend after weekend, so she enlisted Caya for an impressive spread. The women provided thick burgers, mac and cheese, favorite dips and chips, watermelon salad, and homemade cookies for dessert.

As Laila watched them eat with the intensity of wild beasts, she daydreamed about the possibility of adding a daughter to the crew. Would she be different? Would she be a feminine counterbalance to the jostling and noise of boys? Or would she be more of an athlete than Eddie? More of a jokester than Forrest?

Laila knew it was wrong to hope an abandoned sibling of the twins existed in Haiti waiting to be found. Any such calculation was abominable, and she rebuked herself for doting on the idea. If there were any sibling, boy or girl, Laila had an obligation to find the child. Period. It wasn't something to rejoice about. David's work in Miami in the Haitian community years ago had brought the twins into their lives. She had to complete the process and keep the family members together.

But, oh, a daughter.

The boys suggested going out for ice cream, and in an abundance of caution, Laila refused. They must have been full to the gills because there were no serious complaints, even from Forrest, and the group settled in front of the big screen for movie night.

By the time the parent of Eddie's friend picked him up, the group was drowsy, and then some. She could pick up the sleeping Alton, but Eddie had to carry Forrest to his bed. The older boys, droopy-eyed, said goodnight, and Laila, with a cup of tea, sat with a book in the living room. Margaret was long gone, and Caya, late to leave because of the barbecue cleanup, waved goodbye from the foyer.

When the elevator chimed, Laila didn't look up. It would be Caya, back to pick up whatever she had forgotten. The girl was as harebrained as Laila had been at that age, but she'd find her way eventually.

"Don't get up."

When she heard Brick's voice, her hand jerked from her lap and sent the book flying, but she couldn't get up to retrieve it. Brick had trained his gun on her. Claire was by his side.

"Where are the boys?" Claire asked.

The gun was nothing short of a cannon to Laila. The barrel was huge, and at any moment, it could issue deadly fire. Brick's hand was steady. His aim would be good, Laila reckoned. She had no escape.

"Gone," Laila whispered. "At a sleepover."

"You know that's not true," Claire said. "Does Brick need to go get them out of bed?"

Brick started toward the bedroom hallway.

"Don't touch them," Laila said. "They'll sleep until morning. They won't move."

"And David?" asked Brick.

"Tell us now," said Claire.

"You already know, don't you? He's in Miami," Laila answered.

"You're going to help him tonight," Brick said.

"We have a plan," said Claire.

Laila was silent, watching them dominate her living room. Brick had moved back to the center of the room with his back to the balcony, and Claire took a seat on the sofa. Predatory and uniform, both in gray sweats, black t-shirts, and running shoes, the couple displayed an ease that heightened Laila's fear. The barrel of the gun was hypnotic, and Brick aimed it unwavering at Laila.

Claire said something, but her words were noise, nothing Laila understood, not like she understood the gun pointed at her.

"Laila, listen," Claire's voice was raised. "I said I'll stay here with the boys, and you go with Brick," Claire said.

Her voice broke through Laila's focus on the gun, and she looked at Claire. Her nose had a perfect tilt, her eyes were large, and her neck was sleek. Her looks unnerved Laila. It was as if Brick and Claire had always carried weapons of steel and beauty, and she had just come to realize it.

"No," Laila answered. "Never. I'm not leaving you with my kids."

Claire smiled over her shoulder at Brick. She looked back at Laila and nodded approvingly.

"I told him you weren't going to volunteer. Not Mama Bear."

"What do you want?" she asked.

"We need to get out of trouble," Claire said.

"David said he's going to fix it. He'll be back Sunday."

"Is that what he told you?" Claire said. "He's protecting you."

"David doesn't understand the situation," Brick said.

Everything was off balance. A gun was not the solution to the kind of problem David described. He said he had a financial glitch to straighten out. Claire and Brick were threatening to harm her and to take the children hostage.

David is in over his head.

"David was right," Laila said. "You're greedy. Doing this for some kind of real estate! You'll get caught. Both of you."

"Real estate?" Claire started to laugh, then thought better of it. "Is that how David explained the card from Billie? God, Laila, you really think he walks on water, don't you?"

"What do you know about that card?" Laila asked. She got up from her chair to start toward Claire, but Brick quickly drew closer.

"Sit!" he said.

Laila collapsed back onto her chair.

What does Brick have against David? Why is he trying to ruin them?

"The card wasn't real. You! You left the card with David's name on it at Billie's. You want to get us in trouble. That's why you set me up at the flea market," Laila said.

"No to the card, yes to the flea market," said Claire. "It might not have been his smartest move," she said. She leveled an 'I told you so' look at Brick.

"Your arrest could have been a useful distraction," said Brick. "We might have been able to slip out of town. But it didn't work."

"You killed Billie," Laila said. "You killed her and tried to make us look guilty."

"Show her," said Brick.

Claire pulled a cell phone from the pocket of her sweats. She flicked it on and hit an icon on the screen. She turned it for Laila to see. The picture was askew and out of focus, poorly taken as if it were snapped in a hurry. A man's face filled the screen, mouth open in conversation, and unaware of a camera. The man was Jake Hanlon.

"Jake? Bailey Hanlon's Dad?" Laila couldn't guess the relationship of Jake to Claire or Brick. "How do you know him?" she asked. "What's this mean?"

"Billie's phone," said Brick. "That's the last photo taken on Billie's phone."

"Not true," said Laila. "You're making things up. I saw her cloud. I saw the last picture."

"*This* is Billie's phone," Claire said, and she reached the phone to Laila. The screen saver was unmistakably Billie's – a picture of the moon taken through a telescope, the lacunae shining in stark beauty. Whenever Jackson was around, Billie would pull out that photo.

"Oh, my Lord. You killed her. You have her phone? Do you have her computer, too?"

"No. When you left Billie's the afternoon we were cleaning up, I went in the kitchen to make coffee. It was buried in the coffee bean container, and I fished it out," Claire said.

"If that's true, then you should have given it to Benjamin," Laila said.

"*You* would have," said Claire. "But I knew something you didn't. So, I kept it."

"We've got to go," Brick said. "Tell her."

"Who are you?" Laila asked Brick.

"Never mind," he answered. "Claire, come on."

"When I had a chance to examine the phone, there were two important things. Billie had this picture of our esteemed County Commissioner looking angry and up close. And she had turned off the Wi-Fi and data."

"But the picture has a date and time?" Laila asked.

"Saturday night, at eleven forty-five," Claire said. "A last, desperate picture that Billie didn't want on the cloud. She could hide the phone, hoping someone would find it, but she knew she couldn't protect her computer from Jake."

Brick shifted his position, coming around the sofa, closer to Laila. He seemed impatient, and Laila was petrified one of the boys would wander into the room and into the line of fire.

"So, we guess he came to Billie to do a deal. At some point, she said she was going to make coffee, and she hid the phone. But she wouldn't do the deal, and she was killed," Claire continued.

"What's wrong with you? This is all something the police should know," Laila said in a quiet but desperate voice.

"Maybe. But that would be very bad for David," said Claire. "*David* was part of Jake's deal."

"No. You're trying to get back at David. You want to blackmail him or something. And he's not cooperating, and you're going to get back at me now." Laila's terror turned to seething, a fury at having Claire and her henchman in her house, armed and dangerous and close to her children.

"No, Laila. David made his arrangements with Jake on his own. He was paying Jake for favors like right-of-ways and height permits and housing waivers. I could go on, but it's better to get to Brick's plan."

"There's no plan," cried Laila. "The only plan is to tell the police. You have nothing to do with any of this."

"Shhh," said Claire. "The boys."

"Claire, you wouldn't hurt them," Laila said. She got up from the chair again, and Claire pushed her down. Brick moved closer, the gun trained expertly on Laila.

"Jake left the dolphin card as a warning to David. David *knows* that Jake is the killer. I showed him Billie's phone. But he thinks he can buy him off. Promise silence, pay a fat bribe, and let the police wander around trying to find the computer and phone. Make Billie's death into a cold case."

That's what David meant by fixing the situation. Getting the bribe money from Sam.

Brick was watching Laila. "I think she's getting it," he said.

"But Jake won't stop causing your husband major difficulties. David will always be under threat. Jake will never let up—or worse, a bigger Jake will come along and take over the Harrow United account. It's so predictable, it's sad," Claire said.

"What do you care? You care about David? What is he to you?" Laila spat at Claire.

"I like you guys," Claire said. "I always thought you brought a touch of class to Laguna Shores. And your boys are an interesting bunch."

"Claire, please," Brick said. His voice was growing edgy.

"But I'm involved because I've been blackmailing Jake, and he's not going to let me get away with it. Billie's murder was a warning to me, too. He has her computer with all my research and all the proof of his corruption. He now owns *my* leverage as well as evidence that makes it look like I killed Billie." Claire sat back in the sofa and threw up her hands. "I've gotten some money from Jake, but now, he owns my safety. I need to get out of Dodge."

"So go," said Laila. "Go."

"That's what your husband told me, too. He didn't want to help us trap Jake. So, we have come up with Plan C," Claire said.

"I'll give you money, Claire. You and Brick. Go to another city and forget this," Laila pleaded. "I know about your children. I'll help them, too."

Claire narrowed her eyes and stared at Laila with a look of hate so violent Laila looked away and back at Brick. His gun barrel was less threatening than Claire's anger.

"How do you know?" she hissed.

"Research. I did research," Laila sputtered.

A cold smile curled Claire's lips. "Of course, you did. Billie's little offspring. Of course."

"I understand why this is so important to you," Laila offered. Claire's expression hardened into a mask of determination.

"Spare me the empathy. I'm already a felon. If Jake or the police get to me, I won't see my children ever again," she said. "I won't let that happen."

"So, here's how it's going to work," said Brick.

Laila listened carefully. After Brick finished, Claire followed Laila into her bedroom and watched her change into sweats, a t-shirt, and running shoes. Claire insisted she leave the door open when she used the toilet. They marched back into the living room, and Claire took Laila's phone from its carrier bag and inserted Billie's phone in its place.

"See you soon." Claire waved to Brick as he and Laila got on the elevator.

CHAPTER TWENTY-NINE

Friday, Day Thirteen – The Trap

The backyard of the empty house would have been pitch black except for the light spilling from a neighbor's upstairs bedroom. It filtered through the trees and created shadows that shimmied with the breeze. Laila walked through the left side gate, past beds of lilacs and hyacinth that curved around the back deck. She stepped towards the middle of the darkened yard into a splash of light.

She rubbed her feet back and forth in the grass as she waited, hoping to get traction, in case she had to run. If guns were drawn, she was told she should run directly through the break in the bushes into the neighbor's yard.

She whistled lightly, as she had been instructed. Jake Hanlon stepped from behind the box hedges on the right side of the deck. He wore sweats and thick-soled athletic shoes.

"Where is Claire?" Jake asked.

"I have it," said Laila.

"What?" he asked.

"You know what, Jake," Laila said. "Look at it."

Jake took a few steps toward Laila, and the light behind him cast a shadow of his profile on the grass. She opened the pouch resting across her body and drew out Billie's phone.

"Did you bring the computer?" she asked.

He returned to the bushes and brought out a computer. He walked back toward her, the computer in his outstretched arms. A familiar picture of Billie and Jackson on the illuminated screen assured Laila that he was giving her the evidence they sought.

"I don't understand why you. . . ." Jake's thought broke off when they heard a noise from the deck.

Brick was scrambling to his feet. Without a word, gun in hand, he shot Jake in the back. Jake tumbled forward, face down on the ground.

Laila fell backwards onto the grass, a scream of horror gurgling in her throat. Her head snapped back, and her eyes rolled up behind her eyelids, making everything go black. A twirling vertigo made her want to stay on the ground. She wanted to throw up, get the panic out of her throat, and start crawling to her car. A lightning bolt of realization made her open her eyes.

I'm next. The next shot is for me.

She brought her head up and forced herself to look beyond Jake's splayed body. Brick squatted on the deck, keeping his eyes on Laila, and holstered the gun. He picked up a length of rope.

Claire lied. Everything about their plan was a lie.

Laila dropped Billie's phone and pushed herself to her feet. She darted left, toward the neighboring yard, but Brick was faster. He ignored the low stairs and leapt off the deck. She heard him coming and changed directions. If she could push through the box hedges where Jake had been hiding, she might get through to the street, her car, and an escape.

She ran an arc across the back of the lawn then veered toward the hedges. He cut back in front of her, his long legs bringing him into her path. She dodged from one side to another, but he hooked his foot around the back of her knee and she fell on the ground, her full weight bending her right hand back and sending bolts of pain up into her shoulder.

She tried to get up, but her arm was useless. With one knee bent, she pushed her hip up from the ground, but he got behind her. His knee pressed into her back like a rod that could snap her in two. She arched backwards toward him.

The rough hairs of the rope burned her skin as Brick wrapped it around her neck and then slid it back and forth, intentionally creating the most pain he could. Her hands went up to pull it loose, and he tightened his hold. Struggling made it worse, and the rope pressed in on her throat. He twisted her into a full back bend. His hand clapped over her mouth and nose. His fingers were strong and large enough to lock her jaw shut and squeeze her nostrils tight. The tree branches over her head fluttered and whirled, as if they were drunk. Her eyes, starved of oxygen, let the light and shadows blend into gray. As her shoulders touched the ground, wild panic pushed up from her heart to her head, blotting out her thoughts with pounding desperation.

Then, nothing.

CHAPTER THIRTY

Saturday, Day Fourteen – All's Well That Ends

She awoke with her head in his lap and his hand poised for a slap. Her face burned. He must have smacked her several times already.

"Stop!" she gulped. Her throat felt like someone had taken a razor to her esophagus. She wouldn't talk without pain for another week.

"Shut up," he hissed. "And don't faint on me."

"You shot him," she whispered.

"Listen to me," he rasped. "Get this straight. Are you listening?"

She stared up at him, transfixed, thinking about the rope, expecting more pain.

"He was raping you," Brick said. "I caught him ripping your clothes off. He had a rope around your neck."

"You're crazy," she said. "You're insane."

"He lured you here with a story about your son. He said Eddie was harassing the girls at school, and he had pictures of Eddie at a party. Nasty pictures. He got you here, and then his true purpose came out, and he got you down to rape you. The marks from the rope are on your neck."

"Jake Hanlon? He wouldn't know me from Adam," she squeaked.

"Yes, Jake. County Commissioner. Has a hand in every pocket up and down the coast. He'd know you. Don't worry about that."

"Why were you here?" she asked. "What were you doing at this 'supposed' rape?"

"You left Claire with the kids. She got worried and called me. She knew the address, and I arrived in the nick of time."

Laila pulled up her knees, and Brick didn't stop her. She realized that Brick was desperate but not crazed. He had a plan, a desperate plan, but somehow, he needed her in it.

Killing me is not the goal.

Brick's gun was holstered under his left armpit. She had no idea how to use it if she got hold of it, but it would be better off in her hands than his. He was a murderer; she was not.

"What was wrong with the first plan you told me?" she asked.

With her knees up and her feet on the ground, she might be able to roll herself off his lap in one move. She needed to free one hand from his grasp.

"We were going to exchange the phone for the computer. Everyone goes home," she reminded him, attempting to sound reasonable. She tried to make a gesture toward home with her hands. He held them fast.

"You give him the only existing picture that ties him to the murder, while the photo of David and Claire is floating around on the cloud. How would that work?"

"You said you guys would be happy," Laila answered.

"She'd never be safe from that piece of crap. And neither would David. We did you a favor. Now take it."

"We could never convince anyone. What about his body? It was murder."

She shifted her right elbow a few inches to prop herself up but yelped in surprise at the bolt of pain that shot up her arm.

"You hurt yourself?" Brick asked. He lifted one hand, letting her right wrist lie loose on her chest.

"No. *You* fucking hurt me," she gasped.

"That's good. You're plenty angry. He was really rough with you. He deserved what he got," he said.

"No, no. I can't do this! I wasn't raped," she cried.

"Yes, yes you can," he said. "Think it through. You can."

She let her body go limp, her head lagging to one side, pretending her will was bending to his. His face came closer as he nodded at her, as if they had finally reached an agreement.

Suddenly, Laila drove the index finger of her bad hand into Brick's eye, found the curve of his eyeball, and hooked it into the space behind it. He reared back, his hands fleeing to his face. She lifted and twisted her hips, her elbow finding his thigh. She stabbed it down hard and rolled off his lap. Her palm closed around a clump of grass, and she pushed up with her right arm, yelping in pain.

He leaned forward, one hand clapped to his eye, one reaching out and grabbing her arm. Pulling her down, he scrambled to his knees, but instinctively, she tugged away. He lurched forward, got one foot on the ground, and shoved himself toward her. The gun handle tilted out from his holster, and she grabbed it with her left hand.

"You idiot," he growled at her.

"Get back," she said, her voice a thin, painful shriek. She took her own two steps back.

"The neighbors will be out here. You make more noise than a frigging coyote," he hissed.

"I'm calling the police," she said.

"Laila, don't be stupid. Jake is gone, and David's bribes are erased."

"This is to help us? We don't want your help."

"David is up to his neck in this," he said.

"Thanks to Claire with her meetings on the beach with him. You're only going to hurt us."

Laila took a few more steps backward toward Billie's phone, left on the grass near Jake's body. Brick mirrored her, keeping a short distance between them.

"You're going to make a mess, Laila."

"Keep your eyes closed. It'll feel better." She cast a look behind her, trying to spot the phone.

"The police will see the photo, and they'll know what David has been doing. They'll say you and I murdered Jake to protect David and Claire."

"Who are you, really?" she asked.

"Jake hired me to investigate Claire. He couldn't stand her blackmailing. And I took his money and got friendly with Claire. But the thing is, I fell in love with her."

"And her kids? You have so much love for them?"

"She wants to go back to Atlanta, to work her way back to them. If she wants it, I want it."

One more step, and Laila's foot grazed the phone. She stooped, the gun steady in front of her, and grabbed it up. The evidence was all hers.

"And Billie?" said Laila.

"Exactly," he said. "We brought her killer to justice. That's what matters, right?"

"This is not the way she'd want it done," Laila said. She pulled up the dial screen on Billie's phone.

Brick stood, one hand covering the eye she attacked. The other eye focused angrily on the barrel of the gun. "You don't know how to use that," he said.

"It must be ready to shoot, or you would have already tried to grab it from me," she answered.

The gun was growing heavy in her hand, and her arms were trembling, but she kept one finger on the trigger.

"I will walk the police through this whole thing, moment by moment. You and Claire are going to jail," she said.

Brick moved one step closer.

"And David will go to jail, too. Claire has information on every bribe and every favor he got," he said.

"Every bribe? It was one stupid mistake, one bribe for one stupid left turn lane or something like that. It's what developers do."

"No. Claire has records. It's been going on for two years. Jake Hanlon had his hand in every decision, every purchase, what contractor to use for dirt removal, what contractor to use for foundations, where to buy the cement for the foundations, for God's sake. Harrow United was the big fat pig that Jake had trussed and ready for the luau."

"So, Billie knew that? Billie told Jake she knew that?" Laila's voice was as unsteady as her hand; her arm was aching, her shoulder throbbing, her voice box begging for a rest, her emotions working overtime.

"Billie knew that, yes," he said. "We figure Billie saw the patterns in Claire's research and took matters into her own hands. Like a good citizen, she approached her County Commission president and warned him to stop extorting money from her friends. Jake and Billie went to the same church, you know."

"Claire's church," she murmured.

"That's right," he said. "Claire made one, big mistake. She let Billie see her data."

"Why did she do that?" Laila asked.

"She underestimated Billie. She didn't realize how quickly and clearly Billie would recognize what she and David were up to."

She held the gun in front of her, phone tucked in her back pocket, her arms extended despite the pain in her wrist. Tears streamed from her eyes. The gun provided no protection from Brick's words.

"If you tell the police I shot Jake," he began again, "Claire and I might go to prison, but David will go, too. Most likely a few other Harrows will go. The bribes were coming out of Miami, right?"

Laila lowered the gun.

Billie died trying to protect my family and me.

"How long has David known that Jake killed Billie?" she asked.

"Since he heard about that card," he said. "The cute dolphin card."

"He told Claire about the card? David told Claire?" she asked, her voice rising in anger.

"Of course," said Brick. "He thought he could warn her off. Maybe make her see that Jake was too dangerous. He told her she was over her head."

"That's just what I thought about David. He was over his head."

"So now Jake is gone," Brick said. "Don't you see? We all have a chance to survive."

She looked at him and nodded. Her legs trembled. She couldn't run. Couldn't drive, even if she did reach the car.

It might work. It has to work now.

Brick looked at Laila, his one good eye blinking continually, his injured eye beginning to swell shut. "Good to go?" he asked.

"Jake wrecked your eye," she said.

"He was a very bad man," he answered.

He took the gun from her hand and reached for the phone. She handed it over and sunk to the ground. He retrieved the computer from the grass near Jake's body. He found the hose at the side of the house and sprayed them until they sat in a muddy puddle a few inches deep.

"I'll shove this stuff into the wheel well of my car," he said. "I'll bring back a knife for Jake. You know, the one he threatened me with—the reason I had to shoot him."

Laila nodded. The details were swimming now. A gun, a knife, a phone call from Jake, claims about Eddie. The story they must tell had a million details.

"My clothes?" she asked.

"Start messing them up," he answered.

In the grass where Jake had fallen, she lay next to him, rolling in her clothes, soiling them as best she could. She smeared dirt on her cheeks and tousled her hair, mixing twigs and cuttings into her curls. She kicked off her shoes, took off the sweatpants, and was working on staining and ripping her panties when Brick came back and made the 911 call.

"I'm reporting an attack. And there's been a shooting." As if hyperventilating, but still in control, Brick gave the address.

CHAPTER THIRTY-ONE

Saturday, Day Fourteen Plus - The Police Had Questions

Brick held the gun by the trigger so that it hung upside down from his thumb and forefinger. He picked it up from the ground near Laila, although she didn't remembered him placing it there. She had probably closed her eyes, trying to rehearse what would come next.

He offered it to the cop who came into the backyard, shooting arm extended, gun raking back and forth. He made Brick drop the pistol and lay face down on the grass. When the second cop came into the backyard by the other side of the house where Jake had crouched waiting for them just an hour before, he trained his gun on Brick, and the first cop approached Laila.

"Are you hurt?" he asked.

"I don't think so," she answered.

"Can you get up and walk?"

"Pretty sure, I can," she said. She inhaled a sob but not too loudly.

Brick had told her that she shouldn't overdo it. "Cops have seen real crying and fake crying, and they know the difference," he warned.

She didn't have to fake the pain her shoulder caused as she pushed up from her prone position. The muscles had stiffened from the prolonged contact with the cool earth—and from the flood of fear. On her knees, she pulled up her panties and sweats. She stood, holding on to the cop's arm, and twisted around to look at Jake. She had managed to roll away from him, avoiding his form, but now she saw him, splayed out, mouth open in a final grunt.

Her knees gave way, and she sank slowly back toward the ground, clutching the cop's bare forearm. He pulled her back up to a standing position.

"Do you know the dead man?" he asked, indicating Jake's corpse.

"Jake," she answered.

Brick had told her to answer with minimum information. "Make them ask the questions," he advised. "It's not your job to do their job."

"Jake what?" the policeman asked.

"Hanlon."

"How do you know him?"

"Just a little bit," she said.

The cop guarding Brick and the one holding her up both looked into her face, their brows furrowed. She wasn't prepared for the men's eyes trained on her, searching, she realizes now, for a false move or a revealing word.

"How did he die?"

"Shot," she said. "Shot with a gun."

She started to sink again, and as naturally as one might incline to pluck a weed from the grass, she bent and vomited. She let go of the cop and settled fully into her haunches because she knew the nausea hadn't passed. Once more, the reverse surge passed through her bruised esophagus, and she groaned.

Sirens sounded as more vehicles arrived, and the cop led Laila to the front of the house. The policeman kept behind her, a firm hand on her shoulder propelling her forward.

It was okay. Brick had told her to go easily and not worry about him. "I'll take care of my story," he said. "As far as you're concerned, I was an unexpected addition to the scene. I came out of nowhere and ended Jake's attack."

"Am I grateful?" she asked.

"You're traumatized," Brick answered.

That part was true.

The exam at the hospital was a blur. It was busy, and for a while, she was on a gurney parked in a hallway. At some point, she was in a curtained area, and a nurse removed her clothing, a very young female doctor, maybe even a med student who examined her and took some swabs. She was thirstier than she had ever been in her life, but she fell asleep until the morning. The first visitor was Detective Borden, and she asked him for water. He told her to ring for the nurse.

"What happened last night?" he began.

"I went to that house to meet Jake, and he attacked me. He was going to rape me," she said.

"Why did you want to meet him?"

"I didn't want anything," she said angrily. "He called me and told me to meet him there. He said he had some pictures of my son, Eddie—pictures that I wouldn't want anyone to see."

"But we know that's not true," said Borden.

"*Now*, I know that," she said. "Now, I know he just wanted to rape me."

"No, we know he didn't call you. We have your phone, and he never called you."

They have my phone? Oh, of course. Claire is with the kids. She gave them my phone. Brick didn't tell me that part.

"No, not call like a voice call," she sputtered. "He texted me. I erased it."

"We have your phone, and *you* texted him," Borden said.

The nurse came in, and Laila asked for water. She turned away from Borden and stared at the curtained partition. She was shaken, but she remembered the story Brick and she agreed upon. To keep the details straight, she imagined it like a painting she was working on, each character in the scene acting out his or her part. Claire was nestled in the house, caring for her children; Brick was the knight who rode to her rescue; David was the hard-working builder, far away in Miami. And Jake was the snake, luring her into evil, ready to strike, and full of venom. A killer once before, he'd kill again.

Now Borden had blundered in, grabbed her brushes, and splashed black paint across the imagined scene.

"I need to call my husband," Laila said.

"You need to get dressed," he said. "I'm arresting you for the murder of Jake Hanlon. I'll take you in for questioning, and you can make a call from the station."

The nurse came back with water, and Borden read Laila her rights in front of her. When he left, the nurse supervised her getting dressed. The nurse was older, her face creased deeply, her head sparsely covered by dry puffs of red-tinted hair. None of what was happening to Laila seemed to surprise her. Laila remembered thinking she would give nearly anything she had at that moment to exchange places with the dedicated nurse and watch someone else get arrested.

In a way, she did sit back and watch as the movie rolled on—even as the supposedly excellent and expensive attorney that the senior Harrows hired sat confounded by the cascade of evidence against her.

The prosecution started with her text to Jake, which identified the meeting place. According to Claire, Laila had confided in her about a thorny predicament with Jake, and Claire had suggested the house as a meeting place.

"I believed her," Claire said. "I knew Eddie was a handful, and when Laila said he might have done something with his little girlfriend and that the girlfriend's father was livid and needed to talk, well, I believed her story."

Next, the prosecutor pointed to the exchange of texts between Laila and David a mere half hour before confronting Jake. Her message 'This won't be hard' was answered by David's plea, a last-ditch effort, according to the prosecutor, to stop Laila from taking the law in her own hands.

'Stay home,' he texted. 'Take care of our kids.'

Laila's assertion that Claire and Brick had taken away her phone seemed unlikely, given that the police found it locked in David's truck the night of the killing. Claire and the kids, huddled in the condo, sleepless and terrified, wondering what had become of the errant Laila, had told the police as much as they knew about the Harrow vehicles.

Thus, Laila had the means to corner Jake. Very quickly, the prosecutor established her method of murder. The gun had been stolen from a flea market Laila knew all too well. The market manager testified that she had broken into the market two days before the murder. She was thought to have been trying to steal art, but the manager had observed her at the market on other occasions, asking curious questions about vendors' hours and merchandise.

Anyway, as David's supposedly hotshot lawyer had not let her forget, the manager's testimony was but icing on the cake. Only *her* prints were found on the gun.

What wasn't found was Jake's semen—not on her, her clothes, or even on Jake or his underwear. For a man Laila originally claimed was intent on rape, his belt ties loosened, his sweatpants and boxers pushed down, he was remarkably unaroused, mused the prosecutor. A wave of nervous chuckles rippled through the courtroom.

How lucky she had been that Regina and Ken had taken the boys and made sure they were not present for any of the trial.

Laila's lawyer had full-color pictures of the gruesome rope marks on her neck, the best evidence he had for her assertion that Brick set up the charade of Laila's rape to justify his shooting of Jake. The prosecutor, however, neutralized the argument in one of the most searing moments of the trial.

"Was a rope found at the scene of the murder?" he asked Detective Borden.

"Yes," he answered. "It corresponded to the width of the marks on Ms. Harrow's neck."

"Were threads from the rope found on Ms. Harrow's clothing?"

"Yes."

"Were threads found on Mr. Davison's clothing?"

"No."

"Were threads found in Ms. Harrow's vehicle?"

"Yes."

"Were threads found in Mr. Davison's vehicle?"

"No."

"No," the prosecutor repeated, standing front and center, addressing the courtroom. "You did not find a rape scene."

He walked the few steps to the defense table where Laila sat, and turned around to face the jury box.

"But did Laila Harrow intend for you to find a rape scene?"

Laila's lawyer jumped to his feet to voice his objection, and Borden did not answer the question. He didn't really have to.

Besides talent, the prosecution appeared also to have great luck. Detective Cranston had been the beneficiary of an anonymous tip – a spreadsheet dropped on his desk. He and the department's forensic accountants traced the chronology of a collection of payments from Harrow United that coincided with several unusual permitting waivers granted by the County Commission.

Cranston lined up permit applications with accelerated Commission subcommittee decisions with excessive payments by Harrow United to subcontractors throughout the county who then made deposits in Hanlon's account.

David Harrow admitted to illicit business dealings with Hanlon spanning nearly three years. During questioning, he told police that after Jake Hanlon killed their neighbor, he indirectly threatened David and Harrow United. He swore that Laila and he never discussed his knowledge that Jake killed Ms. Farmer or that the famous "dolphin card" was Jake's message to David.

In the light of her actions the night in question, the claim appeared laughable.

"You are testifying, sir, that you never got around to telling your wife that Jake Hanlon, who had been squeezing you dry, also murdered her best friend? You never mentioned to her that your son, Edward, was cavorting with the daughter of a killer?"

The prosecutor allowed a long minute to pass while David processed the question.

"No," he said. He shook his head forcefully. "No," he repeated. He looked at Laila sitting at the defendant's table, and she saw the despair in his eyes.

Brick and Claire made highly sympathetic witnesses. They had loved the Harrows, their generous and fun-loving neighbors, devoted to raising their ambitiously constructed family. Pride of accomplishment was to be expected of energetic and intelligent people.

"Would you say you envied the Harrows?" asked Laila's lawyer on cross-examination.

"I suppose," said Claire. "I'm in real estate. I know success is not that easy."

"Were you particularly jealous of Laila?" he asked.

"She had a great life. The penthouse condo, the clothes, the vacations, a maid and a cook. It looked like a good life, for sure." Claire smiled wistfully.

The lawyer paced thoughtfully in front of the witness box. He turned and looked at the jury, his lips pulled tight, as if apologizing in advance for what he had to do.

"Did you plan to seduce David Harrow when you met him on the beach two nights before the murder? Did you want Laila Harrow's life, or were you just trying to make your lover, Brick, jealous?"

The lawyer stood back so that the jury could see Claire's blushing face.

"Objection!" shouted the prosecutor.

"Overruled," answered the judge. "Answer the question, please."

"I know I shouldn't have gone," she said. She covered her face with her hands.

The lawyer asked the judge to let him show the jury the now-famous photo of Claire and David on the beach. Under questioning as a hostile witness, Ken had admitted to the court that when he showed it to Laila, she had been visibly upset. The judge permitted the jury to pass the image along from member to member.

"Why did you go?"

"He told me he knew who killed Billie." She paused.

Jury members leaned toward her.

"I knew. I knew at some level that he was lying, but I went anyway. He just wanted to talk about sex. Then, I felt sorry for Laila. I wasn't envious anymore."

"Why would a successful developer want romance with a convicted felon?" roared the lawyer. "Would a wealthy and busy father of four, with a beautiful and talented wife, risk it all to pursue the alcoholic mother of two abandoned sons?"

"I know. I know," Claire cried. "It made no sense. He must have been drinking, too. I ran from the beach that night."

The lawyer followed up with more facts about Claire's misdeeds and failures, but Laila could see that it was too late. The prosecution had the police witnesses who pointed out that Laila was terse and dry at the scene of the crime, like someone who had completed an unappetizing but necessary task. Claire was a fallen woman who had righted herself. There was no doubt whom they believed.

Regina made a strong defense witness when she described the loving family David and Laila worked hard to maintain. Under close questioning by the prosecution, however, she admitted that Laila had never visited Regina at her home, and Laila did not, as far as Regina knew, visit her parents, siblings, or in-laws very frequently.

The jury saw a spoiled couple that had gotten their life served up on a platter. Claire was the humble woman who had managed to stay off the tracks of their train wreck, and Regina was an employee Laila had befriended. David's decision to reveal the details behind his bribery of Jake to back up Laila's story of Brick and Claire's involvement backfired miserably. His behavior fortified the version of Laila as a wealthy and idle wife of an absent husband who would take any step to ensure their corrupt lifestyle.

The best opportunity to change the narrative would have been to trip up Brick. If they could show he knew much better than Laila how to engineer a fake crime scene and that he had outsmarted her at every turn, maybe the jury would consider a second scenario.

Yes, Brick knew about crime scenes, and he also knew about trials and juries.

He sat in the witness box with his shoulders slumped forward. His posture told the story of a man who would rather have been any place else. The prosecutor had to extract the information from this most-reluctant witness in bits and pieces.

He had already gone on record with every one of the reporters swarming around Laguna Shores with the earnest comments that the Harrows were the bright lights of the community. They made people feel good. They cared about the old and young. They had spectacular dinner parties, to boot. They had him fooled.

"What did you think when Claire asked you to check on Laila Harrow?" the prosecutor asked Brick.

"I was already irritated," he answered.

"Why?"

"Because she was babysitting the kids."

"Did you not like the Harrow children?"

"No, they're fine. Nice kids," he said.

"So why the irritation?"

"She had just gotten chased around the beach by David Harrow not two days before," he said.

"So, you thought they were trouble?"

"They were their own thing. I thought Claire should stay clear."

"But you answered Claire's call?"

"Sure. I knew Claire had a soft spot for those kids."

"Do you always carry a gun?"

"I have a permit."

"Did you draw the gun when you got to the address Claire gave you?"

"Yes."

"Did you get off a shot?"

"No."

"Why?"

"Mr. Hanlon was already dead."

"What had happened?"

"He had a bullet in his back."

"What did you do?"

"Ms. Harrow was holding a gun."

"Did she point it at you?"

"She dropped the gun. She rushed at me and tried to explain stuff."

"What did she explain?"

"She said to call 911 and get the police. She said they would believe her."

"Did you understand her?"

"I understood I should call 911."

"Did she say anything else?"

"No, she got on the ground."

"Was she hurt?"

"I don't think so, but she dropped hard to one side."

"Had she fainted?"

"No, she was pulling down her pants and. . . ."

"And what?

"She was sort of grinding her bottom into the dirt, getting her underwear dirty."

The image of Laila soiling her clothes in order to get away with murder was the lead story in newspapers throughout Florida. Reporters hounded David's parents so they moved to an undisclosed location. David, out on bail and with his own trial for bribery and fraud imminent, agreed that Eddie and Jackson would be better off with their grandparents. The senior Harrows stated that caring for the older two boys was the best they could do in these circumstances. Regina stepped up to take the twins.

Under questioning, Brick categorically denied he had gone to his vehicle and Laila's vehicle before calling 911, as her lawyer asserted.

"I wouldn't have left her alone in the yard, not in the state she was in."

"Why didn't you check Mr. Hanlon for a pulse?" Laila's attorney asked.

"I wasn't going to get between Ms. Harrow and the gun. That much, I figured out."

Brick, said the prosecutor, was an Everyman who happened to be a policeman. He wanted to please his new girlfriend, so he got sucked into the diabolical plans of the corrupt Harrow family.

The prosecution was firm in their intent to prevent the defense from putting Jake Hanlon on trial instead of Laila Harrow. In his final presentation to the jury, the case became clear.

"Don't get me wrong," he continued. "The victim was no angel, and he had almost certainly murdered Wilhelmina Farmer. But rape was not on his mind that night. Quite the contrary, Laila Harrow lured Jake Hanlon to that isolated backyard with promises of a gratifying sexual payoff if Jake would stop extorting money from her husband. Jake Hanlon was getting the best of both worlds: money and sex. He was not intending to hurt Laila Harrow."

The dolphin card and the threat it represented served to reduce Laila's sentence to nine years with a possibility of parole in six. David got a proportionally stiffer sentence of seven years, but his crimes had been thoroughly planned and executed over a period of three years, his judge said. The damage to the St. Augustine community was undeniable. The judge was running for re-election.

"There's a way to do this," David told her in their last call before being moved to state prisons, she down towards Ocala, he to Raiford.

"What way?" she asked. She closed her eyes to imagine him on their balcony, his arms around her and his voice tender. All she managed to see was David in the prison bus, his hair in a military cut and his eyes cold.

"Every night when the lights go out, we hold each other and tell the good thing that happened that day, the thing that reminded us of how we were and how we'll be. Every night. You say it, I'll hear you."

"You say it. I'll hear you," she answered.

"And we'll be out one day," he said.

"And we won't forget a thing," she said.

Sitting in her prison cell, Laila remembered it all.

Thank you so much for reading *The Laguna Shores Research Club*. If you've enjoyed the book, we would be grateful if you would post a review on the bookseller's website. Just a few words is all it takes! ♥

Acknowledgements

Many helped me produce this novel and these words are too brief to indicate how much I appreciate the support. My Boise writing group, Erin Anchustegui, Glida Bothwell, Judy Frederick and Kelly Jones, I owe you much more than a bottle of Albariño. Beta readers, Kristine Robb, Rita Cook, Gina Hager-Moitoso, Eileen Cobb, Anne Hughes and Barbara Gebuhr, you invested valuable time but there is no way for me to tell you the measure of your help. It's an enormous amount for me to pay forward.

Helen Ladson, I asked you to be a sensitivity reader, and you gave me that insight as well as a full-on character development assessment. Thank you.

Sally Schmeczer Wells you were the shoulder I leaned on. I'm surprised you still have a shoulder.

At TouchPoint Press, from our first contact through to this writing, Ashley Carlson, Kimberly Coghlan, and Sheri Williams, you have delivered solid advice, guidance, and patient editing. Many thanks from this newbie.

To my Boise family, a generation and more of story-telling readers, Isaac, Rebecca, Emre and Saul, I can barely imagine what you will send out to the world. May I be as encouraging a fan as you have been for me.

Finally, Paul, you asked after every workday "And how did the writing go today?" so that I would believe I was a writer. You are priceless, my dear.